HIGHEST PRAISE
HOMESPUN ROMANCE

"In all of the Homespuns I've read and reviewed I've been very taken with the loving rendering of colorful small-town people doing small-town things and bringing 5 STAR and GOLD 5 STAR rankings to the readers. This series should be selling off the bookshelves within hours! Never have I given a series an overall review, but I feel this one, thus far, deserves it! Continue the excellent choices in authors and editors! It's working for this reviewer!"—*Heartland Critiques*

We at Jove Books are thrilled by the enthusiastic critical acclaim that the Homespun Romances are receiving. We would like to thank you, the readers and fans of this wonderful series, for making it the success that it is. It is our pleasure to bring you the highest quality of romance writing in these breathtaking tales of love and family in the heartland of America.

And now, sit back and enjoy this delightful new Homespun Romance . . .

HOMEWARD BOUND
by Linda Shertzer

Praise for Linda Shertzer's previous Homespun Romances:

PICKETT'S FENCE

"A glimpse into small-town living in the western frontier. Linda Shertzer creates some soul-stirring characters who embody the essence and purity of Americana."—*Affaire de Coeur*

National bestseller!
HOME FIRES

"Sweet . . . delightful, charming characters . . . a satisfying, warm read."—*Romantic Times*

HOMEWARD BOUND

LINDA SHERTZER

JOVE BOOKS, NEW YORK

HOMEWARD BOUND

A Jove Book / published by arrangement with author

PRINTING HISTORY
Jove edition / June 1995

ISBN: 0-515-11637-8

A JOVE BOOK®
Jove Books are published by the Berkley Publishing Group,
200 Madison Avenue, New York, New York 10016.
JOVE and the "J" design are trademarks
belonging to Jove Publications, Inc.

PRINTED IN THE UNITED STATES OF AMERICA

10 9 8 7 6 5 4 3 2 1

To my Mom,
Ethel Mae Kreisel
(1927—1992)
who taught me how
to make a happy home

Many thanks to Kelsey Roberts
for always being willing to share
her expertise in Indian lore

One

Ever since he'd boarded the train in Macon, Georgia, Sarah Bolton had been trying very hard not to stare at the thin, pale man with the crutch seated across the aisle from her. Every time her gaze wandered toward him, she could almost hear Aunt Myrtle—may she rest in peace—instructing in her genteel drawl, "My dear, a lady *never* stares."

Being considered unladylike was the least of Sarah's worries.

How was she going to explain everything to her sister Mildred and her husband? How was she ever going to live down the shame and protect her daughter? No words came to mind that seemed adequate.

Day after day, as the train jolted along, she pondered her predicament as she tried to keep Patsy entertained. Heaven only knew it took all her ingenuity to keep her eighteen-month-old daughter content on the long, tiring journey to Cottonwood, Kansas.

Whenever Patsy was napping or amusing herself, Sarah watched the passing countryside through the sooty window. She'd never been far from her home in Savannah, but the unfamiliar countryside bore the same familiar marks of the hundreds of bombardments and the pounding feet of thousands of marching troops. But there was also the bright green promise of new vegetation sprouting through the ruins as the land began to renew itself. If only she and her daughter could make a new beginning, too.

She tried to find some interest in watching the other passengers who boarded the train, then left at their own destinations, and the new ones who took their places. But no one else captured her attention like the quiet man seated to her left.

What a shame a man who had obviously been so handsome once should now be so ill. What a shame a man so weak should be traveling all alone. Her heart ached for him.

But she didn't stare. On the other hand, it really wouldn't have mattered much if she did. He was usually asleep. Even when he was awake he spent most of his time with his eyes fixed straight ahead. It was almost as if he were too weak to give his full attention to anything. Or perhaps his condition was so deteriorated that he was already looking ahead to a glimpse of a better life on the other side of the grave.

But there was always the possibility he'd notice her rudeness. Then what would she do? What would she say?

Suddenly, as if the entire plan had dropped into her head from Above, she knew exactly what she'd say.

She knew she *must* do this, if not for herself, then for Patsy's sake. But it was still a difficult subject to broach, so she waited for the right time and prayed he wouldn't die before she had a chance to speak with him.

Night had fallen. The car was almost empty, and Patsy was asleep. Sarah laid her daughter gently on the bare, hard seat. She cushioned the child's head with her own faded shawl and spread a patched blanket over her. She sat as close to the aisle as she could, then turned to the man. If she was going to do this, she couldn't wait much longer.

His eyes were open. But the only reason she knew he was awake and not dead was because he hadn't keeled over in his seat yet, and occasionally he blinked.

She took a deep breath to bolster her courage. "Excuse

me." She cleared her throat a little to cover her nervousness. She leaned toward him, and a little louder, but not so loud as to be heard by the people seated at the front, she repeated, "Excuse me, sir. I . . . I hope you won't think I'm too forward."

Slowly he turned to her. In the flickering light of the lanterns swinging overhead, his blue eyes were glassy and sunken and ringed by deep circles of purple.

"I mean . . . I know we haven't been properly introduced."

He looked so weary, she didn't think he'd be able to keep his eyes open long enough for her to finish what she'd planned to say. She spoke in a rush.

"I mean . . . I hope you don't mind my speaking to you like this, but . . ."

Her speech trailed off when she saw him smile. At least, she thought it was a smile, as only the corners of his mouth turned up, and just barely. Then she saw that his eyes were no longer so dull, but had a twinkle, and she knew he was definitely smiling.

"Ma'am," he began in a low, weak voice. He coughed several times, and she had to wait until he'd managed to catch his breath again before he could continue. "Ma'am, if you knew how long it's been since a pretty lady talked to me, you'd realize I don't mind at all."

She breathed a silent sigh of relief. He'd called her a lady. He didn't think she was some sort of woman of ill repute, accosting strange gentlemen. Of course, when she finished what she had to say, he might change his mind. Well, even if he did, he was in no physical condition to do anything about it. For that she was doubly grateful, and found the courage to go on.

"If I could introduce myself, sir," she ventured. "I'm Sarah Bolton. That's my daughter, Patricia."

"Jesse Taylor, ma'am," he replied. Slowly, with a great effort, he touched his fingertips to his forehead, doffing a nonexistent hat. He nodded his head. "I hope you won't think I'm rude for not rising."

"No, no. Of course not," she answered quickly.

Again the corners of his lips turned up, this time in a definite smile. His eyes sparkled even more brightly. It was almost as if he were trying to convey to her through his eyes the laughter in his heart that his withered body was incapable of expressing.

"I think, under the circumstances," he continued, tapping with the tip of his gnarled forefinger on the hard wooden seat, "you and I are uncomfortable enough without making things more difficult for each other."

"Oh, I couldn't agree with you more."

On the other hand, how could she jump right in and tell him of her plan to make life a bit more comfortable—for both of them—at least for a little while? She still had to tread very carefully with what she was about to propose.

"I couldn't help noticing you when you boarded the train in Macon."

He gave a little chuckle. "Yeah, I guess it's a little hard not to notice a moving scarecrow on a crutch."

She flushed with embarrassment. She'd barely acknowledged the crutch. But she could hardly admit to the man how very noticeable he himself had been—and still was—to her.

She tried to sound very casual. "Are you from Macon, Mr. Taylor?"

"No, not originally. And certainly not by choice."

She waited for him to elaborate, but he didn't seem willing. She could tell by his speech, though, that he wasn't a Southerner. On the other hand, all that shouldn't matter so much anymore, should it? It certainly wouldn't matter if her plan succeeded.

"I also couldn't help noticing you boarded alone."

"Yes, ma'am," he answered, and managed this time to keep his coughing spell to a few seconds.

"If you'll excuse me for saying so, in your weakened condition, don't you have someone . . . any family who could travel with you?"

"No, ma'am. I have no brothers or sisters, and my parents passed on many years ago."

"Oh, I'm so sorry. Please accept my deepest condolences," she murmured.

She didn't think it would offer him much comfort if she told him he looked as if he might soon be joining his loved ones in the Great Beyond.

"Will you be traveling much farther, Mr. Taylor?"

"I'm not sure, ma'am."

Another terrible question! The man might not even live long enough to reach the next station. Embarrassed again, she almost lost her courage and decided to sit silently until she reached Cottonwood. But she knew she had to press on.

"Do you . . . do you have someone else waiting for you at the end of the line? Some friends? Or perhaps . . . a fiancée?"

"No, ma'am. No one at all."

Sarah tried not to sigh aloud with relief. The man had looked perfect enough for her purposes, but as she talked with him, he seemed to grow more perfect with each answer to her questions.

"What a pity."

Sarah could almost hear Aunt Myrtle's indignation even now at her latest remark. "My dear, a lady *never* prevaricates—unless it's absolutely necessary." She hoped her elderly aunt would agree that this was absolutely necessary.

Still, in order to quiet her conscience in the guise of the ghost of Aunt Myrtle, Sarah asked, "Then why are you going out West—if you don't mind my asking."

"I've heard it's a pretty country I've just finished fighting to keep together. I think I'd like to see a little more of it . . . while I can."

"Do you really think you'll get very far?"

He peered at her, his eyebrows raised in surprise.

"I mean . . . I'm sorry to be so direct. But I . . . well, you do seem to have some extensive injuries." Cautiously she added, "Did you get them in the war?"

"You might say that."

"If you'll forgive me for mentioning this, they do seem rather severe for you to be traveling much at all."

"Of course I forgive you. It's pretty hard to hold a grudge against someone for stating the obvious."

He tried to laugh, but only broke down into another coughing spell. He reached into the inner pocket of his jacket and pulled out a brown bottle. All along this journey, he'd seemed to find great comfort in its contents. She surely wouldn't have picked a drunkard—if she had any other choice.

When he opened the bottle, she expected to be assailed by the telltale aroma of strong alcohol. But upon closer examination of the worn label, she realized he was taking laudanum.

How could he not notice her intense scrutiny? He gave the bottle a little tilt before replacing it in his pocket. "For the pain."

"Of course."

"I was told I'd be lucky if I lived to see another Christmas."

She felt a tremor in her bones. "Are you sure—?"

"I feel like that poor little fellow with a crutch in that Dickens story," he said, grinning again.

"Are you sure—"

"Well, I guess that's better than being compared to the old miser," he added, and chuckled just enough not to set himself off on another coughing spell.

"No, no," she said, and hoped she didn't sound too anxious. "I mean, is the *doctor* sure you're . . . dying?"

"Ha! What do doctors know?" he asked with an uncertain laugh. Then he tapped lightly on the right leg he kept straight out in the aisle. "Morbid infection, ma'am. But I wasn't about to let them amputate."

"But . . . if it could save your life . . . ?"

Then he tapped on what must have once been a broad, muscled chest, but was now a mere shell. "Galloping consumption." He gave a little cough.

She averted her gaze, embarrassed to look him in the eye.

"Yes, I see. I suppose one or the other would do it, but both . . ."

"Yeah, I do have the rottenest luck. Oh, did I mention a lengthy period of near starvation?"

"Oh, dear. Oh, no."

Food had been scarce during the war, but she'd never imagined how badly. She'd mistakenly attributed his emaciation to his illness. Consumption would do that to a person, too, she knew—although he didn't have the customary flushed cheeks that also indicated consumption.

"I'm sorry if it bothers you, ma'am, for me to be so explicit about my . . . illnesses."

"No, no. I'm just dreadfully sorry for you."

"Don't be. I told the doctor I wanted him to be honest with me, so I could hardly kick up a fuss when he was. I think honesty's the best policy."

That's just what Aunt Myrtle always used to say.

"Don't you, Mrs. Bolton?"

Oh, dear. Why did he have to ask her that question, and in that way?

Sarah looked around the interior of the railroad car before replying. Patsy was still asleep. The few other passengers seated to the front were either asleep or else not paying Mr. Taylor and her any mind at all. She felt very relieved to see that. What she had to say next wasn't going to be easy. But he wanted honesty, and so he'd get it. But it was certainly going to be painful for her.

"That's *Miss* Bolton," she replied. She held her chin so low she crushed the frayed ribbon that held her bonnet in place. She watched for his reaction from the corner of her eye.

He glanced from her to the sleeping child, then back again. One eyebrow rose with his growing curiosity. "Oh, I see," he replied slowly.

"No, Mr. Taylor, you don't see." Summoning the courage to raise her head and look him in the eye, she replied, "You don't see at all."

This man had been through an ordeal himself, that was

certain, and had more yet to suffer before the end. But what could he know of what she'd been through in the past five years? What could he understand of everything else she'd be willing to go through, just for Patsy's sake?

"But I still think we can help each other, you and I."

His thin face expressionless, he leaned back, studying her. Then he moved forward a little and tilted his head. His eyes danced with interest. "Just what do you have in mind, Miss Bolton?"

"I need a husband, and my daughter needs a father."

His eyebrows lifted, and he nodded his head. "Don't you think it's a little late now to be thinking about that?"

She chose to ignore the remark. She had a more important point to make. "And you need a place to die."

She noticed a tightening of his lips and a slight misting of his eyes. He was silent as he settled back against his seat.

"I didn't mean to hurt you, but . . . well, you yourself said you preferred honesty."

He nodded.

"Then, please, let me explain before you decide to tell me to go away and not to bother you again."

She held her breath for a second, waiting. What else would a respectable person tell a woman who had the unbelievable audacity to have a child out of wedlock—and then boldly keep it?

"Go ahead, ma'am," he said. She was glad he still addressed her with some respect. "I'm curious to hear what you have in mind."

"It's *not* what you're thinking, Mr. Taylor." She tried to sound haughty, but feared she wasn't succeeding.

"Please don't underestimate me, ma'am," he countered. "I don't believe either one of us is really as wicked as the other thinks." When she made no reply, he continued, "Why don't you tell me what you want?"

She drew in a deep breath and plunged into her story.

"My sister and I were raised by our aunt in Savannah. Mildred married the Reverend Mr. Preston and moved to Kansas six years ago. I stayed with our aunt. But Aunt Myrtle passed away recently, so I sold what property we owned and I'm on my way to Cottonwood, to live with my sister and her husband."

"Is that why you think you need a husband?"

"My brother-in-law is the minister there."

Jesse reached up to stroke his chin. "That sure could complicate matters for you."

"I made up my mind when I discovered I was . . . well, in a family way, that I'd *never* give up my child. I love her too much."

He nodded his head. "I . . . I've been, well, sort of watching . . . both of you playing together during this trip," he admitted. "No, you don't seem the kind of woman who would abandon her child."

"But, as you can pretty well suppose, I can hardly arrive on the parsonage doorstep with a child and no husband. Especially with my brother-in-law and his family needing to set a good example for the townspeople and all that."

"Why don't you just put on widow's weeds and tell them your husband was killed in the war?"

"Because I don't have a marriage certificate or a death notification from the army."

He shrugged. "Those things were easily lost."

"As a war widow, I'd be entitled to some land . . . and I have no way to claim it, and Mildred and the Reverend Preston—and probably everyone else in town—will wonder why I don't."

"That could be a problem."

"But my biggest problem is Mildred herself."

"She's a problem?" he asked. His dark brows drew into a little frown, but the merriment still danced in his eyes. "I never had a sister, but I would've thought yours would be a great comfort to you, as a widow."

She grimaced and sighed. Then she turned to him and peered deeply into his eyes.

"You just don't know Mildred, Mr. Taylor. She's the world's *worst* busybody."

He looked as if he wanted to laugh again, but was afraid to start another fit of coughing.

"When we were children, I used to tease and call her Meddling Mildred."

This time he did chuckle. "I suppose she still lives up to her name?"

She nodded. "After she's done fussing over Patsy and crying over Aunt Myrtle, she'll be asking a thousand and one questions about . . . my child's father. Questions I can't answer."

"Couldn't you tell her Patsy was the child of a friend who passed away?" he suggested. "Then you wouldn't have to worry—"

"Oh, no, Mr. Taylor," she said with an adamant shake of her head. "I'll never have anyone think—I'd never want Patsy to have one second of doubt—that she's anyone's daughter but *mine.*"

"Couldn't you make up something?"

"I'm not a good liar, Mr. Taylor."

"Well, when she asks, couldn't you just sort of break down and cry and tell her you're grieving too much to talk about him?"

"I'm not a good actress, either."

"If you'll allow a poor old cripple to say so, I think you're pretty enough to be on the stage."

It had been a long time since a man had complimented her. She knew she didn't look her best in a twice-turned gown grimy from traveling. She'd never expected him to comment on her appearance, and so favorably. She especially never expected to see such a light in his eyes—a light from deep within that she had the feeling hadn't been kindled in a long, long time. She felt the warmth color into her cheeks.

In order to distract both of them, she continued, "My sister's a firm believer in the verse 'It is not good for man to be alone.' I know her. She'll decide that as a woman alone with a small child, I need to find a new husband."

"But not if you already have a husband who . . ."

"Who is dying. You catch on fast, Mr. Taylor."

He drew in a deep breath. "Well, you are frank, if nothing else."

"I need a husband and a father for my child," she repeated.

"And what will you do after I'm dead? Even though Patsy will have a last name, you'll be a widow for real then. And you'll still need to stop your sister's matchmaking."

"I should be able to get at least a year's peace."

"So I'm good for at least a year, huh?" He folded his hands over his hollow stomach.

"Oh, at least, depending on when you die." Suddenly she realized she didn't want to sound too eager. "Please understand. I don't mean to insult you."

"I've got to hand it to you, ma'am. It sure seems to me you've thought this out all the way through."

"You can't believe how very hard it was for me to approach a strange man." Her nervousness, as well as her need to provide for Patsy, brought out an urgency in her voice that she would rather have kept hidden. "You realize I'm not asking this for myself. If it were just me, I'd set up a shop and make my way through the world alone. But I won't have my daughter robbed of the loving security of a family —aunts, uncles, cousins—friends, neighbors, schoolmates. And even without them, I certainly won't let Patsy go through life with the stigma of bastard."

Mr. Taylor's eyebrows rose. "My, my, you do speak bluntly, ma'am."

"I'm sorry if you find my language offensive, Mr. Taylor. But I think you understand by now that I would do absolutely *anything* for my daughter."

He looked again at the sleeping child. He nodded slowly as he turned back to Sarah. "So you saw me getting on the train and thought I looked like a likely candidate for a dying husband?"

"Yes. Well, no." She could feel her cheeks growing warmer. "Not immediately, anyway."

He chuckled, then nodded toward Patsy and asked, "Before we go any further, ma'am, tell me. What happened to her real father? Why couldn't he—?"

"He's gone," she answered abruptly. She knew she couldn't tell him the truth. But if she protested too much, it might only pique his curiosity, so she remained silent.

She should've figured any man who had the courage to cross the country alone, even when he was so ill, wouldn't be satisfied with a simple answer.

"I mean, I wouldn't want to find out I was a bigamist," he persisted.

"I thought I made that clear, Mr. Taylor. I've never been married."

"Why didn't Patsy's father—?"

"He's just gone, Mr. Taylor," she answered sharply this time. Suddenly she realized that if she argued with him, she probably didn't stand much of a chance to talk him into going along with her plan. A little more gently she continued, "It's . . . it's not important now anyway. And it certainly has no bearing on what I'm asking of you."

"I told you I appreciate complete honesty."

"I'd hope you'd appreciate my privacy even more," she answered softly.

"Very well, ma'am," he agreed. "Sorry to pry."

She nodded and was glad he'd decided not to press the issue further. But the longer he remained silent, the more Sarah began to worry that he might decide to tell her no after all.

She felt more relieved when she heard him clear his throat to speak again.

"You said this was for both of us. What exactly do I get out of this?"

"A home."

He nodded and continued to watch her, obviously waiting for more. She was going to have to make this sound awfully appealing.

"All the gentle comforts of a peaceful, comfortable home. A quiet place to sleep, neat clean clothing, three hearty meals a day."

"With desserts?" he asked with a grin.

A little taken aback by his frivolous question, Sarah took a second to answer. Considering how thin he was, he probably needed all the extra food he could get. "Well, I suppose if you consider that absolutely necessary. . . ."

"And do I get a Christmas present?" he asked, eyebrows lifted expectantly.

She eyed him suspiciously. What if he was lying to her, and she'd gone through all this for naught? "I . . . I thought you said you might not live to see Christmas."

"Just in case. And if I don't, well, my birthday is August fifth. Will I at least have a cake?"

"Yes, Mr. Taylor. Both my sister and I are very good cooks."

"I'll be counting on that."

"Also, the last I heard, there was a fairly good doctor in Cottonwood, and I spent the past few years nursing my elderly aunt."

"So I'll have your personal attention, huh?"

She nodded.

"Will I get a sponge bath every Saturday night?"

Sarah couldn't stop the blush that rose to her cheeks. "Only if you go to church on Sunday morning." She figured that was a safe answer. A man ill enough to require a sponge bath wouldn't be in any condition to go galloping off to church early the next morning.

"Sure. You see, I kind of figured, with your brother-in-law being the preacher, we'd *have* to go."

The very thought of Mr. Taylor's flesh, warm and wet beneath her fingers, made her throat tight. She swallowed hard. "So . . . so, you see, you'll get the best care we can give you to make you comfortable until . . . until your time comes. Then we'll see you get a decent Christian burial, too."

"With lots of flowers?"

What a question to ask! "Yes, as long as you don't die in the winter."

"The choir'll sing?"

"I suppose so."

"And I'll have a good long eulogy? Your brother-in-law *is* a good preacher, isn't he?"

She nodded uncertainly. "As I recall. It's been a while since I've heard him."

"I'll be buried in a nice new suit?"

"I don't see why not."

"Black—not blue."

"Trust me, Mr. Taylor. I have had some experience in what is appropriate attire for the deceased."

"And you *will* cry a lot, won't you?"

"I promise you, I'll give you all the mourning you're entitled to."

"And a headstone?"

"If you like."

"Marble, not just a wooden cross with my name painted on it? Those things fade, you know."

"If I can afford it."

"A big fancy one."

"We'll see what the undertaker has available."

"With maybe a big angel on top pointing heavenward?" He tried to raise his arm overhead to show her just what he wanted, but groaned and dropped his arm. Much to Sarah's surprise, in spite of his obvious pain, he still managed a chuckle through his coughing fit. "I'd hate to have somebody passing by think I'd gone in the other direction."

"You really shouldn't get so carried away with the plans for your interment, Mr. Taylor."

"It might just be the first thing I've done in my life that a lot of people will notice."

Still grinning, he lifted his gaze to meet hers. Now his eyes were truly sparkling with laughter.

What kind of man was this Jesse Taylor, Sarah wondered, who could joke about his own imminent passing? He *had* asked for a Christian burial. He didn't seem to be completely unchurched or irreverent. Even though his earthly form was dying, was his spirit still so full of the joy of life that it shone through his emaciated body?

It was a shame for a man to have to die alone and unattended, to be buried in a lonely grave in a potter's field, unmarked and unmourned. She knew she'd made the right choice in Jesse Taylor.

Suddenly she was all too aware of how close this man was to her—the warmth of his breath, the scent of shaving soap that came from his warm body. She couldn't insult him now and lose her one chance to give Patsy a respectable name. But she couldn't bear to have this stranger so near.

She drew back as quickly as she could manage and still appear polite.

"I'll be honest with you now, ma'am."

Oh, dear! She *had* insulted him. After all her fast talking just to try to convince him, her simple movement had offended him, and he was going to refuse her after all. He was going to tell her she was making a nuisance of herself, and have her put in the baggage car. Or worse, denounce her for the wanton she was, and have her and her illegitimate daughter ejected from the train rather than suffer them to ride with decent people.

"When I boarded the train, I noticed you and your cute little girl, too."

Sarah watched him with wide eyes and waited.

"Oh, don't look so surprised. I might be sick, and they've told me I'm dying, but I'm still a man—and they haven't nailed the coffin lid down on me yet. Your offer of a home and care in return for my name and the good reputation it'll give you and your daughter might be a tad out of the ordinary. But, after all I've been through, to die in the arms of a lady as lovely as you doesn't seem such a bad bargain. Lord knows, I've made worse deals in my life."

Slowly he reached across to take her hand. Did that mean he would accept? She held back. Before he accepted, she must make *everything* absolutely clear to him. Still, it was a subject that was very hard to broach.

"You do realize, of course, Mr. Taylor, that under the circumstances—I mean, that you and I have just met . . . Why, we barely know anything about each other besides our names—and of course, we're not really . . . in love with each other. Well, you must certainly see that this will be a marriage in name only."

He withdrew his hand slowly. "My dear Miss . . . my dear Sarah—and I think under the circumstances, I can call my bride-to-be by her given name. Do I look like a man who is in any condition to do otherwise?"

Two

Jesse watched as Sarah leaned back against the seat and closed her eyes in obvious relief. He'd been watching her on this journey more than she'd ever know— and probably more than he'd ever be able to admit to her.

He'd seen what a loving mother she could be. How she came to be a mother was questionable. Whether she was a wanton or a fallen angel didn't seem to matter right now. She had enough morals left to be a good mother. And she was returning to her sister, the preacher's wife, so she must have repented her wild ways. Even if she wouldn't exactly be a loving wife, she'd probably at least do her duty by him, as she'd promised.

Whenever his final moment came, his last memory would be a glimpse of her. Hers would be the last hand he'd touch. The last voice he'd hear before he answered to his Maker would be hers.

Even if it was to be a marriage in name only—and even if he wasn't in any condition to make it otherwise—and even if she wasn't exactly completely virtuous—he could still *pretend* she was and that he'd loved a woman like that. With a satisfied nod he decided that was all right with him.

Linda Shertzer

She opened her eyes and turned to him. "Thank you for agreeing to do this, Mr. Taylor."

"Jesse," he corrected.

Her green eyes were bright with unshed tears, but she blinked her long, dark lashes and kept the tears at bay. Thank goodness, he thought, she wasn't one of those weepy, wailing, hanky-waving women.

"I promise you, Mr. Taylor—"

"Jesse," he repeated.

"You'll get all the care you need. You won't ever regret—"

"Can't you call me Jesse?" he asked a little more loudly to distract her from her nervous recitation of promises.

She looked around, as if afraid everyone in the railroad car could hear them. "But I hardly know you," she protested quietly.

"But you're going to marry me," he pointed out.

"It's a marriage in name only," she reminded him.

"If I'm giving you—and Patsy—my name, can't you at least use it?"

Her rosy lips curved up in a grin. As he studied her face, it suddenly occurred to him, wasn't a man supposed to kiss his bride-to-be? Even if this was going to be a marriage in name only, couldn't he at least give her one *little* kiss?

After a brief pause she quietly replied, "Very well, if you insist."

His weary heart gave an eager leap, until he realized she was actually answering his request to use his name. He'd really have to do something to stop his imagination from running away with him—especially when he didn't have the strength to do anything to alleviate those feelings. Right now, he'd have to do something to hide his disappointment.

Even though he knew he still had a grin on his face, he lifted his chin a bit and looked down his nose at her, so that he could appear more authoritarian.

"Yes, indeed. I do insist. I mean, after all, you *are* going to promise to love, honor, and obey me." He stressed the "obey" and wished he had the nerve to insist on a kiss. He watched for her reaction.

She pulled back a little more, he noted with disappointment. "Only up to a point, Mr. Taylor," she stated in a cool, firm voice.

So she wasn't one to be cowed, he thought, reaffirming his respect for her. No, he really should've realized that from the beginning.

On the other hand, he really wished she'd have realized he was only teasing—and maybe even teased him back. She'd told him she'd called her sister "Meddling Mildred." She hadn't always been such a serious little thing. The war for the Union had changed them all. Had it changed her that much? Oh, well, he figured, it could have been worse. She could have been fat and bald, with a big hairy wart on the end of her nose.

"I assumed you understood all the stipulations of our bargain," she said stiffly. "I fully expect you to abide by our agreement, so if I need to repeat any part of it for your benefit, let me know."

Oh, tarnation! She *was* going to be a stickler for everything. In that case, he supposed a kiss really was out of the question. On the other hand, something more than a kiss hadn't been out of the question for *somebody*.

"No. I understand completely," he said, even though he didn't, and even though he couldn't agree with her. "But I do have a problem."

"Oh, dear. What is it?"

"How do I know you'll keep your end of the bargain?"

She lifted her chin and stared at him, puzzled.

"How do I know you'll see me buried proper? I mean, I'll be dead. How do I know you won't go through my pockets for loose change, sell my clothes, and toss my lifeless body in the river?"

"But . . . well . . . why, Mr. Taylor!" she sputtered. "You have my word. I'd *never* do such a barbaric thing!"

He grinned. He'd like to tell her how pretty she looked when she was flustered and her eyes were wide and her pale cheeks flushed pink. If only he had the strength—or the time—to make her blush more often.

"I don't think this is a matter we can have put in writing. You'll just have to believe my promise—"

"So, I have your word of honor—as a lady?"

"And I have yours—as a gentleman?"

Jesse nodded. "Well, now that's settled, I guess we'd better get off at the next stop so we can find a judge," he suggested.

"A judge?"

"Or a preacher. To marry us. Which would you prefer?"

"Well, a preacher, of course."

He studied her warily for a moment. "Say, you're not one of those Bible-thumping, hallelujah-shouting, teetotaling fanatics, are you?"

"Excuse me?"

"I mean, I don't mind a hymn—if it's got a nice tune and not too many verses. Or a prayer and a good sermon from time to time—if it's not too long. As a matter of fact, for the past few years, I've been doing a *lot* of praying myself."

"Me, too," she said very quietly.

"But I do enjoy a little sip of good whiskey now and then, even if it has been a long time since I've had one. But well, with your brother-in-law being a minister and all, I just thought maybe . . ."

"Excuse me, Mr. Taylor—Jesse," she corrected herself before he could. *"You* were the one who was planning the big church funeral service with such enthusiasm."

"Well, you're the one with family in the business."

"My sister married him—not I. But if I don't want my sister pestering me until you pass away, we'd better be married by a minister."

"We'll find one at the very next stop," he promised.

She settled back against the seat. He supposed she was contemplating her last few moments as a single woman, maybe even praying. Maybe he ought to be praying, too, but instead he couldn't help watching his future bride.

He let his gaze slip up and down her figure. It had been

hard to tell when she was all wrapped up in her big brown traveling shawl, but he couldn't picture her really fat underneath. From the size of her hands and wrists, she'd looked delicate, almost like some of the porcelain figurines from Germany that rich people kept on their mantels. But he couldn't picture her as a doll.

Try as he might, he hadn't been able to shake the thought that beneath that big shawl was a slender, softly rounded body, sort of like the marble statue of a Greek goddess he'd once seen in a museum. All pale and cool and smooth to the touch. But Sarah'd be smooth and warm. . . .

Jesse'd watched with pleasure and satisfaction when she'd removed her shawl and rolled it up for her daughter's pillow. He hadn't been wrong. She was as delicate as he'd thought she'd be.

No, he didn't have any trouble at all imagining that any man would want to make love to Sarah Bolton. But who had that man been? Had he been some wicked cad who seduced and then abandoned her? Or had she truly been in love with the lucky fellow, and he with her, and he'd been killed in the war before they'd had a chance to marry? Either way, Jesse wondered, what kind of man could make a proper Southern belle like Miss Sarah Bolton forget all propriety?

What a shame it hadn't been him.

He'd never have loved and left a woman who looked like that. And he wasn't the kind of man who'd abandon his child, either.

Patsy was a cute little girl. Well, according to the doctor who examined him when he was released from the prisoner-of-war camp just outside of Macon, he wouldn't be her step-daddy for long, but he'd try to stick around for as long as he could. While he was still on this earth, he'd do the best he could for her, and her mother, too.

The whistle blasted as the train began to huff to a stop. Jesse peered out the window.

"Looks like a sizable town coming up. I see a steeple over yonder." He pointed out the spire, outlined in gold by the rising sun against the still dark backdrop of the western sky. "There ought to be a minister there who'll marry us."

"Without too many questions," Sarah said hopefully.

As the train lurched to a stop, he heard her take a deep, weary breath. She turned and gathered up Patsy.

The little girl was awake now. "Milk?" she mumbled sleepily. She rubbed at her eyes with a pudgy fist.

"In a little while, honey. First we have to get off the train."

"Milk." Patsy nodded, yawned, and laid her head on Sarah's shoulder.

Lucky kid, Jesse thought, watching her.

Sarah reached for her traveling bag.

"I'd help you with that—if I could," he offered her. "But I think I've already got enough trouble getting around on my own."

"That's all right. I've managed this far by myself."

"But you won't be by yourself anymore, Sarah," he reminded her, then added, "not for a while, anyway."

She lifted the heavy bag. "Well, I won't be blamed in any way for hurrying your demise. I bargained to be a widow." With a grin and a lift of her delicate eyebrow, she added, "Not a murderess."

"Mighty kind of you," he replied with a grin. Well, I'll be switched, he thought with a grin. She *did* have a sense of humor. There was hope for her yet.

He tried to rise. It was difficult to stand up when one leg wouldn't bend, and the one that did wasn't strong enough to bear all his weight alone. He managed to pull himself up by the back of the seat in front of him. Balancing on his crutch, he followed Sarah down the narrow aisle of the train, and then descended the small metal steps to the wooden platform.

Piles of boxes and barrels, either ready to be loaded or just unloaded, turned the platform into a confusing maze. People getting on and off the train bustled about. Cows, horses, and crates of chickens contributed to the general noise, not to mention the variety of odors. Sarah, with Patsy cradled closely against her, stood wide-eyed, watching all the hustle and bustle with a look of uncertainty.

"The train won't stop here for long," Jesse said, coming up beside her. "We've got to find a preacher fast."

Sarah looked about, speechless. Jesse reached out to take her by the elbow. She started at his touch. He moved his hand away.

"Well, I know I'm not real clear on how much you'll obey me," he told her. "But for now, try to follow me."

"Follow you?" She glanced from him to the platform and back again with a look of dismay. "Are you sure you'll be able to maneuver through this crowd in your condition?"

He smiled at her. Oh, what the heck! He even summoned up the nerve to give her a sly wink. "You'd be surprised."

He started to limp forward, coughing pathetically and pounding his crutch on the platform loudly as he went. The crowd began to part, making way for him. He could hear Sarah's footsteps and Patsy's call for milk following close behind in his wake.

At last they made it to a quieter spot under the eaves beside the ticket window. Sarah drew up closely beside him. He liked the idea she came to him for protection—although what good he could do in his condition, he didn't know.

Glancing back at the crowd closing in their wake, Sarah released a deep sigh. "Well, I never would've believed. . . ."

"Didn't I tell you? I was Moses in my Sunday School Pageant."

She just looked at him, one delicate eyebrow raised skeptically.

"Well, not really. But I was a great sheep."

"That I'll believe."

"And I have taken advantage of my infirmity before."

"I also believe you'll be trying to do so again."

"You bet," he replied with a wide grin. "See, we're getting to know each other better all the time."

Well, at least she was getting to know him, he thought. But then, he was transparent as a pane of glass, and almost as thin. And Sarah? She was still a little clam—or a tight flower bud. What would it take to make her unfurl? Obviously someone had once found what it was. Could he? Would she let him? Would he even have the time?

No time to think about that now.

Jesse stopped a short, stocky man in a peaked cap. The old fellow wore a dark blue jacket, and unlike a lot of the people there, he looked as though he might know what he was doing. Jesse hobbled up to him. "Excuse me, sir."

"How do." He touched the brim of his cap.

"I suppose you're the stationmaster."

"Yep."

"I noticed there's a church in town."

"Two."

Jesse nodded back to Sarah. "The lady and I would like to see a preacher."

"What kind?"

"Well. . . ."

Jesse was about to answer, "The closest," when it occurred to him he really ought to consult Sarah first.

She'd never actually mentioned what sort of preacher her brother-in-law was. Did it matter as long as the minister they found was willing to marry them? Unsure, Jesse turned a questioning look to her.

"Methodist," she said quietly.

The stationmaster pointed toward the end of the street and muttered, "Right across from you. Can't miss it."

Jesse could see the clean, white steps from where he stood. They still looked an awful long way away.

"Thanks," Jesse replied. "Say, can you tell us how much longer the train will be stopped here?"

The stationmaster pulled out his pocket watch, flipped open the case, and glanced at the bold little face. " 'Bout fifteen minutes."

"That doesn't give us much time," Sarah murmured.

Jesse could detect the worry in her voice. If she was worried, how did she think he felt? How in the world was he going to make it to the parsonage, convince the minister to marry them, stand up through the long ceremony, and make it back in time to board the train without keeling over?

"Where's the other church?" Jesse asked.

The stationmaster pointed in the other direction. " 'Bout a half mile thataway."

"Well, that's out of the question," Jesse said to Sarah.

"Suit yourself," the little man commented with a shrug and began to walk away.

"Excuse me," Jesse called him back. The stationmaster didn't turn completely around, but only turned his head. "If we're not back in time, do you think you could wait just a little longer?"

The man fixed him with an icy stare. "There's mail on that train, son. Can't stop the U.S. Gover'mint."

"But so are our bags," Sarah protested.

"Sorry, ma'am."

"Thanks anyway." Jesse turned away.

Sarah held her ground. "But . . . but . . . we've got to find the preacher, maybe wake him up, get him to perform the ceremony. Please. Couldn't you wait just a little . . . ?"

"Sorry, ma'am," the stationmaster repeated as he moved away, obviously indicating that no matter how much more Sarah rambled on, his part in this conversation was definitely at an end.

"But . . . but . . ."

"Come on." Jesse took the sputtering Sarah by the elbow and began to pull her along. "You might as well try to argue with the platform. We've got to get to that church—fast."

"But you can't go fast. . . ."

"I'm fine."

"You can't. . . ."

You can't arrive in Cottonwood without a legal husband," he reminded her as he hobbled along the wooden sidewalk as fast as he could.

"But what if we miss the train? What about our baggage? What about—"

"You know, all the time you're wasting arguing with me

could be spent getting married." As he continued down the sidewalk, he called over his shoulder, "Follow me."

She pressed her lips together. It didn't take long for her to catch up to him.

Already it was becoming harder to breathe. He needed to cough so badly, but he knew if he gave in, he'd have to stop walking—and he might not be able to start again. So he just kept making little rasping sounds in his throat.

His leg hurt like hell, and he didn't even have time to stop and take a little sip out of his bottle. Once they were married and back on the train, then he'd take a good long swallow of that laudanum, and sleep for a good long while.

Damn! He hoped this woman really appreciated what he was doing for her.

Spikes of pain shot up his leg. He felt like the train had stopped on top of his chest. He could barely speak by the time the parsonage door swung open. "Are you . . . ?"

"I'm the Reverend Morgan," the gruff-looking man in his shirtsleeves answered, snapping his suspenders proudly.

Jesse's head was spinning, and he was having trouble focusing. He could tell the tall, dark-haired man was talking because his thick, bushy beard kept wagging up and down. It was hard to tell exactly what the man was saying because Jesse had the darnedest ringing in his ears.

"We . . . I mean, I . . . We . . ."

"Speak up, son," the man urged.

"We need . . ." Jesse tried to continue, but he had to lean against the white column of the porch for support. He had a hard time stopping coughing, and he didn't think it would look too good to pull out his bottle in front of the Reverend Morgan. The preacher might think he was drunk this early in the day. A sermon on temperance was the last thing he needed—the darned thing might take longer than the entire wedding service. They just didn't have the time.

The Reverend Morgan looked from Jesse to Sarah to Patsy, then back to Jesse. "I think it's a bit too soon to be burying you, son."

"We need . . ."

"Milk," Patsy interrupted.

Sarah boldly stepped forward. "Will you marry us, please?"

"Marry you?" The Reverend Morgan looked at the trio on his front porch uncertainly. "You aren't married yet—or aren't married to each other?"

"We're not married . . . at all," Sarah answered.

"So you need marrying. Well, I guess that's better than a burying." The Reverend Morgan fixed his piercing brown eyes on Sarah. "I take it you've at least had a Christian baptism."

"Oh, yes, sir," Sarah answered.

He turned to Jesse. "You, too?"

"Yes, sir."

"The child's been baptized?"

Jesse paused, waiting for Sarah to answer this question.

"Yes, sir," Sarah answered.

"Er, we're in kind of a hurry, Rev," Jesse managed to gasp.

"Appears to me as if you two were in a little too much of a hurry about two years ago."

"It's not what you think," Sarah tried to explain.

" 'Judge not lest ye be judged,' ma'am." The Reverend Morgan waved his hand. "And I suppose it's better to marry at the eleventh hour than never at all."

He turned back into the house. Jesse was afraid he was going to tell them no after all. Then he heard the man's booming voice call, "Mother, go get the grave digger."

"No, no," Jesse tried to tell him. "We said *wedding.*"

"Of course you did. You need witnesses, don't you?"

"Oh, dear," Sarah murmured. "I never thought of that."

"Good thing I know my job, isn't it?" the Reverend Morgan asked with a merry laugh. He turned back toward the kitchen and called, "Mother, bring some milk and a biscuit, too, for the little one." From a hook beside the door he took his black broadcloth jacket. He tilted his head toward the church next door. "Come with me."

Donning his coat as he went, the preacher headed across

the newly sprung grass. A plump little woman untying a big white apron emerged from the back door of the parsonage. She balanced a cup of milk and a golden brown biscuit in her other hand. A grubby young man with a limp and carrying a shovel appeared from behind the house.

It took every ounce of strength Jesse could muster to push himself away from the column. "Couldn't you just kind of do it out here on the porch, Rev?" he called after the preacher.

"Oh, I don't mind giving you folks the benefit of the doubt as far as marrying you," the Reverend Morgan called back. "But we'll at least do a proper ceremony in a proper place."

"Couldn't we just kind of go on the supposition that God is everywhere?" Jesse asked.

"Nope." The Reverend Morgan opened the church door and disappeared inside.

Jesse, still gasping for breath, managed to hobble across the grass beside Sarah. "Do you . . . do you really think we have time for all this, Rev?" he called as they drew closer to the church.

"Yes, I do. Come on in," the deep voice reverberated from inside—almost like the voice of God, summoning him.

Jesse could only hope this preacher wasn't as long-winded as some of the others he'd had the misfortune to encounter.

Sarah placed Patsy in a pew at the back of the church. Mrs. Morgan handed the little girl the biscuit and the cup of milk.

"Thank you," Sarah said.

"Taddy," Patsy echoed.

"Can't have her going hungry on her ma's wedding day," Mrs. Morgan said, then began to make her way toward the altar.

"Stay here, honey," Sarah told Patsy. "And don't make a mess."

Patsy, her mouth full of milk, only nodded.

The Reverend Morgan had situated himself in front of

the altar. Mrs. Morgan and the grave digger stood in front of and to either side of him, waiting to act as witnesses.

Jesse took his place beside Sarah and whispered, "You have such charming attendants, my dear."

"I didn't have time to make up proper gowns. The one with the limp was so hard to fit."

In the hush of the church, Jesse almost laughed aloud. He was glad to see Sarah show her sense of humor again.

"At least he put his shovel down."

The Reverend Morgan was already thumbing through his well-worn prayer book. "I'm assuming you two want the short version of this here ceremony."

"Well, we do have a train to catch. . . ."

The preacher pulled his watch out of his pocket and glanced at it. "Emmett keeps those trains running like clockwork. Let's get on with it, then."

Jesse looked toward the Reverend Morgan with dismay. From the outside, the church hadn't seemed any bigger than any other church he'd ever been in. But from the inside, he thought it was the longest aisle he'd ever seen in his entire life. It stretched from his feet all the way to the altar, that seemed almost as far away as heaven itself to a poor sinner like him. After all his efforts, he wasn't sure if he had enough strength to make it at last.

Suddenly he felt a gentle hand linking under his elbow. He looked to his left. Sarah stood there, looking up at him with a tiny, nervous smile on her face.

"I'll help you," she whispered. "Lean on me."

He tried to support himself on his crutch and his good leg. He didn't want to lean too heavily on her. She was such a tiny thing, but right now he needed the reassurance she could give as much as she needed his name. Just feeling her beside him gave him the strength he needed to continue.

With a little more assurance, he began to walk up the aisle. The floorboards creaked with each step. The smell of mildewed plaster, dusty hymnals, and decaying flowers assailed his nostrils. He almost choked on it until the soft spring breeze brought the scent of lavender to him. Too early in the year for lavender to bloom, he thought.

It was Sarah. He was suddenly struck with a very vivid picture of her, splashing a little lavender water behind each ear, and some between her breasts, which trickled down to her navel. He could imagine her pulling sheer silk and lace underthings out of a lavender-scented drawer. He could imagine her naked, stepping into her drawers.

He stumbled. Served him right. A man shouldn't be thinking such things in church. But, oh, when he leaned on Sarah, it was awful hard not to. He was glad she couldn't read his mind.

Even when he had to lean on her for more support, it didn't seem to bother her. He guessed she was stronger than she looked.

When they at last stood before the Reverend Morgan, the preacher cleared his throat loudly and, in a booming voice, began.

"Dearly beloved—well!" he exclaimed, looking out over the empty pews. "There aren't any beloveds here, are there? So we can dispense with that."

He turned the page.

"We are gathered here today in the sight of God to unite —what's your name?"

"Jesse Taylor."

"And . . ."

"Sarah Bolton."

"In holy matrimony." He looked down at his book. "And so forth, and so forth, and so forth," he mumbled to himself as he flipped through the pages. He looked up at Jesse and demanded, "Where's the ring?"

"Ring! No ring!" He turned to her. "Oh, Sarah, I'm so sorry."

"That's all right."

"I promise I'll get you one."

"That's all right," she repeated.

"A really pretty one."

"No time for that now, son." The Reverend Morgan

forged ahead. "Do you, Jesse, take Sarah here to be your lawful wife, to love and honor and cherish . . . and all that stuff?"

"I do," Jesse answered.

"Do you, Sarah, take Jesse to be your husband, for better or for worse, for richer or poorer, in sickness . . . ? Well, I guess that's a pretty pointless question."

"Make her promise to obey me, Rev," Jesse couldn't resist asking.

The surprised look on the preacher's face was enough to make Jesse want to laugh. But Sarah's sharp poke to his ribs really made him cough.

"Do you promise to love, honor, and obey him?" the Reverend Morgan continued above the sound of Jesse's coughing.

"I do," Sarah answered softly.

"For as long as you both shall live?"

"Oh, darn, Rev," Jesse protested. "Did you have to bring that up?"

"I do," Sarah repeated, sealing her fate.

The Reverend Morgan closed his prayer book. "I now pronounce you man and wife. Kiss the bride."

Kiss the bride, Jesse repeated to himself. The preacher'd told him to kiss his new bride. Well, he just had to. If he didn't, wouldn't it sort of be like disobeying a direct order from God?

Jesse could only hope Sarah would see it that way.

He turned to her. Would she turn to him in response? He waited. He hoped it was her nervousness that was making her so slow to turn around. He couldn't believe it might be some sort of maidenly modesty. He sure hoped it wasn't that she was dreading touching him.

"C'mon," the preacher urged. "We don't have all day. I know you folks are hoping to catch that train, and my wife and I left a darned good breakfast waiting."

At last Sarah turned to face Jesse.

He knew he looked awful. He hadn't even been able to

shave this morning. But he didn't think he was completely
repulsive, even now. Why then, as Sarah looked up at him,
did her eyes hold such concern—worry—he'd almost call it
fear?

Slowly Jesse leaned toward her. Clinging desperately to
his crutch, he tried to stand firm and not let his poor,
withered body shake with the effort. He was heading for two
of the prettiest lips he'd seen in a long time, and he didn't
want to miss!

His lips barely brushed hers, but he knew immediately.
They were soft and warm, just as he'd imagined—and she
didn't move. She didn't respond to his light kiss in any way
at all. Why, he'd swear she'd never even breathed. Was he
that terrible-looking that he didn't inspire any sort of reaction in a woman? Couldn't she have kissed him out of pity?
Or was this the best she could manage? Was she too polite
to show the true revulsion she felt at his touch?

As he drew apart from her, he noticed a slight trembling
of her lips and a small tear glistening in the corner of her
eye that she quickly blinked away.

Had he been that much of a disappointment? Well, she'd
stressed that part about them not really being in love with
each other. He should have sort of figured she might rather
be marrying the baby's father than him anyway.

What had he expected? A big, hot, wet, passionate kiss?
To all intents and purposes, this was just a business deal. He
didn't know too many business contracts that were sealed
with a kiss.

Had the Reverend Morgan noted the bride's strange behavior? Jesse wondered. In his limited church experience,
he'd found brides usually cried at their weddings. He
guessed the Reverend Morgan had seen more than his fair
share of weeping and didn't think anything of it.

Jesse and Sarah followed the preacher over to a big book.
After the Reverend Morgan noted the date, they signed
their names. Mrs. Morgan and the grave digger signed below.

"Much obliged, Rev," Jesse said, hunting through his pockets. He handed the preacher a few bills.

The Reverend Morgan pocketed the money without even counting it. He handed Sarah a small, stiff piece of paper with lots of lilies and roses, cherubs and curlicues around the edges and, on the lines in the center, their names and the date of the wedding written in a script that had as many curlicues as the border. How could a man who looked and sounded like a bear have such elegant handwriting?

The blast of the train whistle pierced the air, even in the peaceful church interior.

"Go on now. Get your daughter and get on that train." As they hurried down the aisle, the Reverend Morgan called after them, "And next time be a little more . . . well, shoot! I guess it doesn't matter now."

"Come on, Patsy," Sarah said as she threw her shawl around her shoulders and scooped up her daughter. She tucked the marriage certificate into her traveling bag and shouldered it. "We've got to hurry."

Jesse was already heading toward the door. He tried to hold it open for Sarah, but he figured he must weigh next to nothing, as the door kept pushing him back.

The whistle blew again.

"Run ahead," Jesse told her.

"I can't leave you," Sarah protested.

"Yes, you can," he tried to insist as he hobbled along behind her, losing ground with each step. "You've got to get on that train."

She hurried on, but kept glancing back worriedly at him.

"Go on, go on," he urged. "Once you're on the train, you can dawdle with your ticket with the conductor and delay the train."

"Do you really think that'll work?" she called back.

"Oh, yes." What else was he going to tell her?

"I won't let them leave without you," she promised.

"You can't lose me now, Mrs. Taylor," he answered, and tried not to cough anymore.

Mrs. Taylor? That sounded so odd, Jesse thought as he

still managed to move along behind Sarah. Mrs. Taylor had been his mother—once, long ago. Or his grandmother. Funny to think he now had a wife to share that name.

He kept his eyes riveted on her soft little figure as she ran ahead of him. No, sirree. He wasn't going to lose sight of her. He wasn't going to let her get on that train without him.

He was going to arrive in Cottonwood with his wife. He was going to live in a house with her, eat dinner with her. Gosh, would she actually let him sleep in the same bed with her? he wondered as he struggled to place one faltering foot in front of the other.

Was that what kept him moving along in spite of all the times he tripped and his injured leg dragged?

Pain shot through his leg like the first time he'd been struck. The tight fist around his heart began to squeeze unmercifully. He couldn't even draw in enough breath to expel a cough. Even though it was hard to see through the haze of pain, he knew he had to keep moving.

He hoped he was moving in the right direction. It wouldn't do much good to have Sarah on the train and him end up at that church a half mile down the road.

By the way the sound of his footsteps changed, he knew his feet were on the platform.

"You're late," he heard the little stationmaster's voice grumble. He sounded really irritated. "First time in three years I've had a train leave late."

Rough hands on his arms and back lifted him, so he figured someone was helping him up the steps and into the railroad car. Either that or the stationmaster and his friends were making ready to throw him in the river to drown.

The support of his crutch and his free hand gripping the seat backs propelled him down the aisle. He was glad to feel the wooden backs instead of cold splashes of water.

"Mr. Taylor. Right here, Mr. Taylor."

He recognized Sarah's soft voice calling to him. He couldn't see her. His head was swirling, and he was having trouble watching where he was going. He kept bumping into the arms of the seats. Didn't his leg hurt him enough already? Did he have to do himself more damage as well?

The edges of his vision had turned dark and were threatening to close in on him, no matter how many times he closed his eyes and shook his head to clear it. Thousands of little stars sparkled and fell through the blackness.

"Sit down here, Jesse," she told him more softly.

He felt her hands pushing him down into the seat and taking his crutch from him. Her gentle hands rearranged his weary legs so that the stiff one was safely out in the aisle and the other one wasn't all doubled up beneath him. He felt her soft, soothing hand reaching into his coat pocket, brushing against his aching chest. That was enough to make his poor heart feel better already.

Wait a minute! Oh, no! What was she doing? He felt her pulling out his little brown bottle. She wasn't going to throw his bottle away, was she? How would he endure without his bottle? Hadn't she said she wasn't one of those Bible-thumping, teetotaling . . .

He felt the cool glass against his lips. He wanted to gulp it greedily.

"Just a sip now," she admonished him. As she pulled the bottle away she repeated, "Just a sip. I can't have you arriving in Cottonwood looking like you've been intoxicated for the past three weeks. What would Mildred—what would the Reverend Preston—what would all those strangers say?"

"They'd say, 'Have another one, Jesse, ol' boy,'" he mumbled as exhaustion overtook him.

"Hush, now. You've exerted yourself a tad too much."

"They'd say, 'You need a shave, Jess, ol' boy.'" He tried to raise his hand to his chin, but his arm only flailed around aimlessly.

He thought he still had his eyes open, but he really couldn't tell. Everything looked black either way. He could feel Sarah tucking her big warm shawl around his shoulders and up under his chin.

"They'd say, 'You got a damned pretty wife there, Jess, you lucky ol' . . .'"

He let the darkness close in on him.

Sarah watched her new husband as he slept. Anxiously she watched the rise and fall of his chest until she was convinced she'd managed to give him just enough laudanum to put him to sleep, not to kill him.

Now, she thought, at last she could study him without fear of being thought rude. He would've been a handsome man if he weren't so awfully thin. Maybe her good cooking could fill him out a little so he'd make a better-looking corpse for the funeral.

Every so often his dark brows would draw into a deep frown, and he'd moan. His gnarled fingers clenched the arm of the seat until his protruding knuckles were hard and white.

When she'd first seen him do that on the trip, Sarah thought he might be having a bad dream. She knew all too well how terribly real some nightmares could seem. But now that she knew him better, she realized the resulting pallor on his face and the beads of sweat across his brow attested instead to his constant pain.

Poor man. He'd done a lot of good for her this morning— enough to last her and Patsy the rest of their lives. She'd do her best to make sure the remainder of his short life would be comfortable.

"Oh, no. Oh, no. Oh, no." Sarah's repeated mumbling awoke him.

"What . . . what is it?"

He tried hard to focus. He untangled his arm from her shawl and raised his hand to push his hair back from his forehead. He tried to take a couple of deep breaths to help him awaken. His leg had stopped throbbing and settled into the dull ache that he usually was able to endure without more laudanum.

"I should have known," Sarah muttered as she continued to peer anxiously out the train window.

"Indians?" Jesse felt the train begin grinding to a stop.

He might not be able to walk too well, but he could probably still fire a gun if he had to.

"Worse!"

"What could be worse?"

"Mildred."

Three

Sarah peered out the window at the approaching platform and the crowd gathered on it. She felt her heart plummet.

"Oh, Mildred! How could she do this to me?" she mumbled under her breath. In equally hushed tones, she answered herself. "Because she's Meddling Mildred, and she can. That's all the reason Mildred's ever needed."

She thought she was keeping all her complaints to herself. Apparently not.

Leaning toward her across the aisle, Jesse asked, "What's she done to you? Has she done it to me and Patsy, too? Or just you?"

She turned to him, frowning, and demanded, "What on earth are you talking about?"

"Well, I'd like to know what your sister's done so I can either thank her or spit in her direction every time I see her."

She blinked with shock, then turned back to the window. "I . . . I don't think that'll really be necessary—regardless of what she's done."

He'd managed to stand by himself, had crossed the aisle, and was now trying to look out the same window she was.

Instead of leaning on his crutch, or even on the back of the seat in front of them, he placed his hand on her shoulder for support.

She hadn't minded his touch so much when she was helping him down the church aisle. Then she knew she was his only aid. She also knew, then, that she still had the opportunity to escape. But now he crowded her between her seat and the sturdy seat back in front of her. She felt so trapped.

Why did he have to touch her? Why did he have to feel so gentle? If he leaned down and put his face beside hers to see out the grimy window better, what would she do? Would she be able to hear him breathing and feel his warmth on her neck as he exhaled? Would she feel the stubble of his beard burning her cheek? How could she bear to have another man so close?

She must have squirmed under his touch.

"Sorry to get so personal when I know this is just a marriage in name only," Jesse said, patting her shoulder. "But I need you to hold on to. And I guess this is better than losing my balance and falling into your lap."

She tried to hide her gasp and turned quickly to peer out the window. She didn't want to have to look at him, didn't want to have to be so aware of his body so close to hers, didn't want to have to imagine the weight of him pressing on her.

"What's your sister done that's upset you?" he asked.

"It's . . . it's just that Mildred is probably responsible for . . . this." Sarah indicated the mass of people on the platform.

Jesse surveyed the milling crowd. Sarah was silently grateful that he only bent over slightly to see out the window instead of coming too close again.

"You think your sister's responsible for this?"

She nodded ominously.

"It's just a platform full of people, Sarah," he pointed out to her with forced gentleness.

"No, it's not. It's a welcoming party."

"You've got to learn to relax." He patted her shoulder

comfortingly. "You've seen crowds like this at every station we've stopped at."

She heaved a deep sigh. "A great big welcoming party," she insisted.

"Are you sure it's not a lynching?"

She turned to stare at him again.

He was grinning at her, as usual. "I mean, if you really think your sister and these people are all out to get you. . . ."

Honestly, the man had the strangest sense of humor. "Why are you so certain it's a lynch party for me? Maybe you've done something you deserve to be hanged for."

"Not me," he said, shaking his head. "They don't even know I'm coming, do they?"

She grudgingly shook her head.

"So it must be for you. That surly little stationmaster probably recognized you from the wanted poster in his office and sent a telegram ahead. I wonder if it's too late to see if he'd split the reward with me."

"Oh, you must be joking!"

"Don't worry." He gave her another reassuring pat on the shoulder. "I'll put most of my share aside for Patsy's future."

"Oh, honestly!" She grimaced at him and shook her head. "I knew I was taking a chance marrying a complete stranger, but you seemed so . . . so helpless, I didn't think any harm could come from it. I was foolish enough to believe your illness would be confined to your physical ailments. How could I have known you'd be completely insane?"

"You accuse me of being insane? *You're* the one afraid of an ordinary little welcoming party."

"It's not an ordinary welcoming party," she corrected him. "It's *Mildred's* welcoming party."

"Is there a difference?"

"You'll understand once you know Mildred better," she warned.

At last, whistle howling and brakes squealing as the wheels ground on the tracks, the train lurched to a complete stop. He held her shoulder more firmly. She told herself he did it to keep his balance, but she was all too aware of his hand. It was only his hand, she told herself. And it was only her shoulder. There couldn't be anything threatening in that.

If she moved away, he might fall. She couldn't do that to him. The man might be positively bizarre, but she *had* promised to take good care of him. She'd just have to manage to endure his touch—but only for the moment, she consoled herself. Soon he'd move away again. Oh, please, let it be soon.

"I . . . I don't see my sister," Sarah said, still searching through the crowd.

"Yeah, I guess it would be kind of hard to single out anyone. Gosh, she must've brought out the whole town."

"It certainly looks that way."

"Do you know *all* these people?"

"No. Not a one. I've never been here before. Remember?"

He chuckled. "Well, apparently your sister does know everyone in town."

"I'm not surprised. It was the same way in Savannah before she married and moved away."

"Of course. How can you meddle in the lives of people you don't even know?"

Sarah gave him a knowing grin. "Don't underestimate Mildred," she warned. "You've never met her, and she's the reason you married me."

Jesse's hand on her shoulder flattened until his entire warm palm was resting on her. His voice soft and low, he told her, "Don't overestimate Mildred, either."

A silence closed in between them. Sarah wasn't about to break it. She'd told him time and again this was a marriage in name only. Why did she hesitate this time to remind him?

Suddenly he stepped closer to the window and pointed. "Is that her?"

"Where?" she demanded, eagerly pressing nearer to the

window. Then she stopped. "Wait a minute. How would you even know what she looks like?"

"Isn't she the one with the noose?" He laughed and stood as upright as he probably was able when he was coughing that badly.

Even though Sarah was concerned for him, she gave only an obligatory laugh. She was too preoccupied with taking this opportunity to tactfully slip out from beneath his hand. It was a relief not to have to bear his gentle touch any longer—especially not when her awareness of his nearness made her feel so nervous, so . . . no, not numb, the way she'd felt for so long, but strangely enough once again alive. She didn't want to feel alive. Being alive hurt too much.

As she watched all the people on the platform, other problems intruded into her thoughts.

Could she actually succeed with the plan she'd concocted with him? She wasn't a good liar—but then, telling everyone Jesse was her husband wasn't a lie. Of course, he wasn't really Patsy's father, and that would be hard to explain. She could only hope Mildred and everyone else would take it for granted, and no explanations would ever be necessary.

But her biggest worry was Jesse himself. Would he uphold his end of their unusual bargain? He'd said he valued complete honesty, and yet he was willing to perpetrate this scheme with her. Would he be able to lie for her? He couldn't possibly be contemplating deliberately telling anyone they'd been complete strangers before yesterday. Both she and her daughter had everything to lose.

But he'd be losing the things he'd bargained for, too. She didn't think he'd rather die all alone on the prairie, of starvation, or exposure, or his maladies, instead of enjoying wholesome food, a comfortable home, and a proper burial. She'd provide him with clean clothes and a hot bath. She could picture him taking off the dirty clothes so she could wash them while he soaked his tall, thin body in the soapy, warm water. . . .

Without his crutch, he'd need help standing. He'd probably need help getting into the tub . . . and as his wife, it would be her duty. . . .

No, no! She closed her eyes and shook her head hard. She'd better keep track of what was going on around her now, and not let her imagination run away with her.

Maybe this crowd was just a figment of her imagination, too, she thought hopefully. Maybe when she opened her eyes, they would all disappear and she could step out onto the platform to be greeted by Mildred alone. Oh, all right, she'd be willing to be greeted by the Reverend Preston, too —after all, he was family—but she wouldn't allow anyone else in her dreams.

She opened her eyes and took one more nervous glance out the window. She drew in a great gasping breath.

"Oh, no. Oh, no. Oh, no!" She didn't mumble this time, as she had when she'd first seen the crowd. She knew this was more like a groan of despair coming from deep inside her.

She drew back from the window quickly, so he wouldn't see her. She felt her knees weaken and feared she was going to collapse back into the seat. She clutched at the windowsill. When he'd left Savannah, his was one face she'd hoped never to see again. What was he doing here in Cottonwood?

Maybe she'd been mistaken. Maybe it was just someone who bore an uncanny resemblance to him—poor fellow. Cautiously she peeked out the window again.

No, there he was—as tall as ever, straw-colored hair above the crowd, and broad shoulders pushing everyone else aside so he could go wherever he pleased.

How could her sister have invited Deke Marsden to the party, too? How could even Mildred keep a man like him away? It really wasn't her fault. Her sister didn't really know —no one did—why Sarah detested him so.

"What's wrong?" Jesse asked quickly.

"Nothing," she stammered. She managed to release her grasp on the windowsill. She rose and busily began to gather up Patsy and her traveling bag.

"Do you see your sister? Is there something wrong with her?"

"No, no," she mumbled, unable to look him in the eye.

"Well, something's obviously upset you. I thought you said nothing could be worse than Meddling Mildred," he reminded her with a laugh.

"It's nothing."

"It's something," he insisted, blocking her way with his crutch as she tried to move into the aisle.

"Just . . . just never mind," she answered. She scooped up her traveling shawl and tossed it across her shoulder.

"I'll help you if I can, Sarah," he said. The blue eyes that held her gaze were no longer sparkling and mischievous. He seemed to be trying to convey to her all the depth of his sympathy and sincerity. "I think I've already proved I'm willing to do anything."

She lowered her gaze, refusing to accept any attempt he might want to make to come closer. Who knew what would happen if she did?

"I thought we'd also agreed not to ask each other too many questions about the past, Mr. Taylor."

"This isn't the past, Sarah," he said softly. "Whatever upset you is upsetting you *now.*"

She had to get away from Jesse. She supposed confronting Mildred and all those strangers would have to be better than staying and worrying about what else he might ask. She'd just have to hope she could safely avoid Deke, for as long as she could. She had a bad feeling it wasn't going to be easy. Cottonwood didn't look like that big a town.

"Unless this is something from your past that's followed you," Jesse persisted.

She didn't want to hurt him, but she couldn't bear any more of his questions.

"The only thing that's following me right now is you, with your persistent questions—which I thought we'd agreed not to ask." She readjusted the traveling bag on her shoulder and began to push past him again. "Excuse me. I have a sister I haven't seen in six years."

With her lips clenched tightly together, she pushed past him and began to move down the aisle.

She began to descend the steps. After being in the dimly lit interior of the train, she had to blink in the glare of the bright noon sunshine. She felt and heard her sister before she saw her.

"Oh, Sarah! I've missed you so much!" she heard Mildred exclaim and felt her arms wrap tightly around her.

"I've missed you, too."

Then Mildred released her and stepped back. Sarah got a good look at her sister for the first time in six years.

How thin Mildred looked. Oh, no! Was she going to have to worry about her sister's health, too? But Mildred's eyes were sparkling, her skin seemed fresh and glowing, and her dark hair was shining in the bright sunlight. Unlike Jesse, Mildred appeared healthy, but still awfully, awfully thin.

"What are you doing with this little darling?" Mildred demanded, grabbing one of Patsy's soft baby cheeks and giving it a playful pinch.

Patsy cooed and smiled, then pulled away and buried her face shyly in Sarah's shoulder.

"What a sweet angel she is!"

"This is Patsy—"

"The same name as our mother. What a coincidence! Whose little baby is she? And what are you doing with her?"

"She's my daughter," Sarah concluded nervously.

"Oh? Oh! Well, that explains it. How wonderful!"

That was it? No prying questions, no subtle hints for more information. Not a question in the world from Meddling Mildred? How could she be so lucky?

Sarah gave her shoulder a shrug to lift Patsy's face. "Patsy, say hello to Aunt Mildred."

Patsy eyed her curiously, then buried her face again.

"But you never even wrote to tell me you were married, much less that you had a little girl," Mildred scolded.

"The mail's been awful. . . ."

With a pout Mildred added, "Why didn't you tell me in

the telegram? All you said was 'We're coming to Cottonwood.' "

"I couldn't use too many words. Telegrams are awful expensive. I had to save what I could for . . . for the train fare, and milk for Patsy, and food for us, and . . . and . . ." She groped for other excuses.

"Well, naturally, I thought you meant you and Aunt Myrtle. Would it have taken so many words to mention little Patsy here and . . . well . . . ?" She paused and looked around. "Well, I suppose you've brought your husband, too."

Sarah nodded. After all, it *was* the truth.

"But where's Aunt Myrtle?" Mildred asked, glancing down the line of windows on the side of the train.

Sarah drew in a deep breath. This was just one of the many questions she'd been dreading all the way from Savannah, and the one she didn't have any easy reply for. Oddly enough, right now, this seemed to be one of the easiest ones to answer.

"Mildred, I'm sorry to have to tell you, but . . ." she tried to explain as gently as she could, "Aunt Myrtle . . . passed away."

Mildred made a grab up her sleeve for her handkerchief. She gave the lace-edged cotton a grand flip before applying it to her watery eyes.

"Six months ago. . . ." Sarah tried to fit her explanation in between Mildred's loud sobs. "From old age . . . peacefully in her sleep . . . she didn't suffer. . . ."

After the wailing had ceased, Mildred wiped her eyes and tucked away her handkerchief. She looked around again. At last, she seemed to notice that there were other people waiting to get off the train.

"Oh, Sarah, let's get our own grief out of this poor fellow's way so he can leave the train."

"But . . . but, Mildred . . ."

"We'd better hurry, too," Mildred said as she grabbed Sarah by the elbow and began to pull her out of Jesse's way. She leaned a bit closer and remarked confidentially in a whisper that could probably be heard to the end of the platform, "He doesn't look like he's going to live to make it to wherever he's going."

"Mildred—"

"Thank you for being so patient, kind sir," Mildred told him. She waved her hand as if scooting him from the platform. "Please be on your way now. I have a brother-in-law I'd like to meet."

"Mildred! This man *is* my husband."

Mildred gave Sarah a skeptical glance. Then she peered sharply at the stranger who had turned out to be her brother-in-law.

"This is my husband, Mr. Jesse Taylor. Mr. Taylor, my sister, Mrs. Preston," Sarah recited almost automatically. Somehow, in spite of all the commotion, she managed to remember the polite social responses Aunt Myrtle had taught her. She just hoped Jesse would be able to stifle his coughing long enough to greet her family.

"Pleased to meet you at last, Mrs. Preston," Jesse answered. Steadying himself on his crutch, he touched his fingertips to his brow. "Sarah's told me so much about you, why, I feel like I already know you—as a matter of fact, right from the time you were just a little girl. Why, the stories she's told me!"

Would she have to haul off and hit him with her traveling bag in order to shut him up? Sarah worried. Or could she just subtly kick his crutch out from under him? Why couldn't she have given him enough laudanum to make him just drowsy enough to walk off the train under his own power, but too drowsy to say anything that would embarrass her?

"Welcome to the family, Mr. Taylor. I wish I could say I knew you as well as you seem to know me."

So do I, Sarah thought wistfully. How strange to know so little about one's own husband.

Never taking her eyes off Jesse, Mildred leaned closer to Sarah and whispered, "Oh, my dear, but couldn't you have picked a husband that was a little more handsome—not to mention healthier-looking?"

Sarah could hardly admit to her sister that she hadn't exactly been seeking a handsome husband, just one who wouldn't live very long. Then she heard Jesse chuckling over Mildred's remark. He was being awfully pleasant about his first encounter with Meddling Mildred. Now Sarah felt twice as guilty about taking such advantage of him. She'd have to make sure she gave him a *really* nice funeral. Maybe she'd even save up for that marble headstone with an angel on top that he seemed so fond of.

"How on earth do you think he's going to support you all?" Mildred's complaint broke into Sarah's musings. "You don't want to end up like poor Winifred Maxwell, with six children to support on a laundress's pay and a husband who sat on his posterior all day and moaned about how bad his back pained him, when everyone in Savannah knew the man had never in his life done a lick of work that could've caused him such an injury."

"But Mr. Taylor actually has been very ill, Mildred," Sarah stressed.

"So he tells you." Her sister eyed him critically. "Well . . . well, never mind that right now, dear," she said, waving her hand about. "Just as long as he's good to you and Patsy." In her inimitable whisper, she asked, "He doesn't beat you, does he?"

Sarah shook her head.

"No, I guess he couldn't beat an egg in his condition. Well, we'll fatten him up soon enough. Get him working again," Mildred added with a sharp glance back at Jesse.

Sarah heard him stop chuckling, but the coughing continued. Only the two of them knew perfectly well he wouldn't live long enough to fatten up, much less find a job.

"I don't think—"

"What's his occupation, dear?"

"He . . ." Oh, my goodness! She had no idea what her very own husband would do to support them all—if he were in any condition to work. How was she going to answer this question?

"I'm a carpenter by trade, Mrs. Preston," Jesse answered.

"Ah, well," Mildred said with a relieved sigh, "there's always work for a good carpenter out here." Then she turned to Sarah. "But . . . but, well, you see, Sarah, your having a husband is going to cause the Reverend and me just a bit of a problem."

"Problem?" Sarah echoed. She could hardly believe her ears. Her being married was a problem for Mildred and the Reverend? Had she gone through all that fuss with Jesse not to solve a problem, but to create one? "Problem?" she repeated. What was Jesse going to say when he heard about this?

"Oh, my goodness! What's the matter with me? This is a welcoming party," Mildred exclaimed, obviously forgetting all the problems, real or imagined, for the moment. Apparently she had no intention of bringing them back when faced with the prospects of a celebration instead. "There's all sorts of delicious food at the parsonage, made by all the fine ladies at the church."

"What problem?" Sarah persisted.

Ignoring the question as only she could do, Mildred seized Sarah by the elbow and urged her along.

"Come. You can meet them. I'm sure you'll like them very much."

"Mildred, I don't think a big party is such a good idea right now," Sarah tried to tell her sister.

"Then maybe you can tell me, when *is* the best time for a welcoming party? When you're leaving town?"

"No, no. But we've been traveling a long time. We're all very tired and grimy from travel, and it would be very nice to use the . . . um, facilities—and Mr. Taylor's very ill. He's exceptionally weak—"

"Oh, our good food'll fix him up right as rain in no time," Mildred assured her.

"Mildred, you just don't understand," Sarah tried to convince her sister. She should've remembered sooner. Aunt

Myrtle had always said, "Once Mildred's made up her mind, neither hell nor high water'll change it."

"Oh, I understand. But there's no reason to be shy. All the folks of Cottonwood are so nice—I know you're just going to love each and every one of them, just like I do. And they'll love you, too, just like they love me!"

How could Sarah argue with her cheerful, overbearing sister? She should just be grateful Mildred hadn't hired a big brass marching band to precede them to the parsonage.

Hurrying along, Sarah looked back to see what was happening to Jesse. She didn't know how far away the parsonage was from the station. Jesse had barely made it back to the train when they'd been married. Had he had enough time to rest and get some strength back? His coughing had subsided somewhat. How could he survive being caught up and dragged along by this excited crowd?

But Jesse seemed to be doing fine, hobbling along on his crutch between two men. Sarah blinked. Jesse looked as if he'd been trapped between two facing mirrors.

The man to Jesse's right had a florid face and wild white hair that stuck straight up from the top of his head. His spectacles had slipped down his long narrow nose. He wouldn't look so silly if he could've managed to wear a suit that wasn't a garish red and ocher plaid wool and at least ten years behind the style.

The man to Jesse's left, with the same florid face, wild white hair, and slipping spectacles, was obviously the other man's twin. But this man wore a plain, dull, black broadcloth suit that contrasted sharply with his crisp white shirt and black string tie. If the man had had a longer neck, Sarah might be tempted to think he looked less human and more like a vulture. Knowing nothing else about the man, the suit alone seemed to her to be a hint that this was Cottonwood's undertaker.

She hoped Jesse hadn't noticed the resemblance of the man to his occupation.

She didn't like the inordinate amount of attention he was paying to Jesse, either. Why didn't he just whip out his tape and take Jesse's measurements for his coffin right in the middle of the street?

And if the man in black was the town's undertaker, what in the world was the job of his twin? Sarah didn't think too many Kansas towns had clowns.

Fortunately the parsonage wasn't as far away as Sarah had feared. She had no idea how her trunk and other things had been deposited so quickly on the front porch. But considering Mildred was in charge, Sarah knew her sister could manage somehow to get it done or, more likely, bully someone else into doing it for her.

She assumed the other two tattered bags belonged to Jesse. How strange not to know what her own husband's belongings looked like. How much more upsetting to suppose that her nosy sister *did* know.

"Sarah, I know it's been a long time," Mildred said as they climbed the three short steps to the front porch. "You do remember my husband, don't you?"

"Of course," Sarah replied.

"Say hello, dear," Mildred prompted.

"Yes, dear. It's good to see you again, Miss Sarah. Welcome to Cottonwood," the Reverend Preston greeted her. He gestured toward the wide-open front door. "Our house is—"

"Well, of course our house is your house, Sarah," Mildred finished.

Her brother-in-law hadn't changed a bit since the last time Sarah'd seen him as he and Mildred left on their wedding trip—a trek out to Kansas in a crowded, rickety wagon. Sarah hadn't thought it so very romantic at the time, she recalled. On the other hand, what kind of honeymoon had she had?

The Reverend Preston still had the same round face with its benign blue eyes and a placid smile. He never had been able to manage to keep his shock of curling, reddish-brown hair out of his eyes, no matter how much pomade he'd used. Apparently that hadn't changed either. Neither had his single phrase in answer to any comment of Mildred's.

"It's a very lovely house, Reverend Preston," she commented. It truly was, with its white picket fence surrounding the neat green clover lawn and the vivid pink petunias sprouting beside the front steps.

"We're trying, aren't we?" Mildred acknowledged with her usual false humility.

"Yes, dear," the Reverend replied.

"Now, take those things upstairs," she told him, pointing to the baggage on the porch.

"Yes, dear." The Reverend Preston held out his hand for the handle of Sarah's traveling bag. "Let me relieve you of that, Miss Sarah." Glancing questioningly toward his wife, he added, "I'll put it up with the others." He began heading toward the stairs.

Mildred pulled Sarah into the house. The small vestibule led straight ahead to a flight of stairs.

She glanced into the parlor to her left. In spite of the crowd gathered there, she could see the room was immaculate.

Every pane of glass glistened through the white lace curtains behind the drawn-back green velvet draperies. The sunlight bounced off a shining, gold-framed mirror above the fireplace and gave a deep, rich glow to the dark mahogany furniture with its flowered damask upholstery and intricate needlepoint cushions.

"It's lovely. So elegant. . . ."

"Well, it's . . . it's easy to keep a house neat and clean without . . . without children tracking in mud and dragging home frogs and stray dogs and spilling food all the time."

"There wasn't any mail. I didn't know you didn't have any children," Sarah said apologetically. "I'll try to keep Patsy—"

"Oh, don't fret about her," Mildred said, continuing to pull Sarah along.

"Oh, let me see this little angel," a white-haired lady declared, reaching out her plump arms. "She's about the same age as my youngest grandchild, but my son took his family out to Oregon before she was born. I'll probably never get to see her," she concluded with a sigh.

Before Sarah could even ask who she was, the lady had snatched up Patsy and was cooing and cuddling her. Sarah was relieved to see her daughter laugh and make a grab for the lady's nose.

Somehow, in the hustle and bustle, she had lost track of Jesse. Where was he? She listened for his coughing, but couldn't hear a thing. Did it mean he'd improved, or that he was already dead?

"Where's my husband?" Sarah asked.

She searched the crowd in the parlor and the vestibule. The ladies were all fussing over Patsy, who was obviously enjoying all the attention. But Sarah didn't see Jesse there.

She looked as well toward the room to her right, and the larger group that had stationed itself around the heavily laden dining-room table, impatiently waiting for the Reverend Preston to say grace so they could begin eating. Jesse wasn't there, either.

Of course, she did notice there were an awful lot of young men milling around the table. No doubt her sister had bullied them into coming to see her unmarried sister. Some of them even looked disappointed. Poor Mildred—finally to be frustrated in her matchmaking attempts. At least for the time being, Sarah thought with a tinge of sadness.

"Has anyone seen my husband?" she repeated.

"Oh, he's off with the menfolk, no doubt," her sister assured her.

"I don't think so. He doesn't travel very fast on his crutch."

"Don't worry. They'll keep him entertained, filling him in on all the manly gossip in town."

"But I have to take care of him," Sarah protested.

"Oh, Sarah, don't fuss over the man so much! You'll spoil him—if you haven't already. I declare, if I didn't know better, I'd swear you were acting just like a newlywed!"

Sarah sent a guilty prayer heavenward that her sister would never know how close to the truth she'd come.

"You must meet . . . well, I had intended for you to meet . . . so many . . . people. But," Mildred continued with a sigh, "considering the way things turned out, I suppose we'll settle for introducing you to all the fine members of the Cottonwood Methodist Ladies Evangelical Temperance and Missionary Soul-Saving Spiritual Aid Bible Society." Leaning closer to Sarah, she explained, "We removed the word 'Abolitionist' after Mr. Lincoln's Proclamation thing." Pulling Sarah along, Mildred continued her original line of thought. "They're the ones responsible for all that delicious food."

Even after the Reverend Preston said grace, and most of the casseroles and salads were left in ruins, Sarah still hadn't been able to spot Jesse. She'd seen the ladies feeding all sorts of goodies to a delighted Patsy, who gobbled up everything—and she knew she was most likely in for a night of nursing her daughter through a bellyache.

Mildred kept her busy sampling each dish and meeting the lady who'd made it. Sarah was busy thinking up new and different ways of complimenting each lady on her dish—whether she actually found it edible or not! She really hadn't been too fond of the raccoon stew or the roast gopher with skunkweed stuffing. She'd decided she was much too full to eat another bite by the time they got around to the muskrat pie.

She didn't even have the chance to look for Jesse. She'd promised to take care of him until he died and she hadn't even been able to get him a plate of potato salad and a watermelon pickle. She didn't think an invalid would be up to trying to digest possum potpie. Still, she hoped he didn't think she intended to starve him to death!

Sarah was much too concerned about the location of Jesse to recall any of the names to pair with any of the faces, or match them with their special dish. All she could recall was their eagerness and enthusiasm.

"I'd be happy to share the recipe with you," a tall, fair-haired lady offered.

"Thank you," Sarah tried to say graciously as Mildred pulled her along.

"Don't bother getting a recipe from Olive Luckhardt," Mildred warned.

"But she offered—"

"And you'll get it, too—with one very important ingredient missing."

"Oh, she wouldn't!" Sarah didn't see much harm in leaving the raccoon out of raccoon stew.

"Trust me, she would."

"Listen to your sister, Mrs. Taylor," a lady in a brown dress said. "Anyway, I'm sure you're a much better cook than Olive."

Modesty prevented Sarah from responding.

"Course, just about everybody in town is."

"You really should join the Ladies Society and help us with our charitable work," a plump lady in a let-out gown said. "Of course, we'll give you a week or two to get settled in."

"Miss Jemima Finchcroft has a real nice quilting circle meeting at her house each month," interjected a lady with lacy fingerless gloves that had obviously been mended many times. "You do sew, don't you?"

"Well, of course—"

"Then you must come."

"Well, I . . . I'm not really sure yet. . . ." She didn't want to reject their kind offers entirely. After Jesse did finally pass away, she'd probably be grateful for something to keep herself busy. "We'll . . . we'll need to get settled in first."

"Course, there's always the church choir," Sarah heard a familiar voice say.

How in the world could she hear a familiar voice in a town she'd never been to? Why that particular voice? In spite of her forebodings, she turned around to face the woman.

The Widow Marsden still looked as tight and pinched as an uncomfortable shoe, as if someone had made a line of running stitches around her mouth and then pulled it closed. Maybe she wouldn't have so many lines in her pale face if the two long black and gray braids weren't wrapped so tightly around the top of her head.

"I know you sing, don't you, Mrs. Taylor?" Mrs. Marsden spat out her new name as if it were poison. "As I recollect, you always thought you could do everything so perfect, nobody else was good enough to associate with you. And I swear, I'm plumb bamboozled by your choice of husband." Her voice took on a mocking, condescending edge. "He . . . he's just not . . . not Bolton quality."

Sarah could almost hear Aunt Myrtle instructing her, "The test of a lady's good manners is to be gracious in the face of bad." On the other hand, Aunt Myrtle'd admitted many times that she'd like to give Ruth Marsden a good smack in the mouth and a sharp kick elsewhere. Sarah didn't think her welcoming party at her sister's house was the time or the place to carry out her aunt's unfulfilled wish, so she just smiled and tried very hard to sound polite. "Why, Mrs. Marsden, what brings you here?"

"Curiosity," she replied. "It sure as hell ain't the sheer joy of seeing your face again."

All the ladies gasped and placed their hands over their gaping mouths. Only someone as countrified and uncouth as Mrs. Marsden would curse in the Reverend's very own house!

"Well, I hope your curiosity's satisfied," Mildred shot back. "So good of you to stop by, Mrs. Marsden. Do drop by again—in a few years."

Sometimes it was worth having a sharp-tongued sister, Sarah thought with relief as she moved away. But even though Mrs. Marsden had left, her presence there today still gave Sarah reason to worry.

What she'd seen from the train hadn't been a hallucination or a bad dream. If Mrs. Marsden was here, then her son Deke really was in Cottonwood, too. How long could she manage to avoid him? What would she do when she couldn't avoid him anymore?

"Why on earth did you invite her, Mildred?" Sarah demanded as her sister moved her along into a quiet corner of the large, immaculate kitchen. Sarah was grateful to have some peace and quiet at last—and a little time alone with her sister.

"You know, I don't think the choir's the right pastime for you," Mildred said.

"Mildred, why was Mrs. Marsden here?"

"I mean, you really can't sing, you know. You never could."

"What is Ruth Marsden doing in Cottonwood?"

"Well, I could hardly *not* invite them now, could I? What with Mr. Preston being the minister and all—we've a certain obligation to the congregation."

"All of them?"

"Well, they *are* members of our church," Mildred offered as her excuse.

"They?" Sarah repeated. "Then Deke's here, too."

Mildred nodded.

"Why didn't you tell me before I arrived?" Sarah demanded.

"Well, like you said, the mail's been awful. And they haven't been here all that long."

"Are they actually members of your husband's church?" Sarah asked with a feeling of dread. How terrible to see Deke every Sunday, and at each and every church social.

"Of course, the Marsdens never really were in the same social class as the Boltons—or the Prestons," Mildred hastily added, then her mind flitted off to something else. Sarah was pretty used to her sister's habit of never actually answering the specific question asked of her. "But you know, you really ought to consider joining something—"

Sarah shook her head. "I can't do that now, Mildred."

"Nonsense," Mildred insisted. "Emily Norse has a fourteen-year-old daughter who'd be perfect to look after Patsy while you're out."

"I'm sure, but—"

"Louella is Mrs. Norse's youngest, so she really needs to

learn how to care for young ones, not having had much experience at home."

"I can't do that."

"Of course you can. In fact, I've already arranged everything with Mrs. Norse and Louella."

"Mildred, my husband is too ill, and a young girl just can't . . ."

"Well, she's going to have to learn how to care for the sick, too, isn't she?"

"Mildred," she said with exasperation, "I don't think you understand. Didn't you see him?"

"Well, of course I saw him. In fact, I distinctly remember telling you that I didn't think he was all that handsome or healthy-looking."

"Well, handsome or not, I have to take care of him," Sarah insisted. "I mean, he's . . . my husband."

It seemed so strange to call Jesse her husband. The brief memory of the two of them standing before the Reverend Morgan flashed across her mind. She'd always be grateful to him now for giving her additional ammunition against Mildred's meddling—and from her very own arsenal, too.

"*I* have to take care of him. After all," Sarah reminded her sister, "I did promise in church—in sickness and in health, for better or for worse."

"Oh, well . . . I guess you did, didn't you?"

"Because he's sick—very sick."

"Oh, you and I—and Doc Hanford, too, if we really need him—will have Mr. Taylor up and around in no time."

"Mildred, you can't pass his illness off that easily," Sarah told her as forcefully as she'd ever said anything to her formidable sister in her life.

Mildred fixed Sarah with a warning stare. "Don't you let him take advantage of you like poor Winifred Maxwell let that no-good . . . !"

"Mildred, he has consumption and an incurable leg wound."

"So we'll just have to make him up some extra bowls of chicken soup."

"What do you think he's going to do? Soak his leg in chicken soup?"

"Well, he'll just have to learn to live with his wounds, like Bob's done."

Sarah didn't have time right now to ask her sister who in the world Bob was. She supposed, sooner or later, she'd meet him, especially if Mildred considered him an eligible bachelor.

"Mildred, people don't learn to live with consumption. They die from it!"

"I knew that," Mildred answered defensively. Then she went rambling on again, as if she hadn't actually heard a word Sarah had said. "Well, we'll see what Doc Hanford has to say about it."

Sarah didn't want to hear about any of Mildred's harebrained plans for Jesse's miraculous cure, especially when she knew it wouldn't do any good at all. "I really need to find my husband, Mildred, and make sure all those ladies don't feed Patsy so much she has a tummyache. We'll have plenty of time for catching up later."

"No, no, no," Mildred said, detaining her just a little longer. "Not until I see that wedding ring."

"Ring?"

"The little round gold thing that fits on your third finger, left hand," Mildred cued her.

"I . . . well, um, I don't have one."

Mildred threw her hands up in the air. "Oh, just as I feared. He *is* another layabout like that awful Gus Maxwell!"

"No, no. It's not that," Sarah hurried to explain. But what kind of explanation could she offer her sister? "We . . . we wanted to get a really nice one, but with doctor bills and all . . ."

"You mean he was sick like this when you married him? Were you out of your mind?"

Yes, Sarah decided, she must be out of her mind to have done such a crazy thing as to marry a stranger. But half the blame had to go to Meddling Mildred.

"You must've been, because I can't ever recall you being one to be completely infatuated with a man."

Only once, Sarah thought regretfully. And never again.

Mildred leaned a little closer and whispered, "And you still managed to have a child with him in this condition? My, my!"

"Well . . . um, he wasn't always this ill," Sarah answered. She figured she wasn't lying. She'd known from the first time she'd seen him that Jesse had once been really strong and handsome. "It's just been lately. . . ."

"Oh, I understand. Just make sure you get some kind of ring out of him once he's better, dear," Mildred advised. "Now, I need to make sure all the desserts are out! The ladies worked so hard on those cakes and puddings, it'd be a shame to miss a taste of even one." She bustled off.

Sarah continued her search. Jesse wasn't in the dining room or the kitchen. He wasn't in the parlor, although Patsy still was, being pampered and cosseted by nearly every lady there. Thank goodness they'd all stopped feeding her.

Sarah found yet another door. Probably another parlor, smaller than the front one, and therefore little used, she decided as she entered the darkened room—just the perfect place for Jesse to sneak away for a nap.

This back parlor was completely different from the sunny front of the house. The red velvet draperies were half drawn, admitting very little light. The furniture was much darker, too—mahogany with dark blue upholstery. There was even a fancy patterned Turkish carpet on the floor.

As her eyes grew accustomed to the gloom, Sarah could make out a small rolltop desk in the far corner of the room and several heavily laden bookshelves. Oh, dear, she'd inadvertently wandered into the Reverend's study, she was sure. Well, she hoped he'd forgive her her trespasses, she thought as she turned to make her way back out again.

Deke Marsden's large frame filled the doorway, blocking her escape.

Four

Sarah *had* to get away from Deke, but she wasn't sure how she could. Should she try to make a dash for the open door? she wondered as she never took her eyes off him. She was afraid he'd reach out his huge, rough hands and try to touch her. His heavy arms would encircle her, trapping her.

She knew she didn't stand a chance if she tried to push past him. Even if she had the courage to try, she'd never escape him in a struggle. And it would be very hard to explain to Mildred how she'd managed to wreck the Reverend's study within hours of her arrival.

She quickly glanced to her right, then to her left. They were on the first floor. The windows were open. It was still light enough outside to see that she'd only land in the bushes—and thank goodness they weren't roses. Could she make a dash and jump out the window before Deke could catch her?

But her fear kept her paralyzed. Deke was big and strong —and fast. Once, what seemed so long ago, she'd seen how fast he could be, and she didn't want to be the one to try him again.

What if she didn't move? What if she just let out a loud scream right in the middle of her very own welcoming party? That would certainly bring Mildred running—and everyone else, too—and give the whole town something new to gossip about. Aunt Myrtle had always said, "My dear, a lady never gives anyone cause to gossip—at least not on their first meeting."

And Deke hadn't really done anything worth screaming about—yet. What if he'd just followed her in here to say hello after all? If she screamed when he'd only been standing there, then she'd really look foolish! Much worse than being the target of gossip, Aunt Myrtle detested having anyone in her family appear stupid.

"What are you doing here, Mr. Marsden?" Sarah asked cautiously.

"I came for your welcome party, you silly li'l thing," he replied in his thick drawl.

No, it wasn't really a drawl, Sarah thought, recalling some of the softly spoken, eloquent gentlemen of Savannah. Deke didn't sound anything like them. It wasn't that he hadn't been educated. She'd heard his mother had insisted he attend until he'd learned to read, write, and cipher—even though he was the only student late for grammar school every morning because he had to shave. It was the fact that when he spoke, what he said was just plain rude, crude, and coarse.

"Course, I didn't think I'd be welcomin' your husband and young'un, too."

"No, I mean, what are you and your mother doing in Cottonwood?"

"I was just gonna ask you the same thing," he said with a broad grin. "Why'd you come to Cottonwood, Sarah?"

"That's *Mrs. Taylor* to you," she corrected. But as soon as the words left her mouth, she knew she might as well be talking to the rolltop desk.

"Oh, we're old friends, Sarah. We ain't gotta be so formal."

"Yes, we do," she murmured under her breath, and wished she had the courage to argue aloud with him.

Reaching behind him, he closed the door. If she screamed

now, would anyone hear her? She backed up a step. Maybe it would be a good idea to be a little closer to the windows, just in case she needed them.

Maybe if she asked him questions, kept him talking long enough, Patsy would start calling for her mama, or someone else would notice she was missing and come looking for her.

She was surprised to find herself hoping it would be Jesse. Pale and weak, and walking with the help of that crutch, at least his presence as her lawfully wedded husband would put some kind of damper on Deke's obnoxious behavior— even if Jesse didn't look as if he could really do much to defend her honor.

She hoped for Jesse, but she knew she'd probably get her sister instead. On the other hand, maybe right now Meddling Mildred was the better choice. Jesse'd only bargained to give her and Patsy a name. She wasn't sure she could count on him for anything more.

"Shortly after the war ended, Aunt Myrtle passed away," Sarah said, hoping a sad subject would keep Deke from making advances toward her, or at least keep him talking until rescue could arrive.

She paused, but Deke didn't take advantage of the lull to make an appropriate expression of sympathy. Too late, she realized she really shouldn't have expected him to. Nobody should expect Deke to acknowledge that other people had feelings—or that he gave a tinker's damn about them.

She continued anyway.

"I . . . we sold the house in town, and what was left of the plantation, and anything else I . . . we could, and came out here to be with my sister and her husband—as a family."

"Well, ain't that nice."

"What are you doing in Cottonwood?" she repeated, even though she was afraid to hear his answer.

He gave her a smug grin. "Me and my ma live here now, Sarah."

She didn't even bother to correct him about the use of her first name this time when her heart was sinking so fast. This was the answer she'd been dreading to hear.

He gave a short laugh. "What'd you think, that we'd travel all the way out here just to be at your party and then go home again?"

She wouldn't have put it past Deke to cross an entire continent if he'd set his mind on coming.

"I knew you'd moved away from Savannah. I didn't know you'd come here."

"So you noticed when I left, huh?" he asked with a lift of his eyebrows and a widening grin.

"Yes, I did," she reluctantly admitted.

Of course she'd been very aware that he was gone. It was the first time in several months that other fellows hadn't been afraid to ask her for a dance at a party or to go for an afternoon stroll in the park while she could. It was the first time she'd been able to breathe easy for months. In fact, she was downright glad to see Deke go.

"Everyone noticed."

The barkeepers were probably relieved not to have to break up the fights Deke started every night. She didn't want to think about what might have happened to Deke if the military police had caught him. On the other hand, if they had, then maybe she wouldn't have to be going through this unpleasantness with him now.

"Well, sure. I knew I was real popular. So you missed me real bad, huh?" He took a step toward her.

"Of course not," she replied quickly, backing away.

"Not even a little?" he asked with a sly tilt of his head.

She supposed he was trying to be the roguish, charming Deke who thought he could capture the fancy of any girl he set his sights on in Savannah. She felt very sorry for all the other girls who had succumbed to his foolishly flattering, and ultimately false, terms of endearment. Well, it wouldn't work on her. Not anymore.

"Not a bit." She shook her head, but never took her eyes off him. She wouldn't risk letting her guard down for a moment.

"Won't admit it, huh, sweetheart?" He moved a bit closer.

"Don't call me sweetheart!" She wanted to cry with the force of her need to escape him. "I'm a married woman now —and I . . . I was never your sweetheart. Never."

She might as well have told that to the desk, too.

"And here, all this time, you been heartbroken 'cause you never thought you'd see me again."

"I had my hopes. My sister never told me you'd come to Cottonwood." She'd have a word or two with her sister about that later.

"She didn't? Well, well, well. Now, ain't that the darnedest peculiar thing for her to do—knowin' how you females all like to gab just like a bunch of cacklin' hens over who does what when with who."

Sarah could tell from the tone of his voice he wasn't surprised at all. That was the most frightening part of it, but she didn't intend to ask him where he got his information.

"That's all right." With a slow, silent tread he made his way across the dark carpet, closer and closer toward her. He continued to stare at her, almost as if he were a tiger, stalking his prey. "We're all full of surprises for each other, ain't we? I didn't know you'd gotten hitched—much less had a kid. Couldn't have been all that long ago. You wasn't married when I left."

Sarah drew in a sharp breath and held it. What else would he notice? She could only hope Deke wasn't any better at ciphering than he'd been at anything else involving book learning.

"Guess that ol' boy didn't waste no time when he got back from the war, did he?"

She nodded and released a deep breath. Thank goodness most men weren't all that good at guessing the ages of small children. She hoped he wouldn't ask her when her anniversary was. She figured it was just about half a day now.

"I'll tell you, I'm just plumb heartbroken, Sarah."

She wanted to tell him he didn't have a heart to break, but she couldn't find the courage. All she could do was make a feeble gesture toward the door that seemed so far away.

"Please let me pass," she said. "I really need to find my husband and child."

"That feller standin' next to me at the train station, I almost punched him in the nose when he told me you was married."

Sarah wasn't surprised. That was the way Deke usually dealt with people he disagreed with.

"I got to wonderin' what a man like that husband of yours has got that I ain't. Then I got myself a good look at him, and now I'm just plumb flabbergasted. He looks like hell! Real, real weak . . . and pale and sickly. Say, does a sissy-lookin' feller like him write poetry, too, and speak that Frenchie talk, and wear them queer ruffly shirts?"

"I don't know about his literary achievements or his tastes in fashions. I didn't marry him just for his appearance."

"Reckon not," Deke responded with a low chuckle.

He began to move around her, with slow, careful steps—sort of like a buzzard circling a suffering animal, waiting for it to die so he could land and feed—except, unlike buzzards, she knew Deke wasn't the kind to wait until the animal was completely dead.

Each round brought him closer to her. He watched her, his eyes moving up and down her body until she felt filthy just from his gaze.

She wanted to run as fast as she could toward one of those windows and leap. But she remained standing where she was, absolutely still, like a rabbit trying not to be seen—and still knowing perfectly well that she had been.

"There's other parts of a man worth marryin' for besides a face, ain't there, Sarah?"

He continued his low laugh as he shoved his hands into his pockets and began rocking on his heels. His pelvis thrust back and forth toward her. She had no doubts that he knew exactly what he was doing, or that he knew she knew, too.

She could feel her face growing hot with embarrassment. "My Aunt Myrtle taught me to be too much of a lady to respond to that remark, Mr. Marsden," she replied icily, turning her gaze away.

She'd been gone from the party for so long—or maybe it just seemed so long—and still no one had come looking for her. She remembered that Deke only felt good when he was making someone else feel small. Maybe, if she could manage to remain cool and aloof, she could control her own embarrassment and dampen some of Deke's ardor in the process. Then she could make an easy exit.

"I'll thank you to keep such comments to yourself."

"You ain't such a lady you don't know what I mean by them comments," he answered with a chuckle. "I mean, you got one young'un already. Another one on the way maybe, huh?" he asked, blatantly eyeing her stomach.

"No!"

She clasped her hands protectively in front of her. Then she realized she'd perhaps denied his question too forcefully. It wouldn't be a good idea to let anyone even suspect that hers was a marriage in name only. Who knew what little piece of seemingly innocent information someone might turn into a large piece of harmful gossip? She couldn't let that happen and ruin Patsy's future, not after she'd worried and worked and schemed so hard to secure it.

"No, not yet," she repeated a bit more calmly, and lowered her hands.

"What happened to your husband—what's his name?" Deke asked, coming so close to her now that he could actually touch her with a pass of his broad shoulder.

"Taylor. Jesse Taylor."

"What, he get wounded in the war or somethin'?"

She hadn't the faintest idea, and she knew she couldn't let anyone know this. But her fear and anger made her incautious. Suddenly she blurted out, "At least he was brave enough to fight."

Too late, she realized her mistake. What if she told everyone in town one story about his past and Jesse told them another?

But she had another more immediate problem. Deke's face grew red with anger, his fists clenching and unclenching. She was only trying to defend Jesse.

Deke growled and gestured angrily toward the door. "I don't care what kind of lies those bastards out there told you about me!"

How could she have known? And even if she knew, she wouldn't have cared about what happened to Deke after he left Savannah. She'd been glad to see him go.

Then Deke's fists relaxed, and his face regained its normal color. "Anyway," he said with a stiff laugh, "a lady like you should be thinkin' of smooth sheets and lacy pillows to please her man on. You shouldn't fill your pretty li'l head with gossip and lies."

How would Deke know what she should be thinking? Deke wouldn't know a lady if he fell over one!

"You oughtta know me better than to believe that crap, anyway."

Just like Deke—to use language like that in front of a lady, and right in the preacher's own study! Well, he came by it honestly from his mother.

"I *had* to provide for my ma," Deke insisted. "I had to keep her safe. I had to take her away from all those ruins."

Sarah pressed her lips together. What difference did it make? A ruined Savannah looked pretty much like what the Marsden farm looked like all the time.

Aunt Myrtle had always told her, "A lady *never* uses profanity—unless it's absolutely necessary." Sarah didn't think this was the time to tell Deke what she really thought of his statement, although she was sure Aunt Myrtle would heartily approve.

"At least I can provide for my ma—which is more than it looks like your feller can do for you."

She knew Deke would strike back in some way. She was glad he'd only resorted to insults this time.

"I don't think he'll be up to workin' to support you and the young'un anytime soon—like a husband should."

"My husband's been ill recently," Sarah answered. "But he's a carpenter by trade."

"You know, I was kinda surprised to see you with a young'un, specially after seein' that husband of yours. He don't look like he could take care of you like a man should —but you know what I mean by that real good, don't you?"

"My husband wasn't always so ill, Mr. Marsden. And I have promised to love, honor, and . . . obey him, in sickness and in health. Now, if you'll excuse me, I have to take care of my husband . . . and *our* child."

Deke was standing behind her instead of between her and the door. Now might be her chance to escape. She made a quick move forward.

He was even quicker to take one long step to block her way.

"You know, with a husband in such bad shape—not goin' nowhere, not doin' nothin'—a lady could get awful lonesome."

"I have an invalid husband and a young daughter, not to mention a sister and brother-in-law I haven't seen in six years, and a whole town full of people she's dying to have me meet. I'm sure they'll all keep me from ever being lonely."

"Maybe. But you never know. Some night, lyin' in an empty bed, or lyin' beside a man who can't do nothin', even if he wants to, you might get really lonesome. You might 'preciate a visit from someone who can be real . . . friendly."

He reached out to touch the thin tendril of pale hair that hung in front of her ear.

"You know, if you ever get *real* lonely, Sarah . . ."

Even before his rough fingers could brush against her cheek, she cringed.

Ignoring her show of blatant dislike for him, he stroked her cheek with the rough knuckle of his index finger.

Just like Deke, Sarah thought, swallowing hard to keep herself from vomiting on the Reverend's good carpet. It didn't matter what anyone else thought, how anyone else felt, just as long as he got what *he* wanted.

"Please let me pass." She could hear her voice quaver with threatening tears of fear and frustration. She refused to cry in front of this horrible man, ever again.

"Naw. You're a Bolton. Hell, you think you're too good for the likes of me. All you damned Boltons always did think you were too good for almost everybody else. So I'll just wait. Yeah, y'know, from the looks of him, I don't think that husband of yours is gonna live much longer. And when he dies, you're gonna need a new husband."

"I . . . I don't intend to remarry—ever."

"I don't give a damn what you intend to do. All I know is what I want. I want you, Sarah—and I'm gonna have you. I missed you once before. I ain't gonna do that again. Someday. Somehow. I'll have you. And I'll warn you, I ain't a very patient man."

Deke could be a bare-faced liar in everything else, but he always meant every threatening word he ever uttered. She tried to stay calm.

"Sarah!" Mildred burst into the room. "So this is where you've been. We all thought you'd gone out to the necessary and gotten lost." She gave a little giggle. "We were afraid we'd have to go looking for you, and find you wandering out on the prairie, trying to find your way back. I'm so glad I found you. You need to see to Mr. Taylor."

Spotting Deke, Mildred stopped in her tracks and glared at him.

Sarah didn't know whether to hug her sister for her timely intrusion or grab her and shake her for not continuing. The devil with Deke! Was something wrong with Jesse? Would Deke have his opportunity to try to badger her into marrying him far sooner than Sarah had feared? Or had Jesse hit somebody with his crutch, stood up on the dining-room table, and was now loudly singing "Dixie" with his good foot in the bowl of Mrs. Silesky's potato salad?

"Mr. Marsden, what are you doing in here?" Mildred demanded, eyeing Deke disdainfully. "The Reverend doesn't permit anyone in his study unless he's with them. Lots of valuable books and all, you know."

"I don't bother much with books, Mrs. Preston."

"I'm not surprised. But I'll still have to ask you to leave here anyway and join the other guests in the parlor."

"Golly, and I was havin' so much fun in here."

"I should've known you wouldn't know your place in Cottonwood any more than you knew it back in Savannah," Mildred answered, obviously unfazed by his lame excuses. "Against my better judgment and all, but . . . well, I could hardly invite the whole congregation and not you. Although it's not exactly as if you show up regularly for worship or contribute to the collection plate and the building fund with any great frequency—or generosity—either, like everyone else does. Your mother's gone home, Mr. Marsden. I'll thank you to go home, too."

"Sure, sure. I'll go now," Deke told her. "You had lots of food—and other things. I got what I came for—for now."

In spite of his agreeable words, he had a fierce grin on his face, and Sarah couldn't help but notice how cold his blue eyes looked under his lowered brows.

He leaned toward Sarah and whispered, "I'm gonna be in Cottonwood for a long, long time." He brushed past Mildred as he strode from the room, muttering, "Chatterin' old busybody."

"Trash, just plain trash!" Mildred exclaimed, hands placed indignantly on her slender hips. "That's all those Marsdens ever were, that's all they'll ever be. That's what Papa and Aunt Myrtle always used to say, although some folks might've been fooled. Why, I'd bet the man doesn't even know who his own daddy was."

Well, he wasn't the only one here who could make that claim, Sarah thought guiltily.

"I wouldn't be surprised if his mother doesn't know, either. Imagine the two of them, living on that worn-out piece of swampland, farming with one old, half-lame mule— whenever they felt like working, which wasn't that often. I'll tell you, the day they showed up in Cottonwood you could've bowled me over with a feather!"

Without pausing for breath, Mildred walked over to the bookcases, started examining the backs of the fancy, leather-bound books, and continued, "I'll have to check all these volumes tomorrow, to make sure Deke didn't steal

one, thinking to sell it—although who'd buy one of the minister's very own books in his own town, I'll never know. But
that's the only way he and his kind know how to make
money. Papa was right. Trash, that's all they are, that's all
they'll ever be."

"Mildred!" Sarah had to fairly scream to get her sister's
attention.

"Oh? What?"

"What happened to Jes—ah, Mr. Taylor?"

"Oh, dear, yes. Come with me. Your husband's collapsed
on my sofa."

Sarah rushed from the room even faster than she would
have when trying to escape Deke. It just wouldn't be fair to
Jesse if he died on the same day as their marriage. How
would she keep all her promises to him? It really wouldn't
look too good to everyone else in town, either, to have him
die the day he arrived.

Would all the townspeople start to argue, each one blam-
ing the other, and eventually divide up into separate camps
about whose rotten food at the welcoming party had eventually poisoned Jesse? And of course, just on general princi-
ples, she didn't want to see the overeager undertaker get
their business too soon.

Worst of all, it would give Mildred the opportunity to
eventually introduce her to all those single young men she'd
missed today. No doubt, as sensitive as Mildred was, she'd
pick the six most promising bachelors to act as Jesse's pall-
bearers.

The crowd of people in the parlor was so clustered
around the sofa that Sarah couldn't even see Jesse.

"What happened?" she cried, standing on tiptoe to try to
see over their heads.

She heard muttered whispers of "Shh. Poor thing. It's his
wife." The crowd parted to let her pass. Expecting the
worst, she slowly approached the sofa. The curious crowd
closed in behind her.

"Oh, merciful heavens!" Her hand flew to her open
mouth.

Jesse was lying unconscious on the sofa, his feet propped up on the arm. She felt a pang of guilt. She'd promised to take care of him, and then, the one time he needed her, she hadn't been there. She blamed herself, even if Mildred had kept her so busy she hadn't been able to look for him.

Then she noticed someone had arranged a pile of fluffy, tasseled pillows neatly and comfortably under his head. Who else—which one of the ladies there—had been doing the job she was supposed to do? she wondered. As she eyed the ladies, standing to her right and left, all in their Sunday finery for the party, she felt a sharp pang of jealousy. She tried to push it aside very quickly. She tried to tell herself that it didn't matter, as long as someone had taken care of him. But as she imagined another lady ministering to her husband, she was finding it increasingly difficult to listen to her own advice.

"Is he still alive?" she asked, hoping that someone could give her the right answer. She got no answer at all.

She approached Jesse on feet she could barely feel beneath her, with legs that reluctantly supported her. Coming closer, she could see how colorless he looked. His illness already made him pale, but now he looked almost as white as Mildred's lace curtains. His sunken, purple-encircled eyes were closed. Already she missed their sparkle when he laughed.

She wanted to reach out and touch his hand, but was afraid she'd only feel the cold chill of death already resting on his flesh. Surrounded by strangers in a strange town on the sofa in a stranger's home—what a pitiful end for a kind man who'd helped out a strange lady and her little girl on a train.

Then she saw his fingers twitch, and she felt her shoulders relaxing from the tight knot of tension in which she'd held them. She felt more sensible, more logical now. Looking more closely—and objectively—at his hand resting on his flat stomach, she could see his thin chest barely moving up and down as he drew in shallow breaths.

"What happened to him?" she repeated.

"We were just chatting, Mrs. Taylor," the tall man in the black suit replied as he stepped forward from the surrounding crowd. "Pleasant as could be."

Well, chatting with the undertaker would make her nervous, too, Sarah decided, if she were in Jesse's condition.

"One minute he looked as if he was paying attention to me," the man continued, "the next, his eyes rolled up in the back of his head, his head lolled over on the back of the sofa, and the poor fellow just seemed to fall asleep."

"I don't blame him," the man in the awful suit told his twin. "I've been listening to you all my life. He's lucky you didn't bore him to death."

"I'm not used to having them keel over in the middle of a conversation. That's usually your experience, Mel," the undertaker replied. "I'm used to having them lie still when I deal with them."

Without so much as a "by your leave," the undertaker's brother—obviously named Mel—sat down on the sofa beside Jesse. He lifted Jesse's hand from his stomach and placed his index and middle fingers firmly on the inside of the wrist. He'd left a small black leather bag sitting open on the floor at his feet. Sarah could see an array of capped silver and corked brown glass bottles inside and, of all things, a stethoscope.

"Oh, merciful heavens! *You're* the doctor!" Sarah exclaimed. She tried not to groan in disbelief.

"Dr. Melvin G. Hanford, ma'am," he answered proudly. He rose from his seat just enough not to appear impolite, then seated himself again quickly. He nodded his head so that his fluffy white hair waved above his head like ostrich plumes. "Although most people 'round here call me 'Doc.' "

She'd often heard the preacher telling the congregation, "A merry heart doeth good like a medicine," but she didn't think having the town doctor dress like a clown was quite what the Good Book intended.

"Is there anything else you need, Doctor?" Mildred asked, inserting herself between the man and Sarah. "I've already set a kettle of water to boiling and gathered up a few clean sheets."

"Shoot, Mrs. Preston, the man's passed out. He's not having a baby!"

Mildred drew herself up indignantly. "Well! I was only trying to help. . . ."

"Thank you, Mrs. Preston. If you want to be of some real use, you can rustle up a couple of strong men to carry this man to his own bedroom, where I can examine him properlike." Looking up, Dr. Hanford glanced at all the ladies standing in a semicircle around them. "I don't think I can have him strip to his union suit and examine him right here in the middle of your parlor."

All the respectable members of the Cottonwood Methodist Ladies Evangelical Temperance and Missionary Soul-Saving Spiritual Aid Bible Society began tittering behind their hands like a flock of finches.

"Come to think of it, in this nice weather, he might even have foregone the necessary in order to be in the altogether. Can't hardly have him dropping his drawers in the middle of the parlor in that condition, now can we?"

The same ladies all began cackling like a flock of magpies.

"It's upstairs to the left at the end of the hall," Mildred said, taking charge once again.

"How about you, Marv?" Dr. Hanford asked. "You're used to hauling around bodies."

"Happy to help, Mel," the undertaker answered.

Although he'd seemed pleasant enough, Sarah wasn't too happy to have the undertaker handling her husband—at least not yet. But it would've looked so awkward to protest in front of all these people.

"Simon Parker's a strong man. Where's he?" Mildred asked, looking around until one of the ladies pushed a tall, red-haired man into the center of the parlor.

"And Deke Marsden," Mildred added. "He's a big man, too. I don't believe he really listened to me and left. Just like that no-good, lazy layabout to disappear when it comes to doing some real work."

All Sarah could picture was Deke trying to carry Jesse upstairs and "accidentally" managing to drop him on his head.

"No! Oh, no! Don't you dare ask him!" she exclaimed.

She couldn't help herself. But now her protest had left the crowd staring at her, watching for what unusual outburst she might make next.

Desperate to hide her error, she glanced around. She spotted another tall man still in the dining room and still eating. Well, if he'd eaten that much, he certainly owed this family something. She decided a lift up the stairs for Jesse wouldn't be asking too much in return.

"Please help my husband," she asked him, her hand outstretched to Jesse, still unconscious on the sofa.

"Shoot, lady," the man exclaimed with a laugh. His mouth was still full of food, and she was glad none of it came shooting out. "He don't look like he weighs enough to need three men to carry him. I'll bet even a little lady like you could heft him up on your shoulders and carry him all by yourself."

Still chuckling, the man put his plate down. He wiped his mouth across his sleeve, then wiped his palms on the front of his shirt. He strode into the parlor and stood ready to grab Jesse under the shoulders, while Mr. Hanford and the man called Simon each took a leg.

"Everyone! Everyone! That's all there is to see," Mildred announced, clapping her hands loudly to be sure she had everyone's attention. "Mr. Taylor's been taken ill. The party's over. Thank you all for coming. Go home now. Go home."

She started moving about the room, sweeping her arms through the air as if she could shoo everyone home like a flock of chickens. Sarah wasn't surprised when all the ladies scooped up their empty dishes from the dining-room table and their husbands from the parlor and the front porch and headed home. Before the three men could lift Jesse from the sofa, the house was empty of guests.

Led by Mildred, they began to carry Jesse toward the

stairs. Sarah, trailing behind, was grateful they managed to get him upstairs without dropping him or knocking his head on the banister.

Mildred stood at the end of the hallway, holding the door open. "Just put him there, gentlemen," she directed.

Sarah could only get a brief glimpse of the room over the heads and shoulders of the big men. It was pink and white and trimmed with more ruffles, lace, and ribbons than there probably were trimming the underwear of all the ladies in Cottonwood. It looked just like something Mildred would like, Sarah decided.

The men headed toward the bed with their burden.

"Oh, no, you don't." Mildred bustled into the room. "I brought that bedspread all the way from Savannah in the bottom of a trunk, wrapped in tissue just so it would stay clean. You let me fold it down before you put him in that bed."

The men deposited a still-unconscious Jesse onto the clean white sheets. Sarah watched him hopefully. Was it her imagination or did he really have a little more color than the sheets now? Maybe he was improving.

"All right, all right," Dr. Hanford said, ordering the men from the room. "Thank you all very much. He's my patient now. You're just going to have to wait, Marv. I'm not done with him yet."

The man in black turned around and chuckled. "Go ahead, Mel. You just keep trying to put me out of business. Sooner or later, I get them all anyway."

"I know I can't stop you, Marv—and I suppose that isn't really the way Nature intended it anyway—but I can still try to slow you down." Still chuckling, Dr. Hanford closed the door.

Holding her hands tightly together in front of her, Sarah kept staring at the closed door, as if she could see through the solid oak. Was Jesse conscious yet? Was he in any pain? What would Dr. Hanford tell her after he'd examined him? Jesse had told her the other doctor had given him until Christmas. Would Dr. Hanford only give him until the fall?

Or maybe, now that he'd suffered through one of Mildred's parties, Jesse would only last until the Fourth of July.

"See, I told you there were problems," Mildred, standing beside her, said sadly.

"Problems?" Sarah repeated absentmindedly. She didn't even bother to turn to her sister. Her thoughts were still with Jesse on the other side of the door.

"Yes, problems," Mildred stated forcefully.

"Oh, my! Oh, yes, problems." Sarah blinked to bring her attention back to her sister in the upstairs hallway. "What kind of problems?" How could the doctor have managed to tell Mildred something about Jesse that he hadn't told her?

"No, no. I mean I told you there were problems with you having a husband that I didn't know about."

Aunt Myrtle had always told Sarah—privately, of course —"Mildred never misses the chance to say 'I told you so.'" Only Mildred could make a grand crisis out of an extra houseguest.

"And what exactly is wrong with my having a husband?" She tried to curb her anger when, actually, she wanted to tell her sister all the trouble she'd gone through just trying to find the right one.

"Well, I sure hope you like your room," Mildred said. "I decorated it myself."

What did wallpaper and draperies have to do with Jesse being a problem? Sarah couldn't figure.

"I saw a little bit of it. I'm sure the rest of it's just as beautiful," Sarah assured her.

She'd slept in an empty, half-ruined mansion and a deserted, dilapidated plantation with an invalid old aunt and, later, her infant daughter as well. She'd tried to sleep sitting up in a sooty, jolting train with her daughter. She didn't care what the bedroom looked like as long as it had a bed with a decent mattress and a door that closed—and locked. Already her mind was drifting back to the other side of the door.

"*You* probably will like it. I'm not so sure about Mr. Taylor."

"Oh, he's a very easy man to please." Sarah could hardly add, *Just keep him dosed on laudanum.* "I'm sure he'll like it very much once he's well enough to notice."

"Sarah!" Mildred exclaimed. "Are you joking?"

"What's wrong?" She hated the continual interruptions of her thoughts. She wanted to just stand there and worry about Jesse in peace and quiet.

"The room is pink and white and lacy," Mildred pointed out. "It's a lady's bedroom. I had it all set up for you, and the other one ready for Aunt Myrtle—may she rest in peace —but Patsy can stay in there now. You'd never expect any self-respecting man to sleep in that room. The least you could have done was send me a telegram telling me you had a husband! I thought you'd be sleeping in that room alone."

So did I, Sarah thought with a wry twist of her lips that she hoped her sister didn't notice.

"Maybe I could take down the pink draperies, add a little brown or some dark green . . ." Mildred mumbled, half to Sarah, half to herself as plans were already forming in her head.

Suddenly the bedroom door opened, and Dr. Hanford stuck his head out.

"Mrs. Taylor, I'd like to see you in here for a moment, please." He beckoned her with his finger.

Sarah, followed by Mildred, began to make her way toward the door. Dr. Hanford let her pass.

"No, no. Not you, Mrs. Preston," he said, holding his hand palm out to stop her.

"Well, why not?" she demanded. Obviously deeply offended, she drew herself up and crossed her arms over her breasts.

"Because I'm the doctor, that's why," he answered with a grin. "And, sorry to tell you this, but right now you're *not* what the doctor ordered."

He closed the door in Mildred's face. Sarah stood there with her back to the door. She could hear her sister's inimitable whisper, "Well, I suppose I'll just go take care of putting little Patsy to bed. At least *someone* around here needs me."

For once, Sarah refused to allow her sister to make her feel guilty and call her back. At this moment she needed her privacy with Jesse and the doctor more than anything else.

She wasn't really afraid to leave the safety of the closed door at her back and enter the room completely. It wasn't exactly a "bedroom," was it—in spite of all their baggage sitting in a neat pile beneath the far window? It was more like a sickroom. Yes. That's what it was, she told herself, and took another step into the room.

Jesse, his eyes closed, lay very still on the big bed.

In spite of her hesitation to get physically close to him, she supposed she could summon up enough courage to nurse him for as long as he needed her. After all, she'd promised—in sickness and in health. And he would be growing weaker day by day. In a very short while, he wouldn't be any threat at all.

Dr. Hanford had removed Jesse's jacket and vest and opened the neckband of his shirt. Sarah could easily see the pulse beating weakly at the hollow of his throat and the short strands of darker, curling hair rising from his chest.

The doctor had also removed Jesse's trousers in order to examine his injured leg, and had left the sheet pulled back. It was easy enough to see that Jesse actually had "foregone the necessary," as Dr. Hanford had so tactfully put it. Either that, or he hadn't been able to afford anything but his well-worn outer garments in the first place.

She hadn't imagined his lower limbs would be so hairy, or that the bandage on his right leg would cover so large an area. No wonder he'd been in such terrible pain.

She certainly hadn't figured that his shirttail would cling to the outline of his thighs and loins so closely. Thank goodness the man had a shirttail down to his knees—to spare her further embarrassment! On the other hand, if she didn't want to look, she could always just turn her head. Somehow, Sarah found it very hard to tear her gaze away.

But if she wanted to be able to concentrate on what the

doctor was telling her, she knew she couldn't allow such visual temptation to remain.

Turning to the doctor, she whispered, "Shouldn't you cover him up—so he doesn't catch a chill?"

"So you're worried about that now?" Dr. Hanford asked grumpily as he pulled the sheet up to Jesse's chest.

"Of course I am. I'm his wife," she answered with surprise. Why would the doctor think she didn't care? More quietly, so as not to disturb Jesse, she asked, "How is he?"

Dr. Hanford's wild white eyebrows drew down into a deep frown. He'd suddenly changed from the jovial town doctor to a serious physician intent upon his duty.

His dark brown eyes glared at her over the top of his thick glasses set low on his nose. In a stern voice he said to her, "I assume you're already aware of what a sick man your husband is, Mrs. Taylor."

"I . . . I know that," Sarah answered, slowly nodded her head.

"I'm assuming you're also aware of the extremely serious nature of his maladies," he continued in the same tone of voice.

"He's told me."

By the way he'd said "maladies," indicating the plural, she was afraid he'd tell her something Jesse had managed to leave out, or the other doctor hadn't told him.

"Well, if you knew, then why in the gol-durn blasted Sam Hill wasn't he immediately put into bed to rest—where he should be?" Dr. Hanford demanded. "What in the everloving blue-eyed world possessed you to make this poor man sit through a party so soon after an exhausting train trip halfway across the country?"

How could Sarah answer these questions without appearing very disloyal to her own sister? On the other hand, almost everyone in town must already know how forceful the preacher's wife could be. Still, Sarah would never want to deliberately embarrass her sister.

"I . . . I never made him. Ah, he . . . he insisted that

he wanted to," she offered. "Yes, that's it." She sighed and hoped the doctor would believe her.

"Oh, I think I understand now." Dr. Hanford gave her a wry grin. "Sorry for asking, ma'am."

Before the doctor could ask her any more questions or tell her how her husband was, Sarah heard Jesse's hoarse voice. "Hello, Mrs. Taylor. Mighty nice to see you."

His voice was weak and breathless, but it was awfully good to hear him.

"Jesse!" she exclaimed with relief. She hurried to his side. But once at his bedside, she drew up sharply and stood still, her hands crossed modestly in front of her. "Mr. Taylor. How are you feeling? What happened to you?"

Jesse smiled weakly at her. Thank goodness he was awake and speaking coherently. He still knew who she was and, more importantly, who he was to her.

Unfortunately he was coughing again, and his cheeks were growing increasingly pink. His blue eyes were red-rimmed and growing glassy. With a sinking feeling, she realized that what she'd mistaken for improving color was actually the flush of fever.

He stretched out his hand to her. "My dear, it's so good to open my eyes and see you."

She could hardly refuse to take his hand—especially not in front of the doctor. After all, they were supposed to be man and wife in the true sense of the words. Reaching out, she placed her fingers in his warm palm and felt his fingers close around hers.

His fingers were callused, but not harsh, just a healthy toughness from hard work. He was a carpenter, she remembered. He pressed his fingers around hers a bit more and smiled up at her.

The cad! He'd known she couldn't refuse in front of the doctor. And he knew she couldn't pull away now, either.

"What happened, Doctor? What made him faint like that?"

"My corset was too tight," Jesse answered.

Sarah shook her head and gave her hand a little jerk, too,

but Jesse held on tight. "Seriously, Dr. Hanford, what's wrong with my husband?"

"Just plumb tuckered out, as far as I can figure," Dr. Hanford answered.

Sarah stared at him. "Plumb tuckered out! Is that a medical term? I could've told you that—even without a medical degree."

"Now, now, calm down. You know Mr. Taylor's very ill," he began to explain. "That cough sounds awful, and I'm not at all happy with the condition of that leg."

"I'm not too happy with it myself, Doc," Jesse said with a weak laugh.

Sarah still wasn't laughing, not until she got some serious answers. "I knew all that already, too."

"It also appears as if his temperature's rising."

"Then what can we do for him?" she asked anxiously.

"First, no more parties."

She nodded. "I agree. Now just try to convince . . . my sister." She hadn't meant to slip, but didn't doctors have some sort of promise not to tell the secrets their patients told them? Did that also apply to anything the patient's wife might say about her busybody sister?

"Oh, I don't think there's much anyone can do about Mrs. Preston, begging your pardon for saying so," Dr. Hanford answered. "As for Mr. Taylor, I want you to put cool cloths on his forehead if he seems to grow any warmer. Keep giving him cool drinks and warm broth whenever he wakes up—whether he thinks he wants them or not. And this is the most important part right now—he's got to rest as much as possible."

"That's it?" Jesse asked.

"You're not even going to give him an elixir or something?" Sarah demanded.

"Yeah, Doc," Jesse said, licking his lips with exaggeration. "I'm real partial to snake oil."

"Haven't had any snake oil since the last traveling show left town."

"Well, if you're going to be sending us a bill, you'd better give my husband more advice than just 'eat and sleep.' "

Doc showed Sarah the brown bottle that Jesse had been carrying in his breast pocket for the entire trip.

Sarah just grimaced. "I could've told you about that, too. Isn't there something else . . . ?"

"Sorry, Mrs. Taylor. Laudanum is about the best I, or anyone else, can do for him now."

Sarah knew she'd singled out Jesse because he looked like he was dying. While she'd felt sorry for him then, she'd never felt a personal loss. But spending even this little bit of time with him had made her realize she actually liked him. He was a man with strength, compassion, and humor, with feelings that were being hurt and hopes that would never become reality. She felt her heart plummeting at the prospect of losing her newfound friend.

"I just gave him a dose, so he'll be getting right sleepy soon," Doc said as he placed the bottle on the small table in the alcove. "He ought to sleep for a while."

"Thank goodness, too," Jesse said, wincing. "That examination hurt like the dickens, Doc!"

"I'll see you have as much as you need . . . for as long as you need it."

Sarah thought Jesse's eyes looked a bit more watery than usual. He asked the doctor, "How . . . how long do you think . . . ?"

Dr. Hanford shrugged. "I don't know. And I don't like playing stationmaster to heaven—giving people dates and times for when they'll be coming or going when nobody really knows."

He closed his black bag resting at the foot of the bed and headed toward the door.

"I'm not telling either one of you something you don't already know. I just hope you've both come to accept this. If you're in need of spiritual comfort, at least you've come to live in the right house."

"Thank you for everything, Doctor," Sarah said.

"Oh, you'll get my bill sooner or later," he replied with a

chuckle. With his hand on the knob, he turned back. "Oh, and do yourselves both a big favor."

"What's that, Doc?" Jesse asked.

"Don't mention any of this to my brother." He closed the door behind him.

"What's that supposed to mean?" Jesse asked Sarah.

She didn't think now was the right time to tell him that Dr. Hanford's brother, the man he'd been talking to when he passed out, was the undertaker. She hoped he'd been too ill to note the physical resemblance and make the correlation.

She did, however, think this was the perfect time to remove her hand from his grasp.

Jesse shrugged and looked around as much as he could while lying flat on his back. "Some room, isn't it?" he asked.

"It's very pretty," Sarah answered tentatively.

"I take it I'm still in the parsonage."

"Yes."

"What a relief! From the looks of this place, at first I thought they'd dragged me into some brothel!"

"Mr. Taylor!"

"Sorry about the language, Mrs. Taylor."

"I don't think my sister would appreciate your likening her best bedroom to a room in a house of ill repute," she explained indignantly.

He glanced around. "Oh, I'd say it was a pretty logical mistake. From the looks of the trees, I'd say we were on the second floor."

"You're pretty observant for a man who's supposed to be so sick and taking laudanum."

"I'm also guessing this was supposed to be your bedroom." He stopped examining the wallpaper and drapes and turned his gaze to her.

"Yes," she answered a bit more cautiously.

Jesse nodded. "I thought so. It doesn't exactly look like a manly sort of room, does it?"

"Mildred's already making plans to redecorate it for you." She gestured toward the frilly curtains, not so much to point them out to Jesse, but so that she wouldn't have to continue to look into his smiling eyes. "She said something about adding brown or dark green."

"But will *you* like it that way?"

"That doesn't matter."

"Yes, it does, Sarah. After all, you'll be sleeping in here with me."

Five

"Oh, no. Oh, no, I won't." Quickly she turned around and backed away from him until she stood closer to the foot of the bed, where she felt much safer. "I've already made the conditions of our marriage very clear—several times," she said with a sigh of impatience. "I refuse to repeat myself once again just because you weren't listening the other times."

"I *was* listening, Sarah. I don't mean you'll be . . . well, sleeping with me—if that's what you want to call it when you're trying to be polite."

"Definitely, we'll be polite."

"But other . . . well, factors have to be considered now."

"Such as . . . ?"

"Such as, when we made our plans on the train, I didn't know we'd be staying all together in the Prestons' home."

"Where did you think we'd be staying? Did you think I had my own house here? Did you think houses just sort of popped up on the prairie? Or that the Indians are in the habit of erecting large buildings and then just abandoning them?"

Jesse chuckled, then shrugged as best he could while lying down. "Are there only three bedrooms in this house?"

"Yes."

"Guess that doesn't leave much room for rearranging."

"Not much, unless you want to sleep on the back porch."

"Not really," he answered with a small grin. "At least, not right now."

"I'd say now would be the time to do it. By fall, it'll be way too cold."

"I'd say no time would be the time to do it."

"I suppose you're not too enthusiastic about fresh air."

"Oh, no," he murmured, shaking his head emphatically. His eyes took on a sad, faraway glaze. "I dearly love fresh air—more than you'll ever know."

She almost asked him why he so dearly loved fresh air. But they'd bargained with each other never to ask about the past. If she inquired about his, wouldn't he feel entitled to ask about hers? If she broke this condition of their agreement, would he claim the right to modify other arrangements, such as this being a marriage in name only?

"But I don't think the neighbors'll appreciate the fact that I like to sleep in my birthday suit."

Sarah blinked in surprise and fought off the brief thought that, hang the neighbors, Jesse in his birthday suit might not go totally unappreciated.

"Well, you'll . . . you'll get plenty of fresh air while you're here," she answered instead, shaking off her nervousness. She gestured to the three large windows surrounding the alcove and the single small window overlooking the side of the house. "If you need anything, I'll be staying next door with Patsy, in the room Mildred prepared for Aunt Myrtle."

"You *can't!*"

Sarah couldn't decide whether his expression was truly disappointed or if he was really that sick. He certainly *sounded* disappointed.

"I'm sick, and I could sure use a little looking after."

He looked worse than when she'd first seen him. The longer they talked, he appeared increasingly flushed and tired, too. She hoped it was just the laudanum taking effect and nothing she'd said. She especially hoped it was not because of any particular thoughts that came into his mind while he was thinking of her in bed with him.

"I could see if my sister has a little bell or something you could ring if you needed me."

"What if I'm too sick to ring the bell?"

"Then we'll hear the thud as it drops from your hand and come running," she assured him. She waited, watching, until he finally realized.

"You're teasing me. I can't believe you're really teasing me."

"Of course I am. I wouldn't abandon you now. Is there anything you need before you go to sleep? Another pillow? Water? Food?" The offer of good food had seemed to be a big inducement for him to accept their initial bargain. "Did you manage to get anything to eat during the party?"

"Oh, so *now* you're going to worry about me. During the party I seem to recall you weren't anywhere around—"

"Oh, Jesse, please don't be angry. I tried to find you, but Mildred kept me so busy. . . ."

"I know. I was only teasing, too," he responded with a slight grin. "It didn't take me too long before I had Mrs. Preston all figured out. I'm just wondering when I'll figure you out."

He watched her, his eyes hopeful. What could he possibly be hoping for? she wondered.

"There's nothing to figure," she answered bluntly. Then she asked again, "Did you have something to eat?"

"Yes, I did. Yes, indeed," he replied. Was the contented grin on his face caused by the effect of the laudanum or his happy eating memories?

"Did you have enough? Are you still hungry now?"

"Not really." Watching her closely, he added, "Seemed as if every unmarried lady there was eager to see I got a taste of her special food."

"No wonder I could never find you when I looked for

you," Sarah said. "You were surrounded by attentive ladies with food."

"An irresistible combination."

"Which did you like best? The possum potpie or the chicken-fried prairie dog?"

"Neither. I don't seem to have much appetite."

"I didn't either. Are you sure you don't want something more . . . edible?"

"I don't seem to have much appetite for anything," he admitted.

She recalled he hadn't eaten much on the trip out here. She supposed it was because he didn't seem to have much money, either.

"The way all those ladies were treating me, you'd think you were the one that was dying, not me, and that I was the one who'd be needing a replacement spouse."

"In the unlikely event that I die before you, please feel free to remarry. But I don't intend to look for a replacement —ever."

He tried to laugh, but ended up yawning instead. "Oh, you'd never be able to find anyone . . . to replace . . . me."

"My, you're certainly sure of yourself. In that case, I'll leave you here to sleep," she told him as she headed toward the door. "You don't need me bustling around, unpacking and disturbing you."

She heard Jesse chuckle, but it wasn't his usual humorous laugh. It seemed more as if he were finding a lot of amusement in this thoughts. She turned to look at him. His eyes weren't dancing merrily as they usually did. They were soft and searching.

"How did you find out?" he asked.

She looked toward him questioningly. "Find out what?"

"How much you disturb me, Sarah."

She knew he meant something far different from slamming doors and stamping feet. She didn't want to acknowledge his remark. She didn't even want to think about it. If she did, she'd have to acknowledge how much he also disturbed her, and that upset her even more. That made it even more difficult for her to think about staying in the same room with him—right now, not for another moment.

"I really wish you'd stay," he said.

"Jesse, you're forgetting something," she said gently. Belying her gentle words, she picked up a small cloth from the washstand in the corner, and with quick, sharp moves of her shaking fingers she began folding it much more neatly than it needed to be. "I have to take care of Patsy, too."

"Mrs. Preston can help you put her to bed, but you're my wife, Sarah. I need you to take care of me."

"I know, but even though Mildred's her aunt, Patsy's not used to her."

"Patsy seemed to do fine with being passed from one stranger to the other during the party."

"Only as long as they were feeding her," Sarah reminded him.

"If she didn't like your sister, I'm sure you'd hear her crying or fussing or whatever it is little ones do when they're not happy."

"They sort of whine—like you're doing right now—when they don't get their own way."

"But, Sarah, you promised," Jesse whined, just for good effect.

She wanted to laugh, but she was afraid she knew exactly where he was taking this conversation, and she didn't want to encourage him—or give him false hopes. "Don't give me that excuse about promising to obey—"

"Even if you won't keep that promise, we do have a bargain, Mrs. Taylor."

Sarah was almost afraid he'd try that authoritarian tone with her again. But he'd dropped all attempts at pretense and only looked at her in a straightforward, businesslike manner.

"I upheld my end, and I intend to see you stick to yours."

"You're pretty insistent for someone so ill."

"You wouldn't want word to get out that Sarah Bolton Taylor doesn't keep her bargains, would you? What would all the folks back in Savannah say? What would the folks in Cottonwood say? Wouldn't that be a horrible way to begin a new life in a new town?"

"All right, all right! I guess not," she was forced to concede. "Mr. Taylor, you may sound businesslike, but you're the worst whiner I've ever had the misfortune to meet!"

Aunt Myrtle had always maintained, "Gentlemen *and* ladies keep their solemn word of honor. It's just that a lady gets to decide which words she meant." Somehow, in Jesse's case, this didn't seem to apply, and Sarah couldn't yet figure out why.

She'd always tried to heed Aunt Myrtle's advice. In that case, she had to remind Jesse, "I'll stay in here and take care of you while you're ill, but I don't want you to think it'll go any further than that. Once you've improved—"

"Once I'm dead, Sarah," he corrected her softly.

"Oh. Yes, of course," she replied slowly. "I'm sorry. But I never promised to actually *sleep* with you."

"You have to."

"What's the matter with you? I don't think the laudanum made you deaf, although there are times when I'm sure it's made you crazy. How can I sleep in the same bedroom with you?"

"How can you not?" he countered. "Everyone else thinks we're married in a really true marriage, Sarah. Everyone— even the good Reverend—and especially your sister—will start to wonder what kind of marriage we have—and how we managed to have Patsy—if we sleep apart while living in their house."

Sarah opened her mouth to give him an appropriate argument.

"Just think how all those nice church ladies'll grab hold of a story like that and turn it and twist it until it bears no resemblance to the original, and then spread it all over town."

"Oh, they wouldn't . . ." she protested, even though she knew very well from previous experience what some nice church ladies were capable of.

"Either that, or they'll start inviting you over for a cup of coffee and a nice little chat about 'doing a wife's Christian duty and keeping the mister happy, dear,' " he finished in a high-pitched, singsong tone.

"Oh, my." With a deep shiver of foreboding, she realized, "You're absolutely right."

There was no way to get out of it. She'd be sleeping in here with Jesse.

"I guess that's about the only thing you didn't take into consideration when you were . . . making all your plans . . . on the train," he said, giving her a sleepy grin. He raised his hand over his mouth to hide a wide yawn.

Sarah pressed her lips together to try to control herself before saying anything else. Now was probably not the time to tell Jesse that on the train she'd actually planned on him dying soon.

"Yes, Mr. Taylor," she at last conceded. "You're the only thing I didn't take into consideration. When's that laudanum going to start taking effect?"

"Real soon," he assured her, blinking to try to keep his eyes open. "I'm feeling pretty drowsy, and the pain . . . in my leg's eased up enough to let me . . . sleep."

His drooping eyelids were finally closed.

She looked down at the cloth she had folded and found she'd twisted it into a shapeless mass of cotton. Grimacing, she tried to straighten it as much as she could. Then she hung it on the side of the washstand in the corner.

Jesse's deep, rhythmic breathing told Sarah he was at least sleeping peacefully, in spite of his apparent fever.

Sarah moved to stand beside him. She didn't feel too uncomfortable as long as she knew he was fast asleep, and even if he wasn't, he still wasn't in any shape to jump out of bed and make a grab for her.

Reaching down, she placed her palm flat on his forehead. She hadn't expected him to feel that warm.

Retrieving the cloth she'd hung on the side of the washstand, she dampened it, then placed it on Jesse's forehead.

She reached out her index finger to brush away a small droplet of water trickling down his temple into his dark hair.

Her hand lingered just a bit. Almost as if her hand had a mind of its own, her fingers brushed back the unruly strands of hair, smoothing them down into place. Her hand wanted to continue down the side of his face, brush against his curling sideburns, and trail down the short stubble along his jawline.

Sarah quickly pulled her mutinous hand back before it did anything she'd regard as completely scandalous, and Jesse might take as an indication that she was about to amend the conditions of their bargain. It didn't matter that he was in a drugged sleep. She wasn't taking any chances.

She eyed their baggage, that the Reverend Preston had seen fit to bring up here, but she just didn't have the stomach right now for unpacking. Anyway, she might make too much noise, opening and closing drawers and cupboards. She didn't want to waken Jesse.

After traveling in a bouncing train on a hard bench, the bed, with its fluffy feather pillows and crisp white sheets, looked awfully inviting, she thought longingly, even with Jesse sprawled out in it, fast asleep. But she still couldn't allow herself the luxury of sleeping in it—not with Jesse—not with any man. And she needed to be ready in case Jesse woke and needed anything.

The only other place to sleep was one of the two chairs on either side of the table in the alcove. The straight-backed little chair didn't look that comfortable, but it would have to do.

She made certain the draperies were drawn tight. She didn't need for some old busybody to see her silhouette in the lamplight and to realize that Mr. and Mrs. Taylor weren't actually living as man and wife.

What a day! she thought as she seated herself. She watched Jesse, sleeping fitfully in the big, comfortable bed, and tried to make herself just a little more comfortable in the hard little chair.

She found her head nodding, so she tried to count the

roses in the wallpaper. She had to stay awake in case Jesse needed her, especially now that he seemed to be tossing and turning with his fever. Did two half roses make a whole? Could four buds add up to one full-blown rose?

Eventually even the 347½ roses didn't help. Her eyelids were drooping, and she couldn't keep her head from nodding. It was worse than trying to sit through a too-long, too-boring sermon.

She laid her head on her arms on the table and closed her eyes.

Aloud, she murmured to herself, "Did anyone ever have a stranger wedding night?"

"Yoo hoo, breakfast!" Mildred's high-pitched greeting was accompanied by a sharp rapping.

Sarah awoke with a start. She lifted her head from the table. It sounded as if Mildred were trying to kick down the door.

Sarah glanced over quickly to see what the noise had done to Jesse. She blinked with surprise when she saw him sitting up on the edge of the bed.

"What are you trying to—?"

The rapping grew louder. "Rise and shine, you slugabeds! Patsy and I've been up for hours. What's wrong with you two? Breakfast's almost ready."

"Thank you, Mildred," Sarah called, hoping even this small reply would quiet her sister. "I'll . . . we'll be down in a minute."

"I certainly hope so. There's pancakes and fried eggs, sausage and fresh-made biscuits with strawberry jam I put up last spring all by myself."

"We'll just be a minute, Mildred," Sarah replied.

"Beffas, Mommy. Beffas," Patsy called through the door. Sarah could hear her little hand slapping on the wood.

"I'm coming, dear. Goodness, you've been busy with Aunt Mildred, haven't you?"

"Auntie Dread," Patsy repeated. "Beffas."

Jesse clapped his hands tightly over his mouth so that no

one could hear him, but Sarah could see his shoulders heaving heartily up and down. It was awfully hard not to laugh, and Jesse had the advantage of not having to answer.

"I can't wait breakfast forever." Mildred's voice took on a peevish tone. "Are you two coming down or not?"

"Yes, yes." Sarah tried to sound sensible in spite of her urge to laugh.

"Patsy and I'll be in the kitchen, making sure everything doesn't burn or grow cold or even go bad before you slowpokes manage to come downstairs."

After that announcement, Sarah heard Mildred's and Patsy's footsteps tapping down the hall, and Mildred's complaint, "I declare, those two are acting just like newlyweds."

"Auntie Dread?" Jesse repeated, allowing himself to laugh aloud. "Oh, Patsy knows your sister so well already." He laughed so hard, he began coughing again. Still weak, he began to teeter on the edge of the bed.

Sarah quickly came to stand beside him. She couldn't let him fall.

"I have to admit, Patsy's a sharp judge of character. But *you*, on the other hand, are not up to such hilarity," she scolded with a small grin. She shook her head. "I don't have to touch your forehead to see you still have a fever."

"Just a little."

"Don't try to be so brave. Go on, get back into bed again," she ordered.

"What time is it?"

"What does it matter? The only reason you need to know the time is to get it right on your death certificate—if you continue to try to get up. Now, back to bed with you!"

"I don't think too many men get to fill out their own death certificates."

He swung his legs back up onto the soft sheets on the fluffy mattress. She shouldn't have been so curious. She should've closed her eyes. She should've remembered Jesse wasn't wearing anything under his shirt.

Not only did she see his hairy shins—she'd seen them before—but this time she got a glimpse of his knees, and even his upper leg—not as hairy as his shins and calves, but still covered lightly with dark hairs. His legs were thin, as she would've expected. But there was a definition to his muscles that belied his current weakness. What a pity she hadn't met him a few years ago. How she would have loved to have seen him in his full strength and virility.

Stop that! You've had enough of men already, she chided herself as she reached down for the covers. This poor man is here to help you get out of the mess you got into. He's not here for you to ogle shamelessly.

As he lay back on the pillows, she quickly pulled the covers up over his legs.

He nodded toward the closed door. "What in tarnation was that all about?"

"I'm so sorry. I forgot, I should've warned you about this beforehand."

"How could you forget something like *that*?" he demanded.

"Mildred always was an early riser. She liked to make sure that everyone else was, too, and apparently she still does."

"When you go downstairs, tell her if she does it again while I'm here, I'll spit in her direction every time I see her —even in public."

"Ha!" She gave a little laugh. "I've heard your idle threats before, sir."

"You've been reading too many melodramas," he accused.

"No, I become very sarcastic when I'm deprived of my sleep. I can manage, but I'm sorry she woke you, too, when you need to sleep so badly."

"No. I was awake anyway," Jesse admitted. "This leg hurts like the dickens. I should've known Doc Hanford poking around in there wasn't going to do any more good than the other doctor, and it only makes it hurt more." He looked around the room. "What'd you do with my laudanum?"

Sarah retrieved the bottle from the table where Doc Hanford had left it. She quickly brought it over to Jesse.

"Have you been feeling poorly all night?"

Jesse nodded as he took a small sip.

"If you needed something, why didn't you wake me?" she told him with a desperate pleading in her voice that she hoped assured him of her sincerity. Although she didn't want to get into their differences of opinion, she had to ask, "Why do you think I stayed in here in the first place? So you could wake me."

"Oh, I just hated to. With the early morning light coming in the window, shining on your hair, you just looked too darned pretty to wake," he answered with a little smile. It wasn't a silly, teasing grin. It was peaceful, grateful, almost affectionate, if she dared to admit it.

At first Sarah was too embarrassed by his flattery and unusual expression to answer. She didn't believe she'd ever get used to compliments. Then she realized the more embarrassing significance was that he'd been watching her while she was fast asleep. The last gentleman who'd ever watched her as she'd slept had been her daddy at the side of her crib when she was just a baby. There was a big difference when she was a grown woman, and the man was her husband and practically a stranger.

The best thing she knew to do now to recover from her embarrassment was to continue to take care of Jesse.

"But you tried to get up for something," she persisted. "What do you need? I'll get it for you."

"Oh, nothing now. I . . . I had to . . . to visit the . . . facilities."

"Oh." So much for another failed attempt to relieve her embarrassment, she thought as she felt her face growing even warmer.

"Yeah, I figured you'd find it a little hard to help me out on that. Anyway, some things a man just has to do for himself."

"I'm grateful for your consideration," she answered. "But you shouldn't have tried to travel so far at night."

"Since it was too dark to see what was below the window, I didn't think your sister and her husband—or the next-door neighbor—would appreciate me opening the window and—"

"I understand," she interrupted. "But next time, if it's something . . . less personal . . ."

"You'll be the first person I call. I promise."

"Good. You shouldn't overexert yourself like that."

"If you weren't . . . so darned stubborn, I wouldn't have to. . . ."

"I'll try to be more cooperative if you will," she told him.

"I'm stuck here," he said. He tried to stretch his arms out to indicate both sides of the big bed, but the laudanum made his movements awkward. "I'm about as cooperative as a potted plant."

"But nowhere near as quiet."

He smiled and chuckled silently. He managed to raise his hand to ruffle his unruly hair. "I think I need a pruning, too."

"Maybe after your morning nap, if you're up to sitting up for a while, I'll see what I can do for you."

"Why don't you call the undertaker? He's used to working on them when they're lying down."

"*You* are a very sick man," she accused with a laugh. "And I don't mean your leg."

"And you love me for it," he replied.

No, she didn't love him, she wanted to tell him. She couldn't bring herself to say the words. She did *like* him. That was absolutely as far as she would allow herself to feel anything.

"Now, I really have to go downstairs or Patsy and Mildred'll be coming up again," she told him.

"Now, Patsy I'd be happy to see." Then in mock horror he cried, "But not Mildred! Oh, no, not Meddling Mildred!"

"I don't think you should go downstairs."

"Oh, you're so right," he agreed, nodding emphatically.

"Do you want me to bring something up for you on a tray?"

"No."

"Mildred'll be very upset if you don't eat something."

"Mildred doesn't know how bad my leg hurts," he answered, snuggling down into the covers. Obviously he didn't intend to eat, much less move a muscle.

"Remember, Dr. Hanford said you should eat, whether you feel like it or not."

"No, thanks."

"You didn't eat much yesterday—and probably not much for quite a while."

"I haven't been all that hungry."

"Doctor's orders," she reminded him.

"All right. Water," he conceded.

"You won't grow strong on water," she scolded.

"Sarah, my dear wife, haven't you realized by now that no matter what I eat, or drink, or do, no matter how nice you or Patsy or the Prestons are to me, not even no matter how much I pray, I'll never grow strong again?" He closed his eyes and sighed deeply. He didn't move again.

Sarah stood there silently at his side for a long time. She'd ever seen him so hopeless. All the while he knew he was ing, his high spirits and good-natured sense of humor had most made her forget how ill he really was. When he at last stopped joking—and worst of all eating, then she had to at last acknowledge that he was admitting the seriousness— and hopelessness—of his condition.

It took a lot of courage when he was still awake, but she reached out and placed her palm on his forehead. It was still just as warm as it had been last night.

"Why is it you only feel safe touching me when you think I'm asleep?" Jesse asked. His eyes were still closed, and his voice was growing softer all the time.

"If you're asleep, how do you know when I touch you and when I don't?" Sarah countered.

"I'm getting to know you better all the time," he murmured, but didn't say anything else.

"Your fever's not any better, but at least it's not any worse. I'll bring you up some cool water."

"Thanks," he murmured sleepily as he turned over in the bed.

This time she'd manage to get him to drink some water, she planned. Maybe next time she'd get him to try some broth.

She washed her face in the basin. She glanced in the large mirror atop the dresser across the room. She smoothed down her wrinkled dress. Her hair was tousled, but that was easily remedied by her brush.

She would've liked to have changed her dress, but she wasn't sure if Jesse was soundly asleep yet or not. She didn't want to risk undressing in the room and finding out later that he'd been sneaking a peek at her the whole time. Maybe after breakfast she'd come back upstairs and, under the pretense of unpacking for Patsy, she'd have the chance to change her clothes in Patsy's room.

As she descended the stairs, Sarah heard Patsy ordering from the kitchen, "More, Auntie Dread. More ca-cakes."

Sarah stood in the doorway of the neat, sunlit kitchen. Just like Mildred to have a place for everything and everything in its place. She could've predicted her sister would paint the walls a cheery pale yellow and all the woodwork white. She watched Mildred flip three tiny pancakes off the big iron griddle and onto Patsy's plate.

"My, you're a hungry little girl, aren't you?" Mildred asked, pouring on syrup.

Patsy, her mouth already full of syrup-laden cakes, nodded.

"I'd sure like to have a pretty little girl like you," Mildred said wistfully, turning back to pour more pancakes onto the griddle. "Or a bouncing little boy. Or one of each. Or two. . . ."

"Milk, Auntie Dread."

Mildred poured more milk into the small glass.

"Taddy," Patsy replied.

"By now, I'd like to have had two or three," Mildred said

as she turned back to pouring pancakes onto the hot griddle. "It's not fair, you know. Your mommy's so lucky to have you, and I don't have anyone. I'm older than her, you know, by just a little. I got married first. I should have a baby first. You'd think a God who could create such a nice orderly universe would be able to arrange that, too. I . . . I just don't know why it doesn't work nice and orderly like that."

Mildred flipped the pancakes, slapping them down angrily.

"Even that little tramp Margaret Simmons went and got herself in a family way and had to get married. And here I am, a respectable, married, church-going woman—six years now—with no baby at all. It should all go in nice, neat order. It really should, you know. It really, really should."

"Good ca-cakes, Auntie Dread," Patsy said, pointing to her plate. "More."

Mildred poured more batter onto the griddle.

"Good, Mommy," Patsy said to Sarah. Pointing to the empty chair beside her, she told her, "Eat some, Mommy. Eat ca-cakes."

"Oh, Sarah," Mildred said, spilling the pancake batter into one big pancake. "I didn't see you there. How . . . how long have you been here?"

"Oh, I just got here," Sarah said. In order to try to give truth to her story, she asked, "Patsy, honey, have you had anything to eat yet?"

"Ca-cakes," Patsy answered, pointing to her messy plate.

"My goodness, Sarah, she certainly has a hearty appetite," Mildred said. Pouring a cup of coffee, she sat it in front of an empty plate on the table. "Have a seat."

"Where man?" Patsy asked.

"What did you say, dear?" Sarah asked. She understood perfectly well what her daughter had said. She just hoped Mildred had either not understood the babyish words or not understood their underlying meaning.

"Where da man?" Patsy repeated more loudly.

"What man, sweetie pie?" Mildred asked.

"Da hurt man." Patsy was very loud and frowning. Obviously she wasn't too happy with how thick some grown-ups could be.

"Do you mean your daddy?" Mildred asked.

"Daddy," Patsy said with obvious relief.

Mildred turned to Sarah. "Why on earth wouldn't she know to call her own father 'Daddy'?"

Sarah's fingers drummed on the polished wooden tabletop. "Oh, well . . . um, Mr. Taylor's been so ill . . . um, well, he sleeps most of the time, and . . . well, Patsy doesn't see him a lot, and . . . she's so young. . . ."

"Yes, children have such strange little memories, I suppose. I really wouldn't know, having no children of my own —yet. I'll just have to take your word for it."

Sarah couldn't miss the envy in her sister's tone. But she was glad that for once Mildred had decided to agree.

"Where's da Daddy?" Patsy asked. She held a cold pancake in each hand and was slapping them together.

"Don't do that, sweetheart. He's . . . Daddy's upstairs," Sarah answered. It was strange enough to hear herself calling Jesse Taylor her husband. It was absolutely bizarre to hear Patsy call him "Daddy."

"It takes Daddy a little longer to get ready when he's not feeling well," Mildred told Patsy.

"No, Mildred. He went back to sleep."

"Why on earth did he go back to sleep?" Mildred demanded. "I was very clear that breakfast was ready and waiting—and very delicious. I don't think warmed-over pancakes are going to taste very good."

"He . . . he won't be coming down at all this morning."

"Why not? A man needs a hearty breakfast out here."

"He's too sick to come down."

"He's too weak from not eating," Mildred pronounced. "What in the world have you been feeding—or better yet *not* feeding—that man?"

"Mildred, you saw what happened to him yesterday," Sarah reminded her.

"Yes, the poor man just fainted dead away—probably from hunger."

Sarah sighed. As usual, Mildred only saw what she wanted herself to see.

Mildred shook her index finger under Sarah's nose. "I'll warn you, my dear stubborn sister."

Sarah wanted to make some comment about the pot calling the kettle black.

"If that husband of yours doesn't eat more, he'll never get better. You don't want to be a young widow, do you?"

Sarah girded up her courage. Now was the time for her to try again to make the most important point she'd ever had to make to her sister. She just hoped Mildred was really listening—and really paying attention—this time.

Sarah leaned closer to her across the table and peered intently into her sister's eyes. "Mildred, Mr. Taylor will *never* get better."

"Well, certainly not, if you take that terrible attitude of defeat," Mildred answered, drawing herself up indignantly.

"No, Mildred. He's . . . he's been to . . . several doctors. They all say the same thing."

"Oh, pooh." Mildred waved her hand in the air. "What do doctors know?"

"They know that Jesse is dying."

"Well, he may look horrible and act very tired, and if he were my husband, I'd be particularly concerned about his fainting spell, but—"

"Mildred! He is dying! I really am going to be a . . . a young widow."

Mildred slowly lowered herself into the chair across from Sarah. She folded her hands on the table in front of her and peered intently into Sarah's eyes.

Very slowly she said, "You mean, he really is . . . is preparing to . . . to meet his Maker?"

"He's dying," Sarah told her bluntly. "He has a very badly infected leg and galloping consumption."

"Well, how in the world did he ever get something like that?"

"In . . . during the war," Sarah answered uncertainly. She herself wasn't even sure how Jesse became ill. She hoped Mildred wouldn't ask for too many particulars. Or if she did, she'd ask Jesse when Sarah was around. Then Sarah could learn more about Jesse's past without having to embarrass herself by asking. Wasn't that what sisters were for? she reasoned.

"That's so hard to believe. . . ."

"Didn't you notice how he limps and how much he coughs?"

"Well, I've only known him for less than a day. I . . . I just assumed he was stiff from traveling, and that he coughed from all that soot the train puts out."

"No. My husband is dying."

"You mean he's *really* dying?"

"No, Mildred. He's only sort of dying. He's going to lie there pretending until Mr. Hanford goes to nail the lid down at the funeral, then pop up and yell 'Surprise!' and watch all the ladies faint." Sarah was becoming more than a little impatient with her sister's inability to grasp the obvious. "Of course he's *really* dying!"

"Oh, my goodness," Mildred declared, covering her mouth with her hand. Her eyes began to fill with tears. "How awful for you—and poor little Patsy."

Sarah felt guilty that she'd been able to deliver the news so calmly, while her sister—who didn't even know Jesse—seemed to be taking this very hard. Then she realized she knew Jesse only a little bit better than her sister did. And Mildred always took everything to extremes anyway.

"We'll . . . we'll be all right," Sarah assured her. She wasn't good at lying, but she had to give it a try, just to make sure Mildred didn't start prying. "Mr. Taylor has seen to our . . . our future welfare."

Mildred stopped her sniffling. "He has? Oh, dear, now I'm so sorry I said all those terribly mean things when I first saw him, about him not supporting you and all. . . ."

"Don't worry about it, Mildred. He's a very forgiving man." Sarah decided to tell Jesse about her sister's remorseful reaction to his imminent passing. Maybe it would keep him from spitting in her direction every time he saw her, at least in public.

"Did the doctors say anything to you about when this dreadfully sad occasion might occur?"

"No. No, they didn't. Not even Dr. Hanford."

"Oh, he wouldn't tell you anyway," Mildred said with a grimace. "He never tells me a thing, the tight-lipped, miserable old buzzard, no matter how much I try to get him to confide in me."

Sarah would've reminded her sister that this was a horribly unchristian remark to make about the doctor, especially coming from the preacher's wife.

"Just take your older sister's advice and do one important thing, dear."

"What's that?" Who knew what Mildred would suggest?

"The doctor bills can wait. Get yourself a nice wedding ring before he goes."

If she hadn't been so upset at the prospect of Jesse's demise, she'd have laughed. "Very well, Mildred. If it's that important to you, I promise I'll get a ring before he dies."

"Real gold, too."

Sarah nodded.

Then Mildred rose. "Well, whenever it happens, I won't have anyone in town saying that anybody who stayed at Mrs. Preston's died of starvation. I have a reputation in this town to maintain, you know."

"Oh, Mildred," Sarah couldn't resist assuring her sister, "I think the good people of Cottonwood know you for more than just your cooking."

"Well, I try to be versatile," Mildred said, preening. She pulled a tray from a cabinet and put a cup, utensils, and a plate onto it.

"You know, Sarah," she said as she scraped two fried eggs onto the plate. "You're still a pretty woman."

"Why, thank you, Mildred."

"Having Patsy didn't ruin your figure . . . much, and a good corset'll fix that. We'll have to see about getting you one, especially for the funeral. You'll want to look your best there."

Sarah just bit her tongue.

"You're still a young woman, too—only twenty-four by my reckoning."

"Yes," Sarah answered cautiously. She didn't like the turn this conversation was taking—even though she'd known from the start that this was where it would all end.

"That's awfully young to be a widow."

"That's not exactly something a woman plans on when she marries, is it, Mildred?"

"No." Mildred placed a stack of pancakes next to the eggs on the plate. Sarah might have thought the discussion was at an end, except for the fact that she knew her sister too well. "But it's something a wise woman takes into consideration."

"Believe me, Mildred, I have thought of it," Sarah assured her sister. "More than you'll ever know."

"But have you thought about what will happen afterward?"

"Yes."

"I don't think so."

Well, of course, Mildred always had maintained that she was the only one who ever thought anything out to its correct conclusion.

"I think you're going to need a new husband."

"Oh, no. Oh, no. Oh, no!"

Sarah tried to make her protest as strong as possible. She really wanted to just lay her head on the table in defeat. All that work and planning, and her sister had still managed to bring up her remarriage within twenty-four hours of her arrival.

"Come now, I know it's got to be hard to think of another husband when your first isn't even cold in the ground—"

"Mildred! He's not even dead yet!"

Mildred stopped her cooking and tapped her lip with her index finger, obviously thinking hard. At last she said, "Not dead yet. This could be good, Sarah."

"*I* think so. I'm sure Mr. Taylor *definitely* thinks so. He'll probably be glad to hear you agree."

"Oh, be serious, Sarah," Mildred scolded. "This is good. Why, Mr. Taylor could even have a say in deciding who your next husband should be. Then he'd be able to rest in peace, knowing the right man was seeing to his daughter's Christian upbringing and taking care of his wife properly."

Sarah stared at her sister in disbelief. Maybe she wouldn't tell Jesse about this. It would certainly make him want to spit in Mildred's direction every time he saw her.

"Now, you take this upstairs to him—and make sure he eats every scrap of it," Mildred said, pushing the tray across the table toward Sarah.

"I . . . I'll try." It wasn't so much that she wanted to see how Jesse was doing. Only one day in town, and she was pretty eager to get away from her sister already.

"If he won't eat for you, you tell him *I'll* come up to feed him," Mildred threatened.

Sarah rose and took the tray. "I'll tell him. I'm sure that'll be a great incentive. Come on, Patsy, let's—"

The tray rattled and almost slipped from her hand. She'd been so busy arguing with her sister that she hadn't been paying attention like she should.

"Oh, my gosh, Mildred! Where's Patsy?"

Six

The tray clattered to the table. Sarah grabbed her hair with both hands. "Oh, no! Oh, no! Patsy! Patsy, answer Mommy," she called.

"Now, just calm down," Mildred said, coming over to lay a reassuring hand on Sarah's quaking shoulder. "We'll find her."

"How could I not have been watching her? How could I have just let her wander off? Where could she be? Oh, my God, what will I do without her?" She raised her voice and called for Patsy again.

"Oh, Sarah, be sensible," Mildred scolded.

What right did Mildred have to tell her to be sensible? Sarah silently protested. Wasn't Mildred the one who'd just produced a flood of tears because of Sarah's prospective widowhood?

"Cottonwood's not that big a town, and she's too little to have walked too far. She's got to be around here somewhere. We'll find her," Mildred repeated, almost as if she were trying to reassure herself as much as she was her sister.

Sarah turned a complete circle in the middle of the kitchen floor, uncertain of exactly which direction to run first.

"She's wandered out the back door," she decided, heading toward it. "She's such a curious little thing. What if she climbed up and fell in the well!"

"Don't be silly," Mildred said, coming up behind her. "We have a well cover. I've been trying to get the mayor and town council to pass some sort of ordinance or something, so that everyone . . ."

Sarah didn't give a hoot about the mayor and town council—although the idea of obligatory well covers was good. She shook off her sister's hand and dashed toward the well in the backyard.

In spite of the safety implied by the cover, she opened it and peered down into the darkness anyway.

"Patsy! Are you there?" she called.

No answer came.

"Patsy, answer Mommy!"

Still no answer came.

"Patsy, this is no time to play games with Mommy," she warned.

Only silence.

She didn't hear any splashing or gurgling. She didn't see any pathetic little petticoat floating there.

"She's not down there," she said, closing the lid. "Could she have fallen down someone else's well, someone who doesn't have a cover?"

"No, she hasn't been gone long enough to make it to their house."

"But I wasn't watching. I don't know for sure how long she's been gone," Sarah wailed.

"She's only eighteen months old. She doesn't travel that fast," her sister reminded her.

Sarah still didn't feel any better.

"Could she have made it as far as the river?" she demanded.

"I . . . I don't think so," Mildred answered. Her uncertainty was clear.

"I'm not taking any chances."

Sarah ran across the field at the back of the parsonage,

heading directly for the river. She stood on the small, grassy overhang that sloped sharply down to the water.

She looked upstream and down. There was no trace of Patsy.

"Could she have floated away already?"

"In this trickle?" Mildred demanded skeptically. "You're just lucky it hasn't rained in a while. Sometimes this little river can really turn into a torrent."

"Maybe the flood already flashed on by, taking Patsy with it."

"No, no. I declare, Sarah, you are turning into the silliest thing I've ever seen. Patsy didn't even come this far," Mildred said, her usual assurance returned to her voice.

"How do you know?"

"Look." Mildred pointed down to the mud. "See, no footprints."

"Are you sure?"

Sarah and Mildred walked up and down the bank, searching for little prints, but didn't find any.

"Are you satisfied now?" Mildred asked.

"Then where did she go?" Sarah's shoulders stooped as she quickly made her way back to the rear of the parsonage.

She stopped and stood beside the well, holding on to the rough wooden handle to steady herself, hoping she could think of something else that would lead her to her daughter.

She couldn't think of anywhere else to look. Her gaze swept the horizon as far east to as far west as she could possibly see.

"Patsy! Patsy!"

Still no answer.

Mildred was pushing the two large lilac bushes on either side of the porch from side to side.

"She's not hiding here."

"What about the railroad tracks?"

"That's on the other side of Main Street," Mildred answered. "There's a fence all around. To get there, she'd have to have gone out the front door and crossed Main Street."

"Main Street!" Sarah swirled around and headed toward

the back door, followed closely by Mildred. "What if she tried to cross and got run over by someone's runaway wagon?"

"Oh, we'd have heard the screams," Mildred assured her as they made their way through the kitchen. "All the neighbors would've noticed. Most of them would've come knocking on the door to let us know and see if they could do anything to help. Of course, there are some in town who'd only come by to stand and gawk at our misfortune."

"What about some of the farms around here?" Sarah asked as they hurried across the vestibule. "She could be gored by a bull. She could be kidnapped by wild Indians. She could be eaten by a mountain lion!"

"Sarah, there aren't any mountains in Kansas. Now you really are beginning to panic. Am I going to have to get the smelling salts? Or am I going to have to slap you to bring you to your senses?"

"No. I guess I'll be all right."

Sarah stopped at the edge of the picket fence and studied the street. A few carriages rolled by at a sedate pace. Most of the rushing traffic of heavily laden wagons was farther down the street, closer to the railroad station and the shops.

She released her grasp. She hadn't realized she'd clenched the whitewashed pickets so hard that she'd driven small splinters into her palms.

"What about rattlesnakes? Buffalo stampedes?"

"No. They killed off all the buffalo around here."

"Maybe they've killed off all the buffalo," Sarah said, "but they haven't gotten rid of the rattlesnakes." With a wry grimace, she thought, Deke was still in town.

"Oh, my God!"

Sarah gasped and clutched at her heart. She leaned against the fence. Patsy couldn't have wandered outside and been lured away by Deke, she kept telling herself. Even a slimy weasel like him couldn't be that cruel, could he?

What good would taking Patsy do him anyway? He couldn't be thinking of holding her for ransom. One look at

Patsy and herself in their worn clothing should be a strong clue that they didn't have a lot of money.

She tried to swallow the bile that rose in her throat with her next thought. Recalling his rough hands as he'd touched her and piercing eyes as he'd examined her, she shivered. Maybe it wasn't money that Deke wanted in exchange for her daughter.

"Do you see Patsy?" Mildred demanded, rushing up beside her. "What's the matter?"

"What?" She knew she'd cried out. Had she been so overcome with anxiety that she'd actually voiced her fears. "No, I . . . I still don't see her anywhere."

She turned to her sister. Mildred's outstretched arms looked so comforting. She collapsed into her sister's arms and laid her head on her shoulder. She wanted to cry, but she couldn't—not yet. She couldn't give way to the luxury of tears until she knew for certain where Patsy was, and that she was safe and well. Then she'd allow herself to cry with relief. She wouldn't allow herself to think about shedding any other kind of tears.

"There, there," Mildred crooned. "We'll send the Reverend for the sheriff. In no time at all, all the men and boys in town'll be searching for her—and find her—before we can brew another pot of coffee."

Mildred lifted Sarah's head from her shoulder and applied gentle pressure to her shoulders to try to lead her back into the house.

"The Reverend's been cooped up in his study since early this morning. I declare, sometimes I don't think he's ever going to come out. He told me he's still working on his Sunday sermon and doesn't like to be disturbed while he's working, but well, this is just too important. His sermon'll just have to wait." Leaning a little closer to her sister as they reentered the vestibule, she whispered, "I keep trying to tell him they're way too long. He really shouldn't talk so much. Why, the way he goes on and on, you'd think that was the only chance the man ever gets to talk. I keep trying to tell

him, people get bored having to listen to the same person
rattle on and on and—"

"Eat!" Sarah heard Patsy's voice commanding.

Her head shot up, alert.

"She's in the house!" Sarah exclaimed.

Tears of relief, and chagrin at her own foolish fears, began
to well in her eyes. Why hadn't she thought to look inside
first? But she still couldn't allow herself to break down until
she held her little girl in her arms again.

"Where is she?" Mildred asked.

"Eat ca-cakes!" came the imperious command.

"How did she get upstairs?" Sarah demanded, making a
dash for the stairs. Almost tripping over the hem of her
dress, she caught herself on the banister, picked up her
skirts, and continued on.

"I'd say she used the steps like us," Mildred grumbled as
she thumped up the stairs behind.

Sarah slowed as she reached the top of the stairs and
peered into the open doorway of her would-be bedroom.
Patsy stood at Jesse's bedside. She was just about to dash
forward and sweep her daughter up into her arms when
Patsy spoke again.

"Eat ca-cakes!" she ordered, pushing a cold, mushy pancake into Jesse's face.

Sarah drew up quickly. She almost laughed aloud to see
Jesse with a pancake flattened against his face by Patsy's
pudgy hand. Instead she decided to watch quietly from the
hall, hidden from their sight by the door frame.

When Mildred came to her side, she gestured for her to
be quiet and prayed that for once her sister would obey. She
should've remembered that anyone as good at meddling in
other people's business as Mildred would be just as good at
managing to collect information undetected.

Patsy peeled away the pancake. Jesse's eyes were still half
closed. He had a weak smile on his face.

"Eat!"

"No, thank you, Patsy," he told her gently, not even managing to raise his head. "Why don't you go back downstairs to your mommy—like a good girl—and let me sleep?"

"No," Patsy insisted, digging her heels into the carpet. "I bringed you ca-cakes. You gotsta eat dem." She pushed it at his mouth, but Jesse was falling asleep again. He didn't open his mouth and only got a good smearing of maple syrup on his lips.

Sarah almost laughed aloud and gave her position away. Jesse was certainly awake now.

Placing her hands on her hips, Patsy glared at him. "Why you such a hardhead?"

"I'm just not hungry."

"No. Eat ca-cakes." She pushed the pancake into his face again. By now her little fingers had poked holes through the pancake, and some of it was beginning to crumble onto the edge of the bed and the floor. Sarah watched crumbs catch in Jesse's sideburns and syrup trickle through the lacy pillow edging.

"I'm not hungry, Patsy. I'm sick. I need to sleep now."

"Ca-cakes make you better."

Jesse sighed loudly. Sarah could almost hear him thinking that nothing would ever make him better. How could he explain this to a little child? It had taken Sarah quite a lot of talking to explain it to her adult sister.

Patsy tilted her blond head and peered pleadingly up at him. "Please, Daddy."

Jesse didn't reply. His eyes brightened. Sarah could almost see him trying to shake off his enveloping drowsiness.

"What did you say, Patsy?" he asked, leaning forward slightly.

"Eat! Please, Daddy."

Jesse felt his reluctance suddenly fading away. "Who . . . who told you to call me 'Daddy'?"

"Auntie Dread."

At first he was surprised—and more than a little disappointed—that it wasn't Sarah. She was the one who'd wanted everyone to think Patsy was his child. Why wasn't she the one who'd said something to Patsy. Then he realized, and he tried to hide a wry little grin, she was probably glad to see her plan was obviously working.

He was, too. Not because he wanted to fool Meddling Mildred and the rest of the town, even though that was part of his bargain. Not so much because he was fulfilling his part of his bargain with Sarah. It was because no one had ever called him 'Daddy' before, and he found he kind of liked it.

He watched Patsy in an entirely different light. He'd watched her on the train, while she was with Sarah. He'd noticed her curling blond hair and blue eyes, so like her mother's. He hadn't really seen her up-close until now. He'd never noticed the pudgy baby cheeks and the little button nose. He reached out his hand and managed to pat the top of her head. He'd never imagined her curls would be so soft and fine.

"Eat, Daddy." Patsy was once again shoving the soggy pancake into his face. By now, there really wasn't much left.

"Well, all right," Jesse relented, smiling. "But just a little bit. Daddy's still sick, you know."

Patsy nodded. "Open wide."

Jesse opened his mouth. She shoved it in. The little piece was pasty and sweet with maple. He didn't want to ask what other flavors Patsy's grimy little hand had added. He didn't even want to think about how much carpet lint it contained from Patsy's four-legged climb up the stairs.

The pancake didn't feel very good in his mouth, but it sure tasted good. For so long, what little he had to eat was in reality inedible. Then, no matter what he ate, everything tasted alike. But this simple pancake tasted so good, he actually thought he might be able to eat another.

"Good ca-cakes."

"Very good, Patsy," Jesse answered. "Thank you very much for bringing it to me."

"Eat more." She offered the pancake she'd held in her other hand. It wasn't in much better shape than the first.

Jesse tried to pat his stomach. "I can't, Patsy. I'm full."

Her blue eyes narrowed. She placed both hands on her

hips and stamped her foot on the carpet. "Yes'oo can! Eat!" Just as suddenly she tilted her head, peered up at him again, and said sweetly, "Please."

Jesse laughed aloud. "Well, you might be young, but you're certainly a persistent young lady. I'll bet once you set your mind on something, you don't stop until you accomplish it. Just like your mommy, aren't you?"

Patsy grinned at him and nodded. "Just like Mommy."

Jesse laughed. Patsy was a smart little thing. She'd certainly understood every word he'd said, but he knew she couldn't possibly understand everything he'd meant.

"More?" she asked when he'd finished what was left of the second pancake.

"It was really delicious, Patsy. But I'm pretty full."

He could remember when he'd been able to down a good hearty meal and still be ready for dessert and a run around the farm. It was a sobering thought that two little pancakes could fill him up now.

She grabbed his hand with her sticky little fingers. "C'mon. Get up. Eat."

How was he going to talk this stubborn little lady out of this one?

Motioning for her sister to stay behind, Sarah bustled into the room and came to her daughter's side. She scooped her up in her arms, holding her tightly.

"Mr. . . . Daddy can't get up, Patsy. Remember, he's a hurt man."

"Oh. Okay." She squirmed out of Sarah's arms.

"I didn't see you there," Jesse told her.

"My sister is the noisy one in the family," Sarah whispered.

"Is she standing right outside?" Jesse whispered back.

Sarah nodded.

"I get you more ca-cakes, Daddy." Patsy turned quickly and headed for the door.

"Oh, no, Patsy," Sarah exclaimed. She managed to catch the little girl's arm and keep her at her side. "Don't go down those stairs alone."

"Came up 'em 'lone," she stated.

Jesse chuckled.

Sarah turned to Jesse. "Go ahead and laugh, you heartless man. Patsy's all I have and I don't want to lose her. I'm just terrified of her climbing stairs, or trying to go down, and tripping and falling and breaking her neck."

Patsy was struggling against Sarah's light grasp. "Le'go! Le'go! Gotta get ca-cakes for Daddy!"

"I'm not heartless, Sarah," Jesse said seriously. "I know how much she means to you." Then his eyes began to twinkle. "But I don't think you're going to be able to stop this one from getting what she's after." He gave a little chuckle. "She's kind of like you, you know."

"Le'go! Le'go!" Patsy was still pulling toward the doorway. "Gotsta go!"

"Patsy," Sarah said, stooping down to talk eye to eye with the little girl. "Why don't we go down together? We'll make up a nice tray for . . . Daddy's breakfast, just like we used to do for Aunt Myrtle. Do you remember that?"

Patsy nodded, then shook her head and finally shrugged. Sarah didn't think her daughter was old enough to really remember her great-aunt, but at least the prospect of doing something had stopped her whining.

"Oh, I'll take her down," Mildred offered from the doorway, holding out her hand. Patsy ran to her. "I just adore spoiling the child. Anyway, by now everything's cold, and I'll have to cook everything all over again. You do deserve a fresh breakfast, you poor man," she told Jesse. "After all, any meal just might be your last." She heaved a deep sigh. "I wouldn't want you reaching the Pearly Gates and telling St. Peter that Mildred Preston never fed you anything decent."

"I'll tell him everything was delicious, but he'll still kick me downstairs for being a fool who'd rather sleep than eat."

"Anytime you're awake and feel up to eating, just tell me. I'll cook you my best dish," Mildred promised. "After all, a dying man gets a last meal, doesn't he?"

"I think that's a condemned man," Sarah corrected her sister.

"Oh. Well, I'll still feed him. He deserves to go to his Maker with a smile on his lips. And a new suit—blue, not black. You do like lots of flowers and hymns, don't you, Mr. Taylor?"

"Mildred," Sarah pleaded, "please, don't get too enthusiastic about the prospects for a funeral anytime in the near future."

Mildred just looked disappointed.

"Why not?" Jesse demanded from his place in bed. "Maybe Mrs. Preston and I could have a nice long chat sometime. I'll bet, being a preacher's wife, she has some really great ideas for funerals that I never even thought of."

"Why, I'd just love to! How flattering that on our short acquaintance you value my opinion already, Mr. Taylor." Mildred was practically preening. "While you'll probably only get the standard wooden coffin, I've seen some lovely—"

"No! I don't want you two encouraging each other," Sarah protested. It was bad enough when Jesse was planning his own funeral alone on the train. Hearing the two of them making such enthusiastic plans was very upsetting, but she could hardly tell them why. When Mildred and Jesse both shot her surprised looks, she felt compelled to explain, "I may not be able to afford it."

"That should *never* stand in the way of saying farewell properly to a loved one," Mildred replied indignantly. "After all, it's the last thing you'll ever do—"

"Whoa! You sound like you're a partner in the undertaker's business," Jesse said, fixing Mildred with a dissecting stare. There was still a playful grin on his lips. "You're not planning on taking a share of the expenses, are you?"

"I wouldn't dream of such a thing!" Mildred was even more indignant, until she realized he was only teasing. "Oh, I declare, Mr. Taylor," she said with a laugh that Sarah would've sworn was more of a girlish giggle. "You are a caution!"

"Only at times."

"I could also give you a bit of . . . well, confidential observations about some of the most tasteless displays of funerary ornamentation I've ever had the misfortune to witness," Mildred added haughtily.

"I'm sure you could tell a good tale or two about the eccentricities of the neighbors, Mrs. Preston," Jesse answered, still chuckling.

"Well, that'll just have to wait until I fix you a new breakfast."

"Please, please, don't go to any trouble."

"Oh, it's no trouble at all. It's a pleasure, really," Mildred insisted.

"I really wish you wouldn't."

Still holding Patsy's hand, Mildred headed for the door. "Nonsense. It's no trouble at all."

"Bye-bye, Daddy," Patsy said, waving her hand.

"You come see me again, Patsy—with or without pancakes."

Sarah stood silently beside his bed. She wasn't sure yet what to say to him.

Jesse lay in his bed, also silent. But his head was tilted to such an angle that Sarah believed he must be listening, waiting. Obviously he had something to say that he didn't want Mildred or Patsy to share.

At last Mildred's loud, endless, and usually mindless chattering to Patsy drifted away down the stairwell, through the vestibule, and into the kitchen.

Jesse looked up at Sarah. He was grinning, and his eyes were dancing merrily again. He was awake and ready for mischief. She was almost afraid he was going to try to talk her into joining him in that big, soft bed—which looked so inviting.

Instead he said, "She called me 'Daddy.' "

"I heard. Are you unhappy about that?" Sarah asked cautiously.

"No, not really," Jesse answered with what seemed to Sarah to be equal caution.

"Good, because I suppose that's another factor in this bargain that we hadn't counted on."

"Patsy?"

Sarah nodded.

"Excuse me," he said, trying to raise himself up onto his elbow and failing. Flat in the bed, he frowned at her. "Excuse me, but wasn't Patsy the sole reason we entered into this bargain in the first place? I'd say she was the very first factor you'd taken into consideration."

Sarah shook her head. "No—"

"You mean you accosted me and talked me into marrying you just because I was the handsomest man on that train?"

"Don't be silly," Sarah chided him.

She couldn't admit to him that she *had* thought he was the handsomest man on the train. But she could still feel her cheeks growing warm.

"What I did I did for Patsy—and *only* for Patsy," she stressed. "I just never figured she'd be . . . doing things and . . . saying things on her own that . . . that just might jeopardize all our plans."

"I think you're worried about nothing," Jesse told her. "You heard her. She called me 'Daddy.' "

There was a big contented grin on his face. He was obviously enjoying this immensely.

"I don't think we have to worry about Patsy at all."

Sarah shrugged off her worry. "I suppose you're right. I just hope we don't have to continue to worry about Mildred."

"I don't think your sister'll be a problem, either. But I know something that might."

"Oh, dear." Did he know about Deke Marsden and all his threats—past and present? What if he wasn't talking about Deke at all? What could he be talking about? The last thing she needed now was an entirely new problem. "What is it?"

"Bugs."

She stared at him. "Bugs?"

"Bugs," he affirmed.

"Now you're seeing things? You've taken too much laudanum, or the fever's fried your poor brain, or both." She turned toward the door. "I'll go get Dr. Hanford and see if he can do anything for you."

"No, no, Sarah. I don't need the doc. But if I can't get a cloth to wash my face and get rid of the crumbs in the bed, I'll draw every hungry, sweet-toothed bug in Cottonwood."

Sarah wrinkled up her nose. She immediately went to the washstand in the corner. She dampened the little cloth she'd mangled last night, wrung out the excess water, and took a fluffy white towel. Standing beside him, she handed him the cloth, but he didn't take it.

"Little hard to do lying down."

"You sat up to use the . . . um, the facilities earlier. I think you can manage to sit up by yourself long enough this time, too."

"Do you have a mirror?"

They both looked around the room. The only mirror was attached to the top of the washstand.

"I don't think I can manage to pull the whole stand over to you."

"Maybe you could at least get me my crutch. I guess asking you to hold me up so I can walk over there myself is really out of the question."

Sarah didn't answer him. She'd supported him when they walked up the aisle of that strange church to be married. He was thin and weak, but beneath the frail exterior, she could sense a strength that somehow kept him going no matter what. She kind of liked the feeling. And she kind of didn't like it at all. His strength not only kept him going, it seemed to seep out and take hold of her, too. The thought of him holding her was very disturbing.

"I think you'd better just . . . sit up on the edge of the bed," she told him.

Reaching out her hand, she helped him to sit upright. Gripping the edge of the mattress, he managed to support himself on the edge of the bed while Sarah brushed away all the crumbs and dabbed away most of the syrup. She pulled the second pillow over and tossed the soiled pillow and case aside to change later.

"All clean, now," Sarah announced. "I'll talk to Mildred about changing the sheets and doing the laundry later. I don't want to tire you with too much moving around."

"What about my face?"

"I'm coming to that."

"Saving the best 'til last, huh?"

Sarah just cleared her throat and opened the damp cloth. But when it came to finally wiping the syrup from Jesse's face, she hesitated.

How close would she have to stand to him? How much would she have to touch him?

"Trying to figure out how to wash someone's face?" Jesse teased.

"I know how." She was nervous about the very thought of touching him again, while he was awake.

"Well, I just figured since you were taking so long to get to it . . ."

"I'm getting to it." She tried not to show the edginess in her voice that her nervousness gave her.

"I mean, it's probably just like washing Patsy's face—only hairier."

"Oh, it's a little different." She tried to sound nonchalant.

No, it wasn't just like washing Patsy's face, not at all— even without the hair.

In the first place, Jesse was bigger, Sarah thought as she leaned toward him. She couldn't stand that far away and still reach him without losing her balance. The last thing she needed was to lean too far forward and fall right into Jesse's lap. There was no way he could support her. He'd fall over backward, and they'd both land on the bed, tumbled together in the sheets.

Sarah swallowed hard. She supposed there wasn't much else to do but take a step closer to him.

She wouldn't step so close that she could feel his knee through her skirt, she promised herself. But Jesse couldn't lean forward, or he'd fall off the bed. She stepped even closer.

She didn't mean to touch him. It just sort of happened that as she moved closer to him, he shifted his position on the edge of the bed. His knee bumped up against hers.

"Now . . . now look at me," she told him as she tried to move away.

"I am."

"Yes, well. I . . . I want to make sure I get it all."

She began brushing the cloth across his side whiskers, removing the pancake crumbs. He moved his knee again. She could feel the warmth of him even through her skirt.

She moved on to wipe his cheeks. No, he definitely wasn't just like Patsy, she decided as his unshaven whiskers prickled her fingers through the soft cloth. His cheekbones stood higher. His jawline was heavier, more masculine, not at all childlike.

The feel of his face beneath her fingers, and the warmth of his breath so close to her cheek, made the touch of his knee all the more distracting. This shouldn't be. It *couldn't* be. Yet she found herself giving in just a little to the temptation to stroke his strong chin even after the syrup was all gone.

She could see perfectly well that there wasn't any syrup under his chin, and none on his neck. But she ran the damp cloth over his skin anyway. His chin was firm, and he held it high in spite of his illness. His neck felt corded and strong. What would happen if she continued to smooth the cloth down his neck and across his hairy chest?

What would happen? She knew—and she couldn't do it. Not at all. Never!

"Now, hold still and keep your mouth closed," she instructed him.

"I'll bet you've been waiting to say that to me since the moment we met."

"No," she declared forcefully.

"No?"

"Of course not. I had to get to know you better before I wanted you to be quiet."

Jesse closed his mouth, but his shoulders moved up and down as he laughed.

Now came the ultimate trial, Sarah thought, steeling herself for her job. With her index finger poised under a clean section of the cloth, she made ready to dab at the syrup on his lips.

A tiny amber droplet hung poised on the tip of his upper lip. His skin was dry with the fever, so she gently caught the drop on the edge of the cloth. Slowly she smoothed away the remaining syrup. She shouldn't be noticing how finely curved his lips were or how warm they felt to the touch of her finger. She wished she hadn't bothered with the cloth and had used her bare fingers. She definitely shouldn't have been wondering how those warm lips of his might feel pressed against her own.

She finished dabbing at his full lower lip. She was just about to back away when she felt his hands resting gently on either side of her waist.

"Don't touch me!" she cried, pulling back.

Jesse's hands hung at his sides as he stared at her in bewilderment. "What'd I do? I mean, I only put my hands on your waist. It's not like . . . like I reached up and grabbed your boobies."

"You have no right! No right at all!"

She was still backing up. She had dropped the cloth and towel and held both hands up, covering her breasts protectively. Her blue eyes were wide and wild as she glanced from him to the windows and doorway, then back to him.

He wanted to get up and calm her. But he was afraid that any movement he made toward her would just set her to yelling again. There had to be another way to reassure her.

"Calm down, Sarah," he said slowly and softly. "And keep quiet or you'll have Mildred running up here, trying to find out what's wrong. And you know she won't stop until she does."

Sarah stopped glancing around the room and managed to

drop her hands. Her eyes returned to their normal size, and her breathing slowed to normal again, too.

"I . . . I wouldn't have hurt you, Sarah," he told her, keeping his voice calm and soft. "Honestly, I wouldn't. Look at me, Sarah. I couldn't."

"I . . . I . . . I know. I should have told you before. I don't like being touched."

He looked askance at her. "You touch Patsy all the time. You've hugged your sister. You've even touched me before, Sarah," he reminded her.

"Yes. But then, I touched you."

"I see, I think. You don't mind touching other people but you don't like other people to touch you."

"Exactly."

Jesse drew in a deep breath and collapsed back into his bed. "Clear as mud."

A long period of silence passed while Sarah rinsed out the cloth and hung it.

"I won't touch you again, Sarah," Jesse promised her as she walked toward the door. "Not unless you want me to."

"But it's Sunday," Mildred protested. "You *have* to go."

"I feel so guilty leaving Jesse here alone," Sarah lamented. She felt uneasy being alone with him, but she felt even more unhappy leaving him unattended in his condition.

"I don't know why," Mildred commented with a twist of her lips. "All the man's done for the past couple of days is sleep."

"He's still very sick, Mildred," she reminded her sister again. "Why don't you take Patsy?" she suggested. "You enjoy taking care of her, and she loves you already."

"I can't take care of Patsy and play the organ at the same time."

"Oh." Sarah paused. "Yes, I guess 'Stand Up, Stand Up for Jesus' wouldn't sound the same with Patsy's duet."

"You'll only be in the church next door," Mildred said. "If he needs you for anything, you'll hear his little bell."

"It's not a little bell," she told her. Leave it to Mildred to supply Jesse with a large cowbell. "And he's so stubborn, more likely I'll hear the crash as he tries to make it down the stairs."

"Come on," Mildred urged. "You haven't been out of this house since you arrived. He's still asleep after *not* eating the fine breakfast I fixed him, pancakes and sausage and hot apple pie," she added with pique.

"At least he ate all the pancakes," Sarah offered.

"Humph!" Mildred snorted indignantly. "A man needs more than pancakes and syrup to grow strong . . . Oh, sorry. Go! Go on and get your bonnet and come to church," she urged with forced cheer after realizing her slip of the tongue.

"Well, all right," Sarah agreed.

"I have to run on ahead. Get the pump organ going, you know. I'll see you there," she ordered as she left.

Sarah reluctantly went upstairs to retrieve her bonnet and Patsy's little cap.

"You're going to church?" Jesse asked sleepily from his place in bed.

"I'm sorry to disturb you, but we need to use our mirror."

"Church?" Patsy asked as Sarah tied the pink satin bow under her plump little chin.

"That's right, sweetheart." Sarah picked her up and showed her her reflection in the mirror.

"You look so pretty, Patsy," Jesse told her.

"Daddy pretty, too."

"No, no, Patsy," Jesse said with a laugh. "But your mommy's pretty, too."

"Yes. Mommy's pretty."

Sarah put Patsy down. The little girl ran to Jesse's bedside and took his hand.

"It's been a long time since I heard Mildred's husband preach," Sarah said, taking her bonnet from its box in the wardrobe. "I suppose as long as we're living here with them, I ought to attend his services."

Jesse nodded. "That's probably a good idea."

She inspected herself in the mirror as she placed the bonnet on her head and adjusted the bow.

"Yes, indeed. You do look really pretty, Mrs. Taylor," he told her. "I don't think it's going to take you long to find another husband after I'm gone."

She turned to him and said firmly, "I'm *not* looking for one. When are you going to get that through your thick head?"

"Just checking every once in a while."

She shook her head and grinned at him. "Mr. Taylor, you need to find something else to keep you occupied."

He raised his eyebrows. "I already know what else to do to occupy myself. I just can't seem to be able to talk you into joining me."

"I'm going to ignore you now," she announced, taking Patsy's hand, "and take my daughter to church."

"Our daughter," he corrected.

"I see you affa chuch, Daddy," Patsy told him.

As Sarah led Patsy out the door, he called to her, "Say a prayer for me."

She turned and smiled. "I always do."

Shocked at her own behavior, she practically ran down the stairs and across the vestibule. She couldn't let him know she cared too much for him.

It had been a long time since she'd been in a church that didn't show marks of shelling or fire. It had been a while since she'd been able to sit in a church where the congregation didn't suddenly stop talking as she entered, then, after she'd passed, continue their conversations behind their hands. It had been a while since she'd been able to walk into a church and not have people look her straight in the eye and then turn away as if they hadn't seen a thing there of any importance.

Well, no one in Cottonwood knew anything that would harm her or Patsy. Sarah decided that for the first time in a long time she'd actually enjoy the service.

Until she saw Mildred standing at the bright red church door.

"Yoo hoo! Sarah!" Mildred called and waved her hand.

Apparently the congregation was used to the minister's wife's outbursts, as no one turned around or even blinked at the piercing sound.

"We've been waiting for you," Mildred said, just a little less loudly as Sarah approached.

We? Sarah's ears pricked up at the word. There was only one of Mildred—thank heavens! "We" could only mean one thing.

"Sarah, you remember Simon Parker, don't you?"

Sarah nodded politely and extended her hand. "Yes. How do you do, Mr. Parker?"

"Aw, just Simon, li'l lady," he said, grinding the toe of his boot into the grass. He clenched his hat in his hand and was worrying the brim into extinction.

"Mr. Parker owns a real nice farm not too far from town," Mildred informed her.

Why didn't her sister just buy a wagon and advertise from the side stage? Sarah wondered.

"A hundred forty acres, mostly corn, a li'l barley and rye. Got a couple of cows and a bull. Rent him out to the neighbors, make a li'l extra money that way, if'n you don't mind me bein' so blunt, ma'am. Got a li'l flock of Rhode Island Reds—they'll be yours for pin money and all."

"Mine?" Sarah repeated.

"Got a li'l vegetable plot you can plant anything you want in. Put it up for us and sell the extra for pin money, too. And I want you to know I'll raise the young'un like she was my own."

"Yours?" Sarah repeated.

"Mr. Parker attends our church quite regularly," Mildred interjected.

Sarah didn't care if the man lived in the basement of the church. There was absolutely nothing he or Mildred could say or do that would make her want to remarry anyone.

Sarah was perfectly aware of what was going on around her. She still held Patsy's hand. She saw all the people going into the church. She knew exactly why Meddling Mildred had insisted she come this morning. She knew poor Simon Parker had been talked into coming to meet her, knowing all the while that her husband was dying and that Mildred was intent on finding her another one.

But she couldn't manage to say anything, except to mumble incoherently, repeating what Mr. Parker had said. She still couldn't manage to move away—either slowly or as fast as she could. Worst of all, she couldn't figure out why, when she thought of running, it wasn't so much to be away from Mr. Parker but to be back with Jesse.

"I have to go in for the start of the hymns," Mildred said. "Why don't you two sit together and get better acquainted?"

Why don't you bite your tongue, Mildred? Sarah thought grumpily.

"Go on, now. No need to be so shy. You've met before, so it's not as if you're total strangers."

Seeing that her only other encounter with the man had been him carrying her unconscious husband upstairs, Sarah didn't consider herself and Mr. Parker to be bosom friends, either.

"I think I'll sit in the back pew," Sarah said, "just in case Patsy starts to get cranky."

"Oh, no need for that," Mildred protested.

"No, I wouldn't want to disturb the Reverend Preston's wonderful sermon."

"Suits me. Don't really care where we sit, ma'am," Simon said.

"Me neither." Another man's voice cut through the pleasant Sunday atmosphere, turning it as chilly and fetid as a tomb.

Sarah really did want to snatch up Patsy, turn, and run now.

Deke slipped his hand around Sarah's elbow and began to guide her into the church. "I think you said you wanted to sit in the back pew."

She pulled away sharply. "It's a church, not a maze. I think I can find my way by myself."

Without waiting for Deke to protest, as she was sure he would, Sarah forged ahead.

She turned to Mr. Parker and said, "I believe you already asked me if I'd like to sit with you."

She tucked her hand into the crook of his elbow and gave him a little push so he would accompany her through the door. She didn't want to give him any false hopes, but Mr. Parker was big and obviously strong, and seemed good protection against Deke.

Sarah slipped into the first pew available, the back pew to her right. She placed Patsy on her lap. Mr. Parker sat on the aisle.

There wasn't much room left elsewhere, thank goodness, she thought as she positioned Patsy comfortably on her lap. She didn't know the older couple sitting at the far end, but they seemed rather grandparently, like a firm old split rail fence between her and Deke. Mr. Parker was almost like a brick wall.

Mildred finished her prelude, then played a short introduction to the first hymn.

Dutifully Sarah stood, balancing Patsy on the seat with one hand and holding the hymnal with the other. Mr. Parker held his hymnal out for her, but she refused to share with him. That was coming just a little too close to being a couple for her liking—especially in public. Even if Mildred was bound and determined to find her a husband before poor Jesse was even dead, she didn't have to let the whole town know.

There was a commotion to her right. Mildred kept playing; most of the congregation didn't stop singing. Glancing to her right, Sarah felt her heart finish the trip it had begun earlier, right straight down to the pit of her stomach.

Deke had made the old couple stand up, and he'd practically climbed over them, just to scoot across the pew to sit beside her.

"You ain't goin' to get away from me that easy, Sarah," he whispered to her beneath the tune of the hymn.

She tried to keep singing.

"You couldn't even travel from Georgia to Kansas without me findin' you. You can try to hide anywhere you want in Cottonwood, but I'll still find you."

Even though her voice cracked on the high note, she still kept on singing.

"You can act as snotty as you want, but I ain't gonna let you just ignore me."

The hymn ended abruptly. Sarah sat and took Patsy onto her lap again. She took a Bible from the back of the pew and opened it to some of the colorful illustrations in the middle, to keep Patsy occupied while the Reverend offered all sorts of long prayers.

She prayed Deke would go away.

She prayed that Patsy would stay well and grow up to be a lovely young lady with a wonderful family of her own. She prayed that Mildred and the Reverend would at last be able to have children.

She prayed again that Deke would go away—far, far away —soon.

She prayed that Jesse would have an easy death and not have to suffer. She really tried to concentrate hard on this prayer. But every time she began, beneath it all she found herself actually praying that Jesse would grow well and strong—and live for a long, long time—with her.

"I'm gonna marry you, Sarah." Deke's coarse whisper interrupted her prayers.

"I'm already married."

"So you say. But I don't see no ring," he said, reaching out to place his hand on top of hers. It wasn't the kind of affectionate gesture a man would make to his sweetheart. It was the proprietary act of a captor with his prey.

She tried to pull away but couldn't get him to release his grasp. As they tugged, they wrinkled the picture pages Patsy was looking at.

"Hey! Stop! Go 'way, nasty man!" Patsy yelled. She started slapping at his hand. He just laughed.

"Not mess my book. Nasty man!" Patsy balled her little hand into a tight fist and started pounding on the back of his hand. He laughed again.

A few of the people in the pew in front of them were turning around, whispering, "Shh."

"I stop you, nasty man!" Patsy bent down and bit him.

Obviously, Sarah decided proudly, no one should ever laugh at Patsy unless she intended him to. Then, horrified, she watched Deke draw back his fist.

"Everyone's watching," she warned him.

Apparently everyone's opinion didn't matter to Deke at all.

"Remember where you are!" she scolded.

Slowly Deke lowered his fist.

"Miserable damn brat!" he grumbled, holding his injured hand. When he moved his fingers, Sarah could still see prominent teeth marks.

She allowed herself a small grin of satisfied retribution. Then her features grew more stern. "You never change, do you?"

"Not me. But that husband of yours is gonna change. He's gonna be dead and six feet under. Real soon, too. We all know he ain't gonna last much longer."

"I don't intend to remarry."

He ignored her protest, as usual. "You know I ain't a patient man, li'l lady. Hell, anybody'll tell you that, won't they, Si?"

Simon nodded woodenly.

"Matter of fact, the longer I have to wait, the angrier and angrier I get. Why, sometimes I get so angry, I feel like I just want to reach out and grab somethin' and kill it." His grip on her hand tightened.

She swore to herself she wouldn't wince. She'd never again let him see how he could hurt her.

"You know what I mean, Sarah?" He turned and glared at Simon. *"You* know what I mean, don't you?"

Simon coughed, nodded toward Sarah, and moved to another pew.

"And you know somethin', Sarah? Right now, the way I see it, Jesse Taylor's makin' me awful angry."

Seven

"Falling asleep in church, I could understand," Mildred grumbled loudly as she entered Jesse's room. As she set the dinner tray on the small table, she glared at Sarah, standing at his bedside. "Although how a body could fall asleep with a little one to watch out for is beyond me."

Sarah grimaced. Mildred obviously had no concept of the complete exhaustion a person could experience while taking care of one old invalid aunt and one very active baby girl.

"Talking too loudly in church, I could even understand," Mildred continued to complain. "If a body was deaf as a post—which you are not. But I have *never* in all my born days seen anyone bolt from a church the way you did."

"She couldn't help it," Jesse said from his bed. "She's a Bolton." He laughed so hard he started coughing again.

"Oh, hush," Sarah scolded, trying to stifle her own laugh. How could she laugh when she knew it was making him ill? He hadn't coughed this hard for almost a week, she worried, and she wouldn't be responsible for it now.

"What in the world is wrong with both of you?" Mildred demanded of Sarah. "Patsy raising such a fuss, and then you running out of church as if the Hoary Hosts of the Netherworld were on your heels."

"Nothing." She kept her voice light. She couldn't tell her sister why she'd grabbed up Patsy and run from the church. Not in front of Jesse. Not in front of anyone.

"Mommy. I hungry," Patsy said, pulling on Sarah's skirt.

"In a minute, dear."

"It didn't have anything to do with Simon Parker, did it?"

"Who's he?" Jesse asked, frowning with obvious surprise.

"No one," Sarah replied quickly to Jesse.

"He has a name. He's got to be someone," he insisted.

"I hungry!"

"In a minute, Patsy."

"What did he do? What did he say?" Mildred pursued her.

"Who is he?"

Patsy stamped her foot. "I wanna eat *now*!"

"Nothing. He's no one important." Sarah felt as if her head were spinning, trying to answer two questions at once and keep Patsy still. "In a minute, dear."

"If he's not important, why are you seeing him?" Jesse demanded crossly. "I thought you said you didn't want to remarry, ever."

"I don't."

"Oh, Sarah, you *have* to remarry. Think of poor little Patsy growing up fatherless!"

"Think of poor little Patsy growing up hungry."

Jesse apparently couldn't resist the temptation to say something witty if his life depended on it. Fortunately she had more self-control and could resist the temptation to laugh.

"I hungry!" Patsy insisted, tugging harder on her skirt, trying to pull her out the door. "Eat, eat, eat, eat, eat . . ."

Sarah wanted to take care of Patsy, and if it meant running away from Mildred and all her questions, well, so be it. But for some reason she wanted to stay with Jesse. She wanted to make him understand that she didn't give a hang about Simon—or any other man except him. And Jesse didn't seem to want to understand.

"Mildred, our father *and* mother died, and Aunt Myrtle raised us, and we grew up just fine. It's nothing, really."

"I thought you liked him," Mildred said.

"Of course I loved Daddy—what I remember of him."

"I mean Simon Parker!"

"You *like* him?" Jesse demanded.

"I don't even know him," Sarah defended herself. She was beginning to get a terrible headache, being bombarded with questions from both sides.

"Then why'd you sit in church with him?"

"Of course you know him, silly," Mildred said.

She was used to Mildred's incessant, pointless questions. But why was Jesse asking all these questions? Was he jealous? How could he be? It wasn't as if they really loved each other. Why was she making excuses, anyway? She didn't owe him any explanations. She hadn't done anything wrong. Her headache was growing worse all the time.

"Why were you in church with him?"

She gave the only logical excuse she could come up with. "Mildred made me do it!" As soon as the words had left her mouth, she was horrified at how much she sounded like a spoiled little girl, but it really was the truth. "I only sat beside him—not *with* him."

"What did he say to make you run from church?" Mildred asked.

"Nothing!" Sarah's head was positively pounding.

"Don't give me a 'nothing' story, young lady," Mildred scolded, placing both hands on her hips.

"Now you sound like Aunt Myrtle."

"Well, why not? You acted like a child. You deserve to be scolded like a child."

"Mildred, I *have* a child," she said with a sudden inspiration. "Sometimes a child needs to be taken outside. After all, you wouldn't want her crying to disturb everyone while they're trying to listen to one of the Reverend Preston's inspiring sermons, would you?"

Mildred bent down to Patsy's level and pinched her round

cheek. "What! This little cherub disturb anyone? I don't believe that's possible."

"Trust me. You haven't been around her long enough."

Patsy let go of Sarah's skirt and latched on to Mildred's. "Auntie Dread, I'm hungry. *You* feed me."

"Oh, you poor little angel. Does your mommy neglect you?" Mildred stood upright. Her face was beaming with a smug pride that Patsy should come to her.

"I still don't see any real reason to be rushing her out of the church. 'Let the little ones come unto me,' " she quoted. "Just between you and me, some of the Reverend's sermons need to be interrupted. I declare, that man is so long-winded when he gets into that pulpit. After about two hours of his preaching, people start coughing worse than Mr. Taylor. And he never takes the hint!"

"I've hardly heard a peep out of the Reverend Preston since we've been here," Sarah said.

"Trust me. You haven't been around him long enough," Mildred countered. She held out her hand to Patsy. "Come on, sweetheart. You must be starving after all that running around in church. We'll get you a delicious dinner."

"Dessert, too?"

"Of course," Mildred answered. "Then Auntie Mildred will put you to bed and tell you lots of bedtime stories."

"Sing songs, too?"

"Oh, yes. That, too."

Patsy jumped up and down, her pale curls bouncing. She started to nod her head from side to side, chanting melodiously, "Auntie Dread sing, sing, sing, sing. . . ."

Fading away down the stairs, Sarah could hear her sister continue over Patsy's descant, "Poor little thing, you probably don't get sung to very often either, but then your mother's voice never was quite as sweet as my own so you're probably just as well off. No wonder you enjoy my singing so much."

"Auntie Dread sing funny," Patsy replied with a giggle. "Desserts is better."

Sarah couldn't help chuckling. "Mildred always did think

she had a vibrant soprano when actually she's a very trembling alto with impossible aspirations."

"I agree with Patsy. Desserts is better," Jesse quoted with an emphatic nod. "You know, it's funny how Patsy's only my daughter by adoption, and she hasn't been my daughter for very long, yet the most important thing about dinner for both of us is dessert."

"I was just about to say the same thing," she said with a laugh. He gave her an affectionate glance. Oh, merciful heavens! What if the man really could read her mind?

Did he know that sometimes she wished, if he had to depart this life, he'd just do it soon and get it over with? She hadn't thought it would be that hard to lose him as a total stranger. She never anticipated the fact that each day he lived he became more and more like a friend. Watching him try to remain cheerful while he withered away slowly, day by day, was wrenching her heart.

What would he do if he knew that there were other times when she wished he could stay here with her forever?

"What happened in church this morning, Sarah?" Jesse asked as he began to eat.

"Oh, hymns, prayers, pass the collection plate, the usual things," she replied with a shrug.

"Was the choir so bad it drove you out?"

"No."

"Were you embarrassed because you didn't have anything to put in the collection plate?"

"I have money," she asserted proudly, then added sheepishly, "a little."

"Were you embarrassed because Patsy reached in and took money out of the plate?"

"She wouldn't do such a thing!"

Jesse only laughed, and Sarah realized it was just his ornery sense of humor again.

Then he stopped laughing. "Did you have a nice time with that Mr. Parker?"

"I thought we'd agreed not to bring that up again."

"Sorry. I guess it's me being cooped up here all the time and you being let loose on the town—"

"I'm not running wild around the town," she corrected him. "I've only gone out once since I've been here—and that was to church."

"Well, once was enough, wasn't it?"

"Don't be silly."

"You're meeting people."

"You met the same people at the welcoming party."

"But you're also meeting people I don't even know, like Simon Parker."

"He's one of the men who carried you upstairs when you fainted," she tried to explain.

"I was unconscious when we met. That's hardly a basis for a lifelong friendship."

Recalling her unpleasant encounter with Deke and his threat of more unpleasant encounters, she sighed and said, "Jesse, I'm meeting people even *I* don't want to know."

"Do you want to know Simon Parker?"

"I never saw him before and I don't care if I never see him again. To tell the truth, I'm not really partial to big, tall men with bright red hair."

"Are you partial to thin, medium-sized men with brown hair and blue eyes?"

She wasn't about to tell him she was, but only if they walked with a crutch. She passed that question completely.

"Mildred set it up without my knowing. I've already told you how she is."

"She's starting already?"

Sarah nodded.

"I'm not even dead yet. I thought you said I could get you at least a year's peace after I go."

"She . . . you . . . no," she said, shaking her head. "You wouldn't believe me if I told you what she's planned."

"What is it? Another party? A wake?"

"No. I . . . I think I'd better let her tell you."

"I can't wait . . . I think."

"Eat. You'll need your strength for Mildred's plans." She

indicated the contents of his plate for his benefit. "Mildred's famous chicken and biscuits, Mildred's famous creamed corn, Mildred's famous pear conserve, Mildred's famous lemonade, Mildred's famous chocolate cake."

"There's enough here for an army. Why does your sister keep piling up the plate when I've told you all I really don't have much appetite?" He picked up his fork and headed for the chocolate cake.

"No, no. Eat your dinner first."

"I'm a sick man, remember? I might drop dead in the middle of the creamed corn—and who wants to spend eternity with that taste in his mouth?"

"I promise, instead of pennies on the eyes, I'll put a piece of Mildred's famous chocolate cake in your mouth."

"Geez, Sarah," Jesse said as he took a forkful of applesauce, "you have a really morbid turn of mind."

"Me?" she demanded with good-humored indignation.

"And you thought I was weird wanting a nice funeral." Jesse grinned at her and continued to eat. "You know, I really don't have much appetite, and I'd hate to fill up on chicken and not leave room for that cake."

Sarah watched as each forkful continued to disappear from the plate. "Don't worry. We'll save you a big piece for when you're hungry again."

Then, between a bite of chicken and more applesauce, he surprised her by asking very nonchalantly, "I don't suppose your running out of the church was all just a figment of Mildred's famous imagination, was it?"

"No," she answered slowly. Then more quickly she assured him, "But you ought to know by now that Mildred's prone to exaggeration."

"All right. So you didn't bolt from the church. But there still had to be some reason for you to tiptoe very slowly and very quietly out of the church in the middle of the sermon."

"It wasn't important, it's over now, and it'll never happen again," she answered, her irritation evident in her voice. "Won't you please leave the matter alone?"

"No." His reply was much more emphatic. "I can't have

my wife running out of buildings like a lunatic. What will the neighbors say?" He looked up at her and grinned. "That I made you go crazy?"

She hated when he did that! How could she stand firm in her resolve and resist his blue eyes, dancing with mischief?

"We just can't have that, Sarah," he mumbled, shaking his head as he broke off a piece of biscuit with the edge of his fork. He put it in his mouth and continued to eat.

"It starts in church, but next thing you know, you're running out of the bank, the butcher's, the milliner's, the monthly meeting of the Cottonwood Methodist Ladies Evangelical Temperance and Missionary Soul-Saving Spiritual Aid Bible Society."

"I haven't joined yet."

"It doesn't matter. People'll be afraid to invite you over for a visit, not knowing what you might do next."

"I don't know anyone yet who'd invite me."

"Suppose you find yourself overwhelmed by the urge to go running from the house some night? What kind of husband do you suppose everybody'll think I am? What kind of reputation do you think that'll give the Reverend, to have that kind of thing happening in his very own house?"

Sarah pursed her lips and frowned. "Well, you do have a point there. Wait a minute!" she exclaimed as she suddenly realized, "I haven't done any of those things. How can you manage to make me feel so silly about something I haven't even done?" She shook her head. He did have the most amazing effect on her—one that she could never admit to him.

He suddenly stopped eating, placed his fork on the edge of his plate, and peered at her intently. "Just tell me one thing, Sarah," he said very seriously. "When you ran from the church, were you screaming and foaming at the mouth? Did you bite anybody?"

She had so much trouble keeping her lips from turning up in a smile that she decided to stop trying. "No," she answered with a little laugh. "I couldn't find *you!*"

Jesse's grin intensified. So did the gleam in his eyes. He

spread his arms wide, encompassing himself and the big bed. "Me? I'm always right here, waiting."

"You'll be waiting a long time," she said with a wry twist of her lips.

He shrugged and started eating again. He gave up, he just gave up! She couldn't believe it. She was used to him talking, teasing, cajoling—even goading her into some outburst that they could both laugh about later. She was surprised and a bit disappointed in Jesse. Most of all, she was surprised at her own disappointment that he hadn't pressed her. She shouldn't feel that way. It was only talk—just talk. That's all it ever could be.

Suddenly he looked up and gave her a wink. "Do you think there's any chance you'll decide to run from the church someday, tearing off all your clothes on the way?"

"Of course not!" she exclaimed. She tried not to giggle.

"Oh, well. No sense in my coming to church, then."

She should be affronted by his mention of nudity. But all she could feel now was amused by the silly images he conjured in her mind—and a sudden tingling feeling down deep inside at the thought of standing before Jesse and, under his watchful shining blue eyes, slowly peeling away each layer of cloth.

Still, Aunt Myrtle would've expected her to be insulted, and she really shouldn't encourage him in his wayward thoughts.

"How can you think I'd do such a thing?" she asked.

He smiled at her warmly, his blue eyes shining. She felt her skin tingle once again, and a stirring deep inside her that she thought had long ago died.

"I think there are a lot of things you're capable of that you just don't think about yet."

She didn't want to ask him to suggest a few things. She knew darned well that he would, and she had more than a sneaking suspicion she knew what some of those suggestions were.

She decided to counter on her own. "That's all right. There was a moment at the welcoming party when I was afraid you were dancing on the dining-room table in Mrs. Silesky's potato salad."

He stopped and stared at her, his mouth open and a forkful of creamed corn halfway to his mouth. Thick yellow droplets began dripping through the tines.

"Naked?"

"No!"

He shrugged and continued eating. "Oh, well, no. I didn't even eat any of it, much less dance in it. When did this happen?"

"Mildred came running in, telling me I had to see to you," Sarah explained. "She didn't see fit to elaborate, and I just sort of jumped to conclusions."

He put his fork down without having taken the bite. "That's one whopper of a conclusion! Your imagination must be as famous as Mildred's. Does that sort of thing run in your family? Can I expect the same thing from Patsy when she gets older? Will you teach her, or are you all born with the talent?"

"Oh, shut up and eat your famous dinner," she said, laughing.

He ate about half of the chicken. He even tried some of Mildred's homemade conserve on one of the biscuits. Maybe he'd have eaten more if he knew that Mildred's secret ingredient—the one she hid under the washtub and hoped the Reverend never found out about—was Kentucky bourbon. Sarah noticed Jesse did finish the entire piece of chocolate cake.

He might protest he still had no appetite, but she'd noticed lately that he seemed to be eating just a little more each day.

While she hadn't actually been keeping track of the hours and frequency, she didn't think he was coughing as much as he used to, either. He was awake longer during the day, too.

Was that how people with consumption ended their days? Had his poor lungs been so taxed that they just gave up coughing and eventually breathing, too? She could hardly ask Jesse. She wouldn't want him to think she was rushing him along. Maybe she could ask Doc Hanford.

She might be tempted to think Jesse was actually improving. No, that couldn't be possible. He still needed his same dosage of laudanum on a regular basis. He was still limping on the few occasions when he rose and tried to walk, and he still had a low fever. Even the man's illnesses were a complete puzzle to her.

"You know, you're making *me* crazy, Sarah," he told her.

"Excuse me?"

"You're making me crazy. Sleeping in this big comfortable bed all alone and having to watch you trying to sleep in that stiff, uncomfortable chair."

"You don't have to feel guilty," she assured him. "It's not that uncomfortable."

"Knowing that when I go to sleep at night, you stand and change your clothes there at the foot of the bed—"

"How do you know where I—?"

"It's the only place there's enough room for you to change clothes that's far enough away from the windows for the neighbors not to see you," he explained. Grinning, he tapped the side of his head. "Think logically, my dear."

"You do too much thinking for your own good," Sarah said, taking the tray from him. "And I'm not going to make any comments about *your* famous imagination."

She knew he was teasing. He was always teasing. She knew he wasn't awake either, not after taking his laudanum. But there was something about imagining him lying there, watching her, that made her heart beat faster.

Could he see the mended places in her underclothes? she worried. She'd have to ask Mildred which was the best place to buy some more fabric and make some new ones.

Did he think she looked like some awkward, contorted oaf, trying to take off her corset by herself? Did she look clumsy leaning against the wall to balance herself when she took off her shoes and hose?

When she took off her chemise, did he think her breasts hung too low from nursing Patsy? Did her stretch marks show in the dim lamplight? Did he like what he saw? Would he keep watching?

Did it matter? She suddenly snapped herself back to her good senses. Of course not. Considering all their circumstances, it didn't really matter at all.

She handed him his laudanum. "Take your dosage and go to sleep." Then she picked up his tray. "I'm going to take this downstairs and check on Patsy."

"Your sister's taking care of her."

"Mildred's idea of taking care of Patsy is spoiling her rotten. You'll be asleep by the time I come back up."

Jesse chuckled. "You'll only think I'm asleep. I'll be lying here with my eyes looking like they're closed, but actually they're opened just a little tiny slit. I'll be waiting for you to stand right there." He pointed to the spot he'd indicated earlier. "I'll be watching."

"That's not part of the bargain, either," she pointed out.

"We've already had to make a few adjustments," he returned. "One more wouldn't hurt."

"That depends on what that one is." Quickly she left the room.

Run, Sarah! Run!
The footsteps followed her in the darkness.
Faster, Sarah! Faster!
Her skirts tangled around her legs. She couldn't run. Her knees collapsed beneath her. Her ankles turned with every step, making her stumble. She reached out to catch herself as the ground rose beneath her, but somehow she never fell. She just continued to run.

The footsteps drew closer in the darkness. Lights and shadows warred against each other on the rough walls that loomed up on either side of her. Darkness was winning.

The footsteps turned into hands—big, hard, rough hands. Hands that grabbed at her and tore her clothes. Strong arms that threw her to the rocky ground. A big body, hard and heavy on top of her.

She couldn't breathe. She opened her mouth to scream, but couldn't make a sound.

The shame. She wanted to die.

Searing, burning, tearing. Pain that wouldn't stop, no matter how much she cried. Blood.

She screamed.

Jesse sat bolt upright in bed. "What the devil was that?" He looked around him, but the room was completely dark.

"Sarah? Are you awake? Did you hear that noise? What was it?"

He didn't hear an answer, but there was a low sobbing sound in the room.

At last he could make out Sarah's silhouette against the starlit sky visible through the half-open curtain. He realized the sobbing was coming from her.

"Sarah? Did it scare you, too?" She'd seemed such a strong-spirited woman, he could hardly believe anything would scare her that much. "Do you know what happened?"

"Nothing."

Her voice was small and raspy. He could hear it quiver. It was almost as if he could feel her body shaking all the way across the room.

"It sounded like a scream."

"Yes." This answer wasn't much louder than the first one, but it was still just as shaky.

"My God, was that you?"

"Yes."

"Why'd you scream? What's wrong, Sarah?"

His leg hurt, but it was oddly easier to breathe as he got out of bed. He limped to her side and reached out to place a comforting hand on her shoulder.

She sprang from her seat. "Don't touch me!" She screamed again and disappeared into the darkness enveloping the room.

"Hey, where'd you go? I won't hurt you," he told her,

taking a step forward. The big toe of his injured leg struck the leg of the chair. "Yow!" A flood of other words followed.

Sarah didn't spring to his side, demanding to know what was wrong. She was still hiding in the darkness. Now he knew for certain she was more than just scared. Something terrible had happened to her.

"Sarah, where are you?" he asked as he moved the chair aside.

No answer but a low sobbing.

"Sarah, sorry about the bad language. I kind of surprised myself. I haven't used those words in front of a lady in years, and then they were followed by my mother soaping my mouth." He tried to laugh to ease her fears. When he was quiet, all he could hear was her continued sobbing in the dark.

He reached out slowly and carefully to find the lamp on the table.

"Watch your eyes, Sarah," he warned. "I'm going to turn the lamp up."

His fingers groped over the table covering until he encountered the smooth glassy globe of the bottom of the lamp. He inched his fingers up the globe, searching for the wick key.

"I don't want to knock it over. I'm going to be dying here. I'm not so sure about your unbalanced state of mind lately —they may have to lock you away in the attic. I guess the last thing the Prestons need right now is for me to burn their house down."

Again he tried to laugh, but Sarah only continued to sob.

He turned up the wick. The yellow gleam illuminated parts of the room and threw other parts into deep shadows. Sarah was huddled in the corner. Her knees were drawn up to her chin, and her arms were wrapped around her legs. She was rocking back and forth and watching him very carefully.

Thank goodness there wasn't any blood. But the terrified look in her eyes hurt him worse.

"Oh, my God! Sarah!" He rushed to her side. She cringed as he approached. But the wall was behind her, and she had nowhere else to run. "What happened to you?"

She just looked at him with wide eyes. He wasn't even sure if she was really awake, or maybe walking in her sleep, or in some strange sort of trance brought on by hysteria.

"Come on. You remember me," he said. Slowly he reached out to pat her on the shoulder, but she jerked away. "It's Jesse. Jesse Taylor. Your husband," he prompted. "The guy with the cough and the limp."

He wanted to add, "The guy who thinks he's fallen in love with you." Of course, if she snapped out of her stupor, she might slap him for saying a thing like that. On the other hand, maybe she'd like to hear him say it. In that case, he wanted to be very sure she was fully conscious when he told her, and fully aware of everything he meant by it. He'd wait.

Then he became completely aware of the utter foolishness of what he was thinking. He had no time to wait. And even if he told her how he felt about her, he couldn't do anything about it. He'd be dead before the year was out.

"The guy who likes dessert," he added instead, and forced a laugh.

She nodded.

She seemed to have calmed down. He dared to place his hand on her shoulder again. When she didn't run away this time, he continued to rest his hand on her shoulder and pat gently to soothe her.

"Jesse," she whispered.

She knew him. She was definitely awake now. Her hysteria must be waning. Her tear-filled eyes lost some of the fear. He slipped his arm around her.

"What happened?" he asked. "You screamed."

She tried to shrug off his question. "I . . . I just had a bad dream," she told him, wiping her eyes roughly with the back of her hand. "That's all it was—a bad dream."

He held her tightly against him. "Bad dream, my aunt Tillie's drawers! Sounded more like the wail of the banshee."

"Everybody has a bad dream once in a while."

"Sure, but most of them don't send people leaping out of their seats screaming. What the heck were you dreaming about?"

"Nothing, nothing."

"That was a heck of a nothing. You're still shaking from it." He held her tightly in an effort to stop her quivering.

She didn't answer. But at least she'd stopped crying, Jesse noted with relief. It seemed as if she was shaking less now, too. If she was calming down, maybe now she could talk more logically and objectively about what had frightened her so badly. Maybe then he could try to do something to make sure she was never frightened by it again. He felt so helpless trying to battle dreams.

"Come on," he urged. "We've got to get you off this floor."

She drew in a deep breath and tried to rise. Her legs were still weak. Jesse kept his arm around her shoulder, supporting her as he led her to sit on the bed.

"Don't worry. I'll take care of you."

"I'm supposed . . . I promised to take care of you," she mumbled as she allowed him to lead her along. She didn't even seem to mind when Jesse sat her down on the bed.

"Don't be such a stickler for duty," he told her. "We've already made a few amendments to our original bargain."

"I promised."

Even though she protested, Jesse had a suspicion that she was still so bewildered by the nightmare that she wasn't exactly sure of what she was saying—almost as if she were repeating things by rote just to respond to his questions. She didn't even protest when he dared to sit down beside her on the bed.

"Yes, you did. But remember, I promised to take care of you, too."

She nodded.

"We never thought I'd actually have to do it, though, did we?"

"No."

"You wouldn't want me to go back on my part of our bargain, would you?"

"No."

"That might mean *you'd* go back on some part of our bargain. I don't think I'd mind much not having lots of flowers and hymns at the funeral, but I don't think I could stand not being able to have desserts."

He could feel her slender shoulders relax against him just a little. He hoped it was his light, reassuring words making her feel better. Even more, he hoped it was his own comforting nearness that made her feel safe to be with him.

He kept his gentle hold on her, being very careful never to hold her too tightly. She seemed to need the option of leaving his embrace. Only then did she feel safe staying. He'd give her that option. He always would. But in his heart, he really wanted to hold her in his arms and never let her go.

"Now, what kind of bad dream could make you scream like that?"

While she remained close to him, he felt her body tense again. "I . . . I don't remember."

Oh, she remembered all right, he decided. What was so terrible about it that she didn't want to speak of it? "Now you've really got me worried."

"Why?"

"Well, at first I only thought you were a little crazy."

"I beg your pardon," she replied. Some of her indignity was tempered by a large yawn.

"I mean, first you're running out of church for no reason. Then you're screaming in the middle of the night and you can't remember why. Maybe you're in your dotage. How old did you say you were?"

"I didn't."

"Oh."

"I'm twenty-four."

"That's a little young to be going senile."

Sarah just shrugged.

"You know, a long time ago," he began, hoping to distract

her, "before the war, my friends and I used to have a drink or two . . . or three, and talk about life and other things. I seem to remember, the drunker we got, the more serious the conversation turned."

"You must've been really drunk," she said with another yawn. "I can't imagine you talking seriously any other way."

"Well, anyway, they warned me. No matter how sweet a girl is during the courtship, a man never really knows what kind of wife she'll make."

She shook her head, then leaned over to rest her head on his shoulder.

"I . . . I beg your pardon," she said, unconsciously snuggling closer to him as sleep overtook her. "I believe I was very straightforward with you."

"No. You bargained for a dying man and got one. I don't recall bidding for a lunatic."

"You're . . . the lunatic," she answered with a little laugh, then yawned again.

"Well, it serves us both right, then, for marrying complete strangers."

"I think it's too late to . . . cancel our bargain."

"That's all right," he said. He wouldn't want to now anyway.

He could feel her slowly relaxing as she was falling back to sleep. He was glad to see it. Maybe it had been one of those dreams that were terrifying at the moment and then quickly forgotten when confronted with the bright lamplight, and someone reassuring and comforting to share it with.

He waited for some sort of reply. All he could hear was her slow, even breathing.

"Well, short of hearing 'Come to my bed, Jesse' from you, I guess that's the next best thing," he told her as he laid her gently back on the pillow. "At least it shows you trust me. Or that you find me incredibly boring."

She must've been exhausted because she didn't even stir as he lifted her feet into the bed. He brushed the dust from the soles of her bare feet and hoped she wasn't ticklish so that he'd wake her. Her feet were tiny. Her nails were smooth and white. He thought of his own dusty, suntanned feet and callused soles when he was a boy. Sarah had definitely been a pampered city girl.

He had to admit he was sorely tempted to lift the edge of her skirt, to take a peek at her pretty ankle . . . or calf . . . or knee. He shook his head. Only a complete, unregenerate, perverted sinner would take advantage of a sleeping lady—even if she was his wife. He sighed and shook his head, then pulled the covers up to her waist.

He turned down the wick on the lamp. Slowly, balancing himself by holding on to the mattress and the footboard of the bed—and making very sure he didn't stub his toe again —he made his way to the other side.

He'd been to bed with a woman before, a time or two, he reminded himself as he crept into bed beside her. It wasn't exactly as if he and Sarah were actually going to do anything but sleep anyway. It must've been from his exertions in his weakened condition, then. That could be the only reason to account for his insides trembling with the thought of getting into bed with Sarah.

He lay in the bed beside her, watching her features take shape in the starlight as his eyes grew accustomed to the darkness.

He'd only seen her upright before. He'd never imagined she could be this beautiful lying in his bed.

Her pale hair flowed out from her head, cascading over the pillow.

He watched the smooth outline of her slender waist and hips beneath the cool white sheet. Her waist was so tiny—no wonder he'd been tempted to encircle it with his hands the other evening. He sure would like to try to hold her again.

Without her corset, her breasts looked soft and accessible. He liked the way one breast leaned into the other, making two soft, creamy mounds one on top of the other, and deepening her cleavage as she slept on her side.

She'd been losing too much sleep taking care of him, he

decided as he guiltily noticed the dark circles that surrounded her eyes.

He'd never imagined he could feel so terrible lying beside her, and being too much of a gentleman to do a darned thing about it!

Eight

"Yoo hoo!"

"Oh, no," Jesse groaned under his breath. He raised his hand to cover his eyes.

As the mattress shifted, he could feel Sarah just beginning to stir beside him. He didn't need Mildred waking her before he'd had the chance to talk to her, to explain what she was doing in his bed when she'd fallen asleep in her chair.

"Rise and shine, you slugabeds!"

"You'd think after this long she'd come up with another cheery morning greeting," he mumbled.

"Yoo hoo, breakfast!"

With a sudden inspiration, in a high-pitched voice, he called out, "I won't be down, Mildred."

"Sarah, you sound terrible. Have you caught a cold?" she called through the door, then added her own comments. "I just knew you were exerting yourself taking care of that man night and day, and him not appreciating a thing you do."

At first he thought he'd argue with her, but he wasn't sure how long he could force his voice to maintain this high-pitched squeak. Anyway, Sarah never seemed to argue much with Mildred—just with him. He'd keep silent now, he decided, but maybe he would spit—just once—in Mildred's direction for such a snide comment.

"It's the vapors," he answered instead. "Geez! I never thought I'd be using that as an excuse for not getting up in the morning," he muttered to himself at a more normal pitch.

"Oh, yes. Oh, you poor dear. I understand completely. The vapors can be so terribly disappointing."

Mildred's voice had lost its early-morning brightness. She sounded awfully sad. Even the little he'd seen of Patsy and her together, it was easy to see how much she loved children. What a shame they didn't have any. In spite of all her meddling, Jesse felt sorry for her and the poor henpecked Reverend.

"Well, if you need some soothing tea or anything, just ring that little bell," she advised.

Bell, my Aunt Tillie's drawers—it was a darned cowbell! It didn't belong on his nightstand. It belonged in the belfry of the church. If he tried to lift that thing in his condition, he'd end up needing a truss to go along with his cane.

If he kept talking in this voice, he'd need a truss anyway.

"Thank you very much," he called, hoping she was going away. Under his breath, he mumbled, "Now leave me alone the rest of the day—except if you're bringing up food."

"Oh, how could you!" Sarah's eyes were wide open and filled with tears of disappointment.

"Shh!" Jesse told her frantically. "I wasn't really trying to be nasty to your sister."

"No. You're a treacherous, lying cad! How did I get in bed with you?"

"Shh! Suppose Mildred hears you?"

"She'd agree with me."

"Did you say something?" Mildred called through the door.

Sarah's eyes grew wide.

Jesse gestured for her to remain silent. "Just . . . just singing a hymn," he replied in his falsetto.

Sarah's eyes grew even wider as she stared at him in disbelief.

"Would you rather have to answer her yourself?" Jesse whispered.

Sarah pressed her lips together.

"And she wouldn't agree with you," he pointed out. "We're supposed to be married, remember? It's your wifely duty to be here with me."

Sarah grudgingly waited until it seemed a long enough time for Mildred to have gone her way. She lifted the covers, peering under them to make certain she had her clothes on. Seeing that everything was still in the right place, she gave a sigh of relief, then tossed back the sheet and jumped out of bed.

From the safety of her place behind her chair, more quietly she demanded, "How did I come to be in bed with you?"

"You came to be in bed with me."

"What?"

"You came into my bed."

"Not willingly."

"Oh, yes. Very willingly."

She crossed her arms stubbornly over her chest. "I don't believe you."

"You had a horrible nightmare last night, Sarah," Jesse explained.

She looked just like a soap bubble that had suddenly burst. Her shoulders sloped, and her arms hung limply at her sides. Her face had a horrible, stricken look. She moved around and collapsed in the chair.

"You heard me?"

"You screamed louder than a train whistle. I'm surprised half the town didn't hear you and come running, let alone Mildred."

"Oh, goodness. Not Mildred! Did I . . . did I say anything?"

"Mostly 'Leave me alone, Jesse,'" he replied.

"Nothing else?"

"No. You were too upset." He tried to look at her with the most understanding expression he could manage. "Of course, if you're a little calmer now, you might be able to talk about what bothered you."

"No."

Sarah might not really remember talking to Jesse last night, but she knew immediately what nightmare would always set her to screaming. It was the same one she'd had for a long time.

How could she describe her nightmare to him? How could she explain to him—or anyone—what it all meant to her? She couldn't let anyone discover her horrible secret. She might risk her own reputation, but she'd never risk the future of her daughter.

"I mean, when a dream is so bad that I had a hard time trying to get you off the floor and into a soft, comfortable bed—"

"I'll bet you managed that in quite a hurry, too," she commented sarcastically. Maybe if she quarreled with him about something else, he wouldn't be so intent on finding out about her nightmare.

"Sarah," he said seriously for a change, "do you have any idea how hard it is for me to kneel down with this stiff leg, much less stand up again with you in my arms?"

She pressed her lips together. "I hadn't thought of that."

"I had to talk you into standing, then urge you over to the bed."

"You couldn't put me back in my chair?"

"Not if I wanted to keep comforting you—and you really seemed to need someone to help you—"

"Did you by any chance help yourself while we were—?"

He shook his head slowly. He wasn't grinning. His eyes weren't even alight with plans for future mischief. She knew he was completely serious for her benefit.

"No, Sarah, I did not. Oh, I'll admit I was tempted. What man in his right mind wouldn't be? But you were in no condition to . . . to appreciate me." Then he gave her just a little grin. "And as much as I hate to admit it, I'm in no condition to be appreciated. There's no way I could've carried you, kicking and screaming, into my bed."

"Oh." For a moment Sarah sat in the chair silently.

"I'm afraid I wouldn't make a very good villain in a melodrama."

"Couldn't you have tried for the part of hero and placed something between us?"

"I didn't want to wake Mildred and ask her where the extra pillows were."

"A wise decision."

"And if I wasn't in any condition to lift you, I certainly wasn't in any condition to roll up the carpet and put it between us."

"That's true."

"I'd have lain my sword of honor between us but I seem to have misplaced the darned thing during the last crusade."

In spite of her intention to remain serious, Sarah giggled. "I'm sorry. I realize you *couldn't* have . . . hurt me. But I should've . . . remembered you're the kind of man who wouldn't . . . hurt me."

"Well, that's quite flattering, and being the modest fellow that I am, I won't say anything about it. But it must've been a horrible nightmare to scare you so. What was it?"

She nodded, then shook her head. "I . . . I don't remember what it was, only that it was . . . very frightening."

"You fell back to sleep while I was trying to comfort you," he explained. "That's how you came to wake up in my bed. I guess sleep was the best thing for you at the time."

"I guess so."

She sat in the chair, staring at the floor for quite some time. Jesse was just about to believe that she'd fallen asleep again.

"I trust you when you say you didn't . . . do anything to me," she said quietly. "I thank you for . . . for comforting me after my bad dream."

Suddenly she looked up and peered intently into his eyes.

"But it'll never happen again."

"Sarah, you can't predict whether you'll ever have a nightmare again."

"I know. And I'll truly appreciate any further comfort you can give me if that ever happens. But you mustn't expect me to join you in bed again—ever."

There was something peaceful about sitting in the green rocking chair on the sunny white porch of the Prestons' house. The pink petunias were beginning to bloom. The birds flitted from the branches of the two oak trees on either side of the yard down to the grass and white clover, and back again to their nests, with some tasty bug for the nestlings chirping their demands.

Sarah was relieved she hadn't had the nightmare in quite a few nights, and she'd resumed sleeping in her chair. In the shade of the porch, sheltered from the warming sun, she could push the dream far back in her mind, to the point where she could almost forget about it.

She couldn't forget how comforting Jesse's embrace had been, or how strangely, decadently relaxing it had felt for just a moment to lie beside him in the soft feather bed. She really didn't want to forget that feeling.

Every once in a while a wagon or carriage would roll on by. Sarah couldn't always identify the occupants, but they always waved at her, and she waved back.

Patsy was playing with Mildred's black-and-white cat. Apparently Mildred's famous imagination wasn't working very well the day she got the cat. Its name was Kitty. It was amazing how nice Kitty looked in one of Patsy's bonnets.

The snap of the crisp green peapods and the tiny thunk as the little round peas fell into the crockery bowl was comforting. The fresh summer vegetables sort of gave her the reassurance that life did go on after the winter—even if she couldn't explain or even understand precisely how.

"C'mere, kitty cat," Patsy called as Kitty went dashing across the lawn, shedding the bonnet as she ran. "C'mere. C'mere."

"Oh, cats never come when you call them."

Sarah's fingers slipped, and several peas went shooting across the porch.

"Jesse! What are you doing up?" she demanded. She tried to spring to her feet to help him, but the bowl and the pile of unshelled peas in her lap kept her seated.

"Just walking around."

She looked him up and down. At first glance he didn't look much different from the Jesse she'd first met on the train from Macon. He wore the same suit of clothing. After unpacking for him, she knew it was the only one he owned.

He still walked with a crutch. He still needed a shave. But his hair was a little damp from a recent washing and neatly combed. He smelled of bay rum.

Better yet, he wasn't coughing. His skin was clear and, although pale from not having seen the sunlight in a long time, appeared a lot healthier than she'd ever seen him. His eyes still held the mischievous gleam that had attracted her to him in the first place, but they were no longer as blurry and tired-looking.

"I think dressing, coming down the stairs, and coming out here is a little more than just walking around," she told him as she settled back into her rocker and resumed shelling the peas.

"You're absolutely right," he declared, seating himself in the rocker beside her. He made sure he stretched his bad leg out in front of him and laid the crutch beside it for protection. "I guess that's about all the work I'll do today." He locked his fingers behind his head, leaned back, and began rocking lazily in the shade.

Patsy snatched the bonnet from the grass and came running up to him. She rested her elbows on the arm of his rocker.

"Kitty cat runned away," she complained.

"Maybe Kitty's tired, too," Jesse told her.

"Why?" Patsy demanded. "She don't do nothin'—like you, Daddy."

"Hmm." Jesse stroked his chin and looked at Sarah. "Patsy, have you been talking to your mommy again?"

"Yes. You catch Kitty?"

"I don't think so," he answered with a laugh, and patted his crutch. "I can't run."

"Oh. Wanna walk, Daddy?"

"I can't go far."

"Oh. Wanna play, Daddy?" Patsy began to pout and hang on the side of his chair.

"I'm not too good at catching a ball with only one hand when I have to use the other hand to hold my crutch to stand."

"No. You sit. I dress you," she suggested, waving the bonnet over his head.

"No thanks, Patsy," he said, holding out his hand to fend off the dangerous bonnet. "Pink just isn't a flattering color on me. It doesn't go really well with my pale face and bloodshot eyes."

"Oh." Patsy dropped the bonnet to the porch and moved around to the front of Jesse's rocking chair. She began to climb up on his lap.

"Oh, don't do that, Patsy," Sarah warned. "You might hurt Daddy's leg." It was becoming much easier to think of Jesse as Patsy's father.

"Not hurt Daddy!" Patsy declared, as if that was the farthest thing from her mind.

"She's a considerate child—as long as you feed her dessert," Jesse said to Sarah. He reached out to hold the little girl around her pudgy little waist and to help lift her onto his lap. "If you sit just so on my good leg, Patsy, you won't hurt me at all."

"Oh, good!" She wiggled into her seat and cuddled up against his chest. "Wanna sing?"

"Like Auntie Dread?"

"No! Sing good."

Jesse laughed. Sarah couldn't help snicker over her peas.

"All right. I'll sing you a song my granddaddy taught me."

"I hope the words are appropriate for a child, Mr. Taylor," Sarah admonished him with a giggle.

"I sang it when I was a child, and look how wonderful I turned out."

Sarah nodded. "I'm sure you think so." She concentrated more intently on shelling her peas. That way she wouldn't have to think about how wonderful she considered Jesse, too, and how much she was going to miss him when he was gone.

"I couldn't do any less for our daughter."

Sarah drew in a deep breath. "I . . . I didn't think you would," she said softly.

"Sing, Daddy!" She tapped on his shoulder to get his attention. "Sing, sing, sing, sing. . . ."

Jesse began a stirring rendition of "Yankee Doodle" in time to the rocking of his chair. His voice was a clear baritone. Sarah was surprised he had such a good singing voice, and that he managed to go through an entire verse plus chorus without coughing even once.

He began tapping the arm of his chair while Patsy clapped her hands in time.

"Sing, Mommy!" Patsy commanded between verses.

"Sing!" Jesse ordered, too.

"I can't sing," Sarah said bashfully. "Mildred's always telling me—"

"Oh, hang Mildred! Sing!" Jesse ordered.

"Hang Auntie Dread!" Patsy declared and gave a whoop of glee.

Sarah laughed. She found herself joining in the chorus, and even rocking and clapping in time to the music. She knew most of the verses, although Jesse came up with a few she hadn't heard before. Each time Patsy cried "More" Jesse seemed to be able to come up with another one.

She and Patsy both were disappointed when Jesse at last seemed to be running out of verses. Suddenly he broke into one more repeat.

"Patsy and I went into town, with Yankee Doodle Dandy. I had lots of mo-o-ney, and bought her lots of candy."

"Oh, yes!" Patsy squealed and clapped her hands. They all joined him in the chorus.

Sarah laughed so much she found herself reaching out and placing her hand on Jesse's arm.

"My, you *are* talented," she remarked, and tried not to show how surprised she was.

Given such encouragement, he couldn't help but devise one more verse.

"Patsy and I went into town, without Auntie Dre-ad. I saw Simon Parker there, and bopped him on the he-ad."

Apparently it didn't matter to Patsy so much what the verses meant as long as she was included, and they were rendered with great gusto. She twittered with laughter and clapped again.

Sarah laughed, too, but she couldn't help wondering why Jesse was so fixed on disliking Mr. Parker when the man had never done anything against him. Could he really be that jealous?

Jesse was laughing and panting hard after his strenuous performance. But he wasn't coughing, Sarah noted.

"More!" Patsy demanded.

"Oh, Daddy's all sung out," he said. "Maybe tomorrow I'll sing you another song my grandfather taught me."

Patsy reached up and wrapped her arms around his neck. "Love you, Daddy." She planted a big wet kiss on his cheek.

"I love you, too, Patsy," Jesse said.

Then Patsy jumped off his lap and made a dash for the recently reappeared Kitty.

With Patsy now off his lap, Jesse had room to reach across and place his hand on Sarah's. The two of them watched Patsy affectionately as she toddled around the porch in pursuit of the cat.

The affection hadn't left either of them as they turned to look into each other's eyes.

Oh, no. He wasn't going to tell her he loved her, too, was he? Sarah worried. She wasn't going to slip and tell him that she thought she was falling in love with him, was she? She couldn't be. How could she fall in love with any man? How could she be the wife he needed?

She drew her hand back slowly. Jesse tried to tighten his grip on her fingers, but appeared to change his mind and let her go.

"I'm so glad Patsy likes you," she told him. She began gathering up her vegetables.

"I like her. I like her mother—" He leaned closer to her.

Sarah rose. "I have to take these peas in to Mildred, or we won't have any dinner tonight. I . . . I hate to ask you to watch Patsy if you're still feeling ill, but . . ."

"I feel fine," he assured her, drawing in a deep breath of fresh air.

She watched his broadening chest expand as he stretched his long arms out to either side. Was it her imagination or was that jacket fitting him better all the time?

"Go do whatever you have to do to shut Mildred up," he whispered to her. "I'll enjoy playing with Patsy."

Patsy had already managed to settle down again with Kitty in her lap and was busy trying to brush her fluffy tail.

Sarah got as far as the vestibule. She set the bowl of peas on the round table in the center, then grasped the edge to support herself so she could control her own threatening tears.

She tried to swallow a sob that threatened to escape. She didn't want Jesse, sitting so close on the front porch, to hear her and ask what was wrong. That would be as hard to explain as her nightmare, and could have just as many repercussions.

In such a short time, Patsy had grown to love Jesse as the good father she should've had all along. She'd readily taken to calling him "Daddy" and enjoyed spending a little time each day with him in his room, being read to or trying to make towers of her wooden blocks that eventually collapsed on the bumpy mattress.

Patsy'd been too little to realize what was going on when Aunt Myrtle had died. Even before her death, Aunt Myrtle had been too much of an invalid to be of any interest to a little child.

But Patsy was older now. She'd grown very attached to

Jesse. How would her daughter take the eventual death of this man she'd come to know and love as her father? How would she, too, bear his loss? Sarah wondered.

She sniffed back the threatening tears harshly. She gritted her teeth and held her head up high. She couldn't allow herself to go to pieces now. She had a job to do. She had a daughter to raise, and she had peas to take into the kitchen. She couldn't let Mildred see red-rimmed eyes.

"Kitty runned away again," Patsy complained to Jesse.

"Most cats have no appreciation for fashion," he told her.

"I build piles," she said, heading for the dirt in the garden.

"That's a good idea, Patsy," he said. "Piles of dirt are usually so much more cooperative than cats."

Well, a little dirt wouldn't hurt her, Jesse figured as he watched her pudgy fingers scooping up and mounding the dirt. Just so long as she didn't dig up any of Mildred's petunias. And as long as she didn't eat anything she found out there.

His dad had always told him, "You got to eat a peck of dirt before you die." It hadn't hurt him when he was a kid. He figured she'd be all right, just so long as she didn't try to eat too much of it.

He wondered if Doc Hanford knew if there was any way of telling how much dirt he'd consumed to date—a half pint or a teaspoon?—to see if there was any way of figuring out exactly how much time he had left.

"Howdy, young feller! Welcome to Cottonwood."

Jesse looked up to see an old man leaning on the picket fence. His round head was bare except for a ring of white hair over his ears. His pale blue eyes twinkled merrily. He smiled and waved.

"Hi. Thanks."

"Mind if I come and sit a spell?"

"Not at all."

Jesse had no idea who the man was. He could be the minister at the other church across town, or he could be the town drunk, or he could be some kind of maniacal murderer that the sheriff hadn't caught yet. Still, that wasn't any reason to be inhospitable.

The older man opened the gate and closed it behind him. He came limping up the walk slowly. As he drew closer, Jesse noticed the odd cast and glassy stare of the man's left eye. His wide grin showed a row of perfectly even white teeth. Jesse would've bet the farm those teeth owed more to a craftsman's expertise than to Nature's art.

"So you're the Rev's new brother-in-law."

"How do you know who I am?"

"Well, my first clue was your sitting on the front porch of the parsonage, and in the second place, you don't look like the Rev or Mrs. Rev, and seeing as how you ain't a lady or a little child, and I ain't heard of them having any other visitors, there ain't nobody left for you to be."

Jesse chuckled. And he'd had the nerve to tell Sarah to think logically.

"Have a seat," Jesse offered.

"Don't mind if I do," the man said, easing himself into the other rocking chair with a loud sigh.

"I'm Jesse Taylor."

"Pleased to meet you. Most folks 'round here call me Bob In Pieces. I live over on the other side of town, but I wander 'round now and then."

Jesse didn't want to look unfriendly to this new acquaintance in a strange town, but he couldn't quite believe he'd heard Bob right.

Bob In Pieces wasn't your usual American name—or even English or Irish—although it sounded as if he were using English words. He just didn't think a whole lot of people used those two words together in a last name. It might be one of those fancy hyphenated names, but Bob didn't look that pretentious—and weren't those two-name names usually preceded by "Sir Percival" or something sissy-sounding?

Maybe it was one of those immigrant names that was spelled with only consonants and nobody could pronounce in English, so they just did the best they could.

Or maybe Bob was part Indian, and it was one of those long Indian names that were supposed to describe something, like "Duck Sits on Water." But Bob didn't sound foreign, and with his blue eyes and scraggly chin hairs, he didn't look like an Indian. Maybe his name really was Bob In Pieces.

Bob stuck his hand out. As Jesse seized it to give it a hearty shake, he noticed Bob was missing the pinkie and ring fingers.

"Oh, don't mind me," Bob said, smiling sheepishly. "Lost 'em in a big explosion during the war down in Texas."

Jesse wasn't about to hurt the old man's feelings. He reached out to him.

"Glad to meet you, Bob In Pieces," he said. It wasn't hard to understand his strange name now. "I'm sorry. I don't believe I met you at the welcoming party."

"That's all right. I wasn't there."

"Oops, sorry. I didn't mean to offend you." It seemed as if no matter what, Jesse was doomed to say or do something to offend the genial Bob In Pieces.

"No offense taken," Bob assured him, to Jesse's relief. "See, I don't belong to the Rev's congregation, or any other, so I wasn't expecting to be invited. Not that I think there's anything wrong with a man having faith and religion and all that—or going to the parsonage for a party. I just never was much of a one for churchgoing—although there's a few of the fine ladies of the Cottonwood Holier-Than-Thou Bible Thumping Society that are more than happy to tell me I'm heading straight to hell because of it. Tell you the truth, if *they're* going to be in heaven, I'd rather be heading in the other direction."

"Well, I'm glad to meet you now, Bob," Jesse said with a laugh.

"Looks like you and me got a bit in common." Bob tapped on his right leg, then tapped Jesse's crutch. Both gave a solid, woody sound.

"Sorry, Bob," Jesse said, tapping on his own leg.

His finger sank into what little flesh and muscle he

thought he had left. He was busy talking to Bob now. It would be rude for him to keep poking his leg, noting with amazement that he seemed to be gaining weight.

"Mine's still flesh and blood and hurts like the dickens, but I don't think it's going to matter much longer."

"How's that?" Quickly he added, "If you don't mind my asking."

"Morbid infection in the leg. Not to mention galloping consumption," he added, tapping his chest.

"Funny. You don't look consumptive," Bob said, examining Jesse carefully with his one good eye.

"Well, let's put it this way. My chest hurts almost as much as my leg. Matter of fact, it hurt me so much, I think it's finally gone numb. I almost don't feel anything anymore."

Bob nodded. "That's mighty strange. I never heard of that happening. Course I ain't no doctor, friend. Reckon you must be right." He nodded back toward the house. "Does your wife know everything?"

Jesse nodded.

"How'd she take it?"

Bob in Pieces might drop his false teeth if Jesse told him Sarah'd been specifically looking for a husband who was dying.

"She was pretty calm," Jesse said, figuring that was a fairly safe answer and close enough to the truth.

"Strong lady. Figures, her being Mrs. Rev's sister. Mrs. Rev's a good sort, even if she is too nosy for her own—and everybody else's—good. But I guess I ain't telling you nothing you don't already know."

Jesse laughed, but decided it would be wisest not to say anything about his sister-in-law while he was living in her house.

"Darned shame she ain't got more to keep her busy at home—like two or three little ones—instead of gallivanting 'round town, always poking in other people's business, if you know what I mean."

Recalling each early morning greeting, each badgering insistence that Sarah remarry, each bit of sage child-rearing advice Mildred gave, Jesse could only reply, "Oh, I know just what you mean."

"Six years they been married, I reckon, and never a baby." He shook his bald head. "Darned shame. They been talking to Doc Hanford, and praying. Mrs. Rev's been listening to every old wives' tale anyone could tell her. I swear, if there was still an old Indian medicine man out here, she'd be going to him, too, seeing what he could cook up for her —probably skunk cabbage, buffalo fat, and bear grease. Course the Rev don't know 'bout none of this. It's just a good thing none of them traveling snake oil salesmen've come by lately. Who knows what crazy scheme she'd fall for then? She'd be better off with the bear grease."

"Yeah, I guess in that situation, she'd be ready to try almost anything."

Bob leaned back in the rocker and nodded confidently. "Me? I'd put my money on Doc Hanford any day."

"How do you figure that?" Jesse asked. He refrained from remarking that Bob didn't look like any doctor—even Melvin G. Hanford, M.D.—had ever helped him.

"When I lost this leg in that harvester accident, I reckon I'd have died. I was bleeding real bad. Doc sewed me up good. I ain't got no wife, or nobody to take care of me, so Doc stayed at my house with me 'til I was out of danger."

Jesse nodded with appreciation. "It's hard to find a doctor like that."

"And y'know what he charged me for the whole thing?"

"What?"

"Two chickens and a jug of whiskey." Bob leaned closer and whispered, "Make it myself—my specialty—if you'd ever care to try some."

"Much obliged," Jesse answered. "I'll take you up on it, if I live long enough. I hope Doc didn't sample it before he worked on anybody."

"Naw! Not Doc!" Bob nodded toward Jesse's leg. "Have you seen him yet?"

"Just my first day here, when I collapsed at the welcoming party."

Bob slapped the arm of his chair. "Well, if that don't beat all for embarrassing!"

"It could've been worse," Jesse admitted. "My wife's glad at least I didn't dance in the potato salad."

Bob looked at Jesse, one eyebrow raised in a combination of worry and disbelief. "I ain't exactly sure if Doc treats lunatics."

"If he does, I might take my wife to see him."

Bob stared at Jesse now. "You got a mighty strange family, if you don't mind my saying so."

"No," Jesse replied with a laugh. "Just a wife with as strange a sense of humor as mine—if only she'd realize it."

"Well, maybe it wouldn't be a bad idea if you both would visit Doc. Couldn't hurt."

"It might even help," Jesse finished for him.

He pursed his lips and frowned. Bob might have a good point there. Not about Sarah. There was no way Doc could look into her brain to help her with those nightmares. But maybe Doc could examine him again. He'd give him a little more laudanum to help with his leg. Maybe he could even tell him why his chest didn't hurt as much as it used to.

Maybe he could give him a little better hint of how much longer he had on this earth with Sarah.

Nine

"Hitch up the buggy, Mr. Preston," Mildred ordered.

"Yes, dear," Reverend Preston replied, heading for the door.

"Oh, no, that won't be necessary," Sarah protested. "It's a lovely day. We'll walk."

The Reverend stopped.

"Nonsense. Hitch up the buggy."

"Yes, dear." He started heading for the door again.

"But we're not going that far," Sarah insisted. "We can walk—really."

The Reverend stopped and looked to his wife for corroboration.

"Of course it's necessary. Mr. Taylor can't walk that far, and no Bolton should be seen trudging around town like a common washerwoman."

"Humility, my dear," the Reverend reminded her.

"Don't preach."

"Yes, dear."

"Now go hitch up the buggy. We're taking Mr. Taylor to see the doctor," Mildred announced as she retrieved her bonnet from the table and tied the ribbons under her chin.

"We?" Sarah repeated. "You're coming with us?"

The Reverend headed for the door again. But this time he wisely waited there.

"Of course. You don't think you can handle an invalid alone, do you?"

"Yes, I do," Sarah replied, raising her chin proudly. "I know I can. I've done it twice now, if you'll recall Aunt Myrtle. And I was in a family way while I was taking care of her," she couldn't resist adding, just to show her sister how capable she was.

"With a husband away fighting in the war," Jesse added.

Sarah was grateful to hear him embellish her story. She wasn't exactly sure how she was going to cover that part. It also helped answer her own question of what Jesse had done during the war.

Just a little deflated, Mildred carried on, "But . . . but I thought you had the house slaves."

"None of them stayed. Would you really expect them to?"

"Oh. But Aunt Myrtle was just a frail old woman. Mr. Taylor is—"

"A frail young man," Jesse supplied.

Sarah looked at him. He was still young. And he was *definitely* a man—from the soles of his boots to the top of his head, with all the muscles and sideburns and everything else in between. But there was no way anyone could refer to him as frail anymore. He might still walk with a crutch, but Mildred's good cooking and the fresh air and sunshine of Kansas were definitely adding weight to his formerly skeletal form and color to his pale skin.

Sarah could readily see his waist and thighs were filling out just a little. At least his pants didn't hang from him as if he were a curtain rod anymore. His chest was fleshing out very nicely. What was he doing? she wondered. Lifting the bed at night to revive the muscles that he'd certainly once had?

Maybe this was one of the symptoms of the last stages of this disease—that the person swelled up. How unusual that he was swelling up in all the right places.

"You can't sit in the doctor's waiting room alone," Mildred still protested. "I'll keep you company."

"What about Patsy?" Jesse asked.

"Oh, the Reverend can watch her."

"But, my dear—"

She shot him a sharp look, and he gulped.

"Today's the day I make my rounds of visiting the sick."

"Can't you wait until tomorrow?"

He shook his head. "Sorry, my dear. The Jackson funeral is tomorrow. Remember? You'll be playing the hymns."

Mildred heaved a deep sigh. "Oh, my. Oh, yes. People do die at the most inconvenient times."

"Since you've been so gracious in letting us share your home," Jesse said, "when I die, I promise I'll try to arrange a time that's convenient for you."

"Such a considerate man!" Mildred gushed. She shot the unfortunate Reverend a look that definitely indicated that at least at this particular time he was not one of the men she deemed considerate.

She pressed her lips together. "Well, we'll just have to take her with us, then."

Sarah gave a little gulp.

"You can't have Patsy sitting in a waiting room full of sick people!" Jesse protested.

"Think of that floor, Mildred," Sarah supplied. She could see exactly where Jesse was taking this conversation, and she was determined to help him in any way she could. "Why, it's nowhere near as clean as yours."

"Who knows what all those sick people—cattlemen, sheep ranchers, pig farmers—have tracked in? Who knows what kind of diseases they'll be coughing and spitting all over her?"

"We can't subject Patsy to all those dangers."

"You'll have to stay home with her."

"I know it's a great sacrifice on your part not to accompany us, but—"

"There's really no one else we'd trust Patsy with."

"And she does love you so," Sarah finished.

Mildred began untying her bonnet. "Very well. For Patsy's sake."

"Mildred, you're an angel!" Jesse said. Leaning forward on his crutch, he placed a little kiss on her cheek.

"Oh! Oh! What will the Reverend say?" Mildred gushed and giggled, flustered. Her face was turning almost as crimson as her parlor drapes.

Sarah and Jesse didn't say anything until they were safely on the other side of the picket fence.

"I had to do it, you know," Jesse admitted as he slowly limped along the dusty street.

"I'm glad you did. The last thing I need is Mildred and Patsy in the waiting room with me."

"No. I mean I had to kiss her."

"Well, since it was only on her cheek, and since she's your sister-in-law, and since she has done us a great favor in taking Patsy again, I suppose I'll forgive you."

"No. I mean, since she's your sister, I guess that's the closest I'll ever get to kissing you again."

"If you live until Christmas, you can catch me under the mistletoe."

He stopped directly in the middle of the sidewalk in front of the hardware store. Confronting her, he asked, "Is that a promise?"

She turned questioningly to him.

"I know what a stickler you are for promises and I want to make sure of this one."

"Yes, I promise," she answered, very slowly and very definitely, so he would know that she really did mean every word she said.

She expected him to move aside and continue on to the doctor's. Instead, he continued to stand there, blocking her way.

"How about for my birthday?"

She grinned. "Hmm. I'll have to think about it." After all, she didn't want to appear *too* eager. She still wasn't sure she could go through with anything beyond that, and she didn't

want him to raise his expectations for nothing. Who knows?
Maybe the disappointment would kill him.

"How do, Mrs. Taylor," came Bob's cheerful greeting.
"Glad to see you up and around, Jesse. I suppose you're
taking my advice?"

"Indeed I am, Bob."

Bob was sitting on the long bench in front of the general
store, whittling a small, galloping horse. The two fingers he
was missing didn't seem to interfere with his considerable
talent.

"Good morning," Jesse replied. "Say, that's some horse
there, Bob."

"Thanks. I . . . I haven't been able to do much work on
the farm in a while, so I make and sell these toys."

"Got any finished ones?"

"Sure." He leaned down for a small leather bag at his
side. From the interior, he withdrew another horse, a dog
sitting up begging, and two sleeping cats cuddled around
each other.

"How wonderful," Sarah said, turning the two sleeping
cats over and over in her hand. "What details!"

"I'll bet Patsy would love this," Jesse said. Turning back to
Bob, he asked, "How much?"

"Naw. It's for the little one. Take it. Take it," he urged,
waving his hand toward them.

"I can't do that, Bob. I'm . . . I was a carpenter myself. I
know how much time and skill this tiny, detailed work
takes."

"All right. Two bits," he said with a shrug.

"Come on, Bob. A man deserves to get paid fairly for his
work."

"Four bits—and I wouldn't take a dime more, not if you
was to tie me up and make me sit through seven sermons."
He gave his bald head a fierce shake and pounded his fist on
the arm of the bench.

"Well, if you're that determined. . . ." Jesse dug into his
pocket and let the silver coins roll out of his hand into
Bob's.

"Much obliged." Bob pocketed the money and returned to his whittling. "Good luck at Doc's."

As they walked away, Sarah asked, "Who was that?"

"Bob In Pieces."

"I beg your pardon?"

"I know. I couldn't believe my ears at first either. Seems it's sort of a nickname."

She nodded. "I can see why. I don't recall meeting him before."

"He doesn't belong to the Reverend Preston's church," Jesse explained.

"But you know him?"

He nodded.

"Excuse me, but weren't you the man who was complaining about my meeting all these people and you not knowing a soul in town?"

He shrugged. "I guess I was."

"And how did he know where you were going?"

"I guess Bob In Pieces has just got the second sight or something. Maybe it's a gift to make up for the loss of one eye."

Sarah harrumphed with mock indignation. "Not much of a gift if all he uses it for is to see a man with a crutch and a limp heading toward the doctor's office."

"Don't be so cynical," Jesse scolded. "I should've known it would be dangerous to tell you to think logically."

"Now who's cynical?"

As they continued on to the doctor's office, Sarah turned the little cats over and over in her hands. "This really is an exquisite little piece of work."

"Nice detail. I'd do something like that, too, except with my luck the darn knife would slip, plunge into my chest, and I'd end up killing myself. I wouldn't have to wait for the consumption or the leg to finish me off."

Sarah held the carving a little tighter in her hands, trying to summon up the nerve to say what she wanted to say to Jesse. "I . . . I suppose I'll have to keep the sharp knives away from you. You have to last at least until your birth-day."

"Sarah. . . ."

But she refused to take her eyes off the little carving as they walked along. She figured she was safe. He could hardly grab her and demand some kind of explanation in the middle of Main Street with people milling all around.

The bell on the door jingled as they entered. No one else was in the doctor's office.

Jesse looked up at the bell and wiggled the door back and forth a few more times just to listen to the bell's gentle tinkle again.

"Patsy usually plays with small shiny things like that," Sarah commented. "So do crows and magpies."

"Why couldn't Mildred get me a bell like this one?" he lamented.

"Because Mildred never does anything by halves."

After the tinkling of the bell echoed away, they waited, but no one opened the little window to the office.

"Looks like he's not here," Jesse said.

"If the doctor was here, he certainly would've come to stop you from playing with the bell."

"Do you think he's out delivering a baby? Sometimes those things can take all day."

Sarah looked up and gave him a wry grin. "Would you like me to tell you about it sometime, or are you the author-ity?"

"Never mind."

"I hate to think we've come all this way for nothing."

"Oh, we'll just sit here and wait for him," Jesse suggested. "We'll talk and get to know each other better."

Just then Doc Hanford stuck his head out of his office door. Sarah never thought she'd be that happy to see his plumes of white hair and his olive-green-and-bright-yellow-striped suit with a matching yellow vest.

She wanted to get to know Jesse better, but at the same time was a little afraid to find out. And if she got to know him better, did that mean he would demand to know more about her in exchange? She still wasn't ready—didn't know if she'd ever be ready—to reveal that much about herself to him.

"I thought I heard somebody. Hello there, Mrs. Taylor." Doc gave her a polite nod. Then he turned to Jesse and exclaimed, "Holy Moses, Jesse! What in the ever-loving blue-eyed world are you doing here?"

"I came to see you, Doc."

"Well, here I am. But you didn't have to walk all this way. You know I'd have come to your house if you'd let me know you were feeling poorly."

Jesse shrugged. "I just felt like taking a little walk around Cottonwood."

Doc's fluffy eyebrows shot upward, and he stared at Jesse in disbelief. "Well, ordinarily I don't think wanderlust is a symptom of consumption—at least not one to worry about unless you end up in San Francisco."

"You're not getting me to walk that far, Mr. Taylor," Sarah told him.

Doc laughed. "Mrs. Taylor, why don't you just sort of make yourself comfortable out here? There're a few old gazettes to read." He turned back toward the examining room and motioned for Jesse to follow him. "Why don't you come on back here and let me have a look at you?"

The examining room was clean and bright. The walls were whitewashed. Sunlight streamed in the numerous clean windows, making the variety of jars, bottles, and vials lined up on the shelves shine like little jewels. Jesse sat on the hard wooden examining table in the middle of the room.

"So, what really brings you here, Jesse?"

"My health."

Doc laughed. "Sorry. Can't help you. For that you have to go to the hardware store."

"In that case, you wouldn't happen to have a good hammer, would you?"

Doc chuckled. "Nope. Of course, they don't have the laudanum you might need."

"Yeah, I guess I do need some more."

"What do you mean 'guess'? How are you feeling, Jesse?"

"Great."

Doc looked him up and down, his white eyebrows held high. "What do you mean 'great'? You've got consumption and an infected leg. How can you feel great? Did you just get religion or something?"

"No, no. But, well . . . I just don't understand, Doc. I'm supposed to be dying, and I feel good. I know my fever's gone down. I don't cough so much anymore." He gave a gentle pounding on his chest. "My chest doesn't hurt the way it used to."

Doc frowned and pursed his lips.

"Of course, my leg still hurts like the dickens."

"Well, let's take one problem at a time. We'll have a look and see what's going on." Doc pulled his stethoscope out of his pocket and hooked the earpieces in his ears. "I'm going to have to ask you to open your shirt."

After listening and thumping on Jesse's chest and back, and then going over the whole process once again, Doc removed the stethoscope from his ears.

He took a swab of cotton and cleaned off the earpieces, stuck them in his ears again, and tapped on the bellow.

"Don't tell me you're not getting a heartbeat! I got enough to worry about already, Doc."

"No, your heart's just fine," he answered with a little laugh. "So's this stethoscope, although I had my doubts for a minute. I could hardly believe what I was hearing—or not hearing, to put it more accurately."

Jesse frowned. "What do you mean, Doc?"

"I'm not sure yet. Let me listen again."

Doc started to examine Jesse again.

"Breathe in deep. Out."

Jesse followed all Doc's instructions.

"Again. Again. Cough for me. Again. All right, you can put your shirt back on."

Jesse watched Doc, waiting for his report. The fact that the man didn't look directly at him made Jesse worry even more. The fact that Doc just stood there, staring at the floor and shaking his head, made Jesse's heart plummet.

"I . . . I appreciate complete honesty, Doc. It's worse than I feared, isn't it? Just tell me the truth." His fingers were clutching the edge of the table so hard his knuckles were turning white. "Come on! Tell me, Doc."

The longer the doctor waited, the more nervous Jesse became. He'd come in here feeling better than he'd felt in years. Now he didn't think he could ever feel any worse.

"I've lived this long knowing I was going to die soon. I think I can take a little more bad news." Jesse had tried to sound brave, but he braced himself for the horrible, depressing news. At last he could stand no more. In frustration he yelled, "Doc, this is driving me crazy! What is it?"

Doc looked up and stared him in the eye. "I'm sorry, Jesse."

Those were the two words he'd been dreading to hear. And he knew they were just the start of something worse.

"I don't know how this could've happened," Doc said, scratching the back of his head. "I don't know how I could've been so mistaken."

"Mistaken? What is it?"

"Well, slap me silly and call me a horse doctor for having been fooled. You don't have consumption."

Jesse paused. He felt as if his heart had paused, too. His ears were ringing, and he wasn't sure he was still breathing, either, and he was too confused right now to bother to check. At last he was able to ask, "What?"

Doc looked him square in the eye. "You don't have consumption."

"Well, then . . . I . . . well, what do I have?"

"You were in terrible condition when I first saw you, and your chest sounded mighty congested. But I couldn't figure out why you never had the other symptoms—the red cheeks, the coughing up blood. You couldn't have had consumption. I've never seen consumption clear up like this."

"But the prison camp doctor said—"

"Prison camp?"

"Oglethorpe, outside of Macon, Georgia," Jesse told him. "I was a Union soldier, but I guess I wasn't a very good one. I got taken prisoner on my first battle. I spent three years in Oglethorpe."

"Three years? Holy cow! It's a wonder you didn't die a long time ago."

"Just lucky, I guess."

"Three years?" Doc repeated more slowly.

Jesse nodded.

"Then how . . . ?" Doc raised his hand to stroke his chin. He coughed and frowned, and coughed again. "Well then, excuse me a minute here, Jesse, but . . . well, I don't think it takes a whole lot of medical or mathematical knowledge to figure that . . . well, if you were in prison for three years, and your daughter's only a year and a half . . . Well, I never was one to want to make trouble between a man and his wife, but . . . is there something the little woman isn't telling you?"

"Oh . . ." The rest of Jesse's expletive drifted away on his sharp exhale. "Oh, Doc. No, no, it's not Sarah's fault. Just don't ask. Don't make me explain. And please don't tell anyone!"

"Jesse, you cut me to the quick." Doc placed his hand over his heart and lifted his chin proudly. "I'm a doctor. I've taken the Hippocratic oath. And even if I hadn't, I like you and Mrs. Taylor too much to ruin your lives—and the little one's, too. I'll never mention it again."

Jesse managed a sigh of relief.

Doc quickly returned to the original subject. "So, how did this leg injury happen?"

"We had a work gang. Apparently I wasn't working fast enough to satisfy one of the guards, but he was a miserable son of a gun anyway. He didn't want to waste a bullet shooting me, I guess, so he just picked up a big stick and struck me across the shin a couple of times. I got a big cut, but it never would heal after that—not that the camp doctor did any of us much good."

"Who was this camp doctor?"

"I'm not sure of his name," Jesse answered. "In the prisoner-of-war camps usually we just saw whoever happened to be passing through. Even if I knew, I probably wouldn't remember. I guess some of them weren't always the best doctors. And I was pretty sick, after all."

"Well, I can understand his being wrong, but I can't believe *I* could've been so mistaken. But now I see you improving, I've just got to believe I was wrong. The best I can figure is, you just had a really bad cold."

"You're joking."

Doc shook his head. "Why would I joke with your life?"

"How do you reckon . . . ?"

"The prison was damp?"

"Yes."

"And crowded."

"Yes."

"And cold and dark?"

"Yes."

"And not much food, and what there was, was lousy."

"You're absolutely right."

"Not much medical care?"

"Of course not."

"And after you got out, you didn't have any money?"

"Darn little."

"Your clothes weren't in such good shape?"

"All my life's possessions fit in two little bags and on my back."

"So there were times when you were pretty cold and hungry?"

"Sure."

"You've just had a darned good cold that wouldn't clear up. I mean, you really couldn't expect a person to stay healthy in the awful conditions you've been through. As a matter of fact, lesser men would be dead by now."

Jesse didn't know if they were exactly lesser men. It was just that he'd been a lot luckier.

"But now that you've been in the sunshine and fresh air, and eating more and better food, you're improving."

"I still don't believe it."

"Well, I'll tell you what. When you outlive me and come to see me on my deathbed, then you tell me you still don't believe me."

"You mean . . . I'm not going to die?" Jesse could feel his eyes growing wider as the realization of what Doc's words truly meant dawned on him. His heart, so tired for so long, leapt in his emaciated chest.

Doc paused for just a moment before he answered. "Not from consumption."

Jesse shrugged. "Everyone dies sometime, Doc."

"Well, I hate to be the one to remind you, but being your doctor, I guess it's my job. You know, there's still that problem with your leg." He nodded toward Jesse's leg still stuck out straight in front of him.

Jesse felt his heart drop back into his chest, beating just a little more slowly.

"Oh, yeah. That. I knew the diagnosis was too good to be true."

"What did the other doctor tell you about your leg?"

"Amputation," he said quietly. It was still hard to say, much less think about. "But I refused. I figured if I was dying of consumption anyway, I was going out with all my body parts."

Doc nodded his agreement. "I can see your logic then. But I guess things have changed a bit now."

"That's the truth!" Jesse gave a rueful laugh.

"Why don't you let me have another look at that leg," Doc suggested. He helped Jesse lift his leg and place it on the examination table. "It's not as if I'm really expecting this to clear up like your consumption—that wasn't really consumption. But if that other doctor was mistaken about your lungs, he just might've been mistaken about your leg, too."

"I'll keep my fingers crossed, Doc."

"You do that, Jesse. Because I want you doing something else with your hands while I look at this," he said, carefully removing the bandage. "I wouldn't want you smacking me, because this is going to smart a good bit."

Damn, Jesse thought as he clenched his fists and his jaws tightly so he wouldn't yell out. He wouldn't want Sarah, still out in the waiting room, to be scared by anything she heard going on inside.

"Are you done poking around in there yet, Doc?" he asked breathlessly through clenched jaws.

"Almost. Just hang on a bit longer, Jesse. You can take it," Doc whispered encouragingly. But he still kept poking around anyway.

He drew in a deep breath as the sharp pain in his leg subsided for the moment. Beads of sweat trickled down his forehead as he waited for the usual dull ache to set in again.

"Whew! You sure are given to understatement, aren't you, Doc?"

"Don't sit up yet," Doc warned, placing his hand on Jesse's shoulder. "I want your head to clear up a little first. Can't have you falling off the examining table and hurting yourself in my office."

Jesse laid there for a moment, letting the ringing in his ears clear up and his eyes focus clearly again.

"You said you always wanted the truth, Jesse," Doc asked.

Jesse nodded. "Usually. On the other hand, I figured out a long time ago that whenever somebody asks me if I really want the truth, I find out afterward I really didn't want it after all."

Doc reached up and scratched his head, making his fluffy hair wave about. "Well, when you're right, you're right, Jesse. Speaking as your doctor, right about now I guess amputation really is the only thing we can do."

Jesse was silent.

"I'm sorry, Jesse." Doc laid his hand on Jesse's shoulder again. This time he figured it wasn't so much to keep him still as to console him. "I wish I could tell you differently."

Jesse swallowed hard.

"From the looks of it, I'm going to have to take it off above the knee. I don't want to scare you with any of the gory details, but that's going to make it harder to stop the bleeding. It's also going to make it harder to fit you for a wooden leg, and for you to walk on that new leg. You probably won't be able to kneel or anything. I . . . I don't know what else to tell you."

"I've been walking with a limp for years. I've always figured, one way or another, I'd lose that leg anyway."

"Bob In Pieces seems to get along fine on one leg," Doc said encouragingly. "Lots of men do. Ladies, too. And if the fairer sex can do it, you certainly should be able to."

"But Bob said he really didn't have much choice in his situation."

"Well, that's true."

"And Bob doesn't have a wife and a little girl to support. He hasn't just found out he's not going to die from consumption after all."

Jesse sat up. He looked at Doc and shook his head.

"Hell of a choice you've given me, Doc. Do I want to go through a long life with one leg, not being able to do everything I used to do? Will I still be able to support my family like that? Or will I end up sitting on the bench in front of the general store, carving little wooden animals for two bits each?" He couldn't keep the bitterness out of his voice. "Or do I want to keep all my parts and keep my life very short and very, very dull?"

"I can amputate if you want me to, Jesse," Dr. Hanford said gently. "I'm good and fast, and you won't feel too much pain."

"I don't know, Doc. Last time you told me that, it hurt like hell."

"I can help you find a wooden leg, too, if you want. And if you don't choose that, I can supply you with enough painkillers to keep you comfortable 'til the last. It's your leg and your life. The choice is up to you."

"I'm going to need to think about this one, Doc," Jesse answered, getting down from the table and heading toward the office door.

"Sure stands to reason."

"If I let you amputate, it'll be the last standing I do on my own. I'll . . . I'll have to let you know."

"It's a big decision, but don't take too long," Doc warned. "So far you've been lucky the infection has stayed in just your leg. But if it ever starts to spread, gets into your blood, gets up to your heart or brain, it'll be too late to do a thing."

Jesse turned back. "Thanks for being honest, Doc. Can you do me one favor?"

"What's that, Jesse?"

"Let's . . . let's not mention this to my wife."

Doc frowned and stroked his chin. "Don't see why you wouldn't want to at least share the good news with her."

"Because . . . because I want to wait until I decide exactly what to do about this leg."

That wasn't the exact truth. What really worried Jesse was how and when to tell a woman who had bargained for him to die that he wasn't going to.

He knew Sarah had a different opinion from the doctor on what constituted good news. Of course, what Doc didn't know—and what Jesse couldn't explain to him—was that, to Sarah, the fact that he wasn't going to die wasn't exactly her idea of good news.

Mildred set the cup of coffee on the kitchen table in front of Sarah. "So, are you ever going to tell me what Doc Hanford said?" she demanded as she seated herself across from her sister.

"I told you before, Mildred. As soon as I know, I'll tell you."

This was probably a very bad promise to make, Sarah decided, when she didn't even know herself what the doctor had told Jesse. As much as she loved her sister, there were just some things she didn't want her to know.

"Right now, I really don't know any more than you do about what went on in that doctor's office."

Mildred pressed her lips together tightly and shook her head. "I told you I should've gone with you two. *I'd* have made Doc tell you what was going on."

Sarah was silently glad she and Jesse had managed to talk Mildred into staying home. As much as she wanted to know, she didn't want to force it out of Jesse. She wanted him to tell her on his own. If he couldn't do that, there really wasn't much need to worry any further about trust and love between them. She'd do her duty until he died, she'd see him properly buried, and she'd spend the rest of her life raising Patsy alone.

"How many days has it been now?" Mildred asked.

Roused from her reverie, she mumbled, "Three."

"And he still hasn't told you?"

Sarah began tracing the flowered pattern of the coffee cup with the tip of her finger. She shook her head.

"No. I suppose he'll tell me when he's ready."

"Most times men don't know when they're ready," Mildred advised. "Sometimes they don't know anything at all. You have to sort of help them along."

"He's not the same Jesse I married," she admitted. "He still plays with Patsy, but he doesn't joke anymore. Not with me, not with you."

"Just keep asking, dear. You'll wear him down eventually."

"Every time I ask, he just shakes his head and tells me he's thinking." She looked into her sister's eyes. "What could he be thinking about except his . . . his last days on earth?"

She tried to stifle her sob.

Mildred gave a little snort. "Well, if he wasn't in such awful shape, and you hadn't seen with your own eyes that he's only been to see Doc Hanford, I'd be worried he was seeing another woman!"

"Oh, Mildred! How can you think such a thing?"

"Well, in that case, does he read his Bible a lot more lately?"

"Not that I've noticed."

"Does he pray a lot more?"

"I haven't noticed that either."

"Oh, well," Mildred remarked with a sigh, "I guess everybody's got to find his own way of making his peace with his Maker."

"I . . . I just wish he'd . . . talk to me, too. I'd like to tell him how much I'm . . . really going to miss him."

She sniffed again. It was hard to trace the pattern of the cup when she couldn't see it through her tears.

"There, there." Mildred reached out and patted Sarah's hand.

At last she found the courage to admit to herself and out loud, "I . . . I love him so much."

If only she could find the courage to admit this to Jesse. But he wouldn't talk to her.

Sarah was prepared to spend this Saturday night sitting in her chair as usual, watching Jesse in his bed until the laudanum took effect. Lately there didn't seem to be much difference in him whether he was taking his medication or not. He was pretty quiet either way, and awfully glum.

She fairly jumped in her seat when Jesse turned to her and said, "I'd really like to go to church tomorrow, Sarah."

She couldn't help but give a little laugh of joy at hearing him talk again.

"Why, are you curious to see what will happen?"

"No. Not really."

His face was still so serious. Sarah began to worry more. Jesse had seemed so irreverent before—not maliciously so, just humorously. It was unlike him to remain serious for so long, but he apparently had his reasons.

"I . . . I suppose it's logical for a man to want to go to church before he . . . he . . ."

"No, it's not that, either." Then he surprised her even more by asking, "Do you remember our bargain, Sarah?"

"Of course I do," she replied. "How could I not? You've either shoved it down my throat every time it was to your advantage or tried to weasel out of it when it wasn't."

She watched him, waiting for him to laugh with her. She was disappointed when he remained serious.

"Well, now, if you'll recall, you promised me I'd have your personal attention."

"I think you already do," she pointed out to him.

"And I also seem to recall you mentioning that you had experience in nursing invalids."

"Just Aunt Myrtle. Are you going to complain that I haven't been giving you adequate care?"

"Close enough," he said with a satisfied nod. Then he grew serious again. He watched her carefully as he stroked his chin. "Most important, I do seem to recall a promise of a sponge bath."

"Oh, no." Sarah's memory was just as good as Jesse's on this matter. She knew exactly why he'd brought it up. But she didn't think she had nearly enough courage to see her through this.

"Every Saturday night."

"Oh, no. Oh, no." She was shaking her head. "Any man ill enough to need help taking a sponge bath shouldn't be in any condition to go galloping off to church early the next morning," she told him emphatically.

"You wouldn't want Mildred and the Reverend to find out you've been neglecting a dying man's spiritual well-being, would you?"

"Of course not!"

Leaning back in his bed, he grinned at her. "Yes, indeed. I'd *really* like to go to church tomorrow."

Ten

"You know what that means, don't you?" Jesse asked her with a wicked grin on his face.

"I know exactly what you mean." She deliberately didn't return his smile, more for her own benefit than for his. Why did he continue to indicate how much he wanted to be like a real husband to her when all she'd ever done was refuse him? Why, with each attempt of his, did she want to turn him down less and less?

"A bargain is a bargain," he reminded her.

"It was such a small part of our agreement," she said with a forlorn sigh and a careless wave of her hand. She hoped that would let him know exactly how small a part she thought it was.

"But you agreed to it."

"I guess I did." She shook her head. "But at the time it seemed so unlikely that I'd almost forgotten it. Apparently you have a much better memory than I do."

"Maybe next time you'll pay better attention."

"There won't be a next time." At first she'd only made this promise to herself because she didn't want to be beset with needless courtship from another man, gleefully encouraged by Mildred. Now, even though she couldn't ever be a real wife to Jesse, she knew she'd never want anyone else but him as a husband.

"Are you sure you're up to an entire bath? I mean, if you've got such a remarkable memory, you have to recall you really are a sick man. Couldn't something like this kill you?"

"Then at least we'll have saved the undertaker the job of bathing me. Maybe then he won't charge us as much."

"You have an answer for everything, don't you?"

"Only for those things that I really, really intend to get."

"You've been getting yourself up and dressed every morning for a little over a week now," she told him. "I think you've been managing to bathe yourself, too."

"They were just little birdbaths at the washstand," Jesse complained. "They get me clean enough, but right now I need a really good soak in a tub, and I'm going to need your help for that."

"You've been coming downstairs by yourself, too. I don't think you need my help in stepping into a tin tub."

"I go downstairs and sit on the front porch all day. That's as far as I get. Gosh, Patsy was right. I'm getting as lazy as Kitty."

Just to prove his resemblance to Kitty, he slowly stretched himself in the bed. His long arms pulled the nightshirt open at the neck so she could see part of his hairy chest. The nightshirt crept up past his knees. Sarah tried not to look, but his sinewy feet and muscled legs were irresistibly attractive—and she was insatiably curious about his body. She couldn't help notice how his heels, calves, and the backs of his thighs made indentations in the soft mattress.

Would his legs feel that firm, pressing against her own? Thank goodness he'd stopped stretching, and the nightshirt remained in place. She didn't think she could bear to look any farther up, and she didn't think she could resist, either.

"Granted, you just sit there, but you're not entirely useless," she said, just to keep some sort of conversation going.

She could think of a dozen and one uses for Jesse right now, and none of them involved even getting out of that bed. She could hardly tell him that. He was a sick man. The thoughts might kill him, and then she'd have something else to feel guilty about.

"You play with Patsy and the cat and chat with just about anyone who happens to pass by—even Simon Parker."

Jesse grinned. "I've met some really interesting people that way. And Simon's not such a bad fellow after all. Did you know he has a big farm not too far from town, mostly corn, with a flock of Rhode Island Reds he seems to be really proud of?"

"Oh, yes. That was just about the first thing he mentioned to me, too. Did he tell you about the vegetable patch?"

"No. What about the vegetable patch?"

She shook her head. "Never mind. It really doesn't have much to do with you, anyway."

Jesse shrugged and appeared to pass it off. "I'm sure Mildred'll get around to telling me. She tells me Simon doesn't drink or chew tobacco and that he's never missed a single Sunday service—day or evening—in the six years since she's known him."

"Oh, I'm sure Mildred's got a lot of good things to say about him," Sarah agreed.

"Good things? He sounds as boring as all get-out."

"As a matter of fact," she tried to continue in spite of her laughter, "I wouldn't be surprised if Mildred were telling you a whole lot of nice things about every bachelor and widower in this town."

Jesse didn't blink or even make a joke. Apparently Mildred still hadn't informed him of her plans for him to select husband number two for Sarah.

"But I still can't figure out why this one big blond fellow just keeps walking by, shooting me the evil eye. I can't get him to stop and chat, or even wave. He just keeps glaring at me—and I don't even know his name."

Sarah's heart sank, and her stomach churned.

"I can't imagine." She tried to keep her voice very casual.

She knew very well who he was, and she wasn't about to tell Jesse. What in the world was Deke doing walking past the house on a regular basis? Why was he watching Jesse? Or was he really waiting to find her out on the porch some-day—all alone again? Either way, she couldn't bother Jesse with this. He was sick and dying and wouldn't be able to do anything about it anyway. It was just better that he and Deke stayed apart.

"Of course, I'm going to need your help to get to church, too."

"I didn't see you stumble even once on the way to Doc Hanford's," she said in a light tone. She was glad he'd changed the subject. Then she wouldn't look so obvious in having done it deliberately. "The church is only next door, a lot closer."

"The lawn's a little bumpier than the sidewalk. You wouldn't want me to trip and fall over a gopher hole, would you?"

"All right. But I still think you can manage to bathe and dress yourself, and then I'll help you across the lawn."

Jesse feigned the same racking cough he'd used to get them through the crowd on the platform in the town where they'd gotten married. Lying back on the pillows, he threw one arm over his eyes and heaved a heavy theatrical sigh.

Sarah crossed her arms over her breasts and watched him skeptically.

"You can stop coughing and save your lungs and your strength," she told him. "You don't fool me one bit with your blatant—and mighty transparent—bid for sympathy."

He moved just enough to be able to peek out from under his arm with one eye.

"I don't?"

"Not a bit."

"Heartless wench," he grumbled, uncovering his eyes completely.

"We've already decided you don't make a good melodramatic villain, and you can't be the hero because you misplaced your sword."

"Careless fellow, ain't I?"

"I think you're a little too hairy to be the heroine."

He stroked his chin. "What if I shave?"

She wanted to tell him his breasts still weren't big enough to be a heroine, but the last thing she needed to remind him of now was anything pertaining to the sexual characteristics of the human female's body. She shook her head instead and told him, "You might as well give up your aspirations for a career in the theater and stay with carpentry."

He laughed. Then he grew more serious. "I really do need your help, Sarah. I really should have a nice hot bath before I go to church. How would it look—the Reverend's brother-in-law offending all those nice—"

"Cattlemen, sheepherders, and pig farmers?" she jokingly tossed his own words back at him.

"I'll bet *they* all had a bath."

"Don't try to pout with me, mister," she teased. "You've been playing with Patsy too much."

He coughed again and watched her very carefully. She could see his lips twitching with his effort not to laugh.

She only stood there, tapping her foot with impatience—and trying very hard not to laugh, too.

She wasn't going to argue with him anymore. She knew it was futile. She knew she'd lost already, and there wasn't anything she could do about it. He'd have his darned bath, and she'd end up scrubbing his back—or something. She tried to tell herself she was upset about it, but the rest of her body just wouldn't seem to listen.

He was silent for just a moment. Then he threw off the covers, making her jump. He sat up in bed. "You never know. It might be the last hot bath I'll get."

"I'll tell the undertaker to use warm water."

He shifted his legs around and sat up straight on the edge of the bed. He didn't lean to one side or wobble the way he used to. Sarah was glad to see he was capable of moving like this, until he raised his hands and slowly began to unbutton his shirt.

She watched his strong fingers working the flat little white buttons, revealing more of his chest each time one came undone. They were strong fingers, used to hard work when

he had been in better health. What would it feel like to have
those fingers undoing the buttons of her own bodice? How
warm would they feel as they brushed against her flesh and
reached out to cup her breasts?

"Why don't I go ask Mildred to heat some water?" she
suggested as he finished unbuttoning his shirt. But he didn't
answer, and she didn't leave.

He reached down and grabbed his shirttail. He slowly
began to lift the fabric.

She could see the tops of his thighs and his tapering waist.
"Why can't you wear underwear?" she pleaded in desperation.

"Because, sitting in bed for a long time, it tends to bunch
up on me in the most uncomfortable places."

She could feel her face grow warm as she blushed. "I'm
sorry I asked."

"Remember, we agreed to be honest with each other,
Sarah. This is the real, honest-to-goodness me."

She wasn't sure about the honest part, but what she could
see certainly was good!

As he continued to raise his nightshirt, she could see his
navel and the soft swirls of dark hair that surrounded it and
spread up his chest, and grew thicker as it spread down over
parts still covered by his thighs.

"Unless, of course, you'd like to stay around to watch me
take the rest off," he invited.

Stay and watch him? she repeated to herself as she kept
her eyes riveted to his body.

"I think my corset's too tight," she managed to mumble
as she felt her head swim and her chest grow so tight it was
hard to breathe. She blinked, and still kept her eyes on him.

Stay and watch him continue to lift his shirt as each rib
was exposed, she mused. Watch as the trail of hair spreading
upward across his broadening chest was slowly revealed,
until his muscled shoulders were completely bare. Watch
him stand up.

Help him into the tub. The very thought of Jesse's bare

flesh, warm and wet beneath her fingers, made her throat go dry. Her corset was definitely laced too tight!

Her heart was beginning to pound harder in her breast. She could feel a warmth spreading through her at the thought of watching Jesse, of touching him, of his touching her. She swallowed and fought down the urge to stay.

"I'll get the water," she said, quickly heading for the door. She closed it tightly behind her.

Jesse released his shirttail and smiled as it fell down around his hips again. He wasn't in that much of a hurry for a bath that he couldn't wait for Sarah to return with the water before taking off his clothes. He might catch another chill. The last thing he wanted to do was bring his cold back again.

Not now. Not when he'd finally made his decision.

He'd decided he wanted to stay on this earth as long as he could with Sarah. And with Patsy, and Doc and Bob In Pieces, and all his other new friends. Yes, and even with Meddling Mildred and the Reverend Preston—although he'd have to try to find work so he could eventually afford a house of their own—eventually. It would be hard to find work with only one leg.

He'd tell Doc about his decision on Monday morning. Then he and Doc would make arrangements for him to get an artificial leg, and set up a time when he could go to the office alone and have his infected leg amputated.

But tonight, and for just a few days longer, he still had two good knees. He knew he could still function darned well as a husband afterward. But before it was too late, before there wasn't anything more he could do about it, he wanted to rest on those two knees, like the man he used to be, and prop himself up on his elbows above Sarah, and look down on her with love.

He wanted to stand on his own two legs, to bend down and lift her in his arms. He wanted to place her gently in the bed and climb in beside her. He wanted to hold her tightly and watch her hair gleam and her eyes shine with pleasure in the moonlight—or the lamplight—or the sunlight. Heck, all three, while he could!

A man could have his dreams, couldn't he?

He'd noticed the way she looked at him sometimes lately. He'd heard her promise to give him a Christmas kiss, and a birthday one, and he'd heard the little hint of disappointment in her voice at the thought that he might not live until then.

August was still a long way away. If she'd changed her mind about this being a marriage in name only, he wanted to make sure he started it off on both knees—before it was too late.

The only real problem was going to be how to tell her he wasn't going to die now after all. When she'd only bargained for a husband who would last a year at best, how would she react when she found out she was going to be stuck with him for the rest of her life? Boy, this was going to make her really upset!

The knock on the door woke him from his daydreams.

"Come in," he called.

The door didn't open. "It's Sarah. Are you decent?" she called through the door.

"If it's Sarah, of course I'm not decent," he called back. "I am specifically not decent just for you."

"Are you *decent*?" she repeated demandingly.

"Yes."

Slowly the door opened. Jesse saw one blue eye peeking cautiously in. Apparently she decided not to take his word for his state of decency. Satisfied he was still clothed enough for an invalid, she opened the door the rest of the way.

She carried in two buckets of steaming water. The Reverend Preston followed with the big tin tub. Mildred followed with an armful of fluffy white towels and a dish of soap. Patsy followed with the cat.

Jesse made a quick grab for the covers and drew them up all around him. If he'd known Sarah would make a parade out of this, he'd never have joked about being decent or not.

"Gee, if I'd have known it was going to be a party, I'd

have baked a cake," he said with a nervous laugh. What were they all doing here? Did they intend to stay and watch, too?

"I declare, this is the strangest time of night for a bath," Mildred complained.

"Kitty get bath, too," Patsy said, trying to shove the cat in the tub.

"It . . . it was a spur of the moment decision," Sarah offered, putting the two heavy buckets down and rescuing the cat.

"A man never knows when the need for some spiritual comfort'll come upon him, and he needs to be prepared," the Reverend said.

"Just put the tub down there," Mildred instructed, pointing out her specific location.

"Yes, dear." He set the tub in the little alcove that Sarah always used to change her clothing. He turned to Jesse again. "I'm pleased to see you taking your churchgoing seriously now. It's never too late, you know."

"I . . . I'm mighty pleased to hear that, Reverend," Jesse told him. He felt awful guilty, but he supposed he'd have time now to atone for his sins. Going to church was *not* the first thing on his mind in asking for this bath.

"You can go now," Mildred told her husband.

"Yes, dear." He headed for the door, followed by Mildred, who had taken Patsy in tow.

"Just let me know if you need any help," she offered as she stood in the doorway, waiting for Sarah's reply before she closed the door.

Sarah knew if she told her sister she could handle this all by herself, Mildred would give her an argument. So she simply said, "I certainly will. I wouldn't dream of calling anyone but you. Thank you so much for everything, Mildred."

Jesse was glad to see the door close in Mildred's face. He was even more glad to hear Sarah click the little latch that locked it.

But she wouldn't turn around and look at him. She kept

her eyes on the floor while she made her way to the tub. She dipped her hand in the water.

"I think you'll find it comfortable," she told him, drying her hand on the edge of one of the towels.

"I think I will."

She still hadn't turned to look at him. He didn't want to waste his grand unveiling without her to appreciate it.

"I don't want to get my crutch wet," he said. "I think I'm going to need your help getting to the tub."

"Oh, my. All right."

She turned at last. She stood between the tub and the bed, holding on to the footboard.

"It's going to be a little hard for you to help me from way over there," he said.

Slowly she moved a few steps forward.

"Why are you so afraid of me, Sarah?" he asked softly.

She gave a nervous little laugh. "I'm not afraid of you, Jesse."

"Then why are you so afraid of my body?"

She swallowed hard—almost as if he'd discovered some guilty secret of hers—but she didn't answer. He knew she still wasn't ready to trust him. He wouldn't rush her.

"I know I'm not the man I used to be, but is my body so repulsive to you?"

"No!" she exclaimed, and shook her head emphatically. More quietly she replied, "No. You should know by now, Jesse. I don't find you repulsive at all."

"But dangerous?" He tilted his head to one side and tried to look into her eyes. But she was still staring at the floor and not saying a word. "In this condition? Haven't I already proved to you that even if I were in perfect health, I'd never hurt you—no matter what? Don't you believe me by now?"

"How can I believe you won't hurt me when you keep doing things like this?" She swung her hand out to indicate the tub. Then she gestured up and down his long body.

"Like what?"

She gritted her teeth with frustration. "Just like a man—not knowing what he's done to upset a woman!"

"How can my taking off my clothes hurt you? How can asking you to help me bathe hurt you?"

Sarah didn't answer.

What else could he say to convince her that he loved her and wanted her? There was only one thing. "Haven't you figured out by now, Sarah? I'm in love with you."

He heard her draw in a sharp breath. She still didn't say a thing.

"This can't come as a surprise to you."

She shook her head.

"I think from the very first I've been pretty honest about my feelings for you."

He watched her with hopeful eyes, but she still remained silent.

"Isn't now when you're supposed to say 'I love you, too, Jesse'? Or maybe 'Begone! Never darken my door again, you moral reprobate!' "

He waited for her to laugh. Her face remained still and almost emotionless. At last she took a step toward him.

"I thought I was being completely honest with you, too. It doesn't matter what you or I think or say, or how we feel. I can't be a wife to you, Jesse. So just stop trying—"

"Did something go wrong when Patsy was born so you can't have any more children?"

Even in the lamplight, he could see Sarah's cheeks growing red.

"I know that's a sensitive subject, but you're my wife. We can talk about it, can't we? We could go talk to Doc Hanford and see if he can help any—"

"He hasn't managed to help Mildred," Sarah muttered sadly.

"If you can't have any more children, that's not a problem, either. You know I love Patsy like she's my own. I don't need to have more children."

"Not even a son—"

"What? To pass along the castle to when I die?"

She tried not to smile when they—well, at least *she*—were trying to discuss so serious a subject. "If you don't need to

have any more children, then we don't need to . . .
to . . ."

"I need *you,* Sarah." He looked into her eyes with sincere
and dedicated longing—the kind of look that lasts a man a
lifetime, and stays with a woman long after he's gone. "To
be my wife—my real, true wife."

"Wouldn't exerting yourself like that in your condition
. . . kill you?"

"Oh, Sarah, it's killing me not to make love to you!" He
tried to keep the love and the longing in his voice, to keep
out the desperation of wanting to have her and not being
able to do anything about it for so long.

Apparently all she heard was the desperation.

"Get in the tub," she ordered, her voice shaking. "Just get
in the tub. Let's get this bath done and over with."

"Should I undress completely?"

"Do you intend to do your laundry at the same time?"

"Remember, you told me to do it."

"I suppose if I can take care of an eighty-year-old, ninety-
pound woman, I can bear to see you in the tub."

She knew there was a big difference between Aunt Myrtle
and Jesse—and a big difference between how she felt about
both of them. Aunt Myrtle was helpless and completely de-
pendent on her.

Jesse was young, and very handsome and appealing. He
was also stubborn, independent, and unpredictable—and he
made her feel that way, too—wild and foolish. She'd been
foolish before, but she'd never allowed herself to feel wild
and free—the way Jesse made her feel. She'd have to exer-
cise a great deal of caution, as well as self-control, around
him.

She stood beside him. He reached down again to take the
edges of his shirttail. Slowly, almost teasingly, he began to
lift the nightshirt.

Maybe, just maybe, he thought hopefully, what words
couldn't accomplish, his body could do to convince her.

Sarah wasn't halfway across the room now, but standing
right beside him. She had a completely different perspective

of his body as it was slowly revealed to her, one she'd never seen before.

Not just the thighs, not just the flat stomach and hairy chest were uncovered. As he drew off the rest of the night-shirt and flung it carelessly to the bed, she saw his chest and shoulders, fully fleshed and muscular again. His strong arms would be capable of seizing her, holding her down. His chest muscles could press heavily atop her, making it hard to breathe. No, Jesse wouldn't do that, not that way—would he? She hardly knew this man who was her husband. How could she know what he'd do?

She wanted to stay, and she still wanted to back away.

Almost as if he could read her fears, he said softly, "I won't hurt you, Sarah. I promise."

"I know."

"I need your help to stand, Sarah," he said, holding out his hand to her, waiting for her to take it. "I need you for more reasons than you'll ever know."

"I . . . I think I know, Jesse," she answered. Her hand was shaking as she reached out for him. He had only placed his hand in hers. It was up to her to hold him, to support him. "But . . ."

"Don't say anything about that yet. Let's just get me my bath before the water gets cold. I can wait, and we'll see."

Jesse rose from the bed. He waited for Sarah to start moving, to help support him to the tub. She just stood there, holding his hand, completely frozen—except for her eyes.

She was watching every inch of him. He could feel her eyes taking in every part of him—the shape, the color, the depth, height, and breadth of him.

"You look as if you're trying to memorize my body," he said softly.

She opened and closed her mouth, obviously trying to say words that refused to come. Then she nodded, and just as quickly shook her head. But she never took her eyes off him.

"You're looking at me as if you've never seen a man naked before." His stomach twitched under her searching, appreciative gaze.

"I haven't," she murmured.

He blinked in surprise. "Never? Not ever?"

She shook her head.

"But . . . but how . . . I mean, at some time you must have . . . I mean, what about Patsy . . . Didn't her father—?"

She shook her head. "Don't talk about . . . about that. Just be quiet and . . . let me look." She grinned sheepishly; all the while her eyes still swept his body.

He tried to keep himself calm. He didn't want anything his own body did, even involuntarily, to unnerve her completely and send her running. He didn't want to ruin any chance he might have to love her as he'd so often dreamed.

He tried to tell himself bad jokes, and recite boring poetry he'd had to learn in grammar school. He tried to recite his multiplication tables. He tried to think of raw gopher guts with maggoty gravy and moldy brussels sprouts on a dirty plate—*anything* to keep himself from thinking about what he really wanted to think about doing with Sarah. He *had* to keep himself calm.

But just thinking about it made him even more nervous and excited. He tried to recite the multiplication tables again, backward.

"Sarah, I think I should . . ."

"Get in the tub while the water's still warm," she ordered. Her voice cracked when she spoke, as if her throat still weren't working right either. She pulled on his hand to encourage him to get into the tub. "I . . . you . . . I wouldn't want you to get a chill."

He was hoping the water might help him out of this situation by being really, really cold.

He stepped into the tub and sank in up to his hips. "Wow! That's still pretty warm."

"It's good for you."

It wasn't good for him, he silently argued. It wasn't helping him at all.

His long legs wouldn't stretch out in the tub, so he kept them bent at the knees. He leaned back in the tub and rested his head against it, and rested his long arms along the sides.

Now that he'd submerged most of what fascinated her so, she was able to move about and do the things she had to do. She handed him a small cloth and a square bar of soap.

He handed it back to her. "Aren't you going to do it for me?"

"This is just like your birdbaths at the washstand, only wetter." She pushed the cloth back in his direction. "I think you know how. You've done it before."

"Will you at least scrub my back?" He pushed the cloth back to her.

"I suppose since that's the only part you can't reach yourself. . . ." She drew in a deep breath and nodded. Pushing her skirt out of her way, she knelt at the side of the tub. She pushed both sleeves up past her elbows.

Reluctantly she took the cloth and soap. She dipped them both in the warm water of the tub, being very careful not to touch any part of Jesse in the process. She rubbed the soap vigorously across the cloth, then slowly raised the cloth to his back.

He was almost as warm as the water, and a lot more substantial. His skin was smooth. Except for his injured leg, there wasn't a scar on him, at least none worth noticing. His muscles were now firm and resisted her touch when she pressed into them. There seemed to be less bone showing. His knees and elbows didn't seem so knobby.

She smoothed her hand over the tops of his shoulders and felt the smooth ridge of his collarbone joining the swell of muscles at the top of his arm. She was tempted to move her hand farther down, to let the droplets of water trickle down his hairy chest and puddle in his navel.

She couldn't help notice the rest of him, in the shadows between his legs, floating in the water, surrounded by glistening droplets on his dark, curling hair, as if the water itself were conspiring to draw her attention to it. She stifled a little laugh. She didn't need any help from the water.

She was so tempted just to toss the darned cloth away and run her fingers across his shoulders and chest, and anywhere else she darn well pleased. And then what would happen? Something she couldn't deal with—not now, not ever.

"What have you been doing?" she asked and moved on to his back, where it was probably a lot safer. "Lifting the furniture when I wasn't looking?"

"Didn't you notice I'd rearranged the entire parlor?"

"No."

"Next week I'm planning on moving the outhouse."

She giggled. "Warn me first, all right?"

"Sure." Although they were the only ones in the room, he lowered his voice to a conspiratorial whisper. "Let's not tell anyone else and see how long it takes for them to notice."

"Oh, no! We can't do that," she exclaimed, moving on to scrub his other shoulder. Leaning forward, she whispered in his ear, "We've at least got to tell the Reverend."

"Yes, dear," he replied in perfect mimicry of the preacher.

Sarah laughed out loud. She moved the cloth down his back, scrubbing firmly but gently.

"Ah, that feels good, Sarah," he said, leaning his body forward until he could rest his forehead on his raised knees. The lower part of his back was exposed to her now. "That's the best I've felt in a long, long time. Of course, it's not the *absolute* best I could ever feel, but I think, someday, maybe you could help me . . ."

"Don't be greedy," she scolded.

As she peered into the murky water, she could see his lean hips and narrow buttocks. She was *not* about to wash any farther than the small of his back—but that didn't mean she couldn't look. She certainly liked what she saw. Somehow, in spite of her good intentions, she found the cloth dipping lower and lower into the water as she bathed his back.

"Someday you'll have to let me do this for you, my dear."

Quickly she began rubbing his shoulders again. "When I'm an invalid with an injured leg and galloping consumption, I'll certainly remind you of your promise."

He sat upright and twisted his torso around to look at her.

"Sarah, my love, we'll have to find another condition to this part of our new bargain. There's no way in heaven or earth I would *ever* wish for you to be injured in any way, and I'd *never* want you to have consumption . . . like I did— do! Um . . . do."

He'd wanted to be so serious and sincere—and there he went! Making a babbling fool of himself, hemming and hawing. He'd made a slip of the tongue that could easily turn into a disastrous error, especially under these precarious circumstances.

But Sarah was apparently too busy noticing his naked body and the intensity of the emotions in his eyes to bother with his mumbling.

"Will you let me hold your hand, Sarah?" he asked. He knew it was somehow important for her to have the option to say no.

"Yes."

The smile grew on his lips. He reached up a wet hand and placed it on hers. He raised his other hand and placed it on her cheek.

"Come closer to me, Sarah," he whispered.

He raised his hand to run his fingers gently through her hair, leaving four damp trails in the blond strands. He returned to cup her chin in his hand.

"I don't think you want me coming closer to you, for some strange reason. So come to me, Sarah. Come to me now."

His rough, damp index finger teased at her lower lip, moving slowly from one corner of her mouth to the other. She swallowed hard. Inadvertently her tongue darted out to moisten her lips. His fingertip brushed the tip of her tongue before she could pull it back inside.

The warm water spread over her tongue. She savored the taste of him in her mouth and wished for more.

"Come to me, Sarah," he repeated in a whisper.

She could feel his warm breath brushing past her lips, tantalizing them again with the smell and taste of him. She moved a little closer.

"I've wanted you for a long time, Sarah," he whispered in her ear.

"We haven't known each other for a long time," she corrected him.

"I've wanted you from the first moment I saw you. That's my whole life, Sarah."

She closed her eyes, savoring his words of love, enjoying the clean smell of him, and the soft tickle of his whiskers contrasted with his smooth skin as he brushed against her cheek.

"Ever since I saw you and your little girl on the train. You weren't wearing mourning—"

"I couldn't afford it after Aunt Myrtle died."

"And I said to myself, 'Oh, she's married and probably traveling out to be with her husband,' and I knew I had to leave you alone."

He turned completely around in the tub, kneeling to come closer to her. The water in the tub splashed, and she heard the drops of water trickling rhythmically off his body back into the tub.

They were so close that their noses almost touched. He made little passes at the tip of her small nose with his own nose, anticipating the moment when their lips would touch like that.

She could see little flecks of gold and brown in his blue eyes and a gleam that surpassed mischief and longing.

"Do you know how surprised and happy I was to find out you weren't married—and that you wanted to marry me?"

"But . . . but you knew I only wanted to marry you because . . . because I knew you were dying," she said. "I feel so guilty now . . . taking advantage of you that way when, all the while, you felt like this. . . ."

"That didn't matter to me. I just wanted to be with you in the short time I thought I had left to live. Ever since I kissed you on our wedding day, I've wanted to kiss you again and again and again. Kiss me again, Sarah," he said. "Won't you kiss me now?"

Her heart was pounding in her throat. Her body burned for him. Her lips could still feel the warmth of his fingertips. She'd been so nervous and bewildered, and in such a hurry at her wedding ceremony that she barely remembered Jesse's kiss—only that he was the first man who had kissed her with tenderness in a long, long time.

This kiss, she promised herself, she'd remember.

His face was already so close to hers. It would only take the smallest movement forward on her part, just a slight inclination of her head.

Her nose brushed past his, and she held her breath. It felt good to be so close to him. Could she still trust him to let her approach him on her own, and not to press her further?

He brushed the tip of her nose with his own several times, slowly breathing in and out the warm air, scented with lavender, around her.

She closed her eyes and savored the gentle feel of him and the clean smell.

She felt soothed and at the same time excited by his touch. She leaned forward. Her lips pressed against his. They were soft and warm, yet still firm in his desire for her. His lips seemed to blend with hers, almost as if they were made to fit together.

He held her face in both hands now. She raised her own arms to wrap around his bare shoulders. He was wet and warm, smooth and strong. How could she be doing this? How could she hold him like this—and enjoy it so?

Their lips separated for only the space of a breath. His lips descended on hers again. She willingly welcomed him. His kiss meandered to the edge of her mouth, then spilled over to caress her cheek. He eased his hands down her neck until he caressed the little hollow at the base of her throat with his thumbs, and moved on to hold her shoulders. Keeping one hand on her shoulder, he eased the other down her arm and across her back. Moving slowly and gently, he urged her to press her body closer to his.

She had no idea what else to do. She really hadn't had much choice the last time. But this time she felt excited and eager. She wanted more of his kisses, more of him.

She could almost think that they were blending into one person. She wanted to open up to him, to welcome him and become one with him. Forever.

No, she had to keep control of herself. She needed time to take just a breath. She tried to pull back just an inch.

Jesse's hand held her face. His fingers didn't twist around the strands of her hair, didn't dig into her skin. His body wasn't weighing her down so she couldn't move at all. But one hand still grasped her face, and the other held her back firmly—and he wouldn't let her go!

She gave a little cry and pulled back.

"What happened? I didn't hurt you, did I?" he asked.

"No, no. But . . . but . . ."

"I was afraid I was too eager. I've scared you. But . . . but . . . Oh, God! I want you so. Come back to me, Sarah."

"No, no. I'm fine. I'll be fine." She grasped the edge of the tub and rose to her feet.

"You're not fine."

"If we don't get you out of that tub soon, you're not going to be fine, either."

Bending down, she wiggled her fingers in the water. She flicked the excess water off her fingers and dried her hand on the edge of one of the towels.

"The water's gone almost cold."

"Funny, I think it's really warm in here. Maybe the water only feels cold to you because you're so warm, too," he suggested with a teasing grin.

"Maybe," she readily agreed. Then she handed him a large towel and moved away from the tub a step. "I think it's time you dried off and got dressed."

"Dressed?" he demanded. She could hear the disappointment in his voice. She could see his frustration and even a little anger. "Dressed? After all that, you want me to get dressed?"

"Yes." She tried to answer calmly. All the while, she could feel her insides shaking, too, with frustration and fear —and yes, with even a little anger, too. She was angry with Jesse for not keeping his word. She was angry with herself for not being braver. "Yes. Oh, don't you see where this is going?"

He rose from the tub, the towel still hanging in his hand. He was angry. His body was tense—every bit of his body. She could see that very well, and she backed up until she felt the bed behind her. There was nowhere else to go.

"I know damn good and well where it's going—where it *was* going," Jesse told her. "I thought you did, too. And I thought you agreed with me."

"I can't. I just can't." She couldn't stop the tears that flowed down her cheeks. She didn't even try to wipe them away. "I thought you'd be different."

"Different from what?"

But Sarah was too upset and too intent on her own fears to respond to him. "You don't give a damn about how you can hurt a woman's feelings—or her body—except for how you can use it for your own pleasure."

"What? What did I do? How did I hurt you? It was because I tried to hold you, wasn't it?"

She didn't answer.

"Wasn't it?" He demanded an answer—not to be cruel, but to be able to understand what made Sarah so unpredictable and so puzzling.

"You . . . you said you wouldn't . . ." she murmured.

"But I didn't mean to. For Pete's sake, I didn't hold you that hard. And I *do* give a damn about you, Sarah. I give more than a damn. I love you."

"No, you don't. You're no different. You're the same as all the other men."

"Other men?" he mumbled, dumbstruck. "All . . . the other men?" When she'd made him promise never to ask, what terrible thing about her past was there that she didn't want him to know?

She didn't stay around to answer his questions. She'd already run out the door.

"Sarah!" he called after her, but he could already hear the door to Patsy's room slam shut.

Why had she run out, instead of staying to talk it out? Why hadn't she closed the darn door after her?

Jesse didn't dare call for Sarah again. He knew she wouldn't come. He didn't need the entire household knowing he was stuck in the tub.

He quickly wrapped the towel around his hips and tucked the end in at his waist, just in case Mildred went wandering by. He slowly and carefully stepped out of the slippery tub.

If he fell and hurt himself now, who would come to help him? Patsy was too little. He wouldn't mind having the Reverend offer him some help, man to man, but he didn't think he wanted Meddling Mildred coming around. She'd have to know what happened to Sarah, what he'd said to her, what she'd said to him, why she'd run out, and why he was lying buck naked in the middle of the floor.

He wished he knew himself why she'd run out like that. Shaking his head, he wondered if madness did run in the family.

He padded, dripping and barefoot, across the carpet, then closed and locked the door.

It was going to be a long, lonely night, he told himself as he dried the rest of his body. Quite a disappointment after what he'd been imagining.

If she wasn't ready for a little kiss from him, he figured as he pulled on a clean nightshirt, she really wasn't ready to know the truth about his illness. After tonight, she probably couldn't wait to have him keel over and die. She might even try to hurry him along.

What would she say now if she knew he was going to live? How could he tell her? He was such a coward. Maybe he could just put it off for another thirty or forty years, and sooner or later she'd figure it out for herself. Forty long, sad, celibate years. He couldn't stand it!

He settled into bed. Well, he'd had his bath. He might as well go to church tomorrow anyway, he figured.

He wondered if Sarah would still sit in the same pew with him.

He wondered if it was all right for a man to pray to be able to make love with his own wife.

Eleven

So far Mildred hadn't noticed that Sarah'd spent last night in Patsy's room. She hoped she could keep it that way. She also hoped that Patsy could manage to keep quiet about it.

She hadn't exactly slept, though. She'd tossed and turned, staring into the darkness. She'd risen and paced the room, hoping not to wake Patsy. She'd stood at a window and gazed up into the star-filled sky, hoping to find an answer there. How could she fear Jesse so, and yet still feel the need to hold him in her arms and welcome him into her deeper embrace?

She hoped her sister wouldn't notice how red-rimmed her eyes were, or that she couldn't seem to stop yawning behind her hand.

She especially hoped Jesse wouldn't notice. She didn't want him to think that he was so important that she'd been losing any sleep over him. That might only encourage him to be more aggressive. She didn't think she could stand that again. She liked him friendly and harmless, the way he'd seemed on the train.

This morning, Mildred was more concerned with her armload of sheets of music.

Jesse, Patsy, and Sarah followed her through the little cemetery toward the church. It wasn't easy to walk here when she knew that soon Jesse would be among these silent stones—silent at last himself. She was going to miss his sparkling eyes and winning smile, his ready wit and awful jokes. She'd always remember that about him.

What would be his last memories of the woman who had promised to care for him until his dying day, the woman he had fallen in love with, the woman who didn't love him? Or did she? Would his only memory be of her scorning him?

She pressed her lips together and suppressed a deep sigh. She shot a sidelong glance at him.

His head was held high, as if he were trying to soak in as much sunlight as possible while he was still above ground. His light brown hair was collecting the sunlight, too, and bouncing it back.

He drew in great breaths of air. He seemed to be savoring each new scent the breezes brought him—from warm, fresh-baked bread from cast-iron ovens and unfurling rosebuds blooming along white picket fences, to the aroma of the outhouses and the cow manure wafting in from the fields.

He watched the clouds changing shapes as they sailed across the sky. He watched each bird that flitted from one tree branch to another and called greetings or warnings to each other as the humans milled about below.

His blue eyes sparkled with joy. He seemed to be enjoying every step of this walk through the cemetery.

Even though he needed his crutch, he still held her hand with his other hand. She was surprised that he'd even want to bother with her after she'd run out on him last night. Even more importantly, she was surprised to find that she was glad he still tried. His grasp was warm and firm. Every once in a while, his thumb would softly caress the back of her hand.

She wished she could summon up the nerve to press his hand in response, but she smiled to herself anyway. Deep down inside, she was glad Jesse was such a stubborn, persistent man. She was glad they were still friends.

Patsy toddled along at Sarah's other side. It was hard to keep up with Mildred, heading toward her destination with as much intensity as she went after everything else.

"At this rate of speed, we'll be lucky if we make it to church by the time the collection's taken," Sarah said.

"Then we better slow down," Jesse said. "If we time it just right, we'll miss the collection completely."

"Howdy, Jesse. Mrs. Taylor," Charlie Wilson said, tipping his battered hat to them as they strolled slowly toward the church.

"Good morning, Mr. Wilson," she replied.

"Hey there, Charlie," Jesse said cheerfully. "Good to see you again. How's that new horse working out?"

"Just great. How's the leg?"

"Oh, about the same."

After Charlie had moved along ahead of them, Sarah turned to Jesse and said, "You certainly seem to have a lot of friends for a man who only spends his time sitting on the front porch."

"Sitting on the front porch is a greatly underestimated pastime," he replied.

Mildred was waiting for them at the church door. "Mr. Taylor, I didn't know you knew Mr. Wilson."

She was smiling, but Sarah could see the tight little lines around her lips that indicated she was upset. Could it be that she didn't want Jesse meeting people who didn't meet her approval first—or who weren't acceptable prospective second husbands for Sarah?

"I met him one day when he was strolling by," Jesse answered. "We talked about his farm, not too far out of town, and a right promising stud horse he just bought."

"He's also got a wife and three little boys," Mildred added. The disapproval in her voice was quite evident. Then she reached up and stroked her chin thoughtfully. "Although I do hear from Mrs. Thorton, their nearest neighbor, that his wife's doing poorly lately, if he's the one you really like and don't mind waiting."

"What on earth are you talking about?"

"Oh, please don't ask, Jesse," Sarah mumbled her plea. She still had too much of a headache this morning to worry about Mildred's silly plans.

"Of course, if you ask me, I'd be on the lookout for Gustav Hoffmann," Mildred told him with a knowing nod of her head.

"Why should I look out for Gustav Hoffmann?"

"I told you not to ask," Sarah said.

"Oh, Mr. Hoffmann," Mildred called melodiously across the churchyard.

A short, roly-poly fellow turned around. His nose was as round as an apple and just as red.

Jesse leaned over and whispered to Sarah, "He looks pretty harmless to me. Unless he intends to hit me with his pocket watch. Geez, that watch is as big as the cowbell Mildred got for me!"

"Oh, hush."

"Did you call me, Mrs. Preston?" Mr. Hoffmann replied.

"Oh, Mr. Hoffmann," she called in the same voice. "Would you mind coming here for a moment? There's someone I'd just love to have you meet."

"But, Mrs. Preston," Mr. Hoffmann protested as he came ambling across the lawn. "I've already met your charming sister."

"No, no. I want you to meet my brother-in-law," Mildred said.

Many times in her life her sister had made Sarah feel virtually invisible. This time, Sarah decided, was the best Mildred had ever done.

"Mr. Taylor, Mr. Hoffmann owns the bakery in town," Mildred explained. "He's forty-three and has been a widower for three years now, with a grown son. He was born in Switzerland, but he's a good American now. He's a trustee at the bank, plays the fiddle, and has all his own teeth."

"Pleased to meet you, Mr. Hoffmann," Jesse replied, extending his hand. "I won't comment on the personal information Mrs. Preston supplied—none of my business, really."

"Oh, but it is," Mildred protested.

"You have my respect, sir. You certainly look like a prosperous businessman," Jesse continued politely in spite of his puzzlement at Mildred's outburst. "That's quite a handsome pocket watch."

"Thank you. Yes, indeed," Mr. Hoffmann said.

Sarah was sure the baker meant to puff out his chest proudly, but his belly seemed to stand out most.

"Shouldn't you be more worried about his income and the establishment of the store?" Mildred whispered to Jesse.

"I'm not that nosy," Jesse whispered back.

"I brought it with me all the way from Switzerland," Mr. Hoffmann declared proudly. "That is where I learned to make the best kugel—ha, ha! the only kugel—in town. Come try a little sometime. For you, I'll give you one free. And for the little one, *pfefferneusen.*"

"Thank you very much. We will, Mr. Hoffmann. We will. It's been a pleasure meeting you."

"The pleasure's been mine, Mr. and Mrs. Taylor," Mr. Hoffmann said, moving away. "See you in church."

Mr. Hoffmann was still so close Sarah could hear him huffing and puffing, trying to climb the three low stone steps into the church. But Mildred had turned to Jesse already.

"Well, what do you think of him?" she demanded.

"He seems nice enough. We'll have to take him up on his offer of kugel. And that stuff for Patsy, too—whatever it was he called it."

"No, no. What do you think of him for Sarah?"

Jesse turned to Sarah. "Gee, I don't know. Do you like kugel, dear?"

"No, no." Mildred's jaw was growing tight with frustration. "What do you think of him *for* Sarah?"

Jesse turned to take another look at Mr. Hoffmann. He was standing in the doorway, talking to one of the ladies of the Cottonwood Methodist Ladies Evangelical Temperance and Missionary Soul-Saving Spiritual Aid Bible Society. For

Mildred's sake, Jesse pretended to be studying the man carefully. Actually he couldn't care less about him.

"For Sarah? What in the world would she do with him?"

"Marry him, of course!"

"Why?"

"Because she'll need a husband—and Patsy'll need a father—once you're dead."

"Well, thanks for reminding me, Mildred," he said with a grimace.

Mildred sniffed to show her injured feelings. "I was only trying to be helpful. I just thought that if you had a personal hand in choosing Sarah's next husband, you'd rest a little easier, knowing she and Patsy were taken care of the way you'd have wanted."

"*I* get to choose her next husband? She's not done with the first one. I'm not dead yet!"

"You can't pick him when you're dead."

"Doesn't Sarah have a say in the matter?"

"Well, sort of."

"Sort of?"

Mildred leaned forward and, in her own inimitable whisper, declared, "You know widows have absolutely no common sense when it comes to choosing a second husband. She'll probably pick some handsome young man, some smooth-talking drifter that comes along, with lots of hair and muscles and all his own teeth, and no money and no sense at all, and he'll expect her to support him and all his wild women on the hard-earned money you've saved, and he'll neglect poor little Patsy something awful! It's our job—it's our Christian duty!—to make sure Sarah marries a man with money, morals, social position, security, a job."

Jesse nodded. "I see. So that's why you've been introducing me to all these men. To see which one I liked best for Sarah."

"Yes, indeed," Mildred declared proudly. "I figured you could inject some much-needed common sense into the matter. You see, she's been turning down everyone I introduce to her."

Jesse turned to Sarah. "She has?"

"Stubborn thing, isn't she?"

Jesse looked Sarah up and down, then peered directly into her eyes. "I'd say sometimes that could be an admirable trait."

Mildred shrugged. "To each his own. I've been trying to study you."

"Me? I'm flattered," Jesse said, although he wasn't fooled by Mildred's false compliments for a second.

"I've been trying to figure out what in the world she ever saw in you to make her marry you that she doesn't find in any of the others." Mildred shook her head in bewilderment and sighed. "It certainly beats me."

"Well, thanks a lot."

"Oh, anytime I can be of help. I have to go play some hymns now."

Sarah breathed a sigh of relief when Mildred bustled away from them and into the church.

"So, none of Mildred's choices are good enough for you?" Jesse asked.

"I haven't met one yet," she answered as she lifted Patsy to help her up the steps.

"But you thought I was good enough. What is it about me that escapes Mildred—and all the others?"

"You looked so helpless and pathetic." She shot him a mischievous grin as she carried Patsy into the church and slid into the empty last pew to the right.

"I swear," Jesse muttered as he took his seat beside her, "you and your sister are two of the strangest women I've ever met."

"You should've met Aunt Myrtle."

Mildred played the first hymn good and loud.

Sarah felt strange sharing a hymnal for the first time in many years. Jesse's fingers brushed against hers under the hymnal, where no one else could see. Slowly, gently, his fingertips stroked the back of her hand, sending chills up her arms and down her spine. He moved farther up her wrist and tucked his finger under the sleeve of her dress.

She was paying so much attention to how fast her heart was beating that she had trouble keeping in time to the music. The touch of just one finger was sending chills up her arm, and running up and down her spine. If just one finger could do that, what would she do if he placed his entire hand on her shoulder or embraced her with both arms?

This had to stop. Running out of church last week was bad enough. She couldn't faint in church this week. Then what would she do next week for an encore? She didn't dare ask Jesse. She knew his first suggestion was to run out of church taking her clothes off as she went.

She tried to concentrate on singing the hymn instead of on touching Jesse. She tried to listen to the words everyone else was singing so she could figure out where in the song they were, but everything was just a jumble of garbled syllables, with one really loud soprano knocking everyone off the rhythm with her own stirring rendition of "Amazing Grace." It was amazing that Mildred could stay on the beat when no one else seemed to be able to. But then, there weren't many people—not even the soprano—who could outdo Mildred.

Jesse was taller and held the book closer to Sarah's eyes than she was used to. If she tilted the book, she could see better. But then he'd tilt the book back again to his point of view. She was having enough trouble figuring out where they were in the hymn without him confusing her, too.

She was beginning to get just the slightest bit irritated when he started to chuckle under his breath. He'd been doing that deliberately, the scoundrel! She knew she shouldn't be laughing in church. That made it all the more difficult to stop. She grabbed the book more firmly, hoping to make him behave.

She nodded toward her daughter, who'd already found the pictures she liked best and was concentrating on keeping track of the number of sheep at the Nativity to make sure they didn't outnumber the angels in the choir.

"I don't have this much trouble with Patsy," she told him in a voice loud enough to be heard even above the soprano —just as the hymn ended.

Everyone turned around to look at her. She hung her head in the pew and pretended to be very concerned with the contents of the hymnal. There was only one Patsy in this town that she knew of. She couldn't remain anonymous in her embarrassment. Now everyone knew who had the loudest mouth in Cottonwood.

After everyone settled down for prayers and the Gospel reading, Jesse leaned closer to Sarah.

"I really missed you last night," he whispered as he placed his hand over hers.

She didn't pull her hand back. It wasn't so much that she was afraid Patsy would bite him, too. She just didn't want to leave his touch.

"Did you miss me, too, Sarah?"

She leaned so close to him that her bonnet brushed against the side of his head. "I don't think this is the time or the place to talk about it, Jesse," she cautioned in a musical whisper. She sat erect again and tried to concentrate on what the Reverend was saying.

"I think it's a good time and place—unless you intend to go bolting from the church again, this time because of me."

"I will if you keep bothering me," she warned mischievously. "I'll have the ushers throw you out."

"That's just in the theaters, Sarah," he pointed out.

"Then I'll leave," she threatened.

The lady sitting in front of them turned around. "Shh!"

He glanced from Sarah seated to his right to the aisle on his other side. "You're going to have to climb over me and the crutch to get there."

She grimaced.

"Personally, I'm looking for you to try it."

She shook her head.

"Then sit and listen."

"I'm trying to," she said, staring straight ahead at the pulpit.

"Shh!" the lady scolded.

"Not him. Me!"

"Oh."

"I missed you last night, my love. I want you back, even if it's in that silly chair. I want you to be the last thing I see when I close my eyes at night, and the first thing I see when I open them in the morning."

The lady had stopped scolding and had leaned her head back to catch every word.

He turned to Sarah and peered into her eyes so she could see his better. "I . . . I couldn't sleep without you. See. Just look at these bloodshot eyes."

"Oh, I thought that was just your usual coloring."

"Only when I'm not with you. Say you'll come back to me. I need you so much." He looked at her, his blue eyes filled with longing.

"I . . . I need you, too, Jesse, but . . ."

"Your eyes are as bloodshot as mine, Sarah. I know you missed me, too—even if you won't admit it."

"I . . . we'll see."

Obviously disappointed at the end of the conversation, the lady sat upright. Eventually, without anything better to keep her entertained, her head nodded forward as she dozed off.

Sarah sat upright and tried to pay better attention to what the Reverend Preston was saying and what Patsy was doing. It was hard to concentrate on anything else when all she could think of was that Jesse had missed her as much as she had missed him.

She'd join him again tonight. She'd already decided that first thing this morning. She never wanted to spend another sleepless night like that. But she wouldn't tell him right away—just to try to keep him on good behavior for the rest of the day, wondering.

Of course, he was still sick, and she'd still sleep in her chair no matter what. But there was something comforting about just knowing he was in the same room with her.

As the Reverend Preston droned on and on, Sarah glanced around the congregation to see if she could remember anyone and attach names to faces. She couldn't wait to attach a face and name to the lady sitting in front of her.

She caught her breath. Deke had turned around in the pew and was staring straight at them. His eyes seemed to burn red with a look of pure hatred. She'd seen pictures of the devil in books. All Deke needed was horns, hooves, and a tail. He probably kept his pitchfork in his barn.

Thank goodness he wasn't looking at Patsy at all. She was also grateful that he wasn't watching her. But she began to worry when she realized Deke was actually directing that grotesque stare at Jesse.

She stared at the words in her hymnal, but she could still feel Deke's eyes, aiming volleys of death in Jesse's direction.

She couldn't run out of the church to seek the safety of the parsonage the way she had last Sunday. But she had to get her family away from Deke as fast as she could—for Patsy's sake, and especially for Jesse's.

She couldn't wait for the last hymn to end.

Jesse couldn't figure out why Sarah was in such an all-fired hurry to get out of church again this Sunday. It wouldn't hurt if Patsy looked at the pictures in the book a little longer. It wouldn't hurt if the old lady with the big black bonnet got ahead of them as they were filing down the aisle out of church.

"Couldn't stay away from me, huh, li'l lady?" It was the same big blond man who kept giving Jesse dirty looks who came up behind them and whispered in Sarah's ear. Maybe now Jesse'd find out what this was all about.

"Go away, Deke," she said without even turning around. Obviously she knew very well who he was.

Jesse stared at the man. He was the same one who'd walked past the house, casting venomous glances in his direction. At last he'd find out who this hostile man was, Jesse thought. Sarah had called him Deke. Deke who? More importantly he'd find out why the man seemed to hate him so.

It had to have something to do with Sarah, he figured. He hadn't seen Deke give her the same hateful glance. But there was no loving affection there, either. The look he gave Sarah was pure animal lust.

Was he married? He must be, or else Mildred would've

introduced him for Jesse's approval as a prospective husband a long time ago. If he was married, what the heck was he doing staring at another man's wife?

They hadn't been in town long enough for Deke to have developed such a strong desire for Sarah so quickly. On the other hand, Jesse thought, *he* had fallen in love with her at first sight.

But there was something different about the way this man looked at Sarah. And judging from the way she avoided him like a rabid dog, there must be some connection between Sarah and this man in the past—the past that Jesse'd promised her he wouldn't ask about.

"I'm going home now, Mr. Marsden," Sarah announced coldly. The calmness Jesse heard in her voice belied the fear he saw in her eyes and the tight grip she kept on his hand. "I'm going to spend Sunday afternoon with my family. I suggest you do the same. Good day."

"Yeah, yeah, I know," the man continued as he pursued them down the church steps. "That mealy-mouthed brother-in-law of yours and that busybody do-good sister, your bratty daughter, and your weakling husband."

Jesse stopped at the base of the steps. He kept his crutch out in front of him, almost like a boundary over which he defied Deke to trespass. "You seem to know a lot about us, sir, and I don't even know your name."

"Naw, but your wife sure does," the man replied with a snicker that ended up as a sneer.

Jesse didn't like the way the man watched Sarah. He looked like a dog who'd been without food for too long, eyeing a roast of beef he couldn't have. Jesse knew what usually happened in situations like that, too. The first time nobody was watching, the dog jumped up on the table, grabbed the meat, and ran off with it. He had to make sure he never left Sarah alone with that man.

"We . . . we're both from Savannah," Sarah tried to explain.

"Well, now we're all living in Cottonwood," Jesse said. "I

guess it just stands to reason we ought to know each other's names now."

He didn't give a damn about this man or his name, but he wouldn't have the fellow knowing anything about him that he didn't know in return.

"I'm Jesse Taylor." He extended his hand and waited for the big blond man to take it.

He wasn't about to remove the safe barrier of the crutch. He gritted his teeth and prayed he could keep his balance without its support, and not fall over flat on his face at this ignorant bastard's feet. The loathsome scum would probably kick him in the face while he was down. But if he didn't take his hand soon, Jesse knew he was going to start wobbling.

"Deke Marsden," the man replied. He never did take Jesse's hand.

Jesse shrugged and lowered his hand to his side. Not a moment too soon, either, he decided as he quickly regained his balance on his crutch. He figured he couldn't have trembled noticeably because Sarah hadn't made a grab for him.

A few people must've noticed the prolonged interchange between Jesse and Deke. Apparently they already knew Deke Marsden and whatever reputation he might have. They were standing just close enough to hear what was being said, but not close enough to become involved with what might go on.

"Jesse Taylor, huh?" Deke sneered as he eyed him. "So this is the feller Sarah finally decided to marry."

"Unless you're some kind of blood kin, I'll thank you to call my wife 'Mrs. Taylor' now."

"Oh, Jesus Lord!" Deke exclaimed.

The ladies gasped.

"You're as snotty as them Boltons, ain't you? No wonder she married you." Without giving Jesse time to answer, he said, "But you're mighty pale, and skinny, and really sissy-lookin'. You're so weak you can't walk without that crutch. You sure don't look like nothin' special."

"I obviously have sterling inner qualities you simply can't

appreciate," Jesse replied with as much haughtiness as he could muster without breaking out laughing at himself. Now was definitely not the time to laugh. There was too much at stake.

But the people standing about laughed. Hearing the laughter, a few more people gathered and drew a little closer. Jesse saw Deke's face darken as the crowd laughed harder.

Deke spat at Jesse's feet. "I'd like to see just how good some of them inner qualities is when they're all spilled out on the street."

The crowd gasped. Jesse heard comments of "white trash" and "rowdy scum" and hoped they weren't referring to him.

"Well, if I ever get run over by a wagon, I'll make sure you're notified."

"Naw."

Deke's big hands had doubled up into even bigger-looking fists. Jesse had the surest feeling that Deke wouldn't hesitate to use them, either. A blow from one of those would certainly land him in the dirt, he decided. Hell, it would probably kill him! He'd have to be very careful about what he said. More importantly, he'd have to be very careful to watch what Deke did.

"Don't bother, 'cause I wouldn't bother comin'."

"What? After the personal invitation I've just given you?"

More people were gathering all the time. Some were even coming, not from the church, but from the sidewalk.

"You're such a skinny little piss-ant, your guts wouldn't make a good enough puddle for me to stomp my feet in."

"Maybe you could if you didn't have such big feet," Jesse pointed out to him.

The growing crowd laughed.

Deke's face grew redder. "Hell, I could piss a puddle bigger'n you!"

The ladies gasped.

"I wouldn't be surprised," Jesse replied, "since that's probably all you're full of."

"Why, you miserable little snot-lickin' son of a bitch. I don't need no wagon to run over you!" Deke declared. "I'll split your scrawny little belly wide open and spill your lousy guts out all over Main Street with my bare hands."

One of Jesse's eyebrows rose, and his upper lip curled with scorn as he viewed Deke's fists. "Do be sure to wash those filthy things first."

"You ain't such a sissy pants that you're a-scared of a little infection, are you?"

"I don't worry about the little things—like you." He could sure tell Deke a thing or two about infections—but Deke wouldn't understand a word he said.

"The way I hear tell, scarecrow, you're dyin' anyway."

"Is that what you're bothering us for? You want an invitation to the wake?"

"When you're dead and rottin' in your grave, I'm gonna come to your widow, Taylor," Deke continued, shaking his fist in Jesse's face. The crowd began to boo and hiss. "I'm gonna make her my wife this time, for sure. I'm gonna take her to my bed and show her what it's like to love a whole man. A real man who's got all his strength."

"But do you have all your teeth?"

The crowd laughed.

Jesse turned and glanced at Sarah. She was shaking as if she were the one who needed a crutch, and her fear-filled eyes were growing more restless with each passing minute. She clutched Patsy in her arms as if she'd never let her go.

"I'm gonna show her what a woman's supposed to do for her man," Deke continued. "She'll beg for me to stop, she'll faint, but I won't be done 'cause I'm a real man. And I know the only two things a woman's really good for, and the only places she oughtta be—the kitchen and the bedroom."

Some of the ladies were beginning to pull out their handkerchiefs and fan themselves. Jesse knew he couldn't stoop to answering Deke's vulgar threats in the same way or he'd only seem as low as he was.

"I know why you're so angry," Jesse declared with a snap of his fingers. "People of your high caliber require engraved, hand-delivered invitations, don't they? But I have to ask you something important. If I send you an invitation, will you be able to read it or will you need help?"

The crowd snickered.

"You're gonna die, Taylor!" Deke exclaimed. He shifted his feet apart and raised both fists in front of him in a boxer's stance. "I'm gonna kill you. I'm gonna watch you die, and I'll be laughin'."

The crowd began to boo again.

"I'm not going to fight you, Deke," Jesse told him.

"Why not? Too much of a coward, Taylor?"

"No. Too much of a gentleman."

"Ha! Don't gimme that Southern gentleman crap—"

"I'm not a Southerner."

Deke paused and blinked, as if trying to rethink how he could take his argument around this roadblock. But he didn't relax his belligerent stance.

Jesse held his breath and waited for what the man would do next. He wasn't stupid, but he was definitely angry and probably used to being the biggest, meanest kid in the school yard. That might make him careless, to Jesse's eventual advantage. But it also made him wild and unpredictable. Jesse knew he had to be ready for anything.

"Well, don't gimme that gentleman crap, either." Deke gave Jesse a smirk. "I know you ain't gonna tell me you ain't no gentleman."

"You're right, Deke," Jesse said. "But I'm still not going to fight you."

"Why not, you yellow-livered coward?"

"Because I'm too smart."

"Smart, huh?"

"That's right." Jesse nodded. The crowd started to murmur their agreement. "Let's face it, Deke. You're taller than me, stronger than me, and you weigh a whole lot more than me. I've been sick for a long time, so I'm slower and weaker. You probably could kill me very easily, so it only stands to reason, since I have no wish to commit suicide, I'm *not* going to fight you."

"You're not gonna fool me with any of that high-falutin' logic," Deke declared angrily. "Fight me, you damned coward!" He reached out a meaty hand and pushed hard against Jesse's chest.

Jesse knew he didn't have the strength to push back against anyone as big and strong as Deke. He was just glad Deke hadn't used his fist. Instead of resisting, Jesse simply stepped out of the way sideways as quickly as he could without losing his balance. He left his crutch in front of him.

Without Jesse's expected resistance to stop him, Deke continued forward. His foot caught in the tip of the crutch. He sprawled flat on his face in the dirt beyond Jesse's feet.

The crowd began to hoot and holler. The little boys who'd climbed up the big oak tree to get a better look, and were perched out on its largest limb, cheered loudly.

"How'd you do that?" Sarah demanded, surprised.

"Just lucky, I guess." He wished he knew how he'd done it because he had the sinking feeling he was going to have to do it again as long as Deke stayed around.

"You're really gonna die now, Taylor!" Deke yelled as he lifted himself from the grass. "But I ain't gonna kill you quick. I'll make sure you die slowly, so you can watch everything I do to Sarah, just to sort of get her primed for what I'll expect of her when she marries me."

"I'll kill myself first," Sarah managed to cry.

"Don't do that, dear," Jesse warned her calmly. "You'll only make yourself more appealing to Mr. Marsden."

The crowd made all sorts of revolted noises, except for the little boys up the tree, who apparently would cheer anything Jesse said. Some of the ladies actually swooned into the arms of their husbands, who quickly took over the fans and worked them vigorously.

Deke took one step toward Jesse, but before he could come any closer or Jesse could move away, a hail of mud pies rained from the sky onto Deke.

"What the . . . ?"

Jesse turned around. Children on the ground were scooping up mud from around the base of the tree and tossing it up to the little boys who were perched on its branches. The boys were hurling the mud at Deke. There wasn't much he could do against such an onslaught from so many tiny attackers.

Deke moved out of range of the mud, but he still glared at Jesse. "I'll get you, Taylor!" he threatened. "I ain't done with you yet!"

Before Deke could move toward Jesse again, Simon Parker, Charlie Wilson, Mr. Hoffmann, and some of the other men in the crowd stepped in between them.

"Go home now, Deke," Jesse called. "Go home and cool off."

"Cool off by jumping in the lake," some of the boys called from the top of the tree. "Go jump in the lake!" they hooted and hollered after him.

Deke backed away from them all. "This ain't over with, Taylor."

"I know that, Deke. I know."

Jesse and Sarah sat on the porch in the fading evening light. The Reverend was in his study, already working on next Sunday's sermon. Mildred had taken Patsy upstairs for more bedtime stories.

"Why are you so afraid of Deke?" Jesse asked.

Sarah fairly jumped out of her rocking chair. "Deke? I'm not afraid of Deke," she told him with a nervous little laugh.

"Then why do you hate him so?"

"Hate's a pretty strong word."

"Why are you afraid of him, then?"

"Hmm, cautious, maybe. You've seen for yourself what a bully he is."

"Yes. But I've seen real fear in your eyes when he comes near you, Sarah. I've seen the hate in your eyes when someone even mentions him. Now that I've met him, I don't like him either, but something tells me you've got another really valid reason, especially since I know you knew him back in Savannah."

"Well, you can see he's just . . . well, he's just not the kind of person I usually associate with."

"But a strange man on a train is?"

Sarah gave a little laugh. "There's a subtle difference."

"I'm acceptable because I don't drop my 'g's and I don't say 'ain't'? Because I'm a carpenter and he's a . . . a . . . what does he do, anyway?"

"He's a blight on humanity," Sarah replied with another laugh.

"What else is he, Sarah?" Jesse asked. He wasn't laughing anymore. He wasn't even smiling. He had turned in his chair and was watching her intently. His blue eyes shone in the darkening twilight with a piercing gleam, making Sarah almost believe she couldn't lie to Jesse, that he could read her mind anyway.

"What . . . what do you mean?"

"Was there something more that he was to you in Savannah? Did he love you and betray you? Did . . . did you love him? Is he Patsy's father?"

"My goodness, Jesse," she replied with a nervous giggle. She shifted uneasily in her chair and started rocking with a lot more enthusiasm. "If you want to know something, why don't you just come right out and ask?"

"I am asking. Is he Patsy's father?"

"Whatever makes you think that? She doesn't even look like him."

"She looks like you, but he could still be her father."

"No, he couldn't!" she stated firmly.

"But do you still love him?"

"I *never* loved Deke Marsden!" Her hands were tight little fists on the arms of her rocker. "I never could. I never will."

"Did he love you?"

"Deke loves himself, that's it."

"Then who is Patsy's father, Sarah?"

"Look, Jesse, I have a lovely daughter and a husband I'm . . . I'm very fond of."

"I'm glad to hear that," he said with a smug grin on his face.

"Don't get too excited about it." Her hands had relaxed again with his humorous approach to almost everything. "I'm making the best of my life as it is. I don't want to dredge up anything that would ruin it—any part of it. Please, Jesse. Let's just abide by our bargain and not ask any more questions about the past."

"I will, but only because you ask me, Sarah. Only because of you."

Jesse lay in his solitary bed again that night. In the light of the full moon, he could see stubborn Sarah, once again sleeping sitting upright in her chair by the window. She'd still refused to come to his bed, but at least they were in the same room together again. He still had hope she might someday learn to trust him completely.

Hope wasn't what kept him awake tonight. Hope was polite. Hope would let a man sleep peacefully, with the certainty that tomorrow would always be better. Worry was rude. Worry kept Jesse awake tonight.

He'd been lucky with Deke today. He didn't know if it was the protection of the crowd, or the children's mud pies, or—his favorite reason—his own sparkling wit that amused the crowd, got them on his side, and diffused some of Deke's anger.

He didn't know if he'd be able to divert the man's rage next time, though. He knew for sure that in his present condition he wouldn't be able to defend himself, or Sarah, against a man as large as Deke if the fellow decided to actually hit him.

Even if he did spend his nights lifting the bed, as Sarah had accused him of doing, to rebuild his muscles, how could he defeat Deke if he only had one leg?

How was he going to stay alive if he kept the bad leg? How was he going to protect his family if he lost it? Tomorrow he'd talk to Doc Hanford.

Tonight worry kept him awake.

Twelve

"Jesse, I know amputation's the traditional form of treatment for your injury," Doc said as he washed his hands in the enamel basin and dried them on a clean, white towel.

"I've been told that before, Doc. That's why I'm here this morning." He'd taken his seat on the examination table and stretched his injured leg out in front of him. "I need . . . there's . . . there's just got to be something else. There's just *got* to be!"

"I know you've got a lot of reasons to live, Jesse, and maybe some fancy doctor who'd studied at Harvard could help you, but . . ."

"You're all I've got, Doc. You've got to at least try."

Doc scratched his head, making his hair wave like tall white grass in the breeze again. "Well, I must admit, your case really puzzles me, Jesse."

"I hate to hear that, because if you don't know what you're doing, I sure don't. I really don't think the Reverend or the sheriff, or even the blacksmith or the barber, would be any good at this, and I'll be damned if I'll ask Deke Marsden."

"Good decision," Doc said with a wink. Then he regained

his professional attitude. "In your case, however, I've been doing some reading, and thinking, and a little praying, too."

"Well, I can't say as I've been doing too much reading, Doc, but the other things, well . . ."

"Jesse, you've got a perfectly good foot with a perfectly good set of toes without any corns or carbuncles, without even an ingrown toenail. The rest of you looks pretty healthy now, too."

"Thanks, Doc. I'm real partial to all of me, too."

Doc shook his head and chuckled just a bit at Jesse's little joke. He was obviously concentrating much harder on what he wanted to tell Jesse.

"I hate like the dickens to chop off a perfectly good foot just because it's attached to a bum leg."

"It all hurts like the devil though."

"It's just this shin injury standing between a perfectly good body and a perfectly good foot," Doc said, more to himself than to Jesse. "Well, let's see what's been happening under this bandage."

Doc was silent as he unwound the strips from Jesse's leg. Jesse could feel his heart beating faster in fear and anticipation. Doc lifted the bandage pad from the wound. Then he just stood there staring for a moment.

"What is it, Doc?" He was just about ready to jump off the table with nervousness.

"Good golly, Jesse!" he exclaimed in a disbelieving whisper.

"What's wrong?" He no longer thought he'd jump off the table. Now he knew he'd pass out and fall off. He leaned forward, trying to see better what the doctor was looking at. He'd hoped living in the preacher's house might count for something. He'd been doing a lot of praying lately, too. But he really wasn't expecting some kind of miraculous healing. Not really.

But he certainly never expected Doc to exclaim, "It looks worse today than it's ever been!"

"Geez, Doc," he said with a laugh that tried very hard to hide his disappointment. He didn't want to cry—not even in front of his doctor. "Don't try to make me feel better. Just tell me the truth."

"The infection was nowhere near this close to the surface the last two times I examined you," he said, peering closer at the wound. With his index finger, he poked the red, swollen edges of the skin.

"Ouch! What's wrong with it? Does this mean it's finally getting worse? Is it spreading? Is it spreading up or down? Does this mean you're definitely going to have to amputate? How much will you have to cut off? Isn't there any way we could just cut out the bad part and leave the good toes?"

"It doesn't make any sense for your consumption—heck, your cold—to clear up and your leg to grow so bad. What have you been doing to it anyway, Jesse?"

"Well, I sure haven't been rubbing mud in it."

"What've you been doing?" Doc repeated, staring at the festering wound.

"Going to church, sitting on the front porch, eating, sleeping." He could hardly tell Doc he'd been trying to talk his wife into making love to him for the first time. Instead he decided to add, "Taking a bath."

"A good hot bath, I guess?" Doc asked.

"A little too hot, if you ask me and my poor butt."

"And when exactly did this nice hot bath take place?"

"Saturday night. Usually I wash at the stand each morning, but I figured for going to church, I ought to do a little more soaking."

Doc nodded. "I see. I see now."

He stood erect and moved toward a tall wooden cabinet with rows and rows of long drawers down the front. He opened one of the drawers and started taking out long, shiny, wicked-looking steel things and holding them up to the bright morning light, then placing them on a shiny tray. Each instrument made a vicious metallic clank as if it just couldn't wait to bite into his flesh. Even the cheery sunshine couldn't make those tools look any more friendly.

"Uh, say, Doc," Jesse asked nervously. "What . . . what are you doing? What are those . . . things, anyway?"

"Jesse," Doc said very slowly without turning away from his cabinet. He continued to put unidentifiable things on the tray. "We've got a little problem here."

"Doc, you might have a little problem. *I've* had a really big problem since 1863, and what you're holding now isn't making me feel as if my problems are going to go away anytime soon."

"Maybe not right now, but I've got a sneaking suspicion they will. They all will."

Jesse refrained from mentioning that unless he could convince Sarah that he really did love her, and wanted to make love to her—and could figure out an easy way to tell her he wasn't going to die after all—all his problems were nowhere near being solved.

Doc began to approach him with his array of instruments. Jesse was trying to figure out if he was well enough to jump off the table and outrun the old doctor. The only thing that gave him any sort of reassurance was the fact that Doc wasn't carrying a bone saw.

Doc was stroking his chin thoughtfully. "You say you had that bath Saturday night?"

"Yes."

"When was your last hot bath before that?"

"Oh, geez!" Jesse raised his hand to his forehead in puzzlement. "You expect me to remember that? It's got to have been shortly before I went into battle. They're not really partial to allowing prisoners of war such luxuries. Even when the war was over, they just doused us off. The doctor still wanted to amputate." Jesse gave a little laugh. "I got my papers, both shoes, and a crutch, and was on the first train out the next morning. I figured if I was going to die, it was going to be on the move, not lying in some filthy bed in some hovel."

All the while Jesse talked, Doc was "hmm-ing" to himself and stroking his chin.

"I'm starting to find a few more pieces of the puzzle falling into place here, Jesse." Doc was nodding and smiling a

very, very small smile of satisfaction. Jesse's heart felt a few
pounds lighter seeing his expression.

"But, Jesse, we've still got a couple of problems here."

Jesse's heart dropped again.

"Even though nothing showed up the first two times I
examined you, I've still got a good suspicion that there's
something in that wound that got in when you were hit and
won't come out. That's why it won't heal up. I'm hoping it
was the hot bath you had the other night that drew whatever
it is closer to the surface, where I just might—and mind you,
I said 'might'—be able to pick it out."

"That sounded real good, Doc, until you got to the 'pick it
out' part."

"Don't worry. You'll pass out long before I'm done."

"That's reassuring," Jesse said with a wide grin. "Don't
you have something that could help? Isn't there something
you can give me so I absolutely don't feel a thing?"

Doc shook his head sadly. "I'm afraid not, Jesse."

"Don't give me that tale, Doc. We're not from the 'Grin-
and-Bear-It School.' I know such things exist. I know there's
chloroform and . . . and nitrous oxide, and . . . and
other doctor-type stuff."

Doc's head was still shaking. Jesse hoped he wouldn't
make himself so dizzy he wouldn't be able to operate accurately.

"Not around here."

"Then where is it? Let's go get some." Jesse was just
about ready to jump off the table and go running down the
street to the pharmacist.

"Even though the war for the Union is over, there's still
fighting going on," Doc explained. "Most of the medicine
still goes to the sick in the East, very little makes its way out
West, and then usually only to the military forts and out-
posts against the Indians." Doc held up an empty brown
bottle and shook it, as if to prove how dry it was inside.
"See, that's the last of my chloroform. I used it on poor Mrs.
Altman when she had such a tough time birthing the twins. I

don't think a whiff of what's left in here will even get you a good catnap."

"What about my laudanum? That's a mighty nice pain-killer, and it sure makes me sleep."

"I don't have much of it, Jesse. You're going to need every bit of it after the operation—whether you keep your leg or not."

Jesse sighed, and he felt his shoulders sag. "Do I at least get to bite a bullet?"

"Sorry, Jesse, I don't have any bullets here," Doc said as he rearranged his instruments on the tray. "I heal them here, I don't shoot them."

"What'll I do, then? Chew on my toenails?"

"Just the ones on the leg I'm not working on."

"Well, Doc," Jesse said, lying down on the table. He closed his eyes tightly and grabbed the edges of the table. "Go ahead and do what you've got to."

Jesse tensed, waiting to feel the sharp probe and scalpel.

"Unless . . ."

Jesse opened his eyes. "Unless what?"

Doc walked over to his cabinet again and opened the door on the bottom half. He withdrew a brown crockery jug.

"Unless we can get you blind, stinking, falling-down drunk. So drunk you'll pass out until morning."

"Geez, Doc. Why didn't you mention that before? Then maybe I wouldn't have minded you unpacking those awful instruments. Geez, if the stuff was strong enough, I wouldn't have even seen them."

"Oh, we won't have any problem there." Doc uncorked the jug and reached for a beaker on a shelf.

Jesse took the beaker and turned it around in his hand. "Unusual glassware you have. What was in this before?"

Doc leaned over to take a sniff, then shrugged. "Probably urine or sulfuric acid." Before Jesse could say anything, Doc poured a bit of the amber liquid out of the jug into the beaker. "Bottoms up, Jesse."

Jesse was quite willing to obey his doctor's orders. As the

glass approached his lips, his eyes began to water. He cautiously sniffed.

"Wow! What the heck is this stuff, Doc?"

"Whiskey."

"From where?"

"From Bob In Pieces."

He knew all about Bob's whiskey, he figured. Bob said it was good. Doc was willing to give it to him. He lifted the glass.

"To your health, Doc."

"No, Jesse. To yours."

He shot back the contents of the glass. His tongue burned, his eyes watered, and his ears rang. "Real smooth," he croaked in a raspy voice. "Oh, ho! Bob was right. He does make a mighty fine whiskey." Jesse stretched out the beaker to Doc. "Pour me another, please."

"Gladly, Jesse. In a minute."

Doc had been chuckling right along with him—until now. Suddenly he grew very serious.

"Jesse, my boy," he said, placing his hand comfortingly on Jesse's shoulder. "I haven't known you long, but I like you a lot. I got a lot of respect for both you and your lovely wife."

He drew in a deep breath. "So, I want to tell you this before you get too drunk to know what's going on. I want to make sure you completely understand one very important thing. And I hope you won't blame me afterward, whatever happens."

Jesse opened his eyes. "What's that?"

"I'm going to do my best to disturb as little tissue as possible and still examine the wound thoroughly. I hope we'll get out whatever's bothering you." He drew in a deep breath and continued. "On the other hand, you must understand that if I find *any* evidence of gangrene . . ."

Jesse's stomach turned. He knew exactly what Doc was going to say next, and he was powerless to stop him.

"If any uncontrollable bleeding begins, I have no way of stopping it. I'm going to have to amputate immediately—no questions asked."

Jesse stared at the floor and bit his lips so that he wouldn't cry. He must've waited so long to respond that Doc was getting worried.

"Did you hear me, Jesse?" he asked. "Do you understand completely what I've just told you?"

Jesse nodded.

"Do you want a little time to think about this, in case you want to change your mind?"

Jesse shook his head.

"I just don't want you waking up with one leg and saying I never told you."

Jesse lifted his head and turned his biggest smile on Dr. Hanford. "Well, Doc, I've just been putting it off as long as possible, but I guess I can't put it off any longer. And I guess I've really been expecting this for a long, long time. I don't mean to disappoint you, but if I wake up with only one leg, you won't be able to shout 'Surprise!' "

"You're hopeless," Doc said, shaking his head. "Don't you take anything seriously?"

"If I didn't, I wouldn't be here, Doc." He held out his empty beaker. "Now, pour me another, please, and let's get on with this."

"Jesse." The voice called to him from the darkness. "Jesse, wake up."

Funny, I didn't know I was asleep. He giggled.

"Jesse, come on now. Wake up."

He felt a gentle tapping on his cheek that grew more insistent each time the person slapping him called his name.

If he could've lifted his arms, he'd have smacked the annoying son of a gun. If he could've stood up, he'd have kicked the irritating oaf. One the other hand, he wasn't sure if he had one leg or two. He'd look really stupid if he tried to kick the fellow and fell flat on his butt. On the other hand, the way his head was spinning, he'd probably fall anyway.

He started to giggle. The tapping on his cheek wasn't that annoying. He figured he'd stay right where he was.

"Time to get up and go home."

Home? The word penetrated the dizzy fog he was in. Home meant Sarah, her soft lips and her loving care. He had to get home to Sarah. When she saw how drunk he was, she was going to be really angry!

"Where . . . where's my laudanum? Where's my crutch?" he heard himself say.

At least, he thought it was himself speaking. He could tell his lips were moving, but the raspy croaking didn't sound at all like his voice. Worse yet, while he was sleeping, somebody had sneaked in and stuffed his mouth full of cotton. It sure felt and tasted that way.

His head hurt too much for him to open his eyes and find out if there was anyone else in the room with him.

"Laudanum won't do you any good for what you're suffering from." The man sounded like Doc. Jesse wondered if Doc was as drunk as he was. No, Doc never drank. If he did, there wouldn't be any of Bob In Pieces' good whiskey left for his patients.

Jesse decided to try to open just one eye. Then, if he saw anything worth looking at, he'd try to open both of them. He lifted one eyebrow, but the eyelid beneath it wouldn't cooperate and remained closed. He sighed and relaxed against the table. Oh, well, he'd tried.

"Come on, Jesse! Up, up." Doc seized his arm and began alternately to pull on Jesse's arm and slap his cheek. "Go home. Sarah's waiting for you."

Doc's white hair was waving almost orange in the afternoon sunlight. Had he really been unconscious that long?

"You're drunk, Doc!"

"I am not."

"Then why are you wobbling in front of me?"

"I think it's your eyes that are wobbling."

"Oh, yeah." Jesse laughed again.

Doc held out a more traditional-looking cup with a real handle and a real saucer beneath. Steam rose from the contents. That must be the coffee he'd smelled.

"Thanks, but right now I'd rather have the laudanum."

"Not now."

"What . . . what'd you do to me so I can't have my laudanum?"

"Don't get upset. You're just a good old-fashioned drunk." Doc chuckled.

Jesse kept laughing. "Oh, boy! Is Sarah going to be angry!"

"I don't think so. Here, drink this." He offered him the coffee again.

But Jesse still had a million questions to ask. "Why does my leg hurt? It wasn't drinking."

Doc put the coffee cup down on the examining table and held up a small jar instead. Inside the jar was a splinter of wood and bark about an inch long.

"What's that? Do I have to eat it?"

Doc chuckled. "No, I don't think you're going to want this little monster in your body ever again."

"In my body?"

"Look down, Jesse," Doc told him, gesturing toward the end of the examining table.

"I can't. My head hurts too much. Bob In Pieces should be shot for making that stuff!"

"He has been, but somehow he always manages to pull through. I swear, he's one tough old bird! Now, look down, Jesse. Look at your feet."

"Feet," Jesse repeated as his head seemed to be clearing. "Feet—as in two of them?"

"That's right, Jesse," Doc announced proudly, lifting the jar. The little piece of wood rattled against the glass sides. "You owe all your troubles to that prison guard and this little piece of wood he managed to leave in your leg when he hit you. You're one lucky dog to have held off amputation this long. When I probed around, this poked its head out. I grabbed hold and pulled. Son of a gun if it didn't all come out, with a load of putrefaction that had probably been storing up. . . ."

"That's nice. Can I throw up now, Doc? I really don't think my stomach's in much condition . . ."

"A little too much of Bob's good whiskey?" Doc patted Jesse sympathetically on the shoulder.

"No. A little too much of your gory details."

Jesse managed to lift his head from the pillow just enough to see two bare feet that looked exactly like his peeking out from beneath the clean white sheet.

"You're fooling me, Doc," he said. "You really cut off the leg and just stuck it back under there. When I go to stand up, I'm going to leave one leg on the table and fall flat on my face."

"Jesse, you are one sick son of a gun!"

"No, Doc. Not anymore. I'm just one happy man."

"You're still drunk, too. Anyway, if I'd done that, the toenails would be blue."

"Thanks. I didn't really need to know that. Can I throw up *now*?"

"No. First I want to see if you can sit up. Slowly and carefully now. You'd be dizzy anyway from the surgery. I don't want to make any predictions about what you'll do after drinking as much as you did."

In spite of his spinning head, and his uncontrollable urge to laugh, Jesse managed to sit up without falling off the table.

After making sure Jesse wasn't going to go tumbling, Doc offered him the cup of coffee again in a way that allowed for no refusal. Some of the steam had wafted away. Jesse figured it was safe to drink without scalding himself.

"You're going to drink this coffee and try to sober up a little more before I send you home."

"Home." Jesse thought that word had never sounded so good. His head was full of plans to go to Sarah and Patsy, to get a job, to someday buy a plot of land and build a home for the three—or four or five—of them, if he could convince Sarah.

"That's right, Jesse. Home. Home for as long as you live, and thanks to that hot bath and a little help from Above, you're going to be living a lot longer than you thought you would when you arrived in Cottonwood."

Jesse gave a whoop of glee, spilling some of the coffee onto the table and the floor.

"Go home and tell your wife—and live happily ever after."

"Oh, yeah. Somehow, I've got to figure out how to tell Sarah." He hoped Doc didn't notice the uncertainty in his voice about how he was going to break the news to Sarah that he was going to live a good long time. Maybe Doc would just blame his strange voice on Bob In Pieces' potent brew.

"She's bound to wonder where you've been all day."

"Oh, geez," Jesse said as he managed to sit up. "What am I going to tell her?"

"What did you tell her when you left the house?"

"That I was going for a walk with Bob In Pieces."

Doc looked at him askance. "You and Bob going for a walk?" He started to chuckle. "And she believed you?"

"I guess. She didn't ask any more questions."

Doc shook his head. "I thought she was the smart one in the family."

Jesse'd been laughing so much, he didn't know if he was laughing at this latest joke or at one Doc had told him a couple of minutes ago.

Doc eased Jesse to his feet. He handed him his crutch.

"I thought you said I was all better, Doc."

Doc held out the crutch again.

Jesse was still trying to refuse until he actually put his weight on the injured leg. "Yow!" Yellow sparks shot through his blackening vision. When his head cleared again, he muttered, "I thought you said . . ."

"You were pretty well passed out, Jesse," Doc explained. "You don't know the amount of probing I had to do."

"I don't want to. I don't want to throw up."

"That leg's still going to be sore for a few days."

Jesse took the crutch.

"Need some help getting home?"

Jesse hiccuped and continued to laugh. "No. I think I can manage."

Doc stood at his door, watching Jesse. He laughed until he reached the general store, where he started to sing a song that Doc knew he'd never learned in church.

Sarah put down the paring knife and the potato she was peeling for dinner, and listened. She turned to Mildred. "What is that horrible noise?"

"What noise?" Her sister looked up from the chicken in the big cast-iron pan that she was concentrating on frying. Then she tilted her head and listened. "Oh, no. It sounds like some of the nasty little boys in town have tied two cats together again."

"No, no. It's deeper than that." Sarah dried her hands on her apron and headed for the vestibule. "It sounds like a man's voice."

"Sort of."

"It sounds like a man who's very, very happy—"

"I can just figure out why, too. Oh, for Pete's sake!" Mildred complained as she followed her. "Don't tell me Wally Bender's drunk again!"

"Who?"

"Wally Bender. What a mindless dolt!"

"Is that why you haven't introduced him to Jesse or me?" Sarah teased.

Mildred frowned, obviously puzzled. "On the other hand, I don't recall Wally being able to sing that well."

The voice Sarah heard wasn't that wonderful. Wally must really sound like two cats yowling.

"I declare, if that miserable sot knocks down my picket fence and piddles on my rhododendron bush again—in broad daylight, too—I won't wait for the sheriff to haul him off to jail to sober up. I'll shoot him myself."

"Oh, dear, Mildred. It sounds like he's coming closer. Should we get the Reverend?"

"What good will he do? He'll only think it's time to eat, and then I'll have him underfoot."

"Should we get the gun, then?"

Mildred ran to the front window and pulled back the

curtain. She shook her head and started laughing. "Well, Sarah, I have good news and then some bad news."

Sarah couldn't figure out why her sister was chuckling. "What did you say? What do you mean?"

She'd find out herself if Mildred would let her near the window. But Mildred always was one to be sure she had the exclusive rights to reporting all gossip. Sarah wasn't about to open the front door until she knew who was out there and why he was making that awful noise, and until Mildred had the gun in her hand.

"The good news is it's not Wally Bender," Mildred said.

"If that's good news, why do you sound so disappointed?"

"Because I'd really like to shoot that miserable drunk someday and bury him under my rhododendron bush."

"Oh, Mildred! What a thing for the preacher's wife to say!"

"You don't know Wally Bender. My rhododendron bush never has been the same."

"But what's the bad news?"

"Well, Sarah," Mildred said, turning to her with a smug grin on her face, "the miserable drunk who's coming toward our house is your husband."

"Oh, no!" Sarah yanked the door open and rushed outside.

"If he goes one step near my rhododendron, I'm getting the gun," Mildred called after her.

It was Jesse, all right. It looked like Jesse. Although he usually limped on his crutch, at least he could walk in a straight line. He didn't wobble and weave when he walked as he was doing now.

He sounded like Jesse, too, and yet he was somehow different—frighteningly different. His voice was raspy, and he slurred his words. She didn't think her husband knew the words to those kinds of songs. She really hoped Patsy was still napping through this horrible noise so she wouldn't pick up these words as quickly as she had "Yankee Doodle Dandy."

"What on earth happened to you?" Sarah demanded, rushing up to him.

Jesse only laughed.

"I'm used to you making jokes constantly. I'm not used to you laughing out loud at jokes you're telling nobody but yourself."

"Then I'll share." He tried to lean closer to her. "There was this traveling salesman . . ."

Sarah grabbed his arm and tugged. She hoped that would at least make him shut up. It didn't. It only stopped his joke. "What do you think you're doing?" she demanded angrily, trying to drown out his singing.

He only paused long enough to answer, "Singing," then continued his song.

"Hush up! Everybody in town'll think you've gone crazy."

"Hey, at least I don't go running out of the church naked."

"You couldn't run anywhere now if your life depended on it."

"Oh, but I will, my dear. I will."

"What in the world are you talking about?"

Mildred, who had approached at a slightly slower pace, seized his other arm in spite of the crutch. "Oh, merciful heavens, Sarah! He reeks! He *positively* reeks of whiskey!"

"That's right, Mildred," he said. "I'm drunker than a weasel in a whiskey barrel."

"Don't you talk to me, mister," Mildred scolded. She started pulling him forcefully along. "I don't talk to drunks and scalawags who leave their wives at home while they go out wasting their hard-earned money on demon rum!"

"Oh, Jesse! How could you?" Sarah wailed.

Mildred sniffed around him. "Pretty well, if you ask me."

"It was really, really easy," Jesse said between hiccups and laughs. "All I did was get some of Bob In Pieces' whiskey—"

"Oh, I should've known!" Mildred declared. "That man never was worth his salt."

"But he sure is worth his whiskey," Jesse said, and started laughing again.

"But you told me you weren't a drinking man," Sarah said.

"And you told me you wouldn't mind me having a drink or two from time to time."

"You had a little more than two drinks!"

"Yeah, but I haven't done this for a long time, so I figured I had a lot of catching up to do all at once."

"I'm not laughing, Jesse. This is not funny." She glared at him.

"I'd really like to bash this crutch over your hard head," Mildred scolded. "The entire street can hear you. Now shut up!"

"I'd listen to her if I were you," Sarah told him. "She shot the last drunk who came through her yard."

She knew that wasn't the honest-to-goodness truth, but Jesse wasn't exactly worth the truth now, she figured angrily. She was grateful Jesse at least kept enough of his senses about him to finally shut up.

"We've got to get him inside, quick," Mildred said. "I just saw a couple of curtains pull back. Who knows what the neighbors are saying? Who knows what they'll have stretched this out to by tomorrow morning? And by this coming Sunday—well, all I can say is, Heaven help us all!"

Sarah and Mildred managed to get him across the lawn, up the three small porch steps, and into the vestibule. He seemed to be quite willing to go where they were taking him until they tried to take him into the kitchen. Then he started heading for the stairs.

"Where do you think you're going?" Mildred asked, following him.

"Bed."

"Oh, no, you're not." She swung him around, away from the stairs. "You're going to sit in that kitchen and drink as much coffee as you did whiskey. That ought to sober you up."

"Oh, no, I'm not," Jesse said, swinging around to the

stairs again. He managed to untangle himself from Mildred's and Sarah's grip. "I'm going right to bed."

"Bed? It's only six o'clock in the evening."

"My dear wife, I'm drunk. My leg hurts like hell. My head hurts just about as bad. My stomach's churning. If I don't get to bed soon, I'm either going to pass out on the floor and you'll have to carry me upstairs, or I'm going to throw up."

Jesse had completely stopped singing, and he wasn't laughing as much. The golden glow of alcohol was already fading to a dismal brown hangover. Sarah hoped he had a whale of a headache tomorrow, just to teach him a lesson.

"He's got a point, Sarah," Mildred told her. "The monthly meeting of the Cottonwood Methodist Ladies Evangelical Temperance and Missionary Soul-Saving Spiritual Aid Bible Society is here tonight. It really wouldn't look too good to have him lying sprawled out in the middle of the vestibule where the ladies would have to step over him, not to mention having to clean up anything else."

"Brew some fresh coffee, Mildred, please, and make it really strong," Sarah requested. "I'll make sure he stays upstairs the rest of the night and doesn't ruin your meeting."

"Thanks, Sarah."

If Sarah hadn't been so upset and worried about Jesse's unusual state, she'd have been surprised that Mildred had actually thanked her.

As Sarah followed Jesse up the stairs, she heard Mildred complaining below. "Oh, I'm going to have to boil some cinnamon just to get the smell of demon rum out of this house!"

Jesse sat on the edge of the bed, unbuttoning his shirt with shaking fingers. He looked up at Sarah with bleary, bloodshot eyes. "Do you think you could give me a hand here?"

"No." She closed the door behind her and leaned against it, her arms crossed tightly over her breasts. "You got yourself into this situation. You get yourself out of it."

"I helped you out of your situation."

"That was different," she said, and tightly clamped her lips shut. That should be a real good indication to him that that subject was closed.

"I . . . I really could use a hand," he said, trying to look very appealingly up at her.

"I'll give you a hand. I'd like to take my hand to your face," she told him angrily. "Or my foot to your rear end!"

"What'd I do now?"

"It's not just your lungs and your leg that are ruined. You're brain isn't working anymore either."

"What'd I do?" he asked, still struggling with the buttons. "I really would like to get some sleep, Sarah. Couldn't you help me out of these clothes now and scold me later?"

She stepped closer and glared at him.

"Didn't I tell you on the train that in such a small town the preacher's family, even his sister-in-law and brother-in-law, have to set a good example for the townspeople? What kind of example are you, coming home drunk in the middle of the afternoon?"

"A bad example," Jesse replied with a laugh.

"Did you have to sing those filthy songs so loud?"

"That's the way I learned them."

"I'm not laughing, Jesse. For once, all your charm can't change what's happened, or cajole me out of being angry with you. You've embarrassed me and humiliated my sister and her husband. I married you to give my daughter a *good* name—not a drunk's!"

Jesse just sort of gave up on the stubborn buttons. He couldn't concentrate on them and Sarah at the same time. And right now he really didn't feel like concentrating on either one of them.

He flopped backward into the bed. He didn't even bother to take his shoes off once he was comfortably established in bed.

"I know we agreed to a drink or two from time to time, but this is taking a little too much advantage of my good nature."

He closed his eyes. It hurt too much to put up with the sunlight. He wished Sarah'd shut up. His ears hurt too much to try to listen. His nose hurt when he tried to breathe. His fingernails hurt as they grew.

"I never bargained to take care of a drunk, Jesse," she continued to scold.

"You know, if my teeth didn't hurt so much, I'd tell you you were starting to sound just like your sister."

He held his pounding head in his hands. He wished he had another pair of hands that could hold his churning stomach. The smell of fresh-brewed coffee wafting up from the kitchen didn't help any. His leg ached, but then so did every other part of his body.

"As God is my witness, I'll never drink again," Jesse mumbled.

"Am I supposed to believe you?"

"Would you believe me any more if I said it in church? Would you like to get the Reverend in here with a stack of Bibles? Will you believe me then? I swear to you, Sarah, you will never see me take another drink of hard liquor again as long as I live!"

The way his head hurt, this time he really meant it.

But the worst pain of all was when Sarah stood at his bedside and told him, "I thought I could trust you, Jesse. You may not know this, but it's hard for me to . . . to trust most men. I'd really started to trust and . . . and to love you, Jesse. But now? What you've done today just spoils it all."

Thirteen

Run, Sarah! Run!
The footsteps followed her in the darkness.
Faster, Sarah! Faster!
Her legs wouldn't allow her to run, and yet all she could seem to do was keep on running.

The thud of the footsteps drew closer in the darkness. The sound turned into the feel of hands—big, hard, rough hands that grabbed at her and threw her to the ground. They tore at her clothes. A big body, hard and heavy, lay on top of her. More big hands held her down. Lots of hands. Lots of big, hard, heavy bodies.

She screamed.

In the light of the full moon, Jesse could easily find Sarah this time. She was huddled in the corner again. In spite of the whiskey still pounding inside his head, he was at her side immediately. He tried to hold her in his arms, to comfort her, to stop her from shaking.

"Let me go! Let me go! Oh, for the love of God, have mercy! Let me go!" She was crying but did nothing to fight against his embrace. She just kept trying to curl herself up into a little ball in the corner.

"Sarah, wake up! It's me, Jesse." He sat down on the floor beside her. He tried to reach out to enfold her in his arms, but she just cringed and tried to pull away from him.

"No! Oh, stop!"

"Sarah! You're dreaming again. Wake up. It's only a dream."

She opened her eyes and looked around.

"Oh, thank God! It's only you, Jesse."

"Geez, don't sound so happy to see me," he said with a little grin.

She drew in a deep breath and tried to stop crying, but the tears continued to roll down her cheeks. She was ready to be comforted, but she wasn't ready yet to snap out of the aftereffects of the nightmare.

Jesse at last managed to slide his arms around her. She collapsed into his embrace. He placed his hand on the back of her head, gently stroking her disheveled hair. Gently he leaned her head to rest on his shoulder. He was rocking her, as if he were comforting a little child.

"It was just a dream, Sarah," he tried to assure her. "A bad, bad dream—but it's over. It's not real."

"Yes, it is," she murmured. She placed both hands over her face and began to cry even harder.

He stopped rocking for just a second, surprised by her conviction, then he continued. "Some dreams can seem very real. It's especially hard when it's a nightmare."

"This *was* real," she whispered. Her voice, barely audible through her clenched fingers over her face, was hoarse and trembling.

He knew from the first moment he'd seen her that she was a pampered Southern belle fallen on hard times. He didn't try very hard not to sound cajoling. "What horrible thing could've happened to you?"

He felt her pull away from him sharply. Remorseful, he didn't blame her. Who could know what secrets people hid in their past?

"I'm sorry, Sarah. I shouldn't have said that. I just can't—

I don't want to—picture anything bad happening to you. What was so horrible that it gives you such nightmares?"

"You promised not to ask about the past."

"Yes, I did. And you promised not to ask about mine."

She nodded.

"You won't have to ask. I was born and raised in Philadelphia—not one of the better neighborhoods. I was an only child. My parents had aspirations for me, and so did I. I worked hard for a carpenter until I learned the trade and set up my own shop with very respectable—and wealthy, I might add—patrons. My parents passed away, but they'd been very proud of me."

"I am, too," she whispered.

"When the war broke out, I joined the army. At first I spent a lot of time building bridges and fixing broken wagon wheels, but I was itching to get into battle. What a fool! I guess I wasn't a very good soldier. I got caught and spent three years in the prisoner-of-war camp at Oglethorpe outside of Macon."

"That doesn't make you a bad soldier."

Jesse felt her hand slowly disengage from the tight bundle in which she held herself. She placed her hand on his arm and let it rest there. Even in the middle of her own distress, she was the kind of woman who needed to comfort others.

"No, it just means I'm really good at being in the wrong place at the wrong time." He gave a rueful chuckle.

He hoped his light banter would calm her. He hoped that his honesty would make her trust him again just a little more. Then maybe she'd be able to confide in him the horrible nightmare that made her wake up screaming. Maybe by talking about it, she could dispel its horror.

"I'd just been mustered out when you saw me board the train."

Sarah sat, silently cuddled in his arms.

"There now. See what deep dark secrets I've been hiding?"

"How . . . how did your parents die?"

"Cholera."

"I'm so sorry."

"What did you think? That I'd axed them to death?" He grew serious again. "I'm grateful I was one of the lucky ones to survive."

"I'm glad for that. Were . . . were you ever married?"

"Nope."

"I can't believe all the girls weren't after you," she told him.

"Thanks for the compliment. I didn't notice them if they were, and none of the ladies I knew really appealed to me. I guess I was always too busy working."

"What happened to your business when you joined the army?"

"I closed up shop. I figured if I died I hadn't lost anything, and if I lived I could always open another or get a job with somebody else."

Sarah nodded.

"What about you?"

"You said you wouldn't ask."

"I'm not asking. I've just told you everything you could ever want to know about me. Pretty boring, isn't it?"

"No, not really," she said. She leaned a little closer to him. "And you haven't told me everything. I want to know who your friends were, how you liked school, what was your favorite Christmas present, if you ever had the measles . . . or any pets. . . ."

"I want to know the same things about you. But I'll tell you all that later. Right now, I'm hoping you'll follow my good example—remember, you told me I had to serve as a good example—and volunteer to tell me just a little about yourself."

"Oh, no." She shook her head adamantly.

"It's pretty strange loving a woman I don't know anything about."

She looked into his eyes. They were deep blue in the patches of darkness and moonlight through the clouds, and searching for something he must think was very important.

"You're looking for something I can't give you, Jesse," she warned him.

"Yes, you can, Sarah. Or do I have to ask Mildred? I'm sure she'll tell me all kinds of . . ."

"Mildred's . . . five years older than I am, you rotten blackmailer," she began with a little chuckle.

He was glad to hear some lightness return to her voice. "I'm sure she'd be glad to know that was the first thing you wanted to tell me." He tried to hug her closer to him, but he felt her stiffen. He eased his embrace.

"My mother died shortly after I was born. My father raised us with the help of his spinster sister, Myrtle. When he passed away several years later, Aunt Myrtle continued to raise us."

"I'll bet you were spoiled rotten, both of you."

"Yes."

"I'll bet you had a mammy and servants—"

"Daddy had slaves on the plantation, and Aunt Myrtle had a few house servants. I really loved our mammy—but her name was Amalie. We called her 'Amalie,' not 'Mammy,' because that was her name."

"I stand corrected. I'll bet she made sure you never had to lift a finger."

"Not . . . not when I was small."

"That doesn't sound like the kind of life that would lead to nightmares."

"It wasn't—then."

"What happened, Sarah?"

"You said you wouldn't—"

"I'm asking, Sarah." His voice wasn't frivolously inquisitive. It was deep and firm. "I'm your husband and I truly love you. I care about the things that make you happy and the things that trouble you. I can't stay in the dark about this any longer. I *want* to know."

He held her tightly with one arm. She struggled against him, but he held her close.

"Please don't struggle, Sarah," he begged. "I'm having

enough trouble with Bob In Pieces' whiskey without having any trouble from you."

She still squirmed in his arms, trying to escape.

With his other hand, he tucked his crooked index finger under her chin and lifted her face until she had to look him in the eyes.

"I'm breaking our bargain," he declared emphatically. "You can kick me out of here tomorrow, I don't care. But tonight I'm still your husband. I love you no matter what—I always will—and I *have* to know why you cry in your sleep. I *have* to know why you won't let me touch you."

She struggled to rise, but he held her fast.

"I can't stand to hold you like this and feel you fighting against me. It's driving me crazy to want you so—and from the way you look at me sometimes I believe you want me, too. Don't you, Sarah?"

His words made her stop struggling against him, but she still wouldn't completely relax.

"Tell me to my face you don't want me, Sarah."

She looked him straight in the eye and shook her head. Jesse's heart thudded into the pit of his stomach.

"I won't tell you that, Jesse. I can't lie to you and tell you I don't . . . don't have feelings, longings for you."

Jesse's heart rose again. He felt a tingling stirring throughout his entire body, just to think she had tender feelings for him.

"But you won't let me touch you, Sarah. You barely allowed me to kiss you. Anytime I try to get any closer, you run away. Sarah, I love you so much—and you know it. But you still won't let me near you!" He felt so frustrated he thought he would burst.

She said nothing.

"Is it just me? I know you've turned down all the other men who asked you to marry them—or that Mildred thinks you should marry. Is there something about me you find repulsive?"

She shook her head.

"The cough I used to have. The bad leg. Do I have bad

breath and body odor? Maybe you don't like the color of my eyes or hair. If that's the problem, I'll shave my head and wear dark glasses."

"No." She tried not to giggle with the image this brought to mind.

"Sarah, don't you know by now I'd do anything for you? Marry you, give Patsy my name, live with you, fight Deke Marsden for you, put up with Meddling Mildred . . . *Anything!*"

She nodded.

"Then why do you reject me when you know how much I care for you?"

He drew in a deep breath before speaking again. After he said what he had to say, he might find himself sleeping on the back porch after all, and she might show him that the quickest way to get there was out the window—but he had to say what was gnawing away at him.

"Why do you reject me when you didn't reject Patsy's father?"

"That's enough!" she declared, and began to struggle against him again. "I'm not answering any more of your questions."

"You haven't answered any of them yet—at least not the important ones."

She continued to struggle, but he wouldn't release her.

"You can squirm and scream and yell all you want until you wake Mildred and the Reverend, and have them come banging down the door demanding to know what's wrong and threatening to call the sheriff. You can smack me in the head if you want, or kick me anywhere else, too—although I'd really rather you didn't. I'm not about to let you go this time—or ever. Was it Deke you fell in love with?"

"No! I . . . wasn't in love with anyone."

"Why do you always seem to have these bad dreams after you see Deke?"

"I don't."

"Yes, you do. I've kept track."

"I . . . I don't know."

"Is he Patsy's father?"

"No!"

"Who is?"

She didn't answer.

"Who is he, Sarah?" he demanded.

The more she refused to answer, the angrier he was getting. He wasn't angry with her so much as with the man—whoever he was—for backing out on all his obligations to Sarah and Patsy. He was angry with his own frustrations and fears of inadequacy. If she was still in love with Patsy's father, could she ever completely love him?

"Why did you let him and not me?"

"I didn't," she protested.

"Well, you had to get pregnant somehow! Did you love him, Sarah? Are you still in love with him? Is that why you can't bear to have me touch you—because I'm not him?"

"No! I didn't love him. I . . . I hate him!"

"So, it *was* Deke."

"No!"

"I can't believe you're the kind of woman who'd give her body to a man to whom she hadn't given her heart."

"I'm not!"

"Then why did you make love with him and you won't even touch me?"

"Because I . . ." Her voice began strong and angry, then dwindled away to barely a whisper. "Because I . . . I didn't have any choice in the matter. And it wasn't making love. Don't *ever* call it making love."

He frowned, trying to understand. Cautiously he began. "You were . . . ?"

"I was . . . attacked."

"You were . . ." He couldn't bring himself to say the word. Naming it made all too real the fact that Sarah had been raped.

She nodded.

His jaw dropped open. He felt his insides melting with the shock of learning the horror and pain she'd been through.

He thought his arms would go limp, but he didn't want

her to think he was rejecting her now. He held her tightly, and she finally began to cling to him desperately as she started to cry again. He reached up to wipe away her tears—not of fear—but finally tears of release. He wished he could wipe away her hurt just as easily.

He stroked her soft hair to comfort her, but the feel of her against him comforted him, too. She could've been killed or driven mad. She was lucky to be alive. He was grateful he still had her well and whole to love.

"How could this have happened to you? Oh, my poor, precious love."

"I was going out to get Aunt Myrtle some food," she tried to explain. After all her struggles, her voice was flat and devoid of any emotion. It was almost as if she were simply reciting words in another language that had no meaning for her personally. "All our slaves left. Even Amalie. She was getting old, and her son and his family were going out West and she wanted to be with them. I don't know why they all left. We treated them well."

"But a slave's still a slave. I can understand their need to be free. I know what it's like to be imprisoned some place you don't want to be."

She nodded. "We both do, don't we? I can understand that now, but at the time it was hard for me to learn to do all the things I'd always had someone else do for me. It took a while to learn how to cook, how to choose food that was still edible, how to find a store that had anything worth buying. It was late when I finally found something. I'd left Aunt Myrtle home all alone, so I took a shortcut through an alleyway."

"Was Deke waiting for you?"

"No."

"He's always following you around Cottonwood, pestering you. I've heard him talk about wanting to marry you. I know you're afraid of him, but there's no need to protect him if he did wrong."

"No, no. It wasn't Deke."

"You can tell me if it was. I'll get revenge for you finally. I'll . . ."

"Will you listen to me, hardhead!" She grabbed his arm and gave it a little shake. "It wasn't Deke. He left Savannah right before the war started. Most folks said he'd left and took his mother with him so he wouldn't have to serve in the army."

"You didn't think a coward like him would stick around for the battles, did you?" Jesse asked.

"There were three or four men, I guess. They all wore uniforms, but none of them dressed alike. I couldn't tell if they were Union or Confederate."

"Renegades?"

"I . . . I guess."

"And one of them is Patsy's father."

"I hate to think so," she said, hanging her head. Then she lifted it proudly. "But she's *my* daughter, and I love her. Even though . . . even though how I got her was horrible, I love her. I'm raising her the best I know how. She'll grow up to be a lady, but it could've all turned out so differently." Then she hung her head in shame. "I never should've gone out alone."

"You had to. You didn't have anyone to go with you."

"I shouldn't have gone out so late in the evening."

"You couldn't help how time slips away from us all."

"I shouldn't have taken a shortcut."

"You were worried about leaving your invalid aunt alone for a long time."

"I . . . I could've tried harder to fight them off. I should've screamed louder, hit harder, picked up a rock, kicked, bit. But I was so afraid they'd hit me harder and knock my teeth out. It was bad enough they tore my clothes. I didn't have too many left, you know. I . . . I don't know. At times like that, people think of the strangest things, don't they? I just keep thinking I should've done something to fight them off or they wouldn't have been able to . . . It was all my fault."

She started to sniff again. Drops of tears were trickling down her cheeks.

"What? Wait a minute," Jesse said to stop her monologue. "No, no, no. You don't actually believe that, do you?"

"Yes," she answered.

He was truly listening to everything she said, and he heard the small uncertainty in her voice. She probably didn't even know it was there.

"You don't actually believe there was something a tiny little lady like you could've done to fight off three big soldiers?"

"There had to have been something!"

"Like what? Throw rocks or mud pies? Call them nasty names and shock them to death?" He picked up her small hand and kissed it. "Punch them in the nose with this? Be sensible, Sarah!"

"But . . . but Aunt Myrtle always said, 'A lady should choose death before dishonor!' " she protested. She held one finger pointing straight up in imitation of her aunt's sage pronouncements.

"Well, in general I'd say she was right."

"What?" she exclaimed.

"On the other hand, I don't exactly think—and you said so yourself—you didn't have any choice in the matter. Did you? I mean, they didn't exactly ask your permission, did they?"

"No, but . . ."

"The fact that you were upset just now because I agreed with Aunt Myrtle shows you know in your heart she was wrong. You had no choice, Sarah. There was nothing you or any other woman in those circumstances could've done to stop them. And, yes, you are still a lady. I think you're very much a lady."

He held her more closely, but she pulled away even now.

"Sarah, don't run away from me anymore. You know I'm not like those other men. You know I won't hurt you."

She shook her head. "I'm still afraid. It hurts, Jesse. It hurts more than you'll ever know."

"Excuse me, I thought I was pretty much the authority on pain around here."

She sniffed again, and he felt the muscles of her arms tighten.

"No, you're right." He gave her a small apologetic hug and gently kissed the top of her head. "I'm sorry I even tried to make a joke about it. I'll never know the pain and degradation you've known, my love. I wish you had never known it, either."

"Do you know what the worst pain was?"

"No. You don't have to tell me if you don't want to."

He didn't think *he* wanted to know. It was hard enough for him to imagine those three bastards—may they all rot in the hottest fires of hell—doing what they did to the woman he loved. He didn't want to have to hear about it from her own lips.

"The worst part was afterward."

Jesse was surprised.

"I didn't . . . I *couldn't* tell anyone—except Aunt Myrtle, who saw me coming home all . . . torn and bloody—"

"Don't." Jesse's stomach turned. He didn't want to stop her from finally opening her soul to him. There were just some things he didn't want to have to hear, didn't want to have to picture in his mind.

"After I figured out I was in a family way, after I began to show, I couldn't go shopping or walk down the street, I couldn't even go to church without hearing nasty whispers behind my back, or catching the dirty looks all those very proper Southern ladies threw me, or the complete cuts my former friends gave me. Then, of course, there were those wonderful people who never stoop to gossip and subterfuge. They just insulted me to my face. Whore, harlot . . . and some folks used *really* bad language. So we moved to what was left of the plantation outside of town."

A small, proud smile lit her face. "I delivered Patsy myself."

"You're kidding!"

"Who was there to help me? Aunt Myrtle was in no condition to help. The slaves had all left, and I don't blame them now—although I really could've used Amalie's help."

"I wish to God you never had to experience what you did because . . . well, because love really can be a very beautiful thing . . . when it's done right . . . between two people who really care for each other."

She shook her head. "I don't think so."

He held her closer and whispered in her ear. "Would you allow me, Sarah? If you're willing—only if you're truly willing—I'd really like to prove to you that you're so very, very wrong—if you'll let me."

"Oh, Jesse, I . . . I'd . . . I want to tell you yes, that I'll be a wife to you in more than name, but I can't. I just can't!"

She was beginning to pull herself into a tight little ball again. Jesse backed away from her just a little, just enough so she would know he'd never force her.

"I really love you, Sarah. You know I do."

"Yes."

"I want us to have a good marriage."

"So do I."

"Do you love me, Sarah?"

She was silent for a moment, and Jesse began to worry that she'd only been nice to him because he'd gotten her out of an untenable situation, and because she thought he was dying. Maybe she didn't really love him after all.

"Yes, Jesse," she replied very slowly. "I believe I really do love you."

In spite of the seriousness of the moment, Jesse couldn't help but smile like a madman.

"I know better than to try to hug you. But you know I can't think of too many other things I'd rather do right now."

She lifted her head and looked directly into his eyes. "Yes, I do," she boldly asserted. "I really do love you, Jesse Taylor. I think I've loved you since the first time I saw you on that train, too. It's just taken me a little longer to realize it."

Jesse rose to his feet. He extended his hand down to Sarah, to help her rise.

"I think we need to continue our conversation somewhere a lot more comfortable than the floor." He reached back and rubbed his rear. "Kind of reminds you of those hard train benches, doesn't it?"

She placed her hand in his and allowed him to help her to her feet. She followed him willingly to sit on the edge of the bed. He sat beside her, still keeping her hand in his.

He was glad to feel she wasn't shaking anymore. She was smiling as she recalled their first meeting.

"In spite of your illness, I could see the man you'd been— strong, virile, handsome. I love the man inside, too. In spite of everything you've been through, you still look at life with joy, a sense of humor so few people possess. It's not the kind of humor that ridicules others. It's just a sense of joy in living."

"Well, I guess once a fellow's survived a prisoner-of-war camp, anywhere else looks pretty good, and he's just glad to be there."

"You've helped me to see, in spite of everything, that I can look at life with that same sense of joy and humor—if I'm with you."

Suddenly she laughed and held her hands to her cheeks. "Oh, my goodness! Do I sound like some sort of silly old lady who writes bad poetry and drinks gin from a teacup while petting her cat?"

"No. You sound like a woman in love."

"I do love you, Jesse."

"I love you, Sarah. I want to show you how a man *really* treats the woman he loves. Softly, tenderly, gently. No horror, no pain. But you must trust me."

"I do."

"Completely?"

"Yes, Jesse. Completely."

He disengaged his hand from her grasp and reached up to place his hands at her cheeks, as if to cup her face gently between the palms of his hands, but without actually touching her.

"I want to kiss you, Sarah. I know you don't like to be touched, but will you trust me enough to do what I want without my having to constantly ask you?"

She nodded.

"Good, because there are some things you just can't talk about while doing."

"Such as?"

Without answering her, Jesse brought his lips gently down to meet hers. She wasn't as frightened this time. Her lips weren't so tight, but were warm, soft, and responsive to him. Her arms wrapped around his neck as she held on to him.

"There. Did that hurt?" he murmured against her cheek.

"No."

"Then, just to make sure, we need to do it again."

He pulled her body next to his, so that his chest pressed against her soft breasts. He felt her tense just a little, but this time she didn't pull away. He held her close to him and kissed her lips. His kiss brushed lightly against the side of her mouth and wandered gently across her cheek.

When he reached her ear, his tongue flickered out to tickle the small pink lobe.

She giggled. Then she kissed him again. Her lips moved to the edge of his mouth and across his cheek. She flicked the tip of his ear with her tongue. He laughed aloud.

His hand smoothed down her slender white neck and across her shoulder.

"I'm so glad I got on that train, Sarah," he said as his hand moved across her shoulder and up and down her arm.

"I am, too."

Slowly Jesse moved from her shoulder across to try to cup her rounded breast in the palm of his hand. She pulled back.

"Did that hurt?"

"They . . . they squeezed and clawed and . . . and bit."

"Don't." Jesse swallowed the bile that rose in his throat. "I think I need to make certain they didn't leave any scars.

Don't worry, I think you'll find that this can be so different with the right man."

He reached both hands up to the top button of her white blouse. He unfastened the tiny pearl, then moved on to the next one. He made his way down the front of her dress until every button was undone.

With only his thumbs and forefingers, he held the edges of her blouse and moved them farther apart until her garment slipped off her shoulders. He helped the soft fabric slide farther down until he could manage to get her arms out of the dress. He let the material fall to the sheets they sat on.

He ran a single forefinger across the creamy half orbs that showed over the top of the fabric. He reached up to untie the corset cover. One tug on the little white string and the gathers came undone.

"Let me see you, Sarah," he said as he began to slide everything down. "Let me see how beautiful you are."

She shyly raised her arms in an attempt to cover herself, but Jesse shook his head, and she stopped.

"I . . . I looked better before I had Patsy." She tried to explain the gentle swells and the tracery of pale blue veins that blended against her pink nipples and translucent flesh.

"I think you look beautiful just the way you are. Everything you have is the way it is because of our little daughter. I wouldn't have it any other way."

"You're just saying that."

"Then I think I should shut up and do what we both have been waiting for." He reached up to touch one breast with the tips of his fingers. "This is gentle. This is love, Sarah. This is the way a man should treat the woman he loves."

He lightly traced a small circle around the nipple.

She laughed and pulled back. "That tickles."

"It's supposed to." He cradled one breast in his hand. He bent down and ran his tongue along one of the pale veins. "And that's supposed to tickle." He placed another kiss on the pink tip.

"Oh! That doesn't tickle at all," Sarah told him, breathless. "But do it again anyway."

Jesse did.

"Oh, as a matter of fact, I think I like that better."

He reached down for the hem of her skirt and began to lift it. She stood to help him. He leaned forward to kiss her navel.

"It didn't used to have so many wrinkles."

He kissed her smooth stomach. "I think it's beautiful. And it's just my size," he said as he darted his tongue swiftly in and out of her navel. She rippled with laughter.

Her skirt dropped to the floor, to be quickly joined by her corset and drawers.

He drew her closer to him until she stood between his legs. The inside of his knees pressed against the outside of hers. He reached behind her to cup her small buttocks in his hands. Slowly he began to rub his hands up and down over the gentle swell of flesh.

She placed her hands on his shoulders and looked down at him.

"You're so beautiful. Just like I always knew you'd be. Just like I imagined you the first time I saw you on that train."

"Oh, you didn't!"

"Of course I did."

She laughed again, then reached down to begin unbuttoning his nightshirt.

"Oh, you've seen my grand unveiling," he told her. "I don't really have to do anything special, do I?" He didn't allow her time to reply. Reaching down, he stripped off his shirt and threw it behind him. He wasn't sure where it landed, and he didn't really care.

She looked down, her curiosity overcoming her fears and cautions. "This is what's important anyway, isn't it?" Her voice rose nervously.

"No."

"No?"

"*This* is what's important," He reached up and tapped

gently between her breasts, where her heart was beating fiercely within her chest. He didn't remove his hand immediately, but continued to trace random patterns on her skin. "If you love someone with all your heart, she's always beautiful to you, and making love is always right. Everything else is just . . . extra trimmings."

He urged her to sit on the edge of the bed, then to slide back until they both lay side by side in the big feather bed.

He kissed her again and cuddled her in his embrace. His hand roved from her breasts down her slightly rounded stomach. He sidetracked to run his finger along the slender indentation of her waist.

She flinched again and curled up like a vine clinging to a stalk. "How do you know where I'm ticklish?"

He tapped his temple. "I look for the sweetest part of you. I figure that's got to be ticklish. The real trouble is trying to figure out which part of you is the sweetest. They all look good to me."

He continued his journey from her waist, around her navel once again, then slowly downward.

She drew her legs together.

"You trust me, Sarah. Remember?"

She nodded.

"No one else in your entire life will ever love you as much as I do at this moment, and for the rest of my life."

He lifted his hand to settle it on her raised knee. As she regained her confidence in him, she lowered the leg closest to him. She allowed his hand to slide along her thigh until it rested on her hip.

She reached out to put her hand on his hip, too. She looked down with a brief, sidelong glance. "I like to look at . . . just you. . . ."

"I know. I remember my bath."

"I thought it was kind of cute when it was sort of short and floppy."

He nodded. "Well, I don't think that's exactly how a man likes to have himself referred to, but . . ."

"I like it."

"I'm real glad to hear that, because that's usually how I wear it."

"But it changes size." Her sidelong glance turned into an admiring perusal, and a shy giggle of uncertainty. "I mean, I didn't realize . . ."

"That's usual, too, depending on the situation—and the company. Ever since I've been around you, it's been changing size a lot, Sarah."

"Oh, blame me, thank you."

"I can't think of anyone else I'd rather be able to blame for my condition."

"To tell you the truth, I kind of like it this way, too."

"Oh, I guarantee you're going to like it this way best of all."

She laughed and moved closer to him. Jesse could feel his own body growing harder and warmer against her own soft tenderness. She loved him. Her closeness to him meant she trusted him. That was important, too, if he was going to make sure their marriage really would last as long as he lived. And that was going to be a lot longer now. If only he could figure out how to tell her. This was definitely *not* the time to spring some new uncertainty on her. Give her time to learn to appreciate him as a man, then let her know she'd have him around for a long while.

He leaned his weight against her. She didn't protest, and he slowly began to ease himself on top of her.

"It's all right to open to me, Sarah. Trust me. It's good, my love. It really will be."

"I trust you, Jesse."

Her slender thighs moved apart. He settled easily between them and then went no farther—for now. Although his heart burned with desire for her, and other parts of him were feeling pretty singed, too, he wouldn't rush. He had to make absolutely sure that Sarah was ready for each and every step he led her to.

"See, I knew we'd fit together perfectly," he told her. "There's just one more thing. The best part—the best fit of all. I'll be slow, to give you time to change your mind if you want to—but I really hope you won't. I'll be gentle, Sarah. I'm so in love with you."

Moving slowly he lowered himself until he rested on both knees and both elbows. He could feel her soft breasts with their nipples already peaked with desire rubbing against his chest. He could feel the soft triangle of pale hair parting and giving way as he entered her.

She was holding her breath, and there was a hint of worry in her eyes. Her fingers held his shoulders in a tight grip. He waited until he saw the worry fade and her fingernails stopped piercing his skin. He began a slow and careful slide up. She tensed again. He stopped.

"Relax, my love." With one hand he gently brushed away a soft curl that had fallen on her cheek. "I wouldn't hurt you for all the world."

He could feel the tension ease out of the muscles in her legs as they brushed against his sides. Only then did he complete his final, gentle thrust.

"Oh." Her cry was more of surprise than pain. "Oh." Her murmur was one of relief, and pleasure.

He began moving against her, trying not to go too fast and hurt her. It had been so long, and he'd never loved another woman the way he loved Sarah.

His breath came faster, as did hers. He tried to watch her carefully for any indication that she was unhappy or uncomfortable. He could only see her closing her eyes, see the slight smile lightening her lips as she tipped her head backward, enjoying the sensations he was giving her body. He could feel her heart beating faster beneath him in time to his own heartbeat until he thought he would burst.

She released a low, sweet cry as his own body convulsed with deep pleasure.

He held himself above her a moment, small beads of perspiration dotting his forehead. Then he dropped to her side. He reached his arm out to draw her to him and cradle her against him amid the pillows and tumbled sheets.

"Are you happy, my love?"

"Yes."

"Do you see now the difference that love makes?"

"Yes. I think I knew it all along, Jesse. I just needed you to show me."

She cuddled into his arms and closed her eyes in contentment.

"Just one thing," Jesse said. "Now will you tell me why you're afraid of Deke Marsden?"

Fourteen

"I declare, you are the most stubborn man on the face of the earth!" She slapped playfully at his stomach.

He caught her hand, brought it up to his mouth and kissed her knuckles, then turned her hand over to place a kiss in the palm, too.

"I thought you considered bulldog tenacity to be an admirable trait." He bent forward to kiss her lips.

"Not when you're being so nosy about me."

"I'm not nosy about you." He kissed her nose and her forehead. "I'm nosy about Deke."

She pulled back slightly. "He's not worth it."

Jesse wasn't about to be deterred. "What is it about him? Why does he keep pestering you when you've made it pretty clear you want him to leave you alone? Why does it bother you so much to be around him?"

"Because once, long ago, I was very young and very foolish."

"How do you figure that?"

"A long time ago, before the war . . . gosh, I was only about seventeen—"

"Wow! That *was* a long time ago!"

"Don't be a wiseacre. You know I'm not that old. But any

woman who'd think Deke Marsden was something special would have to be very, very foolish." She laughed with chagrin at her own stupidity.

"You thought *he* was special? That *is* worse than foolish. That's . . . unbelievable!"

"Oh, thank you very much. He was much better-looking when he was younger. Time hasn't been kind to Deke."

"Time shouldn't be. He doesn't deserve it. I guess nothing could've made him any smarter."

"I hate to admit it, but he was also made a lot more attractive by the fact that Aunt Myrtle didn't want me to associate with him. She thought the entire family was beneath us."

"If you ask me, Deke should be beneath six feet of sod."

"On the other hand, Aunt Myrtle wasn't too happy when Mildred married the Reverend, either, because preachers don't generally get wealthy, and because he wanted to travel to the West."

"I wouldn't blame an old lady for wanting to keep her family near her."

"I suppose you're right." She shrugged her shoulders. "Of course, Deke was very flattered that a Bolton would pay him any attention at all. As I told you, I was very foolish."

"What made you change your mind about him?"

Jesse watched Sarah's face grow pale. Her eyes grew misty. As she gave a little sniff, her breath caught in her throat.

"What happened? He didn't hurt you, did he?"

"Not me."

He stroked the side of her cheek as he waited for her to continue. Eventually she drew in a deep breath.

"Deke's mother always devoted herself to him. I guess he was all she had."

"That's not much."

"All they ever had was a lot of debts he hadn't paid from trying to live like gentry when he was just a poor dirt farmer —and always would be. I guess he just expected every woman to treat him as well as his mother. He's a very jealous man."

"I sort of figured that. I guess being an only child, he never learned to share and play well with others."

"No, I mean he's a *very* jealous man. When he decides he wants a woman to pay attention to him, he doesn't want her to pay attention to anyone—or anything—else."

"And he wanted you."

She nodded. He heard her sniff again.

"I had . . . a little kitten."

"Oh, no," Jesse groaned. He could figure what was coming, and even though he'd seen what could happen in a war and a prison, he still didn't want to hear what she had to say. Why did it seem to make a difference when it was small and furry?

"I really loved that cat." She shook her head sadly. "Mildred had already left for Kansas. Aunt Myrtle was old and sick and wasn't much company."

Jesse pulled her a little closer to him and reached over to stroke her hair to comfort her.

"Black with three white paws."

"Aunt Myrtle?"

"No, the cat, you idiot! Three white paws. A little pink nose. Pickles."

"The cat had pickles?" He wanted to joke to ease her tension, but he didn't want to appear to be taking her loss too lightly. He held her and stroked her hair in an effort to soothe her.

"No!" She giggled, and he gave her a little hug. "Her name was Pickles."

"If you loved her, why'd you name her something like Pickles?"

"I liked Amalie's watermelon pickles, and I really couldn't see giving such a small cat such a long name like Watermelon."

"That makes sense. It's a good thing you didn't like Amalie's macaroni and cheese."

"I think Pickles is a cute name."

"So do I." He pressed his lips to the top of her head and savored the clean lavender smell of her. He stroked her shoulder and marveled at how translucent her skin looked in the early morning light, almost as if she were an angel heralding the dawn.

Then, as she prepared to continue her tale, her eyes clouded again with sadness and hate.

"Aunt Myrtle wouldn't permit Deke in the house—"

"In spite of her views on death and dishonor, your aunt was actually a very wise woman."

"Deke and I had to stay in the backyard. I was holding Pickles. Deke wanted to hug me. I didn't want to put Pickles down in the garden and have her chasing birds and hunting mice, and getting all muddy. He got really angry. He said I was always paying more attention to the cat than I was to him. He . . . he took her from me and . . . and killed her. . . ."

"Right in front of your eyes? Not that it would've been any better if he'd turned around."

She nodded. "Just . . . just snapped her neck. Like that."

"What a bastard!"

She nodded and didn't even take offense at his language. Jesse guessed she thought the term was pretty accurate—or maybe even way too mild.

"It was only after that happened that I could look back and see how blind I'd been to all his petty cruelties over the years. I've hated him ever since. I was so glad to see him move away. I thought he was out of my life completely. I couldn't believe it when I saw him in Cottonwood."

"Is he the reason you were so upset when the train arrived here?"

"I saw him in the crowd. He's big and blond and hard to miss."

"He still wants you? He still thinks you want him?"

"He doesn't want me. He just can't stand to lose. But I'll never marry a man that cruel. If he'd . . . do that to my pet, I hate to think what he might do if he were Patsy's stepfather. He almost struck her in church."

"Is *that* why you ran out?" Jesse's eyebrows shot up in surprise. "Did anyone see him?"

"I don't know. He wanted to hold my hand, and Patsy tried to stop him. He wouldn't let go of me, so she bit him."

"She *bit* him?"

Sarah nodded and gave a little giggle. "Everybody *heard* Deke."

"That's my girl!" Jesse declared proudly, raising a triumphant fist in the air.

"I'll never marry that man. Never!"

It was almost as if Jesse'd been given this golden opportunity to tell Sarah at last that she'd never have to worry about marrying Deke—or anyone else. Now was the perfect time to tell her he was going to live to a ripe old age by her side.

"Don't worry, Sarah. You won't—"

"Yoo hoo! Rise and shine, you slugabeds. Breakfast is ready."

"Oh, Mildred!" they both moaned together as they collapsed again into each other's comforting embrace.

"Beffas, Mommy! Beffas, Daddy!" Patsy pounded on the door. "Eat good oatmeal. Now!"

"We're coming, sweetheart," Sarah called.

He watched with disappointment as she sat up in bed, preparing to leave him.

"I can't keep that oatmeal warm forever, and I don't think you want to eat black toast. It's all going to burn to cinders," Mildred issued her dire prediction through the door.

"Does she ever sleep?" Jesse complained as he sat up in bed.

When would he ever have another chance like this one, with just the right mood, to make love to Sarah and to tell her that he'd be around to love her for a long time? Then he smiled to himself. Tonight.

*   *   *

"Oh, I declare," Mildred mumbled to Kitty as she carried the clean towels into Sarah and Jesse's bedroom. "I certainly feel sorry for Aunt Myrtle—may she rest in peace—having to put up with Sarah's housekeeping for all those years."

Kitty jumped up and settled on the bed.

"I mean, she's quite helpful to me with the laundry, and cleaning, and in the kitchen, but . . . oh, just look at this bedroom!"

Mildred placed the clean towels and cloths on the washstand. She made sure each towel was folded precisely in thirds, and then hung them exactly halved over the bars. She placed the cloth directly in the center of the towel, with one point hanging down the center, and the two opposite points placed exactly on the top of the bar.

"Maybe it's not her. Maybe it's Jesse who's so careless with his things—although I doubt it. Honestly, she's been married long enough to know how to pick up after her husband properly."

Now that she'd accomplished her task, Mildred started looking for something else to do. It was easy to find. There was Sarah's traveling bag, sitting in the corner on the other side of the bed, as if she'd just tossed it out of the way.

"Just look at that," she complained, pointing to the bag.

Kitty jumped down and walked over to it.

"I suppose Sarah's a firm believer in 'out of sight, out of mind.' She's so irresponsible, she never did unpack that traveling bag."

Mildred tried to pick up the bag.

"Goodness gracious! What does she have in there? The blacksmith's anvil?"

Kitty just rubbed up against it.

Mildred dragged the bag out into the middle of the floor. Kneeling down, she unhooked the latch. The overstuffed bag sprang open.

"Honestly," Mildred grumbled as she surveyed the clutter inside. "A body'd think she'd have needed some of the stuff in here before now."

She stuck her hand inside and started pushing some of the things around. Kitty jumped in the bag and tried to help.

"Well, I suppose she'll thank me for giving her a hand with this."

Mildred pulled out several used handkerchiefs. Kitty swatted at them.

"Ugh!" she said, tossing them to the side for next week's laundry. "If she were any more forgetful, she'd lose her head."

She found three biscuits wrapped in paper. Kitty sniffed them and immediately rejected stale fare. There was a whole uneaten apple. There was a rattle, and a small rag doll with light brown yarn hair and a smiling, embroidered face.

"My, my, my," Mildred whispered to herself. "Sarah has the strangest collection of stuff."

She reached in, thinking she'd probably pull out a pillow or blanket—or perhaps more food. She hoped the biscuits and apple left in there hadn't drawn any bugs or rodents. Mildred shook her hand and grimaced, just thinking about all those terrible, creepy little critters in her house. Well, she just wouldn't tolerate having them here!

Who knew what Sarah had stored in there? Mildred wondered as she continued to explore the bottom of the bag. Her hand touched a crisp little paper.

"Oh, now what's she got in here?"

Mildred pulled out the paper. Well, of course she had to open it. It was a lovely paper—full of curlicues and cherubs, like the marriage certificates the Reverend filled out.

"My goodness, that's exactly what it is!" Mildred exclaimed with surprise.

It was Sarah and Jesse's marriage certificate.

"Now, what in the world is that careless girl doing, keeping her marriage certificate in her traveling bag?" Mildred complained. "Why wasn't it packed away more safely in a trunk?" She gave an exasperated sigh. "I'll have to explain to that irresponsible younger sister of mine about the importance of proper care for legal and sentimental documents."

She certainly would've taken better care of something that beautiful. She couldn't help admire it again more closely.

At least the minister spelled Sarah's middle name right. Most people couldn't understand that Mama had insisted upon "Bevarlea," her maiden name. She was so glad she'd been born first and gotten both grandmothers' names—Mildred Ann—much more sensible names.

So Jesse's middle name was Orville? He didn't look like an Orville, Mildred thought with a wicked little laugh.

Their anniversary was April 29. What a coincidence! Only three days after hers and the Reverend's. She looked more closely—but in 1866. Eighteen sixty-six! That was this year! Goodness gracious, it was the very same day they'd arrived in town, too. It really was a pretty certificate, even if it was dated wrong.

"Oh, please let it be dated wrong," she prayed as an awful premonition crept up on her.

What if the date wasn't wrong? The minister'd been careful enough to spell the names right. He might confuse the day, but he could hardly get the wrong year!

She sat there gaping at the paper. Sarah and Jesse had only been married three weeks. Patsy was eighteen months old. What in the world had Sarah been up to since Mildred left? This certainly wasn't like anything her sister would've done before.

What had Aunt Myrtle said to Sarah when Patsy was born? She'd always been such a stickler for appearances and social proprieties. She'd also drilled into their heads that a lady always chose death before dishonor.

Jesse certainly didn't seem to be the kind of man who'd have forced himself on Sarah, or she wouldn't look so happy married to him. He didn't look too much like a seductive scoundrel, either. On the other hand, he was right handsome and charming, in spite of his illness. Sarah really hadn't been born with too much common sense. Look how silly she'd been about that worthless Deke Marsden. At least she'd come to her senses about that—right abruptly, too, as Mildred recalled.

What would Mama and Daddy say if they knew their very own daughter had borne a child out of wedlock? They should be glad they were dead. This would've killed them all over again!

Still holding tightly to the paper, Mildred rose on shaking legs. This wasn't something that could be easily passed off. The minister's family needed to set a good example in the town. *This* was not a good example!

Of course, she'd be very discreet about this. Even if Sarah was foolish, she was her sister. Even if Patsy was illegitimate, she was blood kin. Mildred could never allow members of her own family to be publicly shamed. After all, someday she'd have children of her own—someday. It just wouldn't be right for the minister's children to have a cousin who'd been born on the wrong side of the blanket, even if her mother and father had married each other eventually.

Mildred made her way down the stairs. It was such a pretty piece of paper, she knew Sarah wouldn't want to get coffee and chicken soup stains on it. She set the paper down on the small round table in the middle of the vestibule so it wouldn't get messed up in the kitchen.

She'd make a fresh pot of coffee, Mildred decided. Maybe even some muffins. She'd take Sarah into the kitchen during Patsy's naptime. She'd sit her down, and they'd have a nice long talk about proper behavior for proper Southern ladies.

Mildred shook the canister. Thank goodness there was just enough coffee left that she wouldn't have to bother with grinding more right now. She really wanted to talk to her sister as soon as possible.

She was stirring the liquid into the dry ingredients for the muffins when she thought she heard footsteps on the front porch. She listened carefully. What a time for visitors! Perhaps it was just someone coming to the Reverend's office for a little chat about spiritual welfare. The Reverend was busy in his study again, and she'd be the one to have to let the person in. If her batter was ruined, she'd have to let the Reverend know how really angry she was.

She listened for the knock on the door, but none came. She still heard a slight rustling sound, but now it sounded as if it was coming from the vestibule.

It better not be that awful Wally Bender. If he peedled on her bushes again, she'd shoot him herself this time! But she didn't hear any more noise. No, it couldn't be Wally. He'd never been that quiet in his life.

She listened again, but heard nothing else. Kitty was sleeping on the floor in the big patch of sunshine pouring in the kitchen window. Jesse'd taken a walk down to see Doc. Sarah'd taken Patsy out early for a walk to the nearest farm so she could see the new little yellow peeps. It must be her imagination.

Mildred finished stirring the batter. She poured it into the muffin tins, then placed them in the oven. She cleaned up the counter. Now she was ready. All she'd have to do was wait for Sarah.

She heard the noise again. It definitely sounded as if someone had opened and closed their front door. It couldn't be Sarah back so soon. She'd use the back door anyway. And Patsy would be chattering like a little magpie. Who could it be?

Mildred quickly dried her hands on her apron and rushed out into the vestibule. No one was there. Nothing was missing, and nothing there was extra, as it usually was if the postman brought a special delivery. She shrugged and went back to her muffins.

"Did you like the farm, Patsy?" Sarah asked as they made their way across the field, returning to the parsonage.

"Oh, yes!"

Patsy was just fine walking on flat floors, or in giving Sarah nervous prostration trying to climb steep flights of stairs. But on the bumpy sod she kept losing her balance,

tripping over gopher holes and hillocks. Sarah held her
pudgy little fingers tightly so she wouldn't fall down.

"Did you like the baby peeps?"

"Yes. Softy littles. Peep, peep, peep," she said in a high-
pitched squeak.

Sarah thought she heard the rolling of thunder far off in
the distance. She looked up. The sky was still blue and
cloudless, although she did think the breeze had picked up a
bit.

"Did you like the sheep?"

"Yes. Softy lambies. Baah, baah, baah."

"Did you like the piggies?"

"No! Dirty. Smelly. Oink, oink, oink."

"You know, Patsy, when you grow up, I think you'll have a
great career imitating farm animals."

The thunder rolled again. Off to the northwest, Sarah
could see just the tips of black clouds, followed by a mass of
dark yellowish-gray clouds, on the horizon.

"Maybe we ought to hurry, Patsy." She began to guide
her daughter toward the little bridge that spanned the small
river that ran behind the parsonage. "You know, we left
Aunt Mildred home all alone."

"Hurry for Auntie Dread." Patsy tried to walk a little
faster. The rough ground made her more unsteady. She
clung more tightly to Sarah's hand.

Thunder rumbled in the distance. Patsy jumped.

To keep her daughter's mind on something more pleasant, so she wouldn't be too afraid of the approaching storm,
Sarah asked, "What did you like best at the farm?"

"Cows," she answered immediately and with great conviction.

"Why?"

"Why?" she repeated incredulously, as if anyone needed
a reason to like cows.

"Did you like the cows' horns?"

"Hard."

"Did you like the cows' 'moo'?"

"Moo," Patsy repeated loud and clear.

"Do you like their moo best?"

"No. Ploppies best. Cows do funny ploppies, Mommy."

Sarah sighed and continued to hurry Patsy back home. So much for the educational trip to the farm. She looked up in amused exasperation.

She noticed the clouds were moving toward them more rapidly. They were also much darker now and seemed to be rolling as if they were being violently stirred. Bright, yellow-white flashes of lightning ripped through the black clouds. Thunder rumbled across the prairie, growing louder as the storm approached. The breeze had turned into a definite wind, pulling at their skirts and rippling through their hair.

"Don't like this," Patsy complained.

"We're almost home, sweetheart."

As they crossed the small bridge, Sarah looked down. The stems of the plants growing at the water's edge were submerged, and the water seemed to be running faster than usual under the bridge.

"I hope Daddy's already home when we get there," she told Patsy. "I don't think he'll be able to run through the rain very well with a bad leg."

"See Daddy." Patsy gave a little jump of excitement.

"I don't think the rain will do his cough any good, either."

"Sing with Daddy. Can't wait." Patsy broke into a loud, stirring rendition of "Yankee Doodle Dandy."

"Yes, Patsy," Sarah agreed as they stepped off the bridge. "I can't wait to see your daddy again, too."

"Funny. She don't favor her daddy much."

When she heard Deke's voice, Sarah stopped so abruptly, she almost pulled Patsy off her feet. She looked around frantically to see where the scoundrel was hiding now. She didn't know if there were any rat holes along the riverbank. Maybe, like the trolls in the fairy tales, he was hiding under the bridge. What a shame she and Patsy hadn't brought home the biggest, meanest billy goat on the farm!

Deke stepped out from behind one of the trees growing along the riverside. She could see a big patch of torn-up grass where he'd obviously been worrying the sod with the heel of his shoe. She could see the fresh gouge marks made with a penknife in the bark of the tree. He must've been standing there for a long time to do that amount of damage.

"You've been waiting for me," Sarah accused. She began to head toward the house with a lot more enthusiasm. "How dare you!"

"Go 'way, bad man!" Patsy ordered. She put her hands on her hips and stuck her tongue out at him. "Bad, bad man! Go *far* 'way!"

Deke chuckled, but Sarah detected no true humor in his voice—not like Jesse, whose happiness and contentment shone through regardless.

"Bad man! Cow ploppies on you, bad man!"

Deke stopped chuckling. "Y'know, if she was my kid, I'd break her of that rudeness. I'd teach her to be polite."

"I don't think you know the difference."

"I'll bet you think that cotton fluff you married is polite, though, don't you?"

"Yes, he is." Sarah wished he were here right now.

"Yeah, I'll bet he even says ''Scuse me, ma'am' before he breaks wind."

"I'm sure that's none of your business."

"Y'know, she's a cute kid, but she don't half favor that man you married," Deke persisted.

"I don't see why you're so concerned about it," Sarah said. "She resembles my mother's side of the family, if you must know. If you took the time, you'd notice how much she looks like my sister. We both resemble my mother actually."

The lightning flashed more brightly, and the thunder rumbled closer. Sarah tried to keep moving toward the parsonage, but Deke reached out and grabbed her wrist.

"Wouldn't know," he answered with a slow shrug of his beefy shoulders. "Maybe. Never seen your ma. Somehow, I'd be more convinced if she had any kinda resemblance to that man she calls 'Daddy.' "

"Le'go my mommy, you bad man!" Patsy yelled. She marched up to him and kicked him in the shin.

Deke pulled back to hit her. She'd never let him hurt her

child. Sarah pushed up against him hard, her small frame knocking his bulk slightly off balance. By the time he stood upright again, Patsy was already running across the field, and falling down, and picking herself up again, just as fast as she could.

"Run, Patsy, run! Go get Auntie Mildred and the Reverend. Tell them to get the sheriff!" Sarah called after her.

"What're *they* gonna do—pray over me?" Deke demanded with a sneer.

"Auntie Dread! Auntie Dread!"

Sarah could hear Patsy's voice fading away as she drew closer to the parsonage. She breathed a sigh of relief. At least her daughter was out of danger from this horrible man —for now.

"Good," Deke said. His large, rough hand still clamped around her wrist. "Got rid of the li'l brat. Then I don't have to worry 'bout her interferin' in me gettin' what I come after."

Sarah swallowed hard. She knew what Deke had come for. She'd try to keep him talking again. It had worked once before—and this time she knew Patsy would be coming back with Mildred, the Reverend, and the sheriff, very soon. Very, very soon, she prayed.

"What do you want, Deke?" Sarah demanded, trying to free her wrist from his grasp. He just held her more tightly. "Why do you think you absolutely can't live unless you get it *now?*"

She looked up. Maybe it would rain now and dampen some of his ardor. The wind whipped her hair around her face, but the sky remained dry.

"You can see it's going to rain soon. Isn't this something you can tell me about inside, so we don't get soaked to the skin and catch our death of cold?"

But the black clouds and the thunder only continued to roll overhead, without any hint they might stop and open up. Deke still hadn't released her, either.

"What do you want, Deke?"

"You."

"You can't have me," she told him plainly. She tried in vain to free her wrist. "Don't you realize that? Don't you realize it's just time to give up?"

"Why can't I have you?"

"I'm married."

"Not for long."

"I don't love you."

He shook his head. "That don't matter."

Her stomach churned as she realized it really didn't matter to Deke.

"Y'know, people back in Savannah used to tell me I couldn't have you 'cause you was better'n me. You was a spoiled little rich girl, and I was just some poor dirt farmer who had to work for a livin'. But my ma knew different. She didn't think there was any girl good enough for me—and she was right."

"Yes, your mother was right, Deke. No woman should be married to you."

"But I just found out different."

"You've finally realized you're no good?" Sarah couldn't imagine where she'd learned these smart retorts, or that she actually had the nerve to say them, especially to someone like Deke. Then she realized, she'd had a lot of practice bantering with Jesse. Oh, she liked it so much better when the banter was friendly and with Jesse!

"Nope," Deke replied, unfazed by her insults.

She should've known he either wouldn't be listening to her or he wouldn't understand what she was saying anyway.

"I found out that *you're* no good."

Sarah felt her legs and arms grow cold and her stomach try to lurch into her throat. "What on earth are you talking about?"

She started tugging, trying to free her hand again. Deke held on tight.

"I just found out the hoity-toity Miss Bolton wasn't married to the baby's father when the kid was born."

"That's . . . that's ridiculous!"

"My ma don't tell me nothin' ridiculous."

"How would she know something like that?" she demanded.

"She seen the paper."

"Paper? What paper?"

Then Sarah recalled. She'd been so overwhelmed with all the commotion of their arrival, with Jesse's illness and surprising improvement, with taking care of Patsy, Mildred's matchmaking, and with Deke pestering her, that she hadn't had the chance to clean out her traveling bag. She hadn't thought there was really anything in there that she'd need. She couldn't believe how wrong she'd been!

She could believe Meddling Mildred would go snooping through there, not intentionally looking for damning information, but just because she couldn't stand to have anything not in order. In fact, she actually should be surprised Mildred hadn't been into it way before this. If she had, Sarah certainly would've heard a scolding she'd never forget.

Mildred hated Mrs. Marsden. She never would've told her about this. Who had she told? Who had they told so that Mrs. Marsden had finally found out?

Now that Mrs. Marsden knew, who else would she tell? Who would they tell? Would Sarah ever be able to show her face in Cottonwood again, or should she just start heading across the prairie for the next town right now, while she was out here anyway?

"Seems my ma went over to the parsonage."

"I can't imagine why. From what my sister says, neither you nor your mother are avid churchgoers."

"I don't need to check in with the Lord. Ma's gettin' old and might think she does, seeing as how she's goin' to be accountin' for herself to Him soon anyway. But *I* don't need nobody's say-so. I do what I want to do."

Sarah silently prayed that the Lord might sort of check in on Deke right now. Well, maybe "check" wasn't quite the right word. How about "smite"?

"My ma looked in the house, but nobody was around, so she went on in. Well, what do you know? There's this paper layin' on the table, where anybody could see. And it says that you and that piss-ant was married three weeks ago. Now, I know Patsy's older'n that. And that man looks like he's been sick for a lot longer'n two years."

"So now you're a medical expert?"

"And I got to thinkin' maybe you ain't as good as you make yourself out to be. Maybe Taylor ain't the baby's father. In that case, who is?"

Sarah wasn't about to tell him anything.

"Maybe havin' a father with a big plantation—that you ain't got no more," he added with a snide laugh. "And a crotchety ol' aunt who always thought she was better'n everybody, and a brother-in-law that's a preacher, still don't make you any good. Maybe you're just as much white trash as people say I am. Maybe it makes you just the right kinda woman for me after all."

"I'm not for you. I've told you—I'm married."

"He ain't gonna live much longer anyway. I'll see to that. And maybe I don't want you for a long time. Maybe I just want a little piece of what you was givin' 'round to everybody else."

"No! I wasn't. Only Jesse, just Jesse."

"Just *me,* Sarah," Deke corrected her. "I don't come in second to nobody, 'specially no damn Yankee. I'll kill that half-dead-already son of a bitch, and then I'll have you, Sarah. We'll send Patsy off to live with your sister—she wants a kid so bad anyway—and I'll be the first and only person in your whole life."

"Wrong, Deke!" Jesse shouted. "You'll always be last. Dead last."

Jesse reached out to pull Deke away from Sarah.

The air seemed to crackle with electricity, then suddenly the sky lit up and thunder rumbled directly overhead. A torrent of rain began to pour down from the sky, soaking them all.

Oh, why couldn't that lightning have struck Deke? Sarah lamented.

"You're gonna be dead, Taylor," Deke threatened. He

released Sarah and tried to grab Jesse at the throat with both hands.

Sarah couldn't believe it. Jesse grabbed both of Deke's hands with both of his hands and held them to his chest. He pulled backward so that the big man was set off balance and tumbled face first onto the wet grass.

What was Jesse doing with both hands free? Where in the world was his crutch? He needed it to walk with. And even if he didn't, he could've put it to good use and clobbered Deke over the head with it.

Deke picked himself up and went after Jesse again.

Jesse was much stronger than he used to be. He breathed better, he weighed more, and he even walked firmly without his crutch. But he'd still been sick for a long time, and he was still no match for the bulk of Deke. What in the world were they going to do?

Well, Sarah figured, if he didn't have his crutch, Jesse still had her. She ran around the two struggling men to the stand of trees, searching the ground for a fallen branch—a nice big branch. It would serve Deke right to be clobbered by a branch of the tree he'd damaged.

But she couldn't find any. The last one she saw was rapidly floating downstream. She didn't care what the schoolmasters might say about a birch rod—smacking at Deke with twigs just wasn't going to be effective enough in this situation!

Maybe something different—like a rock! She looked around, hoping to find a rock big enough to hold and still bash Deke on the head with. All the stones in the riverbed were covered with raging, muddy water. Throwing mud at Deke wouldn't stop him and would only make him really angry.

The storm had swollen the river. It almost reached to the top of the bank and threatened to overflow, sweeping away the bridge. Already Sarah could see the foundation timbers of the bridge bending under the pressure of the flow of the water. Maybe if she waited long enough she could use one of the broken planks to hit Deke.

But there wasn't enough time. There wasn't even enough time to run all the way to the parsonage, explain to Mildred why she needed the gun, and wait until Mildred found it.

She could tell Mildred to run for the sheriff, but she wasn't sure how long that would take. Something had to be done now.

If she couldn't find a weapon, she had nothing but herself to rely on. And Jesse needed her—now!

Sarah carefully watched for the right opportunity—when Deke had his back to her—for her to jump on him, bit his ear, pull his hair, scratch his eyes out. Maybe she'd just wrap her arms around his neck and hold on until she'd cut off all his air. If she were stronger, she'd like to have snapped his damn neck, just the way he'd snapped Pickles!

Good heavens, she thought with alarm, where was this violent streak in her coming from? And where had it been before when she needed it? And would it stay, just in case— Heaven forbid—she needed it again?

"Don't hit my daddy!" Patsy yelled. "Nasty man! Bad man!"

Sarah caught her just before she could run up and try to kick Deke in the shin again. Sarah figured maybe if she and Jesse could manage to get Deke on the ground, Patsy could bite him again.

Sarah turned to see the Reverend, Mildred, and Patsy standing beside her in the pouring rain. "What on earth are you doing out here?" she demanded.

"I wanted to see if I could help."

"Good." Sarah turned to her and held out her hand, palm up. "Where's the gun?"

"Gun? Oh, the gun. Oh, my goodness. Well, I . . . I never thought you might need . . ."

"Never mind, Mildred."

"Mildred! You have a gun in the parsonage?" the Reverend demanded.

"Just a little one."

"We'll discuss this tomorrow."

"Yes, dear."

The Reverend circled the battling men. "Gentlemen, gentlemen, please. This must stop!"

Sarah figured the Reverend might as well be trying to talk to them from the pulpit, as much as they were listening to him.

"Why in the world did you bring Patsy out here?" Sarah demanded sharply of her sister. "Are you out of your mind, taking her out in this storm? Taking her somewhere where she might see her father killed or even badly injured?"

"Well, really, Sarah," Mildred pouted. "He's been badly injured all along."

"Why'd you bring her?" Sarah repeated her demand furiously. She felt her fists clench at her sides. "Are you that afraid you'll miss something?"

"I couldn't leave her alone in the house," she tried to excuse herself, but it was a weak explanation at best.

"Then go back to the house," Sarah ordered angrily. "Now! And don't come back without the gun or the sheriff —or both!"

"Oh, all right," Mildred agreed grudgingly. She looked down for Patsy. "She's gone!"

Sarah and Mildred started looking around for her frantically.

"Oh, my God!" Sarah cried. "She's on the bridge!"

The bridge gave a creaking groan as the support on their side of the river began to give way.

Heedless of the swinging fists, Sarah ran up to Jesse.

"Patsy! Patsy!" was all she could manage to yell in her panic.

She started pulling on his shirt. Then she pulled on Deke's arm. His swing practically yanked her off her feet. She pulled on their shirts again and finally interposed herself between them.

"Gentlemen, gentlemen, excuse me," the Reverend continued to try to get their attention.

"Patsy! Patsy!" she continued to yell, pointing frantically at the collapsing bridge.

Jesse stopped to see what was wrong. Deke apparently

couldn't resist getting in one last shot. He hit Jesse's jaw so hard, Jesse dropped to the ground.

"You sneaky rotten bastard!" Sarah yelled. She reached up and hit him directly on the nose so hard it began to bleed.

"Damn, I wasn't expecting that," he said, wiping away the blood. He gave a low chuckle. "Guess maybe you found out you liked the rough stuff, huh?"

Sarah wasn't paying him the least bit of attention. She'd dropped to her knees at Jesse's side.

"Patsy! Patsy's on the bridge!" she gulped breathlessly.

Jesse sprang to his feet and ran to the edge of the bridge that was still standing. Tangling up close with Deke, he hadn't noticed how hard it was to see in the pouring rain. Now he noticed he could barely see where he was going. He almost fell off the edge of the bridge, but he pulled up quickly enough.

"Patsy, what are you doing there?" he asked. He tried to keep his voice as calm as possible so as not to upset her and send her toppling into the raging water below.

"Don't like fights. Wanna go see peeps again. Piggies. Cow ploppies. Moo."

"But it's raining, dear," Sarah said. She'd come up behind Jesse slowly, so as not to send Patsy running in the opposite direction. "All the little animals are inside with their mommies, so they can stay dry."

"Why? We out here."

"We're going inside, Patsy," Sarah said. "Right now."

"We'll make cookies," Mildred called over Sarah's shoulder.

"Can't."

"Why not?"

She pointed her pudgy little finger down to the wooden planks at her feet. "Can't step."

Jesse drew back and surveyed the bridge. He and Sarah were at the base of one side of the bridge. The support beneath this section had already collapsed, sending the foot planks sailing down toward the Mississippi. Patsy stood on the few planks left on the other support.

"Don't move, Patsy."

"Can't step," she repeated with exasperation, as if she couldn't believe they hadn't understood her the first time.

"That side of the bridge is still attached to the riverbank," Jesse said. "We might tell her to go over there and wait for us, but I hate to tell her to try. It doesn't look like that support's going to last much longer, either."

"What'll we do?" Sarah asked, clinging to his arm.

"I could try to reach her, to pull her across to this side," Jesse offered.

"Be careful," Sarah cautioned.

Jesse lay along the planks. "Hold my feet." Sarah complied. He stretched his long arms out to Patsy. Sarah could hear him groan with the effort. Was it rain or perspiration on his forehead as he worked to reach Patsy?

"I . . . I can't do it," Jesse said breathlessly as he sat back up. "I can't reach that far."

"If you tried to lay out farther on this side of the bridge, and I'd hold on to you . . ." Sarah suggested.

"It's worth a try."

But it didn't work.

"You're too tiny to counterbalance my weight," Jesse explained.

"What if we both held you?" Mildred asked.

"I'll hold you," Deke said.

They all turned to stare at Deke.

"I thought you'd left," Jesse said.

"You wish."

"I didn't think you liked children," Sarah said.

"I don't. Now step back and let me do what I have to."

"Your arms are longer, Deke," Sarah said. "Why doesn't Jesse hold you and you reach Patsy?"

Jesse shook his head. "That bridge'll never hold his weight. And if we're going to do this, we'd better get to it. If this water keeps flowing like this, that bridge isn't going to last much longer."

Deke held Jesse's ankles firmly while Jesse stretched out across the planks. He could feel the impact of the water shaking the wood beneath him.

"Grab Daddy, Patsy. Quick! Quick!"

Patsy stretched out.

Jesse seized her hand just as the last support gave way. He heard Sarah and Mildred screaming above the creaking wood. The cold water closed over his head. He tried to lift Patsy and hold her above the water.

Holding his breath as his ears and nostrils filled with water, he kept his eyes shut tight. He knew he was still holding onto something wooden. He didn't know what. All he knew was, as the current pulled at him and tried to suck him away, his grasp on the wood was the only thing keeping Patsy and him from floating away to their watery deaths.

He managed to pull himself up on the wood, the remains of the handrail. It was clinging to the edge of the bridge by one lone, rusty nail.

"Take her, Deke! Take her!" he yelled as his mouth filled with water and he spit it out again and again.

"Get her!" Sarah cried. "Oh, please, reach her!"

"Nasty man!" Patsy cried and stuck her tongue out at Deke again. She clung to Jesse's neck even more tightly.

"No, no, Patsy. Go to Mr. Deke," Sarah called.

"No! Nasty man."

"Oh, Patsy, now is *not* the time to be picky!"

"Patsy," Jesse whispered calmly in her ear. "Daddy wants you to go to Mr. Deke just so he can give you to Mommy. Pretend Mr. Deke is a big fat piggie you're riding to see Mommy. All right?"

She looked a little doubtful at first. Then Jesse whispered, "Oink, oink, oink."

Patsy laughed and held out her hands to Deke. Jesse relaxed when he felt her weight lifted from his arm.

He grabbed on to the piece of wood and tried to pull himself up. He looked for Deke to give him a hand, but Deke was gone. Jesse hoped he was passing Patsy along to Sarah and intended to come back and get him, too.

He hoped Deke would come back soon. His arms were aching. His fingers were going numb. He'd swallowed enough water to make soup for everybody in Cottonwood, with leftovers.

"Well, son of a gun!" Jesse exclaimed when he actually saw Deke's face reappear at the edge of the washed-out bridge. "Thanks for your help for Patsy and Sarah, Deke. Sorry I underestimated you. No hard feelings, huh?"

"Sure, Taylor, sure."

"Give me a hand up, all right?" Jesse dared to release one hand's grip on the handrail and extended it to Deke.

Deke didn't take it.

Jesse glanced over. Sarah, Mildred, and the Reverend were busy fussing over Patsy—as they rightly should, Jesse decided. He should be there with them, if only he could get Deke to give him a hand out of this water. He looked up to Deke again. Deke was still squatting at the edge of the bridge, grinning at him.

"What's so funny?" Jesse asked nervously. He already had a bad suspicion what was going on.

"I was just wonderin' what kinda funeral they have for folks who just get washed away."

"I haven't washed away yet, Deke," Jesse said. He tried to sound as calm as he possibly could. "Now, give me a hand."

Deke reached down and grabbed the other end of the handrail that Jesse clung to. For just a moment, Jesse thought Deke might actually help him.

He should've known better. Deke wrenched the wood from the plank, nail and all. Jesse felt the water rising up around him.

"Bye, Taylor." Deke gave him a little wave. "I'll take real good care of your wife—'scuse me, your widow."

Sarah looked up from Patsy just in time to see Jesse being swept down the river.

Fifteen

Sarah just stood there, clinging to Patsy and watching the water continue to flow downstream. The rain continued to pour down on her, soaking them all to the skin. She couldn't distinguish the raindrops from her tears.

"I tried to reach for him, but the boards gave way," Deke explained. "Wasn't nothin' I could do."

He reached out to put his big arm around Sarah's shoulder. She was too devastated to protest. He tried to pull her closer to him, so she'd fit into his embrace between the crook of his elbow and his armpit.

Sarah allowed her shoulders to be pulled, but continued to lean her head away from him. She'd rested her head on Jesse's shoulder and knew how wonderfully comforting he could be. Deke could never take Jesse's place. She'd never let him. No man would.

"We really should get Patsy inside now," Mildred said. She reached past Deke and tried to take the little girl from Sarah's arms.

Sarah stood there, still staring and still holding Patsy. It wasn't so much that she didn't want Mildred to take Patsy. It was that she still couldn't manage to move. She just kept staring after where she'd last seen Jesse's head sink below the rampaging water. Every once in a while she'd blink away the tears so she could still see clearly.

"He's . . . he's gone," she murmured. She shook her head and sighed. Then she stated very loudly, "No, he's not. I won't believe it." Angrily she wiped her tears away with the back of her hand.

"Let's take Patsy inside," Mildred urged. "And you, too. If you're in shock and catch a chill, you could die."

"Go inside," Deke urged.

Sarah was surprised at the gentleness in his voice. What was this sudden change in him?

"You must think of Patsy now," Mildred told her. "After all, we can't have her losing both her father and her mother. Although, of course," she assured her, "you know I'd raise her as my very own."

Mildred held out her arms, and Patsy moved into them. Sarah half expected to hear her sister suddenly change her mind and ask her to stay out in the rain. She'd tried everything else to get a child. No, she shouldn't think such horrible things about her very own sister.

"Yeah, go on inside and take care of the kid," Deke said, releasing his hold of her.

"I can't," Sarah said. "You can take her inside, please, Mildred. She likes you. She'll listen to you. You can bundle her up in a nice quilt and give her warm cocoa. You can take her to see Doc, and make sure she didn't swallow too much dirty water to make her sick. But I can't go. It's not that I don't care. I just can't."

She turned away from her sister and continued to watch where Jesse had disappeared.

Mildred shook her head. "I'll never understand putting your husband before your child. Is it because she's—"

"No!" Sarah shouted sharply. She held one warning finger up to her sister. "Don't *ever* say that! Don't even *think* it! I've never thought of abandoning my daughter, and I think you know what I mean by that, Meddling Mildred."

Mildred sniffed indignantly. "No need to bring up old—"

"I'm not trying to insult you, Mildred," Sarah tried to

placate her. "I know Patsy's in very good hands with you or I'd never leave her. But Jesse has no one. Only me. And I can't abandon him, either."

"I understand, Sarah," the Reverend said. "Leave her alone, Mildred."

"The wind's died down, and it's not raining as hard. I . . . I just need to . . . to watch for Jesse."

"He ain't comin' back," Deke said.

"Don't say that! Don't *ever* say that!"

"All right. I . . . I'll go see if I can't round up a couple of folks to look for his body. At least you can give him a decent burial."

"You can't have a burial if you don't have a body," Mildred corrected him. "You have a memorial."

"Oh, 'scuse me, Mrs. Rev," Deke said, his lip curling and one eyebrow lifting in an effort to look haughty and scornful. "Not bein' a minister myself, I ain't familiar with all them technical terms."

Mildred turned to Sarah, indicating exactly how much she wanted to ignore Deke. Sarah figured if the Reverend wasn't still here, she'd have probably given Deke a good piece of her mind—in no uncertain terms.

"Now, we don't do many memorial services, as you can well imagine," Mildred told her. "But we can have a really lovely one for Mr. Taylor, if you want."

"Will the choir sing? Will you have lots of flowers?" Sarah demanded.

"Oh, I'll be happy to help you arrange the entire thing," Mildred offered.

Obviously her sister had missed the entire joke.

The mention of planning a funeral brought to Sarah's mind the fun she and Jesse had had planning his—although she hadn't realized it at the time. She hadn't known then how bright even the most dismal aspects of life could be with Jesse by her side. But she knew now how very much she was going to miss him.

Maybe, if she tried to remember him every waking moment, she could still have just a little of Jesse's dauntless spirit with her—and she could teach Patsy to have it, too.

"I'm sure the Reverend'll give a lovely eulogy." Once Mildred got started on a plan, it was hard to get her to stop.

Merciful heavens! She was sounding almost as bad as her sister, planning a funeral for a man who might not be dead. He *couldn't* be dead!

"No! I won't hear any more plans. He *can't* be dead!"

"Come along, Mildred," the Reverend said, placing his arm around her shoulder. "Get the little one inside and stay there. I really need to go out and see how the folks are who live down the way. Their place always floods, and Mrs. Hedges just had a baby."

"Come on, Sarah," Mildred said. She reached out the arm that wasn't holding Patsy and placed her hand on Sarah's arm. "If he's been in the water that long, he's going to be pretty chilly, and he'll need a nice big pot of steaming hot coffee. At least let's go inside and get it ready for him."

"That's the first thing you've said that makes sense," Sarah told her sister. She gave one last, longing look down the swollen river. Then reluctantly she began to follow Mildred and the Reverend across the backyard.

After the coffee was brewing, Mildred said, "I think we ought to take Patsy to see Doc."

"Why don't you go, Mildred? I can't think straight right now. You know I trust you to do what's best for her."

"All right," Mildred agreed grudgingly. "But I want you to sit here in this parlor and don't move. I don't want to find out you've been outside again."

"Yes, Mildred," Sarah answered.

"No, no, no," Patsy told her, shaking her finger at her. "Don't be naughty, Mommy. Not outside!"

Mildred gathered up a large shawl and wrapped it around herself and Patsy. She closed the front door tightly behind her.

Sarah poured herself a cup of coffee. She sat at the kitchen table and hung her head in her hands, trying to think of what she was going to do next. She refused to believe that Jesse was really dead. But, just in case, what would she do?

She supposed she could still live here with Mildred and the Reverend—for a little while anyway. Eventually she'd have to get a job. Maybe she'd try the little millinery shop she'd seen in town, or see if Doc needed a nurse. She certainly had the qualifications. She could take in sewing, or if worse came to worst, she could take in laundry.

If she could save up enough money, maybe she could eventually buy a small house for Patsy and her—away from the river!

And this time she'd definitely have to make at least one mourning dress—if only to have one to wear to church. People were going to talk about her enough. She wouldn't have them saying she didn't dress appropriately.

She smiled to herself. Jesse would've enjoyed her little joke.

She'd known from the very beginning that she'd eventually have to go into mourning for Jesse. Wasn't that why she'd initially chosen him? But at the time his death had seemed so remote. She had felt almost a perfunctory sort of sympathy for a man she barely knew.

But she'd come to know him so much better. And she'd come to love him more than she ever thought she could love any man. She wasn't just going to miss his cheerfulness, even in the face of his awful jokes. She was going to miss the strong feel of his body beside hers in the bed. She'd miss his kiss, his embrace, his gentle yet passionate lovemaking.

Now she knew she'd mourn for him and miss him for as long as she lived.

The knob of the front door rattled loudly in the silence of the house as someone twisted it. She lifted her head, trying to hear more. The door opened and closed very quietly.

"Mildred?" she called. Mildred would never enter her own home that quietly. Mildred never entered anywhere that quietly. Patsy should be chattering, too, unless she were already asleep.

Was the Reverend back already from helping the people whose houses had flooded?

She sprang to her feet. Maybe it was Jesse! She headed toward the front door. Maybe she only thought he'd drowned. Maybe he'd found some sort of log to cling to, or anything else that had come floating downstream.

She pulled up sharply when she entered the vestibule. Deke was standing by the table, looking around.

"Did you find him?" she managed to ask.

"Nope."

"Who else is helping you?"

"Nobody."

"I thought you said you were going to organize . . ."

"A search party? What makes you think I'd go lookin' for a feller I'm glad is dead?"

"Then what are you doing here?"

"Don't you know?"

"No."

"Mildred's taken your brat to see Doc. Rev's gone." He chuckled. "Jesse's gone for sure. Looks like it's just you and me, Sarah. Just us. That's the way it should be. The way I'd always meant it to be. And you did, too, at first."

"I don't anymore."

"I've told you before, it don't matter. You'll marry me anyway now."

"No, I won't," she insisted, shaking her head.

"Yes, you will."

"What makes you so sure?"

" 'Cause if you don't, I'll tell everyone 'bout you and Taylor and the kid."

"I . . . I thought your mother'd already told everybody in town."

"Naw! Why would she want to go and do a stupid thing like that? Don't you know the only reason to know gossip 'bout somebody else is so you can use it against 'em? If everybody knew your kid was a bastard, wouldn't do me no good. But it'll do me good now, 'cause I know, and nobody else does. And you don't want them all to find out. You know, too, Sarah, that unless you marry me, I *will* tell the whole town."

She looked him straight in the eye. "Of course I won't marry you. I never would, I never will."

"Not even to keep this information out of the hands— and chattering mouths—of the Cottonwood Methodist Ladies Evangelical Temperance and Missionary Soul-Saving Spiritual Aid Bible Society? What would they say about Mildred and the Reverend—havin' such a fallen woman in the family?"

What would they say indeed? Sarah wondered. She couldn't hurt Mildred, not after all her sister had done for her. But she could *never* submit to Deke!

"I wish you'd fallen in that river," she told him. "But around here, there are laws against poisoning somebody's water. Just go away, Deke."

"Then I guess my ma won't have no choice. She'll just have to make sure everybody knows. . . ."

Sarah suddenly remembered she was a Bolton, by golly! She was a Taylor, too, by marriage. Jesse's parents may not have been wealthy, but his father had been an honest businessman, and they'd been proud of their son. She came from good blood and she'd married good blood. She didn't have to put up with this sort of thing from a mere backwoods dirt farmer. She raised her chin proudly and glared at him as haughtily as she could—which, after years of watching Aunt Myrtle, was considerable.

"Coming from your mother, I don't think many people will give that tale too much credence."

"Too much what?"

"Credence," Sarah repeated, saying it slowly as if Deke weren't very bright. "Nobody's going to believe something a person like you says about a person of my social standing." She gracefully placed her hand over her breast in false modesty.

Her insides were shaking. She'd never held the same beliefs as Aunt Myrtle—that Boltons were somehow better than the rest of mere humanity. But, just for now, she had to make Deke feel as though he really were beneath her, and that any petty gossip he might spread about her and her daughter wouldn't make a bit of difference to her. She had to carry off the act.

"Well, then, I guess Ma'll have to do what she has to do. And I have to do what I have to do."

"You don't have to do anything but get out of here, Deke. Now go. Just go!" Sarah extended her arm to point to the door. Before she could lower it, Deke had seized her by the wrist again.

"Well, now, wait a minute," he said as he pulled her closer to him. "I ain't done yet. There's only one more way I know to get you to be mine, Sarah—and that's to *make* you mine."

"Oh, no!" She pushed hard against his chest. She'd been through this before, and she never wanted to repeat the terrifying experience.

She'd scream, but who would hear her? The parsonage's closest neighbors were the silent ones in the cemetery. She didn't think they'd be much help right now.

Deke wouldn't let her go. As a matter of fact, it seemed, the harder she pushed, the more he laughed. Twisting her arm behind her, he dragged her into the parlor.

"Seein' as you're such a high-falutin' lady, I don't suppose it'd be right to bed you down on the wood floor. I suppose you're used to clean, good-smellin' linen sheets on feather beds, ain't you? And somebody else putting them on, too."

"I'm not used to this at all," she informed him, trying her best to remain haughty. "Now, let me go!"

"Nope."

Deke dragged her down to the floor. He was trying to kiss her, but his full lips only slobbered more saliva down her cheek. His free hand grabbed roughly at her breasts. He was trying desperately and clumsily with his feet and knees to part her legs, but she was doing her best to keep them together.

His rough groping brought back a flood of memories of being assaulted in the alley.

She felt so small against his big body. Small and helpless. Deke would get what he wanted, and there was nothing she could do about it. She started to whimper again and tried to draw herself up into a little ball.

"Oh, no! Deke, don't do this. Please don't do this. Not in the parsonage! Oh, for the love of God, have mercy! Let me go!"

All her cries didn't stop him at all.

She hated him more and more. She still hated the men who had hurt her the first time. She hated the thought of having to explain to her little daughter why Daddy wouldn't be singing with her anymore. She was going to hate spending the rest of her life without Jesse, the man she loved. She'd had just about enough of all this.

"Now, stop it!" She brought her fist down hard on the side of his head, making sure she got his ear in the process.

He wobbled, startled by the sudden blow. His hands stopped their infernal, constant, and very irritating groping of her body. One hand flew up to cradle his injured ear.

She took this opportunity to hit him again and again, until he leaned over. She doubled her legs up over her stomach, between Deke and her, and gave a great push. He toppled over onto his side. Sarah quickly sprang to her feet.

He managed to stagger up. He shook his head a couple of times as if to clear it.

He couldn't have had that much clearing to do, Sarah thought. He couldn't have that much in his head.

Suddenly Deke lunged for her again, but she'd seen what Jesse had done earlier. She waited until he was almost upon her, then quickly stepped out of the way. He fell for it again, she thought with a triumphant chuckle. How stupid could this man get?

Before he could even raise himself from where he'd sprawled headlong on the floor, Sarah had grabbed the poker from the fireplace. She brandished it in front of her, more like a heavy club than a classic épée. She didn't care what she looked like. There were no spectators here, no judges keeping points. She just wanted to make sure she was protecting herself. She didn't really want to run him through. She just wanted to keep him away.

He looked up and sneered at her. "You think I'm worried?" he asked, surveying the small brass poker. He sneered at the slender weapon and at the slender woman who thought she was going to use it. "I'm tough. Even if I wasn't tough, I still wouldn't be worried. You might be able to hit me with your fist, but you're too much of a lady to use a weapon on an unarmed man."

Sarah's eyes narrowed, and she started to laugh without humor. "Don't give me that Southern lady code of honor crap, Deke. I'll fight you off with everything I have."

Deke blinked at her in surprise. "You said 'crap.' "

"When you knew me before, I wouldn't have said 'cow ploppics' if I'd had a mouthful. I'm different now. I've changed. And I'm not going to let you—or anybody else— take advantage of me any longer."

Deke quickly glanced around the room.

"No, Deke. There's no small, helpless, innocent creatures around here for you to take your anger out on." She was glad Mildred had taken Patsy away. She hoped Kitty had the wisdom to be hiding under the bed upstairs.

"There's still you, Sarah."

"I'm not that innocent anymore, Deke. And I'm certainly not helpless. I'm a lot stronger than I've ever been—and I want you to know and remember always that it's because of Jesse. I owe everything to Jesse. I'll never be a coward again. I'm not afraid of you anymore."

"Leave my wife alone!"

Jesse appeared at the door. He was soaking wet. His clothes hung on his body and dripped onto the floor. He'd taken a wide-legged stance in the doorway. His long arms were spread out to lean from one doorjamb to the other. His entire body appeared larger than life. He looked like an angry man bent on revenge.

"Sweet Jesus! It's a ghost!" Deke shouted. Sarah could see his knees begin to buckle, but he quickly recovered.

"Worse, Deke," Jesse said. "I'm real. I can do more damage this way—and I've come back to get even with you."

"What happened to you?" Sarah cried.

"I washed up onto the riverbank not far from here and rushed back as soon as I got my breath—and just in time, too. How I got in the river is another story—one that I think the sheriff would like to hear."

"Sheriff?" Sarah murmured.

Deke started to shift from one foot to the other. "You're crazy, Taylor. You're clumsy and fell into the flooded river tryin' to save the kid. I didn't do nothin' to you."

"Just tried to push me under when I looked to you for help."

"You can't prove a thing, Taylor."

"Yes, I can, Deke."

Deke stood there shaking his head. Sarah could see him shifting his weight from one foot to the other. He was planning something—and knowing Deke, she could pretty well figure what. She'd have to be ready for almost anything. If only she could warn Jesse.

"No, you can't, Taylor," Deke argued. " 'Cause a dead man ain't got nothin' to say."

Deke suddenly lunged at Jesse. Sarah was ready. She brought the blunt end of the poker down on top of his head. Deke's bulk crashed to the floor.

Sarah raised the poker to strike him again, but Jesse's hand grabbed it and stopped her.

"My, you're a feisty little devil, aren't you? Remember, we just want to knock him unconscious, dear. We don't want to kill the nasty man."

Sarah gave him a wry smile. "We don't?"

"Charity and forgiveness, my love."

"Yes, dear," she said in a near imitation of the Reverend.

Jesse looked from Deke to Sarah to Deke's inert body again. "Still, I'm very impressed."

"And I didn't even break any of Mildred's knickknacks," she said, preening. Suddenly she stopped and looked panic-stricken again. "Oh, my goodness! I hope he doesn't bleed on the carpet."

"The sheriff should be coming soon to cart him away to jail, anyway," Jesse told her, watching Deke cautiously again. "He can bleed all he wants there."

"The sheriff's coming so soon?"

"I saw him at the flooded riverside. He said as soon as he'd finished there, he'd be here." Jesse looked down at Deke again and shook his head. "Attempted murder isn't going to be easy to get out of."

"Me?" she asked in alarm. She quickly put the poker back in its slot.

"No, him!"

She gave a laugh and rushed into Jesse's arms. She threw her arms around him. He held her in his strong embrace. He kissed her lips. She frantically starting kissing his lips, his eyes, his cheeks, and his ears.

"Easy, easy. Remember I just escaped from a watery grave."

"I'm so glad you're alive!" she kept repeating. She continued to hold him as if she never wanted to let him go ever again—and she didn't. She kissed him everywhere she could think of that wasn't covered with clothing. She intended to get to the other parts later.

"Easy, easy. The sheriff'll be showing up soon. Probably Mildred, Patsy, and the Reverend, too. We can't have them catching us like this."

"I'm just so glad to see you alive! I was so afraid you'd drowned."

"Me, too. It would've been such a shame, too, so soon after I'd just gotten my lungs back in working order again."

"Yes, you're breathing again."

"I've always been breathing. It was the coughing that was a problem."

"That's all gone now."

Jesse nodded. "That's because . . . well . . . I really had hoped for a more intimate, gentle, romantic setting when I told you this, Sarah." Still keeping her in his embrace, he reached up one hand to stroke her damp hair. "But, all things considered, I guess there's no time like now. Just promise me one thing."

"Certainly. What's that?"

"Promise me you won't be angry and throw things at me, especially that poker, all right?"

"I don't understand exactly what you're talking about, but . . . all right."

Sarah was watching him with a puzzled frown on her face. Jesse drew in a deep breath and began.

"Remember how I told you the doctor at the prison had told me the coughing was galloping consumption—and that I'd die before the year was out?"

Slowly Sarah nodded. Had all this running around speeded him along his heavenly way? He didn't look like a sick man.

"Well, the doctor was wrong."

Sarah's heart contracted with a sharp, painful squeeze. She had been losing him, she had him, she lost him to the river, he was back, she was losing him to consumption again, more quickly than she'd expected the first time. If somebody didn't make up his mind soon, she was going to scream!

"Does this mean you have less time?" she asked cautiously.

"No. It means I don't have galloping consumption. Heck, it's not even trotting!"

"What?" She stared at him, her blue eyes growing wider as she realized the true meaning of what he was saying.

"I had a bad cold."

"You mean all this time a mustard plaster and a bowl of hot chicken soup would've cured you?"

"Sort of. That and the fresh air, and good food—"

"I'll be sure to tell Mildred."

"And all the wonderful care I was given."

"Does this mean you're going to live?"

"Yes."

"But what about your leg?"

"Seems the prison doctor was wrong there, too. Last

week Doc Hanford managed to pull out a little piece of wood that was stuck in there. That's why I was so drunk—no other anesthesia."

"That's a likely story."

"I just saw him again this morning. He says I'm going to be fine."

"You're going to live," she repeated slowly.

Jesse nodded.

"You're going to be alive and well and strong again?"

"Yes. Oh, I should have a pretty big scar on my shin—"

"Well, all that hair should cover it up."

"I'm glad you're taking this so well."

"Taking it well! Of course I'm not taking it well. I want to jump up onto the rooftop and shout! I want to go dancing down Main Street!"

"Naked?"

"No. I'll save that for what I want to do indoors with you."

"Hmm, I see we think alike."

He gave her entire body a boldly warm glance that sent shivers up and down her spine.

"You realize, of course, that I can't ask you to marry me."

"We're already married, silly. Or were you so full of laudanum that you don't remember that?"

"Oh, I remember very well. I also seem to remember that on laudanum there really wasn't much I could do about it."

"Not that I would've let you, at the time."

"But I can do something now, Sarah, my love. My only love. What I can do is spend the rest of my life proving to you not only how well I've recovered, but also how beautiful and gentle true love can be."

"I think that's a wonderful idea," she replied, laying her head on his chest. She was so glad to hear his heart beating, and prayed they'd spend the rest of their lives together.

If you enjoyed this book, take advantage of this special offer. Subscribe now and…

Get a Historical

No Obligation

If you enjoy reading the very best in historical romantic fiction…romances that set back the hands of time to those bygone days with strong virile heros and passionate heroines …then you'll want to subscribe to the True Value Historical Romance Home Subscription Service. Now that you have read one of the best historical romances around today, we're sure you'll want more of the same fiery passion, intimate romance and historical settings that set these books apart from all others.

Each month the editors of True Value select the four *very best* novels from America's leading publishers of romantic fiction. We have made arrangements for you to preview them in your home *Free* for 10 days. And with the first four books you

receive, we'll send you a FREE book as our introductory gift. No Obligation!

FREE HOME DELIVERY

We will send you the four best and newest historical romances as soon as they are published to preview FREE for 10 days (in many cases you may even get them before they arrive in the book stores). If for any reason you decide not to keep them, just return them and owe nothing. But if you like them as much as we think you will, you'll pay just $4.00 each and save at *least* $.50 each off the cover price. (Your savings are *guaranteed* to be at least $2.00 each month.) There is NO postage and handling—or other hidden charges. There are no minimum number of books to buy and you may cancel at any time.

FREE
Romance

(a $4.50 value)

Send in the Coupon Below

To get your FREE historical romance and start saving, fill out the coupon below and mail it today. As soon as we receive it we'll send you your FREE Book along with your first month's selections.
